# OPENING SHOTS
# Volume Two

# OPENING SHOTS
## Volume Two

### MORE GREAT MYSTERY AND CRIME WRITERS SHARE THEIR FIRST PUBLISHED STORIES

**Edited by LAWRENCE BLOCK**

CUMBERLAND HOUSE
NASHVILLE, TENNESSEE

Published by Cumberland House Publishing, Inc., 431 Harding Industrial Drive, Nashville, Tennessee 37211

Cover design by Gore Studio, Inc.
Page design by Mike Towle

Library of Congress Cataloging-in-Publication Data is available.
ISBN: 1-58182-218-9

Printed in the United States of America
1 2 3 4 5 6 7 8 9 — 06 05 04 03 02 01

*This one is dedicated,*
*with respect and affection,*
*to the late Fred Dannay . . .*
*and indeed to all those editors*
*who bought our early stories*

# CONTENTS

# An Opening Shot . . .

A YEAR AGO, I was sitting right here at my desk, tapping away at the keyboard, trying to find a way to introduce the first volume of *Opening Shots*. Even as I performed that happy chore, I knew it was one I'd have to repeat. Because it was clear to me that there would be more than one book of first stories, with their authors reminiscing about the circumstances and effects of that initial sale.

Typically, commercial success is what generates a sequel. In films, certainly, the motto "Nothing succeeds like yesterday's success" is manifested in the parade of films (most of them undistinguished) with a numeral, Roman or Arabic, after their titles. (Or some variation on the theme: *Return of the Magnificent Seven. Thunderhead, Son of Flicka.*) But you'll note that no one ever rushed to make *Return to Ishtar*, or *Howard the Duck Part Two.*

Sometimes, though, you know ahead of time. In my own series, only with Matthew Scudder did I know before writing the first book that I'd be keeping continuing company with the character. (Back in the early seventies—the twentieth century's, not mine—I knew going in that I'd be doing three books about Scudder. But I didn't have a clue I'd still be writing about him after fifteen books and over a quarter of a century. To paraphrase Eubie Blake's observation on his hundredth birthday, if I'd had any idea he was gonna last that long, I'd have taken better care of him.)

With Evan Tanner and Bernie Rhodenbarr, I had no initial intention of writing a series, but found myself moved to start a second book about the character before the first saw print. With Chip Harrison, the commercial success of *No Score* probably played a role in the origin of the sequel, *Chip Harrison Scores Again*, and unquestionably made the publisher more receptive to the idea of another book about the lad.

Anthologies are different, of course; they require relatively little inspiration on the anthologist's part. It wasn't inspiration that convinced me a year ago that there'd be further installments of *Opening Shots*. As with

9

another anthology series of mine, *Master's Choice*, it was the sheer appeal of the finished volume that struck me.

So here we are again, with twenty-four solid stories by twenty-four outstanding writers. Some of the stories are remarkably mature, professional work. Some are more obviously early work, before the writer's skills reached anything like full development. But they're all a pleasure to read, and in each of them you see the seed of the writer's development. (That last is less true of the couple of stories written after the writer had already become established as a novelist, but I think you'll find those examples interesting in their own right.)

Each writer has included an introduction, and these introductions, I have to say, are worth the price of admission all by themselves. Writers, it seems to me, are never more eloquent or more interesting than when they reminisce about their early days, and recalling one's first success seems a spur to anecdotage for most of us. If you're at all interested in writing, or merely in writers, I think you'll find the intros as absorbing as I did.

You may be struck, too, by the role played by the late Fred Dannay in the gestation and/or publication of so many of these stories. Half of the Ellery Queen writing team, Fred was the founder and longtime editor of *Ellery Queen's Mystery Magazine*, with a Department of First Stories as a perennial feature. He was quite brilliant at discovering and publishing authors who would go on to have distinguished careers, and, as you'll see, was quirky enough to spark some marvelous recollections. It's been said of Fred that he never met a title he didn't want to change, not necessarily for the better. Many of this volume's stories had their titles altered, by Fred or some other magazine editor, and in several cases the writers have been happy to have their original titles restored.

The Fred Dannay connection, if you will, helped me solve a personal problem. I included my own first story, "You Can't Lose," in the first volume of *Opening Shots*, even as a combination of superstition and greed has led me to include a story of my own in each of my anthologies. But how could I supply a second first story for *Opening Shots 2*?

As you'll see, I found a way. Open one door, however, and another one slams shut. Because I can see a problem developing already.

What am I going to do next year for *Opening Shots 3*?

—*Lawrence Block*

# OPENING SHOTS
# Volume Two

# Final Rites

## DOUG ALLYN

## Doug Allyn's Introduction:

*"Final Rites." A very, very scary story. For me. Rereading it for the first time in fifteen years brought it all back.*

*It's the first story I ever sold and one of the very first I wrote for a creative writing class at Mott Community College in 1985. I'd been writing less than a year at the time.*

*The prof, an author named Edmund G. Love, who'd penned (literally) bestsellers in the fifties, wouldn't read student novels. All the components of good fiction are present in the short story.* Learn your craft, people. Write short.

*I turned in a tale about a rich witch who played the stock market. No reaction. Ed didn't mention it in class or return it.*

*Undaunted, I submitted a tale about a Chinese grave robber. Ed discussed everyone's work but mine.*

*Felt like I was back in third grade. Screwing up. Again.*

*When Ed asked to see me after class, I half expected him to bounce the manuscripts off my noggin and boot me out. Instead, he said my writing style might actually be salable. He suggested I read mysteries, specifically,* Ellery Queen *and* Alfred Hitchcock's *mystery magazines.*

*Bought one of each and* really *liked the stories. A surprise. I've always been an omnivorous reader. Though I'd admired many authors who wrote mysteries, Lawrence Block and Elmore Leonard for example, I never thought of them as "mystery writers." I just liked their books.*

*Impressed by the work in the magazines, I wrote "Final Rites" for Ed, who told me to submit it to* Hitchcock. *Cathleen Jordan bought it, and it won the Robert L. Fish Award as the best first story of 1985.*

*My wife and I made a fairy-tale trip to New York for the Edgar Awards, met Isaac Asimov and Dick Francis. I even danced with Mary Higgins Clark. A magical time. Then and now.*

*More importantly, we made new friends, I acquired an agent, and I got into this endlessly fascinating, frustrating Game.*

A very scary business.

Because looking back, I realize how unlikely it all was. What if Ed Love hadn't been such a perceptive teacher? Or Cathleen had been in a reeeally surly mood when this story landed on her desk? What if, what if, what if?

My grandmother once told me that sometimes it's better to be lucky than good. Know what? My grandmother was right.

"Final Rites." A very scary story.

# Final Rites

## DOUG ALLYN

HE DIDN'T LOOK MUCH like the law. In his grubby sweat suit and sneakers he looked more like a Class C high school coach during a losing season. Snoring softly, feet on his cluttered desk, a Detroit Tigers baseball cap tipped forward over his eyes—Norman Rockwell would have loved it. I rapped on the desk.

"Sheriff LeClair? I'm Sergeant Garcia. Lupe Garcia."

One eye blinked open, briefly. "They're not here."

"I haven't told you what I want yet." I eased cautiously down on a battered office chair upholstered in argyle blanket, wondering why I'd bothered to wear my good suit.

"Algoma's a small town. . . . Garcia, is it? I found a note when I came in this morning. Said a guy from the Organized Crime Task Force was flying up from Detroit to see me. I take it you're him. I also take it you're here about Roland Costa and his son, since the only thing anybody from Motown wants to talk to me about is them. If I need help on a hot car or a runaway, nobody gives me the time of day. Anyway, they're not here. They were in town a couple of weeks ago to bury Charlie, I haven't seen 'em since."

"I'm not surprised. Neither has anyone else."

He tipped his baseball cap back and looked at me for the first time. We were of an age, but he had more miles on him. A lot more. His eyes were red-rimmed and he looked exhausted.

"Are you saying they've disappeared?"

"They had Charlie brought to Algoma for the funeral," I said, "and that's the last time anybody saw them."

"So they've disappeared," he shrugged. "That's not uncommon for people in their line of work, is it?"

17

"Did you see them when they were here?"

"Difficult to miss 'em. They were driving a Lincoln limo that must've been a block long. We don't see many cars like that up here in the boondocks."

"Was a woman traveling with them?"

"No woman. Just Roland Costa and Rol Junior. They had a room at the Dewdrop Inn the day of the funeral, and they were alone. Why?"

"Charlie Costa had a girlfriend, Cindy Kessel. She's been talking to the D.A.'s office about buying immunity for herself with information about Charlie's operations. She's missing, too."

He grunted, massaging his stubbled face with work-roughened paws. I noticed the single gold strand around his right wrist. "Look, I'm afraid I'm not really awake yet," he said. "A little retarded kid wandered away from Camp Algoma yesterday. Found her at sunup this morning, in good shape considering, but I haven't been to bed, and I've gotta wait on a call from the National Guard commander to tell him we won't need any troops for the search. Tell you what, why don't you grab breakfast across the street at Tubby's, and I'll be along as soon as I can."

"If they stayed at a local motel, I could . . ."

"Look, Garcia, this isn't Detroit. This is my town. I said they're not here and they're not. Now maybe we can get a line on 'em, but you're a stranger here so nobody's gonna tell you squat and they might just forget what they do know. So get yourself a cuppa coffee and wait for me, okay? Please?"

"All right, I'll wait a bit. Don't be too long."

"You get homesick you can sit in the supermarket parking lot and sniff the exhaust fumes. I'll be over as soon as I can." He tipped his cap back down and was asleep before I was out the door.

He was right about one thing at least. Algoma was definitely a small town. A single paved street lined with tacky little shops, supermarket at one end, self-service gas station at the other. Like most northern Michigan towns, it had probably been a lumber camp once; God only knew what kept its economy afloat now.

Tubby's had no yogurt, no fresh granola, and no air conditioning. The pale August sunlight beating through the smeared windows made the room considerably warmer than my toast, which wasn't very, and I shed my tie and sport coat. Passed the time trying to decide whether the place was named after the waitress or the cook. It was a toss-up. LeClair came in just as my third glass of iced tea arrived. He'd pinned his badge on his cap.

"Christ," he said, sliding into the red vinyl booth. "My call didn't get through, so about four o'clock I got sixteen National Guardsmen arriving on a wild goose chase, or I should say, *another* wild goose chase, counting yours. Okay, so you wanna fill me in?" The waitress brought him coffee in a mug with a chip out of it, and he nodded his thanks.

"I already have," I said. "They came here. They apparently never came back. That's really all we know."

"So what brings you all the way up here? You got a warrant for 'em or anything?"

"No, but if I can find the girl, we may just get a shot at them. We know they're into shylocking and narcotics, but they're very cautious people. Without the girl . . . anyway, it's fairly basic police procedure to keep track of the bad guys."

"No kidding? Gosh, I wish I had something to take notes on. You see, I usually wait till folks do something illegal, and then I arrest 'em. Pretty unsophisticated, I guess."

"Why did they bring Charlie all the way up here to be buried?"

"Roland and Charlie grew up here. Their old man was a bootlegger back in the thirties, or so I'm told. After Prohibition he moved on to bigger things in Detroit, but the family still has a good-sized cottage on the river. They come up for a month or so in the summer, and sometimes during hunting season."

"You know them then? Personally, I mean."

"Yeah," he said, sipping his coffee, "I've known 'em since I was a kid, and everybody else in this town, too. So?"

"So nothing. I was just asking. Look, have you got some kind of a complex about being from the sticks? Or don't you like Chicanos, or what?"

He carefully placed his coffee cup on the table between us, and took a deep breath. "Garcia, I'm tired. I've been up for over thirty hours now. I know nothing happened to those clowns in Algoma because if a chipmunk craps in the woods around here, I hear about it. I'd like to go home, go to bed, maybe say hello to my wife so she remembers who I am, but instead I'm gonna nursemaid you around until you're satisfied there's nothing here because it's part of my job and because I noticed your Vietnam bracelet. Okay? But don't expect me to be cheery about it. I haven't got the energy."

"Terrific," I said. "So why don't we get on with it, and I can be on my way. Where do you suggest we start?"

"We see Faye at the Dewdrop," he said, rising, gulping the last of his coffee. I noticed he didn't bother to pay for it. I paid for mine.

FAYE AND THE DEWDROP Inn were like a couple who'd been married too long. They resembled each other, and both had seen better days. Her red hair was carelessly rinsed, matching the blush of surface capillaries in her cheeks, and both she and the ramshackle motel needed tidying up. If she was pleased to see us, she managed to conceal it.

"Morning, Faye. I need a look at your slips, if you don't mind."

"Wouldn't matter if I did, would it? Here, help yourself." She pushed a battered recipe file box across the counter.

"Roland Costa and Junior stayed here the day of Charlie's funeral, is that right?"

"If that's what it says there. No law against it, is there? They add a little class to this town, you ask me." Her diction had the forced precision of a serious drinker.

"There's no checkout time on the card. When did they leave?"

"Hell, Ira, there's no times for half the people that stay here. I can't be at the desk every minute. Folks pay in advance and that's what I'm in business for, not to . . ."

"What time do you *think* they left?" LeClair interrupted.

"I already told you I don't know," she said sullenly. "Now if you don't mind, I got things to do."

He stared at her for a moment, frowning. She traced a gouge in the scarred countertop as though she'd never seen it before.

"All right, Faye," he nodded, flipping the box lid shut. "I guess that'll do it. For now."

"GEE," I SAID, "IT'S a good thing you came along, LeClair. She might not have told me a thing."

"She seems a bit . . . edgy," he conceded, keeping his eyes on the dirt road ahead as he skillfully piloted my rented sedan through the potholes on the road north from the village. Except for an occasional farmhouse, the countryside was as empty of people as the back of the moon.

"Faye's been known to be a bit light-fingered with her guests' belongings," he added. "That's probably all it was."

"I'll keep that in mind."

"No need to," he said curtly. "With luck you won't be in town long enough to need a room. We'll visit the cemetery and talk to the groundskeeper, Hec Michaud, and that should do it. You can get back to Motown, and maybe I can get to bed."

He slowed as we approached a line of elderly houses huddled beside a clapboard church, and turned in. The cemetery covered most of a hill behind the church, an island in a sea of cornfields. The tombstones were a hodgepodge of styles and sizes, but the lanes were swept, the grass neatly trimmed, and not everyone in it was dead.

Two men were working on a plot about halfway up the hillside, or to be precise, one man was working, digging mechanically in a waist-deep grave, while the other sat with his back against a weathered headstone sipping from a can of generic beer. He was fortyish, barrel-shaped, with a stubbled moonface and wispy spikes of steel-gray hair poking out from beneath his greasy engineer's cap. He lumbered to his feet as we climbed up, smiling with beery good fellowship. "Welcome to Lovedale, gents. It ain't much as cemeteries go, but it's home. Hey, Paulie, quit diggin' for a minute. We got comp'ny."

The digger was younger, mid-thirties, lanky, an open apple-pie face and sandy hair. A deep welt of a scar ran from his left temple to the nape of his neck, the hair bordering it bone white. Despite the heat of the day his sweat-stained denim work shirt was buttoned at the cuffs and throat. He clambered eagerly out of the hole with a grin like an April morning.

"Hey, Ira, good to see you."

"Good to see you, too, Paulie. Looks like Hec's got you doing most of the work, as usual."

"Ahh, Paulie don't mind," the beer drinker said. "Strong as an ox and twice as smart. Right, Paulie?"

"Sure, Hec. You want me to keep shovelin'?"

"Take a break, Paulie," LeClair said. "I've got some questions for you both." Hec's smile remained fixed, but his grip tightened on the beer can.

"You want a beer, sheriff? Paulie, run up to the tool shed and get Ira a cold one."

"I don't want a beer, Hector, and Paulie isn't paid to be your errand boy. I want to know . . ."

21

"Who's this guy?" Hec asked, nodding warily toward me. "Maybe we don't wanna answer no questions with him here."

"This is Sergeant Garcia from Detroit. We're working together."

"What kinda work you gonna be doin'?" Hec sneered. "Bean pickin' season's over."

LeClair pushed two fingers into the heavier man's chest, backing him up. Michaud lost his footing in the loose earth and sat down hard in the open grave. Without spilling his beer. He stared up at LeClair more in surprise than anger, and a momentary flicker of satisfaction showed in his eyes.

"You had no call to do that, Ira," he said slowly, "none at all."

"Maybe not, Hec," LeClair said, kneeling at the edge of the grave, "but there are a few things I've been meaning to discuss with you for a while, and today's as good a day as any. If I were you, I'd just stay in that hole for a bit while we have our little talk. Paulie, you take Sergeant Garcia up to the tool shed and get him a beer. He'll have some questions for you, and you answer 'em. Okay?"

"Do what he says, Paulie," Hec said from the grave. "Maybe he'll wanna talk to Billy, too, while you're up there."

I was puffing when we reached the tool shed. The climb hadn't affected Paulie at all. He took two beers from a cheap foam cooler and handed me one. "You in Vietnam?" he asked. I nodded.

"I thought so. I seen your bracelet. Ira's got one, too. I been meaning to get one, but . . . hey, you know, I had a friend there who was Mexican. I think he had a lotta names. You got a lotta names, too?"

"Sure," I said. "Lupe Jose Andrew Mardo Flores Garcia." My saints' names rolled off my tongue with surprising ease. I hadn't spoken them in years.

"Flores," he exclaimed eagerly, "hey, that was my friend's name. It means 'flower,' right?" I nodded, and I couldn't help smiling. His mood was contagious.

"Well, okay, Flower, why don't we pick out a comfortable hunk o' dirt here and we can sit and drink our beers. Ira said you wanted to ask me something?"

"Maybe you should ask Billy to come over," I said, glancing around uncertainly. "That way I won't have to ask the questions twice."

"You can ask him from here if you talk loud enough," he said. "He's buried over there by the fence next to Major Gault."

I took a long, thoughtful pull at my beer before glancing over at him. He was watching my reaction out of the corner of his eye, deadpan. "Gotcha," he said softly, the smile finally breaking through. "Don't worry, Flower, I'm not bananas. I talk to Billy sometimes, but only to get a rise out of Hec. I know he's dead. I damn near died with him. We was friends in high school, got drafted together, same outfit in Nam. We was even in the same foxhole when this Cong grenade drops in. We both tried to throw the damn thing out and wound up knocking ourselves cockeyed instead. It would have been pretty funny except then the grenade went off and Billy came here to Lovedale, and I wound up at the Vet's Facility in Grand Rapids for two years. Believe it or not, it's nicer here at Lovedale."

"How long have you been working here?"

"I'm not really sure," he said, frowning. "Major Gault's been here since 1864 or '62, and Billy's stone says 1973, but I'm not very good at numbers anymore so I can't say exactly how long I've been here. That's a funny thing about cemeteries. Time doesn't matter much anyway. Like, the major and Billy lived maybe a hundred years apart, but now they're here together, probably swapping war stories and stuff. At least, I hope so." He lapsed into silence, sipping his beer.

"About three weeks ago there was a funeral here. Charles Costa's. Do you remember that?"

"Sure I remember it. It's only numbers I have trouble with, things like that."

"Sorry, I didn't . . . well, anyway, were both you and Hector working that day?"

"Nah, just me. It was on a Saturday and Hec don't like to work Saturdays. It was a funny one, though."

"What do you mean, funny?"

"It was the biggest send-off I ever seen. See that big ugly hunk of marble with the cedars planted around it, like they were keeping it separate from the riffraff in the rest of the cemetery? That's Costa's. Really something, isn't it? And you shoulda seen his casket. It must've been standard size, but it sure looked bigger, burnished copper with burled walnut inserts. Probably weighed a ton. Maybe that was the problem."

"Problem?"

"After the funeral, the director couldn't get the mechanism that lowers the box to work, but that isn't what I meant about its being funny. The funeral director wasn't a local guy, he was from Detroit, Claudio something or other, and he must've had a dozen assistants with him, dressed like head-waiters and scrambling around here like a school gym on prom night putting out flowers and stuff. Then, after all that, nobody came. Just Rol Costa, Jr., and his old man. Just the two of 'em."

"They were here, then? You saw them?"

"Yeah, I know Rol from school, and I've seen his old man around. They showed up in this big Lincoln, stuck old Charlie in the ground, and that was that."

"And no one was here other than the funeral people, you, and Hec?"

"I already told you Hec wasn't here," he said, with a trace of irritation. "Hec don't like working Saturdays."

"It looks like you do most of the work even when he's here."

"Could be," he shrugged. "Look, maybe Hec takes advantage of me a little, but I don't care. I'm just glad to be out of that hospital and doing something, even if it's only digging graves. Besides, sometimes Hec stands up for me, like with old lady Stansfield. She's got a house near the west fence, and she don't like me, you know? When we had a complaint about me working without a shirt, I knew who it was, and I asked Hec to talk to her about it and he did. He don't get many complaints about my work, though. This place looks pretty nice, doesn't it, Flower? Maybe not to move into, but you know what I mean."

"It looks good, Paulie," I agreed. "Anybody can see you work very hard. When did the Costas leave?"

"Right after the funeral, I guess. I'm not sure 'cause I was asleep behind the tool shed."

"Thanks," I said. "I appreciate your help." Without thinking I slipped the thin gold band from my wrist and handed it to him.

"Hey, Flower," he said, his eyes widening, "you don't have to give me nothing. I mean, I'm just glad to have somebody to talk to, you know?"

"It's all right, Paulie, I . . . I've got another one at home. Take it, please."

"Well, thanks. I've been meaning to get one, but . . . well, thanks a lot." He eased it carefully on his wrist, admiring it as it caught the glint of the morning sun. "I wish I had something I could . . ." He fumbled in the pocket of his faded work shirt. "Here, you want a couple of joints? It's not bad stuff."

I accepted one of the crudely rolled cigarettes and sniffed it. It was pure, uncut. "Where did you get these?"

"You ever do a long boonie recon in Nam?" he asked, smiling slyly.

I nodded.

"Well, that's how I got it," he said. "I just lived off the bounty of the land."

I glanced around, and for a moment the cemetery and the fields around it had the scent of danger, like the jungle, but only for a moment. "I think I'd better be going," I said, getting to any feet. "I see the sheriff's helping Hector out of his hole."

WE DROVE MOST OF the way back to town in silence, each of us in his own thoughts. "Paulie said they were here, and then they left," I said finally. "You get anything from Hector?"

"Nope, and I don't think he'll vote for me in the next election, either. He said he wasn't here the day of the funeral. That about wrap it up for you? I can't think of anyone else."

"I can't, either. Look, I appreciate your help on this thing."

"No charge," he sighed, "it comes with the territory. You know, if I'd been awake when you came in this morning I could have saved us some running around. The Costas are a hard lot, all of 'em, and they grew up around here. There's no way anything could have happened to 'em in a place like Algoma."

"You're probably right," I said. "Still, checking things out is part of the job. Paulie mentioned a funeral director named Claudio. Mean anything to you?"

"Rigoni's Funeral Home. They do work out here sometimes, but they're based in Detroit. Legitimate, as far as I know."

"I'll look them up when I get home, but it doesn't sound like much."

He pulled the sedan over to the curb in front of his office. "Well, here we are. Sorry things didn't work out for you, but I told you so. You going straight back?"

"Maybe I'll do a little sight-seeing," I said. "I don't get out of the city much, and you've got a nice little town here."

"We like it. If you need anything else I'll be in my office at least until those Guardsmen get here. I'll have to thank 'em for coming, I guess, even if it's for nothing. I really oughta find an honest job. Have a good trip, Garcia."

He flipped me a mock salute and strode off.

I drove around for a bit, wondering what people found to keep them in a town six blocks long. I pulled in at a storefront office with "Village of Algoma" stenciled crudely on a plywood sign in the window.

The clerk literally dragged himself to the counter, a stroke-shattered old hulk of a man with a paralyzed leg, an arm strapped to his belt, and one side of his weather-beaten face sagging like so much melted wax. His cheek was further distorted by a huge cud of tobacco. He leaned his good arm on the counter and spat a stream of brown juice in the general direction of the spittoon against the wall. Dead center. "Do somethin' for ya?" he asked.

"I'd like to see a plat book for the county, please."

"Got one right here." He pulled a slim folder from beneath the counter and flipped it open to Algoma County. "Some of these titles ain't current, but I know most of the landholders around here. Any particular parcel in mind?"

I traced the line of Lovedale Road north on the map with a fingertip. "Here, the land around the cemetery."

"Well, there are houses north and south of it, but . . ."

"No, I'm interested in these fields around it to the west. All of that property seems to be owned by . . . somebody named Lund?"

"Max Lund," he nodded. "He don't live in Algoma no more, but he still owns the land."

"It has corn growing on it now."

"He's farming it on shares. I believe Hec Michaud is working some of it. He put in some raggedy-ass corn this spring. Hec ain't much of a farmer."

"I thought he was in charge of the cemetery."

"He is. You from the city?"

I nodded.

"Figured so," he said, and spat another stream toward the spittoon. "You see, in a town like Algoma, a man can't make it with just one job. Most folks do a little of this and that to get by. Hec does the cemetery, paints houses, and does a little farmin' now and again."

"How about the sheriff?" I asked. "He do a little farming, too?"

"Sometimes," he said, examining me carefully with his good eye, "sometimes he does."

LeClair was sleeping in his office chair, his grubby jogging shoes up on his desk. I let the door slam behind me, and he jerked awake with a start.

"You back again?" he said, groggy and still half asleep. "I thought you'd left. Those Guardsmen here yet?"

"I haven't seen them," I said, sitting on the edge of his desk. "I've got a little time to kill before my plane'll be ready. Thought maybe we could have a goodbye smoke." I took the joint from my shirt pocket and placed it on his desk. "Have one on me. It's bomb weed."

He stared at me blankly.

"Go ahead. You'll feel better and nobody's here but us cops."

A slow flush rose above the collar of his T-shirt. "Garcia," he said tightly, "I noticed Paulie was wearing your bracelet when you came down the hill today. That was a nice thing to do. So, because of that, and since you're a city boy and don't know any better, I'll give you thirty seconds to flip that reefer in the wastebasket and get the hell out of my office, or I'm gonna throw your butt in jail."

"Open it up," I said, "take a look at the weed."

Still scowling, he tore the paper apart, spilling the leaves on his desk. He picked one up and sniffed it. "This is green and it hasn't been cut. I'd guess it's local, right? Where did you get it?"

"From a guy who knows how to live off the land. As an informant he'll have to remain anonymous, of course."

"Sure," he said dryly. "Gee, I wonder who it could be? Where did he find it?"

"In the cornfields near the cemetery. There's an area to the southwest where maybe every fourth plant is marijuana."

"Hec Michaud!" he said, slamming his fist on the desktop. "I knew something was wrong out there today! I could feel it in my bones, but I thought it had something to do with the Costas. How much do you figure is out there?"

"I don't know, a couple of bales, maybe. Enough."

"And you thought maybe I was in on it, didn't you?"

"Sorry," I shrugged. "Like you said, I'm from out of town."

"*Sorry* doesn't quite cover it. Where the hell do you get off assuming I was corrupt? Or don't they have honest cops in the city anymore?"

"You're right, it was stupid of me. I mean, what kind of graft could you get around here anyway? Chickens and ducks?"

"I manage to scrape by on my salary. Dumb, maybe, but . . ."

"Look, I've already apologized, okay? And you might as well accept it 'cause it's all you get. You'd have wondered, too."

"Yes," he conceded, grudgingly, "I suppose I would have. All right, apology accepted, for now. At least I'll have something for those Guardsmen to do when they get here. You want in on the collar?"

"No, it's not what I came here for, and I haven't had anything to eat all day. I'm gonna pop over to Tubby's for a sandwich. Maybe I'll stop out later to see how it's going."

THE HARVEST WAS IN full swing when I pulled into the cemetery. A dozen National Guardsmen in green fatigue uniforms were hacking industriously away in the corn and carrying the marijuana plants to a pile at the edge of the field, where LeClair and two Guard officers were conferring. I noticed Hec Michaud sitting disconsolately in a jeep, handcuffed to the steering wheel. I walked over. "Hey, meester," I said, "ju know where an hombre can find a chob pickin' beans?" He just stared at the dashboard. No sense of humor.

"Hey, Flower, come on up! I got bleacher seats and cold beer!"

Paulie was sitting with his back against the tool shed on the hill, observing the proceedings. I made the long climb and sat next to him. He passed me a can of generic beer. "Quite a show," he said.

"So it is," I said. "Look, I'm sorry if this . . . puts a crimp in your recreation."

"Hell, Flower," he grinned, "I can't smoke that stuff. I have enough trouble keeping track of things as it is. Hec gave me those joints, probably so I'd keep my mouth shut. Maybe I should have. I'm sure gonna hate losing my job here."

"I don't see why you should."

"Maybe you don't," he said quietly. "but you're going to because if they keep searchin' in the direction they're going now, they're gonna find the car."

I turned slowly and stared. "What car?"

"A silver Lincoln." His voice was a whisper now, and he wouldn't meet my eyes. "Hec was gonna hide it in the field and then get rid of it later, but it got stuck, so we just covered it up."

"The Costas' car?"

He nodded.

"When did this happen?"

"You mean when did we hide it? I'm not sure," he said, frowning. "It was after the casket got stuck . . . but I already told you that, didn't I?"

"You told me it got stuck, but you didn't tell me the rest, did you? Paulie, it's going to come out anyway now. I want you to tell me what happened. All of it. Just take it slow. Now, you said the casket got stuck?"

"Well, I didn't know it was stuck at first. I was sacked out behind the tool shed when this guy Claudio wakes me up. He's havin' a heart attack because his box is jammed in the frame, and everybody's gone but him and Mr. Costa. So I went and took a look at it. It was jammed all right, but we got a crank here in the shed to lower 'em manually if that happens, so I came back up here to get it. On the way back I could hear Claudio and Mr. Costa arguin' clear across the cemetery. Finally, Claudio went stompin' over to his hearse and drove off, which was odd because the director's supposed to see the casket's lowered and the vault lid is in place before he leaves. Mr. Costa was just standin' there lookin' at the coffin when I came up behind him. That's when I noticed it. Charlie's million-dollar box had a little hunk of red cloth sticking out along one seam. Not very neat. Mr. Costa'd noticed it, too, 'cause that's what he was starin' at. He jumped a foot when I walked up. He told me to lower the box, and I said the funeral director was supposed to be there. 'Mr. Rigoni's been called away and I'll take full responsibility,' he says. 'You just lower it, and here's something for your trouble,' and he holds out a hundred-dollar bill. That's a lotta money, right?"

"Yes," I said, "that's a lot of money."

"I thought so, too. I'm not very good at numbers anymore, but I figured there was something wrong, you know? So I said I couldn't lower it by myself, I'd need help. He started to argue, but he noticed me staring at the box. His eyes kind of narrowed and he just turned and walked down to his car and tore out of the cemetery, spraying gravel all over the place.

"I knelt down and took a closer look at the red cloth. It moved. Just a little, like something was trying to pull it back inside the coffin. So I rapped on the lid. 'Is anybody in there?' I said, feeling really stupid. It was the first time I ever tried talking to a stiff when I wasn't just trying to get a rise out of Hector. Still, it seemed like the cloth had moved."

"What did you do?"

Paulie shrugged. "Well, there wasn't nobody there but me and that box, so I unscrewed the lid dogs and opened it. She sat up and I sat down. Hard. A lady in a red dress, with blood on the side of her head, groggy, and maybe blinded by the light. 'Help me,' she said."

"Cindy Kessel," I said. "Charlie's girlfriend."

"She was mumbling about not saying anything about Charlie's business," he nodded, "but she was just sort of rambling, like she was in a daze. Then she must have come out of it a little because she looked down at who she was sitting on. Her eyes rolled up and she fell back down on old Charlie. He didn't seem to mind."

"What happened then?"

"Well, I didn't know what she was to Charlie, but I didn't figure she belonged in the same box with him, so I hauled her out and shut the lid. I wasn't sure what to do. She needed help and nobody was around and I didn't want to just leave her there, so I picked her up and jogged over to Mrs. Stansfield's. The old lady doesn't like me much, but I couldn't think of anyplace else to go.

"I hammered on the door but nobody came and the damn thing was locked. I was tired from the run, my head was pounding . . ." He took a deep breath. "The girl . . . Cindy? Is that her name?"

I nodded.

"She was still unconscious. I could see the dust of Costa's limo coming back and I knew I had to do something, so I put my shoulder to the door, got it open, and set the girl inside. Then I ran back to the grave, keeping low. I didn't want Costa to know where I'd been, and it was kind of fun anyway, like being back in the army.

"Mr. Costa had brought his son with him, Rol Junior. Do you know Rol?"

"I know who he is," I said. "He's a . . . rough customer."

"I knew him from school," Paulie said, "mean as a snake. Mr. Costa said he'd brought him along to help with the casket. I said okay, but he musta noticed I was breathing hard or something because he looked at me kind of funny, and then he checked the box. I hadn't screwed the lid dogs back in. When he looked at me again, his eyes had gone as dead as Charlie's. 'Where is she, boy,' he says, 'what have you done with her?'

"I just played dumb; which ain't too hard for me. 'I don't know what you mean,' I says.

" 'We got no time for this,' Rol Junior says. 'He'll tell us when I show him what his guts looks like,' and he pulled an eight-inch blade. Man, that thing flicked open in his hands like magic."

"What happened?"

"He wasn't no soldier," Paulie shrugged, "he was just a guy with a knife. My head doesn't work so good since the grenade got me and Billy, but I can still understand a guy with a knife. He came straight at me, which was a big mistake. I snatched his knife wrist and spun him around into a choke hold, keeping him between me and his old man. Mr. Costa pulled this ugly little automatic, and he was circling around trying to get a shot when the girl screamed, and he looked away. That was an even bigger mistake." He took a long pull from his beer.

"Where are they now, Paulie?" I asked quietly. "Are they in the car?"

"The car? Nah. I figured that monument stone of Charlie's was too big for one guy anyway, but it's just about right for three, and it says 'Costa' on it, right?"

"And the girl, Paulie? What about the girl?"

"She's still staying at Mrs. Stansfield's. I went over there later to talk to her, but she was pretty weak and couldn't say much. I'll bet she's glad to be out of that box, though."

"I imagine she is," I said, releasing a long, ragged breath I hadn't realized I'd been holding. "Paulie, we're going to have to tell Ira about this, you know."

"I wanted to in the first place, but Hec said I'd get in trouble. I think he just didn't want anybody snooping around here. One good thing at least, Mrs. Stansfield seems to like me a little better now. Maybe she was only grouchy before because she was lonely."

"Maybe so," I said, frowning. Something he'd said was gnawing at the back of my memory. "Paulie, didn't you tell me Mrs. Stansfield's house was west of the cemetery?"

He nodded. I stared across the fields of golden corn that ran unbroken to the pine-covered hills on the horizon. The setting sun was hanging above them like a single fiery eye. "Paulie, there is no house west of the cemetery."

"Sure there is," he said, with a trace of irritation. "That stone one, over by the fence. Mrs. Stansfield's been there even longer than the major, since 1852, I think, or maybe '51. I'm not very good at numbers any more."

"WHAT DO YOU THINK will happen to him?" I asked.

"You tell me," LeClair said, slumping back in the seat of my rental sedan. He looked utterly exhausted but his eyes were bright, almost feverish. He was watching the men in the rear of the jeep ahead of us as we followed the small convoy back to Algoma in the gathering dusk. Paulie was talking animatedly with a couple of Guardsmen, their smiles occasionally visible in the flickering headlights.

"Can you see Paulie on the stand at the coroner's inquest?" he said softly. "They'll tear him apart. He'll go to Ypsilanti for a three-month psycho evaluation, then back to the Vet's Facility if he's lucky, and maybe prison if he's not."

"That's probably how it'll go down," I conceded. "He killed two people, and at least contributed to the death of a third."

"Actually, I don't know whether he did or not," LeClair said thoughtfully. "I only know what you told me. I'm just a small-town sheriff, and the Costas and Stansfields are rich, influential folks. I might be very reluctant to order an exhumation on the word of some poor, brain-damaged vet."

I glanced over at him. "You can't be serious."

"I don't know," he said. "I'll give it to you straight. I don't give a damn about what happened to the Costas, I'm just sorry it happened here. I feel bad about the girl, but she should have been choosier about her playmates, and there's no helping her now. That only leaves Paulie. He's already been ground up in the machinery once, and I really hate to see him fed back into the hopper again."

"Three people are dead."

"You're wrong, sport, a lot more people are dead than that. They got their tails shot off while Roland Costa's son was using his draft exemption to learn the family rackets, and Paulie Croft was getting his head rearranged so he could be a gravedigger instead of a trucker like his old man. So I'll tell you what I'm going to do, Garcia. Nothing. Nada. I'm dumping it on you. You decide who owes who what, and then let me know. Okay?"

"That's not fair," I said flatly.

"No kidding?" he said, stifling a yawn, "Well, we don't have to be fair. We're the law. And don't worry about Hec. I can handle him."

"You've got to be hallucinating from lack of sleep," I snapped, "or maybe all this fresh air's affected your mind. You could never get away with anything like that."

"You're probably right," he admitted, "but at least I'm covered if we get caught. I'll just scuff my toe in the dirt and say I was taken in by a smooth-talking slicker from the big city. I don't know what your excuse could be, but that's your problem."

The faint sound of laughter from the jeep ahead drifted past us on the wind, and I could see the streetlights of the village glowing in the distance. Both of them. "I don't know, either," I said slowly, "but maybe I won't need one. I mean, what could possibly happen to anybody in a hick town like this?"

# Don't Kill a Karate Fighter

## WILLIAM E. CHAMBERS

## William E. Chambers's Introduction:

*The incident that sparked enough creative genius in me to write a publishable short story for the first time occurred in the autumn of 1971. My wife Marie and I lived on the top floor of my mother-in-law's two-family home on Greenpoint Avenue in Brooklyn. My wife's two younger brothers, John and Stanley, had found a pair of abandoned kittens in the yard that fronted the house. They adopted the cats and named them Abraham and Strauss. Now Abe, a quiet cat, stayed near home and minded his own cat-natured business. Strauss was an explorer, a seeker of adventure and truth. And he found both.*

*One Saturday morning I awoke to find my mother-in-law in a state of alarm and my two young brothers-in-law perplexed because Strauss had climbed the tree next door and couldn't get down. Marie and I coaxed him with food and tried talking to him in our best rendition of cat-language, all to no avail. So, we called upon New York's Finest. Well, two patrolmen responded almost immediately. At first they seemed reluctant to take on this case. I think they were going to flag it over to the ASPCA. But my brother-in-law John explained that Strauss was a very expensive cat imported from Germany. The patrolmen bought into this story and went back to the precinct. They returned a while later carrying a long, hollowed-out tube with a looped rope, nooselike, I thought, jutting out of one end, and a long flat board. The cops followed me up to the roof, and then the fun began.*

*Marie had a brainstorm and brought a huge feathered pillow, known as a poduszka to the people of Poland, and placed it at the foot of the ladder leading up to the roof. (Marie's family is Polish, and Greenpoint is the largest Polish enclave on the East Coast.) Meanwhile, one of the officers rested the board between the roof and a tree branch and leaned over the edge of the roof and tried to coax the cat toward the loop. (I held the back of his belt to keep him from going over the edge.) The other cop stood below to help if the cat fell down and got hurt. The roof officer's gentle pss-ing and sss-ing worked. Strauss rubbed against the loop, the body inside the belt I was holding jerked, and a thrashing cat was dragged along the board and pinned neck-first to the tarpaper.*

35

I fetched this feline by the scruff, released the rope, and held him over the roof hatch. Terror would not aptly describe what I saw in his eyes when I released him to a feathered landing below. He hit the poduszka on all fours and seemingly ricocheted across stairs, a banister, and walls until he disappeared into my mother-in-law's apartment below. From that day on, Strauss seemed to appreciate and emulate the more quiet doings of his brother Abraham. I, on the other hand, pondered more creative uses for that noose-ended tube as you will see when you read "Don't Kill a Karate Fighter."

# Don't Kill a Karate Fighter

## WILLIAM E. CHAMBERS

NEVER MARRY A KARATE fighter!

I did and look at the shape I've been in. My problems began immediately after the honeymoon. It was my bowling night. I'll never forget how my little wife's voice drifted across the lawn as I climbed into the car.

"Be back by midnight, honey, or I'll break your butt!"

The trouble was she could, and almost did!

I arrived home about two. The home was totally dark. Not even a night light. I thought nothing of it as I staggered through the door. I couldn't see a foot in front of me and I mean that literally because it was definitely a hard, calloused foot that crashed into my body one inch from my groin.

I'm certain it was either the edge of Margot's palm or an axe-handle that creased my neck. But upon awakening and finding nothing broken, I concluded she wasn't really too angry.

Actually, she has a soft spot for things she considers helpless. Why, she wouldn't harm a polar bear that didn't have it coming.

And so I continued to ignore her admonitions. After all, a bachelor of thirty-five develops some hard-to-break habits. Like golf with the fellows on Saturday or the Thursday night poker games.

However, after several mornings of awakening with severe headaches and knowing I hadn't been drunk the night before, I began to appreciate Margot's point of view. Or at least accept it.

That's how things stood for quite a while.

Our romance had begun one night when I attempted to defend her from a masher.

But that was a laugh!

Margot was sitting alone at a table in Tammy's, a fashionable discotheque. Her dress was low on the boulders—uh—shoulders and high on the thighs. Every time she crossed her legs or took a deep breath the entire male patronage suffered from pleasurable eye strain.

One big guy did more than strain his eyes. He was broad, blond, and cocky. He swaggered up to her table.

"Shall we dance?"

"No!"

"No?"

"No. We shall not dance. Remove yourself."

"Come on now, sugar. You wouldn't want to spoil my rep."

"Your rep for what? Ballet dancing?"

"Listen—"

"The lady said no."

That was me. Perfect timing. My voice cracked beautifully. He turned warily and looked right over my head. I waved my handkerchief and rasped, "Here I am. Down here."

He looked and guffawed.

Little did he know I boxed in college. He was still laughing when I fired my devastating one-two combination. He was still laughing when I jumped up and down, wringing my aching hands. Then his fist struck like a triphammer and the floor slapped my back.

Suddenly two dainty little hands flashed and his collarbones snapped. Right then I fell for her.

"You beast!" She kicked him in the teeth and my heart was captured.

"Thank you for helping me," she cooed as my third attempt to rise was successful.

"Think nothing of it. Your life and virtue are safe with me. You shouldn't have even bothered to interrupt."

"But he was beating you up."

"Nonsense. I'd just let him pound me, then when his arms dropped from exhaustion, I'd give him the old one-two."

She blinked incomprehendingly, but when I laughed she did also. "You've got guts. Just like my mother. I like that."

"You got muscles. I don't know if I like that." My eyes told her I wasn't serious. She had the kind of muscles you liked.

I walked her home that night and kissed her on the doorstep. I mean I kissed her on the mouth while she was standing on the doorstep. I even patted her fanny. She must have liked it because I left in one piece.

That following Saturday she invited me to dinner.

"Waldo, this is my mother, Mrs. Otto."

Her mother stepped back, allowing the barbell she'd been pushing overhead to drop to the floor, and extended her hand. "So you're my daughter's hero?"

Her eyes registered surprise above her broken nose. We shook hands and I began to cry. "What's the matter with him?"

"It's—it's hayfever, Mrs. Otto. Sometimes my eyes tear."

"Come upstairs and have some carrot juice. Great for the eyes."

Holding my right wrist with my left hand I guided my damaged fingers upstairs.

Over a dinner of raw vegetables, broiled liver, and high protein crackers, Margot recounted a somewhat trumped-up version of my heroics. Her mother didn't talk much. She just chewed, growled, and nodded. Finally, she said: "Waldo, you don't look like much but neither does a mongoose. Yet they kill dangerous snakes."

This remark made Margot beam. The old lady had really fallen for me.

Ours was an exhausting courtship. Sitting-up exercises during the day and busy nights on the mat. Fighting, not wrestling.

Finally, we were married. Her mother paid for the reception and half the furniture. But her special gift was a cement block never before touched by human hands. Margot shattered it on the bridal table while her mother wept with pride. She placed some of the fragments under our pillow that night for luck. It was worse than cookies in bed.

We took a cruise through the Caribbean. The long lazy days in Haiti gave us plenty of time to exercise in our hotel room. This is where I finally dissented.

At first she tried to soften me by wearing a topless karate uniform. But I stood firm. While she was demolishing boards I was damaging bone. What good's a bridegroom with swollen hands? On the last day of our honeymoon, I absolutely laid down the law.

"I quit! I'm through knocking myself out to be a human woodchuck."

"Quit! Why, you mouse. How could I have ever compared you to my mother?"

Thus the ordeal began. Under her deft tutelage, I developed such admirable skills as dishwashing, rug-beating, housecleaning, and other things, while she pursued the very feminine art of shattering roof tiles or splintering oak boards.

It was really becoming unbearable. I wanted to escape but divorce was out. Imagine my telling a judge: "It's just terrible, Your Honor, the way she whips my ass."

Too humiliating. There would have to be another way.

One night, while watching my dainty little wife barehandedly damage more wood than a forest fire, the idea occurred to me. Would it really alter the world's future to remove this female James Bond? I gave it serious thought as Margot stood, hand raised, breathing deeply.

Her blue eyes glittered. Suddenly the basement Japanese gymnasium echoed a feminine shriek. Her hand flashed and a red brick exploded like a grenade.

She turned to me and said: "I have good news."

"You're booked to fight Joe Frazier?"

"Ha! Ha! No. Mama's going to spend the holidays with us."

"Wonderful. You can work out together. Does she still have our spare house key?"

"Of course."

The following day was very mild for November. I sat in Central Park feeding bread crumbs to the pigeons and pondering my dilemma. I was about to terminate my lunch hour by blowing up the bag and bursting it when suddenly the police arrived.

A cat, it seems, had climbed into a tree and was unable to come down. One of the patrolmen extended a hollow, tubular pipe toward the animal. A cord had been inserted through the pipe, forming a loop at the extended end. The cop controlled the cord at his end. He gained the cat's confidence by gently petting it with the pipe. Then quickly slipping the cord around its neck, he jolted the animal from its perch.

An idea clicked. On my way home that night I bought a long steel pipe and some cord.

I decided to kill Margot on Thanksgiving eve. That way I'd have something to be thankful for. I'd do it during her workout and dump her body by the sump. I'd tell the police I had gone to bed early and she had gone out jogging. Who could prove differently?

I put my plan into effect the very evening of its conception by entering the basement, apron and feather duster in hand.

"Honey, I think I owe you an apology."

"What for?" she asked, unleashing a barrage of kicks and punches against the heavy bag.

"I realize I've been rather selfish. I'd like to resume training."

She checked her flying roundhouse kick and smirked. "I thought you'd come around sooner or later."

"Well, I have. I've even got a few tricks up my sleeve I want to try with you."

I worked out regularly for the next few days.

Margot was delighted. Especially when I pulled a few dirty tactics I had learned from a friend of mine whose hobby was being an after-hour gladiator in Brooklyn's saloons.

"Turn around and close your eyes and I'll attack you," I would say.

She always complied eagerly. Once I tried a stranglehold with a garrison belt and another time a full nelson from behind. Each time I ended on my butt. Margot was in ecstasy.

"Waldo, this is such fun! Do you know any other tricks?"

"One or two. You'll see."

Everything was going as planned.

Thanksgiving eve, while she was doing her barehanded Paul Bunyan act, I prepared to strike. She was breathing deeply and concentrating. An innocent concrete block was abruptly obliterated.

"Margot. Another trick. Stand close. You close your eyes."

"OK. Fine."

I quickly secured my pipe from behind the stairs, slipped the noose over her head and yanked the cord. She thrashed like a hooked flounder but the six-foot rod kept me safe from her deadly punches and mule-like kicks.

As she grew weaker, I pulled harder. She dropped to her knees, her struggles reduced to feeble finger gouges and elbow thrusts.

"Waldo! Just what do you think you're doing?"

The sweat under my arms froze. The pipe slipped from my hands. I turned to face my mother-in-law, the Kung-Fu* queen. She immediately adopted her Praying Mantis stance. Behind me, Margot began to recover. I could tell by her snarl. I closed my eyes and waited. What else could I do?

Margot must have snap-kicked me from behind because my knees gave out just as "Mama's" fist zeroed in on my chin. Fireworks exploded in my brain while an army marched right over me.

I came to feeling like something a dinosaur had chewed up and spit out. Everyone was looking at me. My mother-in-law, my wife, the police— the police! Thank God, I was saved.

A plainclothesman gave me the spiel about my rights.

"Don't bother," I told him. "I'm guilty. Just carry me out of here."

---

*Kung-Fu is an Oriental method of self-defense similar to karate. Its techniques simulate the movement of wildlife creatures such as the praying mantis.

Once safely in their arms, I worked up the guts to address Margot. "What brought her out here tonight?"

"I told you she was coming for the holidays."

"Christmas and New Years!"

"Thanksgiving, too."

"Lucky for you."

The old lady made a menacing move but the patrolmen pulled their guns. They knew her reputation. However, Margot's features softened as she fingered the burn on her throat.

"I—I am lucky. Self-defense is based on outwitting your opponent. And all my training was useless before your superior cunning."

I cocked an eyebrow suavely. "Naturally," I said.

"Oh, Waldo. I've been so wrong about you. If you can only forgive me—if you'll only have me back, I'll never, ever lay a finger on you again."

Tears welled up in her eyes and my jaw slackened. The cops were so shocked they dropped me.

"Clumsy idiots!"

That was the old lady. Now she was sniffling. Margot knelt beside me.

"Please say yes."

"No more," Margot said. "I promise."

"You got a deal."

I kissed her long and hard even though my swollen lips hurt. It was the least I could do.

# Entrapped

## HARLAN COBEN

## Harlan Coben's Introduction:

*I don't write a lot of short stories. To date, I've written only three. This one, "Entrapped" is my very first.*

*I have nothing against the short story form, actually. It just really isn't me. I like reading and writing novels. Novels are a commitment, a long-term relationship. Short stories I've always viewed more as a one-night stand—fun, a jolt, and when I was young, embarrassingly quick.*

*Drum roll. Thank you, I'm here all week.*

*I'm not sure what the inspiration for writing this story was. I like to start with what seems an impossible situation and then figure my way out of it. This time, a young woman reports her husband missing. When she gets home, a man is there who claims to be her husband. Everyone believes him. The problem is, he's not her husband.*

*What I especially enjoyed about writing the story was the viewpoint and gender: first-person female. Originally I called it "The Imposter." When I sold it to Mary Higgins Clark Mystery Magazine, they changed the name. I'm used to that. The titles I've given my previous four novels have all been changed. But that's okay. I'm lousy with titles.*

*I really dig this twisty tale. I hope you do too.*

# Entrapped

## HARLAN COBEN

"My husband is missing," I said.

I waited for Sergeant Harding's reaction, but he seemed preoccupied—if not enamored—with the half-eaten croissant in his right hand.

He was fiftyish, I guessed. His suit looked like it'd been stored in a laundry hamper since the Watergate hearings. So, actually, did he.

With a sigh, Harding put down the croissant and picked up a pencil. He flashed me a smile with teeth the yellow of a Ticonderoga pencil. "Well now!"

I tried my best not to swoon.

"How long has your husband been missing, Mrs. . . . ?"

"Kimball," I said. "Jennifer Kimball. My husband's name is Edward and he's been missing for two days."

He wrote it down, barely looking down at the notepad. "Address?"

"Three Markham Lane."

"Markham Lane?" he repeated. "Isn't that where those ritzy new mansions were just built?"

I nodded, adjusting the gold bracelet on my hand—a gift from Edward—and crossed my legs. His eyes brightened and followed, slithering along my flesh like earthworms.

"My husband and I just moved to New Jersey last week," I explained. "From Arizona, outside Phoenix."

He looked surprised. "You from this area originally, honey?"

Aside from perhaps "babe" or "sweet-buns," there are few things I enjoy more than being called "honey" by a charismatic hunk who possesses that rare combination of boss threads and top-drawer dental hygiene. "Why on earth would you need—"

"Look, Mrs. Kimball, I'm on your side." He spoke in that patronizing tone some men get around me. "I want to find out what happened too, okay? But put yourself in my position. You move out here from Phoenix and a day or two later your husband disappears. I have to consider the possibility that there may have been a lover's tiff or—"

"There was no lover's tiff," I interrupted. "My husband is missing. His car is gone."

"What kind of car?"

"1997 blue Mercedes 500," I said. "Burgundy interior. Brand new."

He whistled low. "500, huh? Jersey plates or Arizona?"

"New Jersey. AYB 783."

He jotted it down. "What does your husband do, Mrs. Kimball?"

"Edward is an international trader," I said vaguely. "But he hasn't had time to rent an office here yet."

"Does he have any friends or family in the area?"

"None."

"Do you have a photograph of him?"

I reached into my purse with fumbling fingers and plucked out a small photograph of Edward.

"Nice-looking man," Harding commented.

I said nothing.

"How long you been married?" he asked.

"Six months."

His phone rang. "Harding," he answered. "What? Oh, good. Fine." He replaced the receiver and rose. "Well, Mrs. Kimball, we'll do a little checking and see what we come up with."

I was dismissed.

I CONFESS TO HAVING expensive taste. So sue me.

The car—my cuddly baby—is a Jag. She is a powerful, sexy machine. Edward wanted me to get a Mercedes like his—more reliable, he claimed—but I was not to be dissuaded.

I drove up our circular driveway and parked by the front door. But when I put my key in the lock, the door was already unlocked.

Strange.

I eased it open. If I had been trying to do it quietly, I had failed miserably. The door squeaked like a dog toy. I stepped inside, my heals clacking loudly against the marble floor. Then I looked around. Nothing. I meant that almost literally. Very little of our personal belongings had been delivered yet. The large foyer was almost bare.

Then I heard footsteps coming from the other room.

I shivered and backed toward the door, preparing to sprint.

"Jen? Is that you?"

He burst in the foyer, smiling at me. "Hi, hon. Where were you?" He was about six feet tall with wavy dark hair. Fairly run-of-the-mill in the looks department—not bad, not great. He was also a complete stranger. I had never laid eyes on the man in my entire life.

Logic would probably have dictated that I run, but fleeing had never been my style. "Who are you?" I snapped.

The man looked at me, puzzled. "Are you joking?"

"I am two seconds away from screaming," I said. "Who are you?"

"Are you feeling okay, Jen?"

*"Who are you?"*

His puzzled look gave way to a weary smile. "Okay, Jen, let's have it."

"What?"

"Why are you still mad? I thought we had this all straightened out."

"I'm calling the police."

He watched me walk toward the phone but did nothing to stop me. "You're serious."

"Of course, I'm serious. Who are you?"

He looked at me with what appeared to be genuine concern. "Jen, I think you better sit down."

Should I run? To hell with it. I would call Sergeant Harding and see how this guy reacted. I picked up the phone, keeping my eyes on him. He continued to watch with a mix of confusion and concern on his face. I started to dial when I glanced down at the table and gasped.

"Honey, what is it?"

I barely heard him. My hand reached down and picked up a silver key chain—Edward's key chain.

"They're just my keys, Jen," the man said.

I whirled toward him. "Where did you get these?"

"Will you stop it already? Stop pretending you don't know your own husband."

My husband?

I dropped the key chain and dashed outside. So much for my no-fleeing style. The impostor followed, calling my name in a gentle, pleading voice. I veered left and headed toward the garage. When I peered inside, I felt something in my brain stretch taut.

A 1997 blue Mercedes 500. Brand new. I checked out the license plate. New Jersey. AYB 783.

The man came up behind me. "It's just my car."

I spun toward him. "I don't know who you are or what you're trying to pull—"

"Pull? What the hell are you talking about?"

"How did you get his car?"

"Whose car?"

"Edward's!"

"Please stop it, Jen. You're scaring me."

"I'm calling the police."

He shook his head in what appeared to be resignation. "Fine. Call them. Maybe they can tell me what alien scrambled my wife's brain."

I strode back into the house with the man a few paces behind me. I kept glancing back, wondering when he was going to attack, preparing for his imminent pounce. But none came. Surely, he would never allow me to place the call. Once I spoke to the police the gig, as they say, would be up.

I picked up, my hand trembling as though the receiver were a jackhammer. The man moved closer to me. I stepped away and to my surprise, he raised both hands in a surrender salute and backed off. "Whatever I did, Jen, I'm sorry. You have to believe me."

The phone on the other end was picked up. "Livingston police."

"Sergeant Harding, please. This is Jennifer Kimball."

"Hold on a moment." I heard the phone ring again. Then: "Harding."

"Sergeant Harding, this is Jennifer Kimball."

"Well, hello, Mrs. Kimball. Find your husband?"

I felt oddly like a tattletale who just yelled for the teacher. I expected the bully to run away now that an adult was coming. But the Edward impostor kept still as a Rodin.

"No," I said slowly. "But a strange man broke into my house."

"Is he still there?"

"He's standing right in front of me. He says he is Edward."

"Your husband? I don't get it."

"Neither do I, Sergeant. He has Edward's keys and Edward's car, and he claims he is my husband."

Pause. "Well, what is he doing?"

"Doing?"

"Is he trying to escape?"

"No." I imagined how crazy this must have sounded to Harding so I could not really blame him in the least. But of course, I did anyway.

"Mrs. Kimball, would you mind putting him on the phone?"

"If you want."

I handed the phone to the mystery man. "He wants to speak with you."

"Fine," he said, taking the receiver. "Okay, joke's over now," he said into the phone. "Who is this?"

I could barely hear the tinny sound of Harding's voice through the receiver; the impostor's words, however, were quite clear: "What police force? Oh come on now. The joke has gone too far." Pause. "Fine, I'll put you on hold." He pushed down the hold button and pressed for the other line.

"What are you doing?" I asked.

The impostor's face remained set. "Your friend on the phone," he began while dialing the phone, "claims that he is a Sergeant Ronald Harding of the Livingston police. I'm calling the police department myself, to end this little charade once and for all."

I was stunned. How far was this guy going to take this?

He said nothing while waiting for the connection to go through.

Then: "I would like to speak with Sergeant Harding." Pause. "What? So you are a police officer. My God. I apologize, Sergeant, but something very odd . . . yes, of course I am Edward Kimball. No, I do not know what this is all about. My wife left this morning and . . . she said I was what?" He turned and looked at me tenderly. I returned his tenderness with my best hell-spawned glare. "Sergeant, I do not know what is going on here. . . . yes, we had a little fight but . . . fine, that's a good idea. Jen, he wants to speak to you." He handed me the receiver.

"Yes, Sergeant?"

"I'm coming out there right now," Harding replied. "Do you want to stay on the line with another officer until I arrive?"

"I'll put it on speaker-phone," I said. I hit the button and replaced the receiver. "Just hurry."

"On my way."

"He'll be here in a few minutes, Jen," the impostor said. "Try not to upset yourself, okay?"

"Give it a rest already," I said with a sigh. "And stop calling me that."

"What?"

"Jen. That's what Edward calls me."

"Now, honey, I know this move has been stressful but—"

As he rambled on, an idea came to me. You see, most of our belongings had not yet arrived from Arizona, but a few had—including a box of Edward's personal belongings. And what had Edward immediately unpacked from the box and put on the night table next to his bed? Our wedding photo.

That would be my indisputable proof that this guy was an impostor. Case dismissed. Lock him up for breaking and entering and maybe something much worse.

"Jen?"

I tried to smile. "I'm going to go upstairs for a few minutes, uh, darling." Play along, get along—that was my new credo.

"Good," he replied. "Why don't you splash some water on your face? Maybe it'll help clear your mind."

"I'll do that."

MY LEGS FELT LIKE spaghetti strands as I made my way up the grand staircase. This man could not possibly imagine he could get away with taking Edward's place. He must be insane, I thought. An escaped mental patient. . . .

Oh, God, maybe that's it! Maybe he really believes he is Edward. Maybe he stole Edward's wallet and because of some short circuitry in his brain, he now thinks he is my husband.

*Stay cool*, I told myself. *Don't upset him. If he really is unstable, who knows how he'll react if I continue to confront him? Sergeant Harding will be here soon. Just stay calm.*

"Jen, are you all right?"

His voice made me jump. "Much better," I sing-songed, doing my best June Cleaver on happy pills. "I'll be down in a minute."

I tiptoed toward Edward's night table in the bedroom. Relief washed over me when I spotted the familiar silver picture frame. But when I picked up the wedding photograph, my heart slammed into my throat. I closed my eyes and opened them again. But nothing changed.

There I was, wearing white and lace, looking the way a man dreams about his bride looking on his wedding day. And standing next to me with a tan face and bright smile, wearing a black tuxedo with a white tie and cummerbund, was the impostor.

"Jen?"

I dropped the picture and heard it crash. He was leaning against the door frame, his arms crossed like the casual guy in a Sunday circular. "Get away from me," I said.

"It's okay, Jen. Sergeant Harding is here."

Harding rounded the corner as if he'd just been introduced on Leno. "Hello, Mrs. Kimball," he said, spreading his hands. "So what seems to be the trouble?"

"This man is claiming to be Edward," I said.

"Oh, stop it," the man countered. "This has gone far enough."

Harding turned to the impostor. "Where have you been the past two days?"

"Right here, for crying out loud. Jen and I were unpacking. We just moved from Arizona. Look, Sergeant, I am sorry about all this. We had a little disagreement this morning, but I thought it was all settled. Here,"—he walked over to the shattered frame—"this is our wedding picture."

Harding examined the photograph. "Is this your wedding picture, Mrs. Kimball?"

I shook my head. "He must have done something to it," I said. "Trick photography or something. He's about the same height as Edward but aside from that, they look nothing alike."

The phony Edward stepped forward. "You have to face reality, Jen," he said in a soothing tone. "Did I fake all of these IDs too?" He handed Harding a Fendi wallet—Edward's Fendi wallet. I gave it to him for his birthday. There were three picture IDs. All read Edward Blaine Kimball. All had the mystery man's picture on them.

Harding examined the items carefully and then looked at me.

"They're fake," I said. "All of them."

Harding nodded, but he was humoring me now. "Mr. Kimball, do you mind if I talk to your wife alone for a minute?" In other words: I'll straighten out the hysterical bimbo for you, bub. Part of the job.

My voice was strong and measured. "He's not Mr. Kimball, and I am not his wife."

Harding ignored my outburst and kept his eyes on "Edward," who nodded his consent and left the room. Once we were alone, Harding closed the door, took a deep breath, and rubbed his face. "You know how this looks, don't you, Mrs. Kimball?"

"Like I'm raving mad," I replied evenly. "But I'm not. He is not Edward. He has fake IDs and he tampered with our wedding photo. He must be a lunatic of some kind. He must. . . ."

Harding held something in front of my face and my words drifted off. Reality, something that was always so firmly planted for me, was being ripped up by the roots. "No. . . ."

"This is the photograph of Edward you gave me no more than an hour ago," Harding said. "Take a look at it."

I shook my head.

"Take a look, Mrs. Kimball."

I looked. It was a picture of the impostor.

My head spun. I felt faint, though I had never fainted in my life. It couldn't be, it just could not be. . . .

"There are two explanations," he continued, "for what's going on here. One, you are not a well woman, Mrs. Kimball. Two, you are a spoiled brat who craves attention—and let me tell you, lady, I don't appreciate your involving the police in your little mini-drama." He flipped the photograph onto the bed in undisguised disgust. "Get professional help, Mrs. Kimball. I'm a busy man."

He stormed out of the room. I could not move. Somewhere in the distance, I heard a door close and then: "Jen? Are you all right, honey?"

My head did not stop spinning until, mercifully, I passed out.

I HAVE ALWAYS DREAMED a lot. Since I was a little girl, my sleep had taken me on vivid, nocturnal voyages which do not fade away when I am awake. I remember everything, which is not always good. I do not claim to be a prophet, and I do not believe we see the future in dreams but, well, let me tell you what I saw.

I could see myself standing in an alley. I was watching from afar, like Jimmy Stewart in *Rear Window*, helpless to prevent whatever horror might befall my other self. The stench of spoiled garbage was overwhelming. Broken cinder blocks, overturned trash cans, and shattered glass lay sprawled like the wounded. A single light bulb at the end of the alley cast the only illumination. I stepped forward.

Up ahead, I could see Edward's Mercedes. I took another step, and suddenly I could see a whole lot more. Resting on the steering wheel was Edward's head—or, at least, what was left of it. Blood covered his shoulders and dripped off the dashboard, forming a murky puddle on the floor near his feet.

Now I could see someone was in the car next to him. But who? I squinted and then saw who it was. No surprise really. It was the Edward impostor. He reached into the pocket of Edward's custom-made English suit and took out his wallet. He pocketed the money, checked the ID, and then the impostor turned and looked at me—looked straight into my eyes—and smiled.

I sat up in the bed, gulping down deep breaths. A light film of perspiration coated my skin.

"Feeling better?" The impostor stood in the doorway, that horrid dream smile still pinning his lips.

I stood and stumbled a few feet in his direction. "Please," I said, angry with myself for sounding so weak. "Tell me what you want. I'll do anything you say. Just stop. . . ."

He started toward me but when I backed away again, he sighed and shook his head. "I have work to do," he said in a tone of surrender. "I'll be downstairs in the study."

And then it dawned on me. I suddenly knew how I could prove he was an impostor: Edward's aunt.

Rose Kimball was Edward's only living relative. The old goat was over seventy and lived in Boston, but she would know this guy was a fake in two seconds. Rose and I, to be honest, had never been very close. To be more precise, the old goat hated me. Like many people I have come across, she equated beauty with gold-digging and thus took an immediate dislike for me.

But now Rose would be my salvation. She knew Edward better than anyone and would be able to tell just by the voice that this man was an impostor. I reached for the phone next to the bed and quickly dialed her number. After four rings, someone answered: "Hello?"

"Hello, Rose."

"Hello, Jennifer." Her tone could frost a wedding cake. "What can I do for you?"

For once, her snootiness did not bother me. The important thing was that she had recognized my voice right away. "Someone wants to talk to you," I said. I put my hand over the mouthpiece. "Edward! Your aunt is on the phone."

The impostor picked up the extension downstairs. "Rose? Is that you?" He knew her name.

"Oh, Edward, I'm so glad you called."

The hope soaring inside me nose-dived. "That's not Edward!" I shouted.

"What are you talking about?" Rose snapped.

"It's all right, Aunt Rose," the impostor said in a maddeningly calm tone. "Jen has been under a little strain lately."

"I'm not under any strain! You're not Edward! Tell him, Rose. Tell him you know he's a phony."

"I most certainly will not," Rose huffed. "I warned you about her, Edward."

"She'll be fine, Aunt Rose. I think it's the move. How are you feeling?"

They chit-chatted for several minutes before saying their heartfelt good-byes. I sat there with the phone in my hand, my mouth agape. The impostor did not even sound like Edward.

My head felt like it was splitting in two; nothing made sense to me anymore. Before my call to Rose, I could see how the whole thing could be possible, if not rational. You see, my dream earlier had provided a possible explanation for this whole thing: the impostor had simply pushed Edward's body out of the car and decided to take his place. He had somehow tampered with the wedding photograph and might have even paid Harding off to switch the wallet pictures. I'm not suggesting that this made sense, mind you, but at least it was within the realm of possibility.

But not now. Aunt Rose would never go along with such a scheme. She could not be bought (the old goat had more money than God) and more important, she loved Edward unconditionally. There was no way she would go along with such a stunt, no way at all, unless. . . .

But no, that was impossible—impossible and irrational and utterly ridiculous. Better not to think of it . . . which left me with only one other possibility, a possibility that kept poking me with a long finger: Maybe I had indeed lost my mind.

Maybe I was going through some sort of nervous breakdown. It's not the kind of thing you can look at very objectively, but only someone completely insane would not begin to question their own sanity after all this.

"Edward?" I called down sweetly. Donna Reed on saccharine.

"Yes, darling?"

"I'm going to take a long hot bath. Can we talk after that?"

"I'd love that. Don't worry, darling. You're going to be all right. I'll take care of you."

Oh, right, sure. I went into the bathroom and turned the water on. I had no intention, however, of taking a bath. I tiptoed down the stairs, passed the study door, and headed into the yard. A minute later, I was in the garage, standing over Edward's car. I am not sure what I was looking for. Bloodstains perhaps. A clue of some kind. But I found nothing. The front seat was spotless, just as Edward himself had always kept it. There was just one little problem.

The interior color was not the same.

Edward had a specially designed burgundy interior. This car—the impostor's car—was gray.

I almost cried out. This was not Edward's car, and I was not insane. The man in my house was not Edward. Part of me felt relief. Part of me felt mounting terror. It brought me back to an earlier fear, a fear that swept through me when Rose insisted that the impostor was indeed her nephew. There was only one way Rose would go along with such a lie: if Edward told her to.

There, I said it. I knew, of course, that this was not possible. I would sooner believe that Rose could be bought off than believe that Edward was somehow behind all this. Yet, the more I thought about it, the more bothersome it became. Eliminate the impossible and what do you have left?

I quietly opened the door of my Jag and slid into the seat. As I pulled out of the driveway, I glanced behind me. Through the study window, I saw the impostor talking on the phone, watching me.

IT TOOK ME HALF an hour to find the alley—mostly because I had to make sure I wasn't being followed. When I got there, everything was exactly as I had seen in the dream—the darkness, the bare light bulb at the end of the alley, the stench that could paralyze a zebra.

Holding my breath, I hurried toward the Dumpster. It would have been quite a spectacle to those who know me to see Jennifer Kimball down on all fours in a filthy alley, reaching through the buzzing flies for something under a Dumpster. But those people did not know what Jennifer Kimball had gone through in the past. But not anymore. Not ever again.

I felt around until my hand hit metal and pulled it into view. A gun—a .38 actually, Smith and Wesson. I checked the chamber. I was sure there was going to be blanks. It was the only explanation for everything that was going on. I emptied the five chambers that were left intact.

The bullets were real. No blanks.

I dropped the gun as though it were on fire. Yet again, nothing made sense, absolutely nothing. It was as though I had woken up one morning and all the laws of nature had been changed. E did not equal MC squared. The Atlantic Ocean was a land mass. The earth was flat. And the clear line between life and death was suddenly very blurry.

I turned the corner and was greeted with yet another surprise that tore at my sanity with sharpened claws: a 1997 blue Mercedes 500, brand new, New Jersey plates AYB 783. Just where it had been in the dream.

I moved closer to the car and peered through the back window. There was a body slumped across the front seat, the head resting on the steering wheel.

With something past horror, I realized that my hand was grasping the handle. The car door swung open slowly. I swallowed and reached in to pull the head back. At the last moment, as I stared at the dried blood on the burgundy interior, I had a second to wonder why, if Edward was behind all of this, he had not let the impostor use his own car. And in that split second, the answer came to me: Edward's Mercedes was state evidence and needed in another scheme.

The head on the steering shot upright and smiled at me. "Hello, Mrs. Kimball."

I jumped back, tripping over a can and falling to the ground. I clambered back up as he got out of the car and faced me. Suddenly, everything made sense. All the pieces were coming together. And it wasn't a pretty picture.

"It can't be," I shouted, though in truth I knew it had to be. It was the only thing that fit. You see, Edward was not behind all this. Edward was indeed dead.

"It's over, Mrs. Kimball."

Sergeant Harding stepped out of the Mercedes as a police car pulled in behind us. Two men got out and pointed guns at me. One was the Edward impostor.

I swung my head back toward Harding. "I don't . . ."

"Understand?" he finished for me. "I think you do. We found your husband's body here the night he was murdered."

Time to play Dumb Dora. "Murdered?"

"You killed him, Mrs. Kimball, just like you killed your first husband."

Time to play Grieving Widow. I produced a tear in my eye. "Gary died in a car accident."

"His car went over a cliff and into a ravine," Harding agreed, "but you pushed it. You also collected a half-million-dollar insurance policy on him."

Shocked. Insulted. Confused. "What are trying to say?"

"When we found Edward Kimball's body," he began, "his ID still had your Arizona address. The only emergency number listed was for Mrs. Rose Kimball, an aunt who lived in Boston. When we told her what had happened, she immediately suspected you. Now, I've listened to a lot of weird old ladies, so I did not pay much attention until I did a little background check. Edward Kimball had recently purchased almost three million dollars' worth of life insurance. Imagine that."

I'd been conned. Me. "This proves nothing."

"Right again," he continued. "You were very smart about it. You knew your husband the international trader was actually a drug dealer and as a result, his murder would look like a hit. But like Rose Kimball, I suspected otherwise. So we came up with the idea of creating another Edward."

"I still don't—"

"You were right, of course. The wedding photo was a little bit of trick photography. The IDs were police forgeries. We picked up another Mercedes but we couldn't get one with the burgundy interior so we used a gray one."

"So you wanted me to think Edward was alive?"

He shrugged. "We were playing a little mind game, that's all. You knew you shot him in the head. But after all of this, you began to have doubts. You began to wonder if Edward had somehow survived, if he had somehow discovered your plan and pulled a fast one on you—switched your real bullets for blanks, used a little ketchup to make everything look nice and bloody. And now maybe he was wreaking revenge on you with this impostor. That was what you thought, wasn't it?"

I was too busy looking for a way out to respond.

His face was so damned smug. "So you came back here to check the gun for blanks and prove to yourself that Edward was alive," he continued. "And once you turned that corner, Mrs. Kimball, you gave it all away. There was only one way you could have known where the gun was or about this alley. Because you killed him."

I spotted a sliver of light. "Can I borrow a cigarette, Sergeant?"

He tossed me a pack of Marlboros. I took one out and lit it. I expected to choke and start coughing hysterically—I have never tried a cigarette before—but I found it rather pleasant and somewhat comforting. "Suppose I had not thought Edward was behind it?" I asked.

"Excuse me?"

"Suppose," I continued, "that instead of doubting Edward's death I began to doubt my own sanity. Suppose my already fragile mind was pushed to the brink by your heartless scheme?"

Harding looked at me, a little lost now.

I turned toward the impostor. "Edward, will you take me home now?"

"Huh?"

Yes, it was time to play Ms. Insanity Plea. Paint me Victim of Overzealous Police. Juries loved that. I threaded my arm in the impostor's. "Sergeant Harding wants to lock me up, Edward. He thinks I killed you. But here you are, alive and well. You know I would never harm you. I love you. You're my husband. They think I've done something awful to you. Well, we'll just have to hire the best lawyer in all the land. . . ."

# Yellow Gal

## MICHAEL COLLINS

# Michael Collins's Introduction:

*"Yellow Gal"* *was first published in* New World Writing No. 11 *in 1957. (New World Writing, NAL Mentor, was one of two showcase anthologies of "new" fiction, poetry, and essays from major paperback publishers in the late forties and early fifties. The other was* Discover, *I think, from Pocket Books.) Unless you count war a crime, it was my first crime story. It was also the biggest event in my young writing career. Everyone wanted to be in those two anthologies, and my appearance in* New World Writing *led directly to the publication of my first two novels—*Combat Soldier, *and* Uptown, Downtown. *(Neither title was my original; some things never change.)*

*J. Bradley (Brad) Cumings III was the NAL editor who bought "Yellow Gal," and he later bought both my novels. We became friends, and my writing career was off to a good start. Alas, Brad was a heavy drinker, as so many of us were back then, both editors and writers, but he was an alcoholic and couldn't handle it. Eventually, it ruined his career, and my promising start went with him. But he remained a good friend until his far-too-early death some years ago. He was a fine editor, a gentle man, the sixteenth John Cumings to be born in this country, descended from the Red Comyn who claimed the throne of Scotland in the twelfth and thirteenth centuries, and related to half the Atlantic seaboard, including Judge Thayer, who presided at the Sacco-Vanzetti trial. Republishing this story makes me miss Brad more than ever.*

# Yellow Gal

## MICHAEL COLLINS

THAT NIGHT A WARM rain fell on the old river city. Charlie Johnson limped slowly toward the cafe that blinked red and yellow through the wet haze like the distant lights of signals on the tracks guiding to a town with a bar where you could sing for supper and a bed. Forty years is a long time, but the cafe was the same. A little brighter, maybe, with its neon signs, but the same cafe, and the girl would be waiting inside. He made himself walk slowly from the concert hall to make sure the girl would be there first, telling himself all the way that he was crazy.

*Charlie, you're crazy!* The moment he stepped from the train that morning, the moment his feet touched the platform, he told himself he was crazy. *Charlie*, he said, *Charlie, you're a damned old fool.* But maybe it was just the feel of the platform under his feet: hard, respectable, not shifting like the loose gravel of the roadbed the first time he came to this city, sliding down the embankment with his guitar over his head. Maybe it was the people meeting him—the polite, respectful people who carried his bag and guitar to the long, black automobile and drove him to the hotel where they wouldn't have let him in the door that first time in the city.

Now he limped down the dark, wet street toward the cafe, and some of the people who passed on the street, bent against the rain, smiled at him, but he did not recognize anyone. That was what being old meant when you were famous. They knew him, but he didn't know them. He wondered if it was better to be old and famous, or old and unknown. You didn't know damn anyone anyway.

In the old days it was different. Into a bar, unsling the guitar, and sing as long as they'd buy a drink and listen. He didn't know anyone then either, starting to play alone, but always ending with harmonicas, banjos, and sometimes a horn all around like it was his hometown. It didn't matter no one knew him in the old days, they damn soon did. Now, up in New York, they came and sat where he couldn't touch them, and no one had a banjo or harmonica, and they listened polite to his music that was just music to them.

"Charlie Johnson," he said aloud, "you are plumb damn swamp-water crazy."

Hundreds of letters like hers. Kids who wanted to see what a real live jailbird singing-legend was like. Goddamned kids who never had no idea what he was singing about. But her letter was different. He told himself her letter was different. This one he had to go and answer. This one he had to tell to meet him in the old cafe where he met Jenny forty years ago.

"You ain't jus' crazy, Charlie, you is soft in the head."

Maybe he done it because she wrote she liked "Yellow Gal" the best of all his songs. That song come with him out of the swamp the first time, right across Mississippi, through Tennessee, and all the way up North. Up North and right into the goddamn penitentiary. That time the husband come at him with his knife low the way he should. Low and fast, too fast, creasing his side and past when he brought the bottle down on the husband's skull. The knife was under the body when they took it away. That was all that saved him that time. Five years for manslaughter, and he sung his way in and out with "Yellow Gal." It was his song. The others, the ones they shouted for from the big money seats in the big halls, they were other men's songs.

"Jenny" was his song, too. He always ended with "Jenny."

He stood on the stage, tall and white-haired, his thin old body in a black suit, and sang for anyone who knew what he was singing about. He sang the deep hopelessness of thin black men meeting in unpainted temples under the thin rain of scrub pine forests.

> We shall walk through the valley in the shadows of death,
> We shall walk through the valley in peace;
> If Jesus himself shall be our leader—oh,
> We shall walk through the valley in peace.

He sang the songs of dusty men in pits and quarries and turpentine forests; the songs of sweat in the sun of railroad roadbeds; the songs of men chained together and swinging hammers to make ballast for roads they would never use.

*Take this hammer—Whah!*
*Carry it to the Captain—Whah!*
*Take this hammer—Whah!*
*And carry it to the Captain—Whah!*
*If he asks you—Whah!*
*Was I laughin'—Whah!*
*Tell him I was cryin'—Whah!*
*Tell him I was cryin'—Whah!*

He sang the sun on his back, the rain in his eyes, the heat of raw whiskey running inside. He sang the smell of sweat, the smell of the swamp where he was born, the smell of a hard woman on a hard mattress late at night, the wail of a freight train slowing for a curve.

He liked to sing, and tonight had been a good concert, but he was tired and should be in bed back in the hotel, not walking through the rain in the narrow streets of a city of his youth. A lot of years and a lot of distance. Forty years. Jenny was a field woman with big hands, and a long razor scar on her face. That was all he remembered except the long nights and Jenny laughing, smelling of sweat like a woman should at night. He sat in the big chair her grandmother done left her and listened to her sing as she cooked his supper. She taught him the song "Jenny." That was why he called her Jenny. He didn't remember her right name. He sat in the big chair and watched her feed the kid he hadn't seen since they sent him up again after she died.

Limping on his bad leg, he crossed the street that smelled sour with the stink of wet garbage in the back alleys. He crossed through the falling rain to the red-and-yellow cafe. Rain made his leg ache, but he never minded too much because it was the rain that saved him the time he got the bullet in that leg. He never did know if the man he left on the ground was dead or not. Just ran through the wet woods on the hillside. In West Virginia it was, like old John Hardy. Only he wasn't caught like poor John. The rain had hidden him and covered his scent and a day later he was three states away.

She was the only white person in the cafe. After twenty-five years or so in New York he was used to white girls, and black girls, and yeller girls, and brown girls, and he couldn't say why he jumped inside when he saw this girl. Maybe it was just he hadn't expected her to be small and round, with black hair that hung below her shoulders and was shiny even in the dim light of the cafe. A small, straight nose. Soft red lips said every night was Saturday night with her. Small breasts moved high under the tight silk of her white blouse. Her straight gray skirt clung close over her belly showing its curve when she breathed. There was a time, he thought, when she wouldn't have left the section alive.

"Hello," she smiled. "I'm June, June Padgett, Mr. Johnson."

"Like you wrote," he said. "Glad to meet you."

"It was a wonderful concert, Mr. Johnson."

"Call me Yeller," he said. "They always called me Yeller in here. They knowed it didn't mean nothing like it sounds. Yeller Johnson, on account of I'm so black." He laughed, shaking his long, thin frame.

"I thought it might be because of the song," she said.

"Guess maybe that," he laughed. "Always wore a yeller shirt in them days, too."

His trademark back then, that shirt. It was Pete's shirt. Jenny give it to him when he came to her after they killed Pete. He carried that shirt through prison the second time and put it on the first day he come out. Wore it all the time, even on the roads where the railroad bulls could spot him a mile off in it. Wore it all the way to Frisco where he got "discovered" like he'd just been born or something.

"Always liked yeller," he said. "What you drinkin', honey?"

"Gin and ginger ale," she said.

"You can bring me a little rye, son," he told the waiter. The hell with the doctors. When you're sixty-nine you ain't got time for worrying about dying young. Like Pete when he asked him if he was scared. *"Sure I'm scared, kid, but I wasn't fixin' I should live forever."* Old Pete.

"Tell me about yourself, honey," he said. "You sing?"

"Oh, yes, Mr. Johnson. I sing ballads mostly. . . ."

He could not decide where he and Jenny was sittin' that first night, or any other night. He thought it was in the corner near the bar where the juke box was now. But he wasn't sure. Forty years makes a lot of changes.

". . . I can't sing like you—more like Susan Reed. Do you like Susan Reed, Mr. Johnson, she's not as—"

Somehow, the girl looked a lot like Jenny. The only trouble was that he couldn't remember what Jenny looked like. Forty years he'd been singing about a girl named Jenny, who wasn't named Jenny, and who he couldn't really remember. He tried to remember Jenny, but he was tired and the whiskey was hot in him, and his head ached when he tried. He remembered a lot of faces, but which one was Jenny? Maybe all of them was Jenny.

"This is my friend Eddie," the girl said, holding the sleeve of a small man who stood beside her. The man was really only a boy. "He plays guitar. I asked him to come down and meet you."

"That's okay," he said, shaking the boy's hand. "That's fine."

"Can I get you a drink?" the boy asked. He had a guitar case and leaned it against the wall behind them. Charlie wondered if it was a good guitar.

"Never turned down a drink in my life," he said. "Make it rye."

"Eddie plays good guitar," the girl said, "like Sam Madison a little."

"Sam's great," the boy said, returning with the drinks. "I heard him last year and—"

The whiskey was very hot inside him, and smooth, easing the pain in his leg, loosening the old muscles until he felt ready to run over a mountain again. Sam Madison was old Red Madison's boy, at least Red figured he was but had to admit that Sam's mother was mighty popular and Red wasn't all the time sure where she was while he was blowing his trumpet nights. Sam was a good singer, except maybe he sang a little too much like the cover-charge customers wanted. They were talking about Josh and about Sonny, who was one of the best, maybe because he was blind and didn't have much cause to play except like he wanted to play. They talked about Bessie who just sang the way things are and who was dead now.

". . . yeah, Sam's great, but he can't sing things like 'Jenny' the way you can, Mr. Johnson," the boy was saying. "I can't tell—"

Jenny was Pete's woman. Pete killed Jenny's old man to get her, and they got Pete for that. Pete liked him. He was only a kid then, in for that first killing over the yeller gal.

*"You was lucky this time, kid, but they'll get you just like they got me," Pete said.*

*"Not me, Pete. I aim to live a while."*

*Pete laughed at that, an easy laugh that made the deputies look around for help when they had to take Pete in. "Hell, boy, a good man ain't gonna live no long time, 'specially if he's poor 'n black 'n got the gals in his eye. You got the good liquor and no-damn-backtalk look in your eye. If them don't get you, the gals will sooner or later. You jus' like me, kid. You better live whiles you got time.*

*"What you wanna live for you gotta slack up to make it?" Pete said. "If he got the feel to get livin', ain't much man if he worry about livin' old."*

He laughed out loud, thinking of what Pete would say if he could see him now. Yeller Johnson: old, white-haired, with money in the bank, and talking to a white girl in the same town where Pete killed his man to get Jenny. Pete would have one hell of a laugh on himself.

"Did I say something funny?" the girl said, smiling at him.

He waved his hand to the waiter. "Hell no, honey, just thinkin' of something. What's yours, son?" he asked the boy.

"Just beer, Mr. Johnson."

"Play somthin' for me, son," he said.

The waiter came and he ordered gin and ginger ale, beer, and more rye for himself. The boy got his guitar out. It was a shiny new guitar, but the boy handled it well.

"What'll I play?" the boy asked.

"Anythin' son. How 'bout 'Rock Island Line'?"

The boy began to play and he swung back to the table and listened. As he listened, he knew that Pete would not be laughing. Pete wouldn't even know him.

*"You ain't Yaller Johnson, mister. Shuffle off. Yaller Johnson's dead. Killed a long time ago like I said he would. I know Yaller Johnson."*

He could hear Pete real plain, standing right there behind the white girl, sneering at him.

*"I am too Yeller Johnson, Pete. Listen, I'll play you a little tune like I done 'fore they come for you. That'll show you. Listen, Pete. It's Yeller Johnson, Pete."*

*"I don't hear you, mister."*

*"Listen, Pete, I'm singing for you like I always done. I'm singing, Pete."*

"What did you say, Mr. Johnson?" the girl asked.

The whiskey made her seem to float very near, very close, smelling of perfume and sweat.

"I thought you said you'd sing," she said. "I'd like that."

"Me, too," the boy said, laying his guitar down.

He blinked. He opened his guitar case and took out his old guitar. It wasn't the same guitar as forty years ago, but it was old enough. The bartender turned off the juke box to listen.

"'Yellow Gal,'" the girl said, touching his arm.

He ripped into the fast, happy drive of the old song he had brought from the swamps where there wasn't much to do but work and sing and drink your own liquor and find a woman, and where it was worth staying alive just to spit at the swamp sitting like a giant cottonmouth waiting for you to crack.

> *I went home with a yeller gal,*
> *I went home with a yeller gal,*
> *Didn't say a thing to the yeller gal,*
> *Didn't say a thing to the yeller gal.*

He took the song through the dry hills of Texas and up into that Memphis factory where he got a steady job because he had to go and marry Susy

Washington who had four kids of his in three years and hated his guts until he made money in New York and the whole passel tracked him down with their cotton-picking hands itching in his pockets.

> *She was pretty and fine, oh me yeller gal,*
> *She was pretty and fine, oh me yeller gal,*
> *She wasn't none of mine, oh the yeller gal,*
> *She wasn't none of mine, oh the yeller gal.*

Singing the song for pennies on the streets of the old South Side, and in all-night speakeasies when Louis and the King were riding high and stood a touch when his luck got real low. The King was dead now, dead and gone, leaving the blues in the royal garden, the blues in the alleys where he sat watching the yeller gals pass by.

> *She was long and tall, the yeller gal,*
> *She was long and tall, the yeller gal.*
> *She was my downfall, it's the yeller gal,*
> *She was my downfall, it's the yeller gal.*

Singing on a slow freight that stretched from coast to coast and twice back. Singing behind the bars of big jails and little jails. The jails he knew and the jails he didn't know. The other men's jails.

> *Got thirty years for the yeller gal,*
> *Got thirty years for the yeller gal.*
> *Yeller, oh me yeller, oh me yeller gal,*
> *Yeller, oh me yeller, oh me yeller gal.*

Ending on the long, low, descending note like the fade of a faint fog-horn out in the delta.

"Beautiful," the girl said. "Now 'Jenny.'"

Jenny was Pete's woman. They killed Pete because of Jenny. Pete didn't think about that. The only thing worried Pete was what was gonna happen to Jenny.

"*I killed her old man and they gonna kill me. Ain't left that gal no man 'tall," Pete said.*

"*Yaller, you go get Jenny when you gets out. Tell her I said for you and her to stick together. I'm givin' her to you. You tell her," Pete said.*

*"I ain't wantin' your woman," he said.*

*"I ain't 'bout to need no woman," Pete said. "You do like I say."*

Jenny taught him the song. She sang it like no one ever sang it. He always figured he never would have run out on Jenny. He wasn't ever tired with Jenny. Heaving sacks all day at the mill, but he wasn't ever tired. Never too tired for bed, never too tired to play and sing all night. Not with Jenny. He nearly killed the cop who shot her in the mill riot. They sent him up the second time for that. Only what did Jenny look like?

"That's wonderful, Mr. Johnson," the girl said.

"I like it," he said. "Call me Yeller, honey."

"Who was Jenny, Yellow?" she asked, smiling at him.

"She was a gal kinda like you," he said.

She smiled again and picked up his scarred right hand. Her hand was so small she could hold only three of his thick, bent fingers. He felt her thigh against his under the table. His hands sweated on the guitar strings.

"We all ready for another round?" the boy asked.

He nodded, and the boy got up and walked to the bar. He slid into the hard sadness of "Empty Bed Blues." Full beds and empty beds. The girl sat listening with her chin propped on one hand, eyes closed, lips parted. There ain't nothing so empty like an empty bed. The girl sang along with him under her breath, her lips moving with the music. So many empty beds, the ones he was in, and the ones he had left the women in, and all of them fading into the empty bed the night Jenny was killed. Jenny had a scar. But what did Jenny look like? He leaned across the table and kissed the girl's mouth.

Her eyes opened wide—leaped open. With a soft gasp she jerked back. He held her arm, holding her close, the muscles strained in his back. He dropped his guitar, pulled her to him, pulling her closer as she fought.

She screamed.

The boy at the bar whirled around, a glass in each hand. The glasses fell and smashed on the floor. The girl tore loose, stumbled up and across the room to the boy at the bar.

"You goddamn old bastard!" the boy cried, stepping closer, trying to shake the clinging girl away.

"Don't, Eddie, please, he's drunk," the girl cried.

"I'll kill him," the boy raged, pulling free.

"Please, Eddie, let's go."

Roaring with laughter, he leaped. His fist caught the boy full on his angry face. The boy went down dragging the girl with him, blood running over his chin onto his white shirt. The girl struggled to get up, her skirt up to her waist. He watched the boy, but his eyes saw the girl's long white thighs. He saw her blue silk pants. Blue silk, tight to her smooth body and dark at the crotch. The boy stumbled to his feet. The girl wore bright blue pants. It was worth fighting for a girl who wore bright blue pants.

As the boy swung the bottle he felt his knife spring open in his hand. He sidestepped the boy's wild swing of the bottle, moved in low with the knife. Low and close across the boy's arm. Just a little cut. Just a small one. The bottle fell to the floor, rolling across the room into a corner. The bottle was bloody. The boy held his arm. Outside in the street the girl was screaming.

*"Get him out of here!"* someone shouted.

Hands pushed him toward the rear of the cafe. Hands gripped his arm, pushing. The girl out in the street, screaming, and the boy leaning on the bar holding his arm.

Then he was outside and running. The rain splashed on his face. His guitar bounced against his back. No shiny black case now. Over a fence he was in an alley. The rain cool on his face. His leg did not ache any more. Turning, twisting, he limped through the alleys until the noise from the cafe was gone. As he ran he laughed. He laughed until he could no longer run from the pain in his sides.

Leaning against a wall, he laughed so much the tears washed down his face, rippling across the deep wrinkles like shallow water over rocks, faster and wetter than the rain. He slid down the wall into a sitting position, his back against the wall, his legs stretched before him in the inch-deep alley water. He unslung his guitar. Man, he could use that girl in the blue pants. Oh man, but he could use a woman. A low-down yeller woman who raped him with her eyes, who wore blue pants and squeezed with her long, brown, field-muscled legs. In the falling rain of the alley he began to sing.

> *Oh, big fat woman with the meat shakin' on her bones.*
> *I love my woman and I tell the world I do,*
> *I love my woman and I tell the world I do,*
> *Oh Lord, I love my woman, tell the world I do,*
> *She was good to me, just like I's good to you.*

His fingers were wet and slippery on the strings. The music would not come right. Dropping the guitar, he lay flat on the ground, staring into the low, dark sky. Mouth open, he let the rain wash through him. He started to laugh again.

"Pete," he shouted, "Pete man! What you think of this one?"

The sound of a car engine hummed into his mind. It grew louder slowly, very slowly, as if the car was creeping along the street and stopping at each corner. The car was looking for something.

"Charlie," he said, "that means cops."

Struggling to his feet, he picked up his guitar and ran away down the alley. At the first corner he turned into a street. Limping fast, he was in the middle of the street before he could stop. A police car sat parked under the nearest street lamp. Two policemen stood beside it.

"There he is!" one policeman shouted, and then ran toward him calling out, "Hold it now, hold it!"

He shook his head, and looked wildly up and down the street. The policeman reached to hold him. Laughing, he swung his guitar, felt it smash against the policeman's face. The other policeman ran from the patrol car to help his partner. He dropped his broken guitar into the gutter. One of them shouted to him again. He ran on, limping over the broken concrete. He whooped aloud as he ran. He felt good, good. He ran and laughed.

When he heard the shots behind him he began to weave and dodge, running more slowly, running in irregular spurts to confuse the shooters. At the corner he turned to see where they were.

It felt as if he had run full into a brick wall. He was still running, but his legs didn't move. The wall lay on top of him, pressing him down into the wet street. He heard voices. Jenny was looking down at him, the long scar standing out white on her black face. She grinned at him. He wondered if her pants were blue. The voices kept talking, talking. Talking so loud he could not hear Jenny. She raised her skirt so he could see the color of her pants. They were blue. He laughed happily when he saw them.

"He's trying to talk," a voice said.

"I didn't mean to hit him," a voice said. "Jesus! He just turned and stopped. Jesus!"

"Shut your fat yap, he's trying to talk!"

"I just wanted to scare him, for Christ sake."

"Always the gun! You gotta go for the gun."

"The poor bastard's laughing."

"Wait 'till the papers get this."

"Shut up! All of you! Where's the friggin' ambulance?"

Jenny was trying to say something. He wished they would stop shouting. If he kept running maybe he could get away from the voices. Pete was way ahead, running fast with that easy run that could drive a hound into the ground. He ran faster to catch up, like a turkey through the corn, boy, like a turkey through the corn.

*"We're long gone, Pete man, we're long gone,"* he laughed.

Pete laughed, too, running alongside.

*"Come on, Pete, run, man, run!"*

The rain washed all over him. He could feel it wet inside. Wet and warm, like Jenny in the dark on the old iron bed. Wet and warm and dark. He ran faster. The more he ran the more he laughed. He could hardly hear the voices at all now.

"All the fuck he does is laugh!"

"Goddamn that ambulance!"

Then he did not hear the voices anymore. Jenny and Pete stopped running.

They were grinning at him.

# Together

## JEFFERY DEAVER

## Jeffery Deaver's Introduction:

*My experience with the short-story form goes back to the distant past.*

*I was a clumsy, chubby, socially awkward boy without the least aptitude for sports and, as befit someone like that, I was drawn to reading and writing, particularly the works of short-story writers such as Poe, A. Conan Doyle, and Ray Bradbury.*

*When I was in junior high school and my teacher would assign writing projects, I'd invariably try my hand at a short story. I didn't, however, write genre stories, as did the writers I just mentioned, but, with youthful chutzpah, I created my own subgenre of literary short story. These tales usually involved clumsy, chubby, socially awkward boys rescuing attractive girls from life-threatening situations that were both spectacular and highly improbable, like my hero's daring mountaineering rescue set just outside of Chicago, where my family lived at the time (it was the Midwest, for God's sake; you had to drive two hundred miles just to see a hill!). I call these stories "literary," by the way, because the rescuees came to see that there were social and philosophical values far better than those embraced by jocks on the football and basketball teams.*

*The stories were met with about the reaction you'd expect from a teacher who'd spent the hours offering us the entire pantheon of literary superstars as models to emulate in our own writing. I was a solid A-for-form, C-for-content short-story writer.*

*In high school I finally came to abandon the theme of the socially inept youth (as a writer, I mean; it still dogged me as my personal style) as well as the short story genre itself, and I turned to poetry, songwriting, and, eventually, journalism.*

*In my late twenties and thirties I began to write suspense novels and pretty soon they occupied 100 percent of my time as an author. I read short fiction in* Ellery Queen, Alfred Hitchcock, Playboy, The New Yorker, *and occasional anthologies. I often thought about writing stories myself, but I just didn't seem to have the time, working as I was at a full-time job while trying to crank out a novel every twelve to fourteen months or so.*

But a few years after I quit my day job to write full time, a fellow author, compiling an anthology of original short stories, asked if I'd consider contributing one to the volume.

Why not? I asked myself, and plowed ahead and wrote one.

I found, to my surprise, that the experience was absolutely delightful—and for a reason I hadn't expected. In my novels, though I love to make evil appear to be good (and vice versa) and to dangle the potential for disaster before my readers, nonetheless in the end good is good and bad is bad, and good more or less prevails. I think too much of my readers to have them invest their time, money, and emotion in a full-length novel only to leave them disappointed by a grim, unsatisfying ending.

Ah, but with a thirty- or forty-page short story, readers don't have the same investment. The payoff in this case isn't a roller coaster of plot reversals involving characters they've spent a lot of time learning about and loving or hating, set in places with atmosphere carefully described. Short stories are like a sniper's bullet. Fast, shocking, and to the point.

As a result of this insight, I felt liberated. In writing a short story, all bets were off. I could now make good bad and bad badder. I've been writing about three stories a year since then.

"Together" is the short story I mention above, my first published one. Unfortunately, as with much of my writing, I can't say much about it since it features several plot turns, which I don't want to hint at for fear of lessening the surprise. It's typical of the no-holds-barred, read-at-your-own-risk short story that I enjoy writing.

I believe it was an interviewer in England who, commenting on one of my recent short stories, said that it was yet further evidence that I was compellingly "sick and twisted." I don't think I ever received a higher compliment as an author.

# Together

## JEFFERY DEAVER

"A FEW PEOPLE, A very few people're lucky enough to find a special kind of love. A love that's . . . more. That goes beyond anything that ever was."

"I suppose so."

"I *know* so. Allison and me, we're in that category." Manko's voice dropped to a discreet whisper as he looked at me with his barracks-buddy grin. "I've had a barrelful of women. You know me, Frankie boy. You know I've been around."

Manko was in the mood to perform and all I could do was play both straight man and audience. "So you've said, Mr. M."

"Those other girls, looking back, some of 'em were lovers. And some were just, you know, for the night. Wham, bam. That sort of thing. But till I met Allison, I didn't understand what love was all about."

"It's a transcendent love."

"*Transcendent.*" He tasted the word, nodding slowly. "What's that mean?"

Just after I'd met Manko I'd learned that while he was poorly read and generally uninformed, he never hesitated to own up to his ignorance. That was my first clue as to the kind of man he was.

"It's exactly what you're describing," I explained. "A love that rises above what you normally see and experience."

"Yeah. I like that, Frankie boy. Transcendent. That says it. That's what we've got. You ever love anyone that way?"

"Sort of. A long time ago." This was partially true. But I said nothing more. Although I considered Manko a friend in some ways, our souls were worlds apart, and I wasn't going to share my deepest personal life with him. Not that it mattered, for at the moment he was more interested in speaking about the woman who was the center of his own solar system.

"Allison Morgan. Allison *Kimberly* Morgan. Her father gave her a nickname. Kimmie. But that's crap. It's a kid name. And one thing she isn't is a kid."

"Has a Southern sound to it." I'm a native of North Carolina and went to school with a bevy of Sally Mays and Cheryl Annes.

"It does, yeah. But she's not. She's from Ohio. Born and bred." Manko glanced at his watch and stretched. "It's late. Almost time to meet her."

"Allison?"

He nodded and smiled the trademarked, toothy Manko smile. "I mean, you're cute in your own way, Frank, but if I gotta choose between the two of you . . ."

I laughed and repressed a yawn. It *was* late—eleven-twenty. An unusual hour for me to be finishing dinner but not to be engaged in conversation over coffee. Not having an Allison of my own to hurry home to, or anyone other than a cat, I often watched the clock slip past midnight or 1:00 A.M. in the company of friends.

Manko pushed aside the dinner dishes and poured more coffee.

"I'll be awake all night," I protested mildly.

He laughed this aside and asked if I wanted more pie.

When I declined, he raised his coffee cup. "My Allison. Let's drink to her."

We touched the rims of the cups with a ringing clink.

I said, "Hey, Mr. M, you were going to tell me all 'bout the trouble. You know, with her father."

He scoffed. "That son of a bitch? You know what happened."

"Not the whole thing."

"Don't'cha?" He dramatically reared his head back and gave a wail of mock horror. "Manko's falling down on the job." He leaned forward, the smile gone, and gripped my arm hard. "It's not a pretty story, Frankie boy. It's not outta *Family Ties* or *Roseanne*. Can you stomach it?"

I leaned forward, too, just as dramatically, and growled, "Try me."

Manko laughed and settled into his chair. As he lifted his cup, the table rocked. It had done so throughout dinner but he only now seemed to notice it. He took a moment to fold and slip a piece of newspaper under the short leg to steady it. He was very meticulous in this task. I watched his concentration, his strong hands. Manko was someone who actually enjoyed working out—lifting weights, in his case—and I was astonished at his musculature. He was about five-six and, though it's hard for men—for me at least—to appraise male looks, I'd call him handsome.

The only aspect of his appearance I thought off-kilter was his haircut. When his stint with the Marines was over, he kept the unstylish crewcut. From this, I deduced his experience in the service was a high point in his life—he'd worked factory and mediocre sales jobs since—and the shorn hair was a reminder of a better, if not an easier, time.

Of course, that was my pop-magazine-therapy take on the situation. Maybe he just liked short hair.

He now finished with the table and eased his strong, compact legs out in front of him. Manko the storyteller was on duty. This was another clue to the nature of Manko's spirit: Though I don't think he'd ever been on a stage in his life, he was a born actor.

"So. You know Hillborne? The town?"

I said I didn't.

"Southern part of Ohio. Pisswater river town. Champion used to have a mill there. Still a couple factories making, I don't know, radiators and things. And a big printing plant; does work for Cleveland and Chicago. Kroeger Brothers. When I was in Seattle I learned printing. Miehle offsets. The four- and five-color jobs, you know. Big as a house. I learned 'em cold. Could print a whole saddle-stitched magazine myself, inserts included, yessir, perfect register and not one goddamn staple in the centerfold's boobs. . . . Yessir, Manko's a hell of a printer. So there I was, thumbing 'cross country. I ended up in Hillborne and got a job at Kroeger's. I had to start as a feeder, which was crap, but it paid thirteen an hour and I figured I could work my way up.

"One day I had an accident. Frankie boy, you ever seen coated stock whipping through a press? Zip, zip, zip. Like a razor. Sliced my arm. Here." He pointed out the scar, a wicked-looking one. "Bad enough they took me to the hospital. Gave me a tetanus shot and stitched me up. No big deal. No whining from Manko. Then the doctor left and a nurse's aide came in to tell me how to wash it and gave me some bandages." His voice dwindled.

"It was Allison?"

"Yessir." He paused and gazed out the window at the overcast sky. "You believe in fate?"

"In a way I do."

"Does that mean yes or no?" He frowned. Manko always spoke plainly and expected the same from others.

"Yes, with qualifiers."

Love tamed his irascibility and he grinned, chiding good-naturedly, "Well, you better. Because there is such a thing. Allison and I, we were fated to be together. See, if I hadn't been running that sixty-pound stock, if I hadn't slipped just when I did, if she hadn't been working an extra shift to cover for a sick friend . . . if, if, if . . . See what I'm saying? Am I right?"

He sat back in the creaky chair. "Oh, Frankie, she was fantastic. I mean, here I am, this like four-inch slash in my arm, twenty stitches, I could've bled to death, and all I'm thinking is she's the most beautiful woman I ever saw."

"I've seen her picture." He'd showed it to me a dozen times. But that didn't stop him from continuing to describe her. The words alone gave him pleasure.

"Her hair's blonde. God blonde. Natural, not out of a bottle. And curly but not teased like some high-hair slut. And her face, it's heart-shaped. Her body . . . Well, she has a nice figure. Let's leave it at that." His glance at me contained a warning. I was about to assure him that I had no unpure thoughts about Allison Morgan when he forgot his jealousy. He added, "She's twenty-one years old."

Echoing my exact thought, he added sheepishly, "Kind of an age difference, huh?"

Manko was thirty-seven—three years younger than I—but I learned this after I'd met him and had guessed he was in his late twenties. It was impossible for me to revise that assessment upward.

"I asked her out. There. On the spot. In the emergency room, if you can believe it. She was probably thinking, *How do I get rid of this bozo?* But she was interested, yessir. A man can tell. Words and looks, they're two different things, and I was getting the capital M message. She said she had this rule she never dated patients. So I go, 'How 'bout if you married somebody and he cuts his hand in an accident and goes to the emergency room and there you are? Then you'd be *married* to a patient.' She laughed and said, no, that was somehow backward. Then this emergency call came in; some car wreck, and she had to go off to another ward.

"The next day I came back with a dozen roses. She pretended she didn't remember me and acted like I was a florist delivery boy. 'Oh, what room are those for?'

"I said, 'They're for you . . . If you have *room* in your heart for me.' Okay, okay, it was a bullshit line." The rugged ex-Marine fiddled awkwardly with his cup. "But, hey, if it works, it works."

I couldn't argue with him there.

"The first date was magic. We had dinner at the fanciest restaurant in town. A French place. It cost me two days' pay. It was embarrassing 'cause

I wore my leather jacket and you were supposed to have a suit coat. One of *those* places. They made me wear one they had in the coat room and it didn't fit too good. But Allison didn't care. We laughed about it. She was all dressed up in a white dress, with a red, white, and blue scarf around her neck. Oh God, she was beautiful. We spent, I don't know, three, four hours easy there. She was pretty shy. Didn't say much. Mostly she stared like she was kind of hypnotized. Me, I talked and talked, and sometimes she'd look at me all funny and then laugh. And I'd realize I wasn't making any sense 'cause I was looking at her and not paying any attention to what I was saying. We drank a whole bottle of wine. Cost fifty bucks."

Manko had always seemed both impressed by and contemptuous of money. Myself, I've never come close to being rich, so wealth simply perplexes me.

"It was the best," he said dreamily, replaying the memory.

"Ambrosia," I offered.

He laughed as he sometimes did—in a way that was both amused and mocking—and continued his story. "I told her all about the Philippines, where I was stationed for a while, and about hitching around the country. She was interested in everything I'd done. Even—well, I should say *especially*—some of the stuff I wasn't too proud of. Grifting, perping cars. You know, when I was a kid, going at it. Stuff we all did."

I held back a smile. Speak for yourself, Manko.

"Then all of a sudden, the sky lit up outside. Fireworks! Talk about signs from God. You know what it was? It was the Fourth of July! I'd forgotten about it 'cause all I'd been thinking about was going out with her. That's why she was wearing the red, white, and blue. We watched the fireworks from the window."

His eyes gleamed. "I took her home and we stood on the steps of her parents' house—she was still living with them. We talked for a while more, then she said she had to go to bed. You catch that? Like she could've said, 'I have to be going,' Or just 'Goodnight.' But she worked the word *bed* into it. I know, you're in love, you look for messages like that. Only in this case, it wasn't Manko's imagination working overtime, no sir."

Outside, a light rain had started falling and the wind had come up. I rose and shut the window.

"The next day I kept getting distracted at work. I'd think about her face, her voice. No woman's ever affected me like that. On break I called her and asked her out for the next weekend. She said sure and said she was glad to hear from me. That set up my day. Hell, it set up my *week*. After work I went to the library and looked some things up. I found out about her name. Morgan—if you spell it a little different, it means 'morning' in German. And I dug up some articles about the family. Like, they're rich. Filthy. The house in Hillborne wasn't their only place. There was one in Aspen, too, and one in Vermont. Oh, and an apartment in New York."

"A *pied à terre*."

His brief laugh again. The smile faded. "And then there was her father. Thomas Morgan." He peered into his coffee cup like a fortune teller. "He's one of those guys a hundred years ago you'd call him a tycoon."

"What would you call him now?"

Manko laughed grimly, as if I'd made a clever but cruel joke. He lifted his cup toward me—a toast, it seemed—then continued. "He inherited this company that makes gaskets and nozzles and stuff you'd recognize even if you didn't know what it did. He's about fifty-five and is he *tough*. A big guy, but not fat. A droopy black moustache, and his eyes look you over like he couldn't care less about you but at the same time he's sizing you up, like every fault, every dirty thought you ever had he knows it.

"We caught sight of each other when I dropped Allison off, and I knew, I just somehow *knew* that we were going to go head to head someday. I didn't really think about it then, but deep inside the thought was there."

"What about her mother?"

"Allison's mom? She's a socialite. She flits around, Allison told me. Man, what a great word. *Flit*. I can picture the old broad, going to bridge games and tea parties. Allison's their only child." His face suddenly grew dark. "That, I figured out later, explains a lot."

"What?" I asked.

"Why her father got on my case in a big way. I'll get to that. Don't rush the Manko man, Frankie."

I smiled in deference.

"Our second date went even better than the first. We saw some movie, I forget what, then I drove her home. Parked in front of her house. Took us an hour to say goodnight, you get what I'm saying?" His voice trailed off. Then he said, "I asked her out for a few days after that, but she couldn't make it. Ditto the next day and the next, too. I was pissed off at first. Then I got paranoid. Was she trying to, you know, dump me?

"But then she explained it. She was working two shifts whenever she could. I thought, This's pretty funny. I mean, her father's loaded. But, see, there was a *reason*. She's just like me. Independent. She dropped out of college to work in the hospital. She was saving her own money to travel. She didn't want to owe the old man anything. *That's* why she loved listening to me talk, telling her 'bout leaving Kansas when I was seventeen and thumbing around the country and overseas, getting into scrapes. Allison had it in her to do the same thing. Man, that was great. I love having a woman with a mind of her own."

"Do you now?" I asked, but Manko was immune to irony.

"In the back of my mind I was thinking about all the places I'd like to go with her. I'd send her clippings from travel magazines, *National Geographic*. On our first date she'd told me that she loved poetry so I wrote her poems about traveling. It's funny. I never wrote anything before in my life—a few letters maybe, some shit in school—but those poems, man, they just poured out of me. A hundred of 'em. She told me she really liked the ones I wrote about Florida. That's where I went on a vacation with my mom. The only real vacation I ever took with her. When you grow up in Kansas, man, seeing a beach for the first time, it does something to you. It *does* something.

"Well, next thing I knew, bang, we were in love. See, that's the thing about . . . *transcendent* love. It happens right away, or it doesn't happen at all. Two weeks, and we were totally in love. I was ready to propose. I see that look on your face, Frankie boy. Didn't know the Manko man had it in him? What can I say? He's the marryin' kind after all.

"I went to the credit union and borrowed five hundred bucks and bought this diamond ring. Then I asked her out to a movie and a burger after. I played it real cool, you know. I was going to give the ring to the waitress and tell her to put it on a plate and bring it to the table when we asked for dessert. Cute, huh?

"That day I was working the P.M. shift, three to eleven, for the shift bonus, but I ducked out early, at five, and showed up at her house at six-twenty. There were cars all over the place. Allison came outside, looking all nervous. My stomach twisted. Something funny was going on. She told me her mother was having a party and there was a problem. Two maids had got sick or something. Allison had to stay and help her mother. I thought that was weird. *Both* of them getting sick at the same time? She said she'd see me in a day or two."

I saw the exact moment the thought came into his mind; his eyes went dead as rocks.

"But there was more to it than that," Manko whispered. "A hell of a lot more."

"Allison's father, you mean?"

But he didn't explain what he meant just then and returned to his story of the aborted proposal. He muttered, "That was one of the worst nights of my life. Here I'd ditched work, I was in hock because of the ring, and I couldn't even get five minutes alone with her. Man, it was torture. I drove around all night. Woke up at dawn, in my car, down by the railroad tracks. And when I got home there was no message from her. Jesus, was I depressed.

"That morning I called her at the hospital. She was sorry about the party. I asked her out that night. She said she really shouldn't, she was so tired—the party'd gone to two in the morning. But how 'bout tomorrow?"

A gleam returned to Manko's eyes. I thought his expression reflected a pleasant memory about their date.

But I was wrong.

His voice was bitter. "Oh, what a lesson we learned. It's a mistake to underestimate your enemy, Frankie. You listen to Manko. Never do it. That's what they taught us in the Corps. *Semper fi*. But Allison and me, we got blindsided.

"The next night I came over to pick her up. I was going to take her to this river bluff, like a lover's lane, you know, to propose. I had my speech down cold. I'd rehearsed all night. I pulled up to the house, but she just stood on the porch and waved for me to come up to her. Oh, she was beautiful as ever. I just wanted to hold her. Put my arms around her and hold her forever.

"But she was real distant. She stepped away from me and kept glancing into the house. Her face was pale and her hair was tied back in a ponytail. I didn't like it that way. I'd told her I liked it when she wore it down. So when I saw the ponytail it was like a signal of some kind. An S.O.S.

" 'What is it?' I asked her. She started to cry and said she couldn't see me anymore. 'What?' I whispered. God, I couldn't believe it. You know what it felt like? On Parris Island, basic training, you know? They fire live rounds over your head on the obstacle course. One time I got hit by a ricochet. I had a flak vest on but the slug was a full metal jacket and it knocked me clean on my ass. That's what it was like.

"I asked her why. She just said she thought it was best and wouldn't go into any details. But then I started to catch on. She kept looking around, and I realized that there was somebody just inside the door, listening. She was scared to death—*that's* what it was. She begged me please not to call her or come by, and I figured out she wasn't talking to *me* so much as saying it for whomever was spying on us. I played along. I said okay, if that's what she wanted, blab, blab, blab . . . Then I pulled her close and told her not to worry. I'd look out for her. I whispered it, like a secret message.

"I went home. I waited as long as I could, then called, hoping that I'd get her alone. I had to talk to her. I had to hear her voice, like I needed air or water. But nobody picked up the phone. They had an answering machine but I didn't leave a message. I didn't get any sleep that weekend—not a single hour. I had a lot to think about. See, I knew what'd happened. I knew exactly.

"Monday morning I got to her hospital at six and waited just outside the entrance. I caught up with her just before she went inside. She was still scared, looking around like somebody was following her, just like on the porch.

"I asked her point-blank, 'It's your father, isn't it?' She didn't say anything for a minute then nodded and said that, yeah, he'd forbidden her to see me. Doesn't that sound funny? 'Forbidden.' 'He wants you to marry some preppy, is that it? Somebody from his club?' She said she didn't know about that, only that he'd told her not to see me anymore. The son of a bitch actually threatened her!"

Manko sipped his coffee and pointed a blunt finger at me. "See Frankie, love means zip to somebody like Thomas Morgan. Business, society, image, money—that's what counts to bastards like that. Man, I was so goddamn desperate. . . . It was too much. I threw my arms around her and said, 'Let's get away. Now.'

"'Please,' she said, 'you have to leave.'

"Then I saw what she'd been looking out for. Her father'd sent one of his security men to spy on her. He saw us and came running. If he touched her I was going to break his neck, I swear I would've. But Allison grabbed my arm and begged me to run. 'He has a gun,' she said.

" 'I don't care,' I told her." Manko laughed. "Not exactly true, Frankie boy, I gotta say. I was scared shitless. But Allison said if I left, the guy wouldn't hurt her. That made sense but I wasn't going just yet. I turned back and held her hard. 'Do you love me? Tell me. I have to know. Say it!'

"And she did. She whispered, 'I love you.' I could hardly hear it, but it was enough for me. I knew everything would be fine. Whatever else, we had each other.

"I got back into the routine of life. Working, playing softball on the plant team—hey, you and me, we threw some balls together, Frankie. I'm a hell of a catcher. You know that."

"I'd never want to be a runner with you guarding home."

"Knock your ass clean back to third base. Am I right?"

He was indeed.

"All the time I kept writing her poetry, sending her articles and letters, you know. I'd put fake return addresses on the envelopes so her father wouldn't guess it was me writing. I even hid letters in Publishers Clearing House envelopes addressed to her! How's that for thinking?

"Once in a while I'd see her in person. I found her in a drugstore by herself and snuck up to her. I bought her a cup of coffee. She was nervous as hell, and I could see why. The goons were outside. We talked for about two minutes is all, then one of 'em saw us, and I had to vanish. I kicked my way out the back door. After that I began to notice these dark cars driving past my apartment or following me down the street. They said MCP on the side. Morgan Chemical Products. They were keeping an eye on me.

"One day this guy came up to me in the hallway of my apartment and said Morgan'd pay me five thousand to leave town. I laughed at him. Then he said if I didn't stay away from Allison there'd be trouble.

"Suddenly I just snapped. I grabbed him and pulled his gun out of his holster and threw it on the floor, then I shoved him against the wall and said, 'You go back and tell Morgan to leave us alone or *he's* the one's gonna be in trouble: You got me?'

"Then I kicked him down the stairs and threw his gun after him. I laughed, but I gotta say I was pretty shook up. I was seeing just how powerful this guy was."

"Money is power," I offered.

"Yeah, you're right there. Money's power. And Thomas Morgan was going to use all of his to keep us apart. You know why? 'Cause I was a threat. Fathers are jealous. Turn on any talk show. Oprah, Sally Jessy. Fathers *hate* their daughters' boyfriends. It's like an Oedipus thing. Especially—what I was saying before—with Allison being an only child. Here I was, a rebel, a drifter, making thirteen bucks an hour. It was like a slap in his face— Allison loving me so completely. She was rejecting him and everything he stood for." Manko's face shone with pride for Allison's courage.

Then the smile vanished. "But Morgan was always one step ahead of us. One day I ditched work and snuck into the hospital. I waited for an hour, but Allison never showed up. I asked where she was. They told me she wasn't working there anymore. Nobody'd give me a straight answer, but finally I found this young nurse who told me her father'd called and told 'em that Allison was taking a leave of absence. Period. No explanation. She didn't even clean out her locker. Jesus. All her plans to travel, all her plans with me—gone, just like that. I called the house to get a message to her, but he'd changed the number and had it, you know, unlisted. I mean, this guy was in*credible*.

"And he didn't stop there. Next, he comes after me. I go in to work and the foreman tells me I'm fired. Too many unexcused absences. That was bullshit—I didn't have more than most of the guys. But Morgan must've been a friend of the Kroegers. I was still new, so the union wouldn't go to bat for me. I was out. Just like that.

"Well, I couldn't beat him at his game so I decided to play by my rules." Manko grinned and scooted forward. Our knees touched and I felt all the dark energy that was in him pulse against my skin. "Oh, I wasn't worried for me. But Allison, she's so . . . ." As he searched for a word his hands made a curious gesture, as if stretching thread between them, a miniature cat's cradle. He seemed momentarily despairing.

I suggested, "Fragile."

The snap of his fingers startled me. He sat up. "Ex*actly*. Fragile. She didn't have any defense against her father. I had to do something fast. I went to the police. I wanted 'em to go to the house and see if she was okay. But also it'd be a sign to her father that I wasn't going to take any crap from him." Manko whistled. "Mistake, Frankie. Bad mistake. Morgan was one step ahead of me. This sergeant, some big guy, pushed me into a corner and said if I didn't stay away from Morgan's daughter, the family'd get a restraining order. I'd end up in a cell. Then he looked me over and said something about, did I know all sorts of accidents could happen to prisoners. It was a risky place, jail. Man, was I stupid. I should've known the cops'd be on Morgan's payroll, too.

"By then I was going crazy. I hadn't seen Allison for days. Jesus, had he sent her off to a convent or something?"

Serenity returned to his face. "Then she gave me a signal. I was hiding in the bushes in a little park across the street, watching the house with binoculars. I just wanted to *see* her is all. I wanted to know she was all right. She must've seen me because she lifted the shade all the way up. Oh, man, there she was! The light was behind her and it made her hair glow. Like those things, you know, gurus see."

"Auras."

"Right, right. She was in a nightgown, and I could just see the outline of her body beneath it. She looked like an angel. It was like I was gonna have a heart attack, it was such an incredible thing. There she was, telling me she was all right and she missed me. Somehow, she'd known I was out there. Then the shade went down and she shut the light out.

"I spent the next week planning. I was running out of money. Thanks again to Thomas Morgan. He'd put out the word to all the factories in town, and nobody'd hire me. I added up what I had and it wasn't much. Maybe twelve hundred bucks. I figured it'd get us to Florida. Give me a chance to find work with a printer and Allison could get a job in a hospital."

Then Manko laughed. He studied me critically. "I can be honest with you, Frank. I feel I'm close to you."

So I was no longer Frankie boy. I'd graduated. My pulse quickened and I was deeply, unreasonably moved.

"Fact is, I look tough. Am I right? But I get scared. Real scared. I never saw any action. Grenada, Panama, Desert Storm. I missed 'em all, you know what I'm saying? I was never *tested*. I always wondered what I'd do under fire. Well, this was my chance. I was going to rescue Allison. I was going up against the old man himself.

"I called his company and told his secretary I was a reporter from *Ohio Business* magazine. I wanted to do an interview with Mr. Morgan. She and I tried to find a time he could see me. I couldn't believe it—she bought the whole story. She told me he'd be in Mexico on business from the twentieth through the twenty-second of July. I made an appointment for August 1, then hung up fast. I was worried somebody was tracing the call.

"On the twentieth I staked out the house all day. Sure enough, Morgan left with his suitcase at ten in the morning, and didn't come back that night. There was a security car parked in the driveway, and I figured one of the goons was inside the house. But I'd planned on that. At ten it started to rain. Just like now." He nodded toward the window. "I remember hiding in the bushes, real glad about the overcast. I had about a hundred feet of exposed yard to cover, and the security boys'd spot me for sure in the moonlight. I managed to get to the house without anybody seeing me and hide beneath this holly tree while I caught my breath.

"Then it was dues time, Frank. I leaned against the side of the house, listening to the rain and wondering if I'd have the guts to go through with it."

"But you did."

Manko grinned boyishly and did a decent George Raft impersonation. "I broke in through the basement, snuck up to her room, and busted her out of the joint.

"We didn't take a suitcase or anything. We just got out of there fast as we could. Nobody heard us. The security guy was in the living room but he'd fallen asleep watching the *Tonight Show*. Allison and I got into my car and we hit the highway. Man, *Easy Rider*. We were free! On the road, just her and me. We'd escaped.

"I headed for the interstate, driving sixty-two, right on the button, because they don't arrest you if you're doing just seven miles over the limit. It's a state police rule, I heard somewhere. I stayed in the right lane and pointed that old Dodge east southeast. Didn't stop for anything. Ohio, West Virginia, Virginia, North Carolina. Once we started crossing borders, I felt better. Her father was sure to come home from his trip right away and call the local cops, but whether they'd get the highway patrol in, I had my doubts. I mean, he'd have some explaining to do—about how he kept his daughter a prisoner and everything." Manko shook his head. "But you know what I did?"

From the rueful look on his face I could guess. "You underestimated the enemy."

Manko shook his head. "Thomas Morgan," he mused. "I think he must've been a Godfather or something."

"I suppose they have them in Ohio, too."

"He had friends everywhere. Virginia troopers, Carolina, every-where! Money talks, you know what they say. We were heading south on 21, making for Charlotte, when I ran into 'em. I went into a 7-Eleven to buy some food and beer, and what happens but there's a couple of good ole boys right there, Smoky hats and everything, asking the clerk about a couple on the run from Ohio. I mean, *us*. I managed to get out without them seeing us and we peeled rubber outta there, I'll tell you. We drove for a while, but by then it was almost dawn and I figured we better lay low for the day.

"I pulled into a big forest preserve. We spent the whole day together, lying there, my arms around her, her head on my chest. We just lay in the grass beside the car and I told her stories about places we'd travel to. The Philippines, Thailand, California. And I told her what life'd be like in Florida, too."

He looked at me with a grave expression on his face. "I could've had her, Frank. You know what I'm saying? Right there. On the grass. The insects buzzing around us. You could hear this river, a waterfall, nearby." Manko's voice fell to a murmur. "But it wouldn't've been right. I wanted everything perfect. I wanted us to be in our own place, in Florida, in our bedroom. That sounds old-fashioned, I know. You think that was stupid of me? You don't think so, do you?"

"No, Manko, it's not stupid at all." Awkwardly I looked for something to add. "It was good of you."

He looked forlorn for a minute, perhaps regretting, stupid or wise, his choosing to keep their relationship chaste.

"Then," he said, smiling devilishly, "things got hairy. At midnight we headed south again. This car passed us then hit the brakes and did a *U*-ie. Came right after us. Morgan's men. I turned off the highway and headed due east over back roads. Man, what a drive! One-lane bridges, dirt roads. Zipping through small towns. Whoa, Frankie boy, I had four wheels treading air. It was fan*tastic*. You should've seen it. There must've been twenty cars after us. I managed to lose 'em but I knew we couldn't get very far in that Dodge."

"So you split, zip?"

He winked. "I knew that part of the state pretty good. Had a couple of buddies in the service from Winston-Salem. We'd go hunting and stayed in this old abandoned lodge near China Grove. Took some doing, but I finally found the place.

"I pulled up outside and made sure it was empty. We sat in the car, and I put my arm around her. I pulled her close and told her what I'd decided—that she should stay here. If her father got his hands on her, it'd be all over. He'd send her away for sure. Maybe even brainwash her. Don't laugh. Morgan'd do it. Even his own flesh and blood. She'd stay and I'd lead 'em off for a ways. Then . . ."

"Yes?"

"I waited for him."

"For Morgan? What were you going to do?"

"Have it out with him once and for all. One on one, him and me. Allison begged me not to. She knew how dangerous he was. But I didn't care. I knew he'd never leave us alone. He was the devil. He'd follow us forever if I didn't stop him. She begged me to take her with me, but I knew I couldn't. She had to stay. It was so clear to me. See, Frank, that's what love is, I think. Not being afraid to make a decision for someone else."

My friend Manko, the rough-hewn philosopher.

"I held her tight, and told her not to worry. I told her how there wasn't enough room in my heart for all the love I felt for her. We'd be together again soon."

"Was it safe there, you think?"

"The cabin? Sure. Morgan'd never find it."

"It was in China Grove?"

"Half-hour away. On Badin Lake."

I laughed. "You're kidding me."

"You know it?"

"Sure I do. I've lived all over the state. It must've been in the woods, on the western shore?"

"Yeah, in the woods."

"That's a pretty place."

"It's *damn* pretty. You know, as I drove off I looked back and re-member thinking how nice it'd be if that was our house and there Allison'd be in the doorway waiting for me to come home from work."

Manko rose and walked to the window. He gazed through his reflection into the night.

"After I left I drove to a state road. There, for everybody to see. Leadin' off the hounds. Here's Manko. Come and get me. I got twenty miles before they caught up with me. Was a roadblock that did it. I drove the car into this ditch and ran. Then I circled around and hid in a grove of trees. I just waited. About a half-hour later this black limo shows up."

"Morgan?"

"In person. The police had the car out of the ditch by this time and Morgan comes up and looks inside then walks back toward the limo. All this time, I'm just hiding there, waiting. Finally his bodyguards wandered off.

"That's when I made my move. No sneaking up, no cheap shots. I walked out of the trees toward him. He saw me. He looked shocked for a minute, but then he came right at me. I give him credit. He might've called for help. But he didn't; he just ran at me screaming, 'Where's my daughter? Where's my daughter?' I dragged him into the woods, away from his men and the cops, and we went at it. Man, what a slugfest! Him and me, rolling in the dirt, opening skin right and left. See this scar? Was his knuckles did that. I paid him back though, Frankie. That was his day to hurt and hurt bad. Finally I got him down and put a choke hold on him. I squeezed and squeezed. I couldn't stop myself. I felt him getting weaker, gasping for breath. I had him. Man, what a feeling!"

Manko touched the window delicately, as if sensing the temperature, then he turned back to me.

"I let him go. I could've finished him. Easy. But I just stood up, left him in the dirt. I laughed at him. A couple of his men came up and grabbed me, but the police pulled them off. Morgan and I just stared at each other. I remember thinking how easy it would've been to kill him. That's what I'd been planning to do, Frank. I suppose you figured that out. Trap him and kill him. But the funny thing is, I didn't need to anymore. I knew we'd won. Allison was safe from him. We'd be together, the two of us. We'd beat Thomas Morgan— tycoon, rich son of a bitch, and father of the most beautiful woman on earth."

Silence fell between us. It was nearly midnight and I'd been here for over three hours. I stretched. Manko paced slowly, his face aglow with anticipation. "You know, Frank, a lot of my life hasn't gone the way I wanted it to. Allison's either. But one thing we've got is our love. That makes everything okay."

"A transcendent love."

A ping sounded and I realized that Manko'd touched his cup to mine once again. We emptied them. He looked out the window into the black night. The rain had stopped, and a faint moon was evident through the clouds. A distant clock started striking twelve.

A solid rap struck the door, which swung open suddenly. I was startled and stood.

Manko turned calmly, the smile still on his face.

"Evening, Tim," said a man of about sixty. He wore a rumpled brown suit. From behind him several sets of eyes peered at me and Manko.

It rankled me slightly to hear the given name. Manko'd always made clear that he preferred his nickname and considered the use of Tim or Timothy an insult. But tonight he didn't even notice; he smiled as he shook the man's gray hand.

There was silence for a moment as another man, wearing a pale blue uniform, stepped into the room with a tray, loaded it up with the dirty dishes.

"Enjoy it, Manko?" he asked.

"Ambrosia," he said, lifting a wry eyebrow toward me.

The older man nodded, then took a blue-backed document from his suit jacket and opened it. There was a long pause. Then in a solemn Southern baritone he read, "Timothy Albert Mankowitz, in accordance with sentence pronounced against you pursuant to your conviction for the kidnapping and murder of Allison Kimberly Morgan, I hereby serve upon you this death warrant, issued by the Governor of the State of North Carolina, to be effected midnight this day."

The warden handed Manko the paper. He and his lawyer had already seen the faxed version from the court, and tonight he merely glanced with boredom at the document. In his face I noted none of the stark befuddlement you almost always see in the faces of condemned prisoners as they read the last correspondence they'll ever receive.

"We got the line open to the governor, Tim," the warden drawled, "and he's at his desk. I just talked to him. But I don't think . . . I mean, he probably won't make the call."

"I told you all along," Manko said softly, "I didn't even want those appeals."

The execution operations officer, a thin, businesslike man who looked like a feed and grain clerk, cuffed Manko's wrists and instructed him to remove his shoes.

The warden motioned me outside and I stepped into the corridor. Unlike the popular conception of a dismal, Gothic death row, this wing of the prison resembled an overly lit Sunday-school hallway. His head leaned close. "Any luck, Father?"

After a moment I lifted my eyes from the shiny linoleum. "I think so. He told me about a hunting lodge near Badin Lake. Western shore. You know it?"

The warden shook his head. "But we'll have the troopers get some dogs over there. Hope it pans out," he added, whispering, "Lord, I hope that."

So ended my grim task on this grim evening.

Prison chaplains always walk the last hundred feet with the condemned, but rarely are they enlisted as a last-ditch means to wheedle information out of the prisoners. I'd consulted my bishop and this mission didn't seem to violate my vows. Still, it was clearly a deceit, and one that would trouble me, I suspected, for a long time. Yet it would trouble me less than the thought of young Allison Morgan lying in an unconsecrated grave, whose location Manko adamantly refused to reveal—his ultimate way, he said, of protecting her from her father.

Allison Kimberly Morgan—stalked relentlessly for months after she dumped Manko following their second date. Kidnapped from her bed then driven through four states with the FBI and a hundred troopers in pursuit. And finally . . . finally, when it was clear that Manko's precious plans for a life together in Florida would never happen, knifed to death while— apparently—he held her close and told her how there wasn't enough room in his heart for all the love he felt for her.

Until tonight her parents' only consolation was in knowing that she'd died quickly—her abundant blood in the front seat of his Dodge testified to that. Now there was at least the hope they could give her a proper burial, and in doing so offer her a bit of the love that they may—or may not—have denied her in life.

Manko appeared in the hallway, on his feet the disposable paper slippers the condemned wear to the execution chamber. The warden looked at his watch and motioned down the corridor. "You'll go peaceful, won't you, son?"

Manko laughed. He was the only one in the place with serenity in his eyes.

And why not?

He was about to join his own true love. They'd once again be together.

"You like my story, Frank?"

I told him I did. Then he smiled at me in a curious way, an expression that seemed to contain a hint both of forgiveness and of something I can only call the irrepressible Manko challenge. Perhaps, I reflected, it would not be this evening's deceit that would weigh on me so heavily but rather the simple fact that I would never know whether or not Manko was on to me.

But who could tell? He was, as I've said, a born actor.

The warden looked at me. "Father?"

I shook my head: "I'm afraid Manko's going to forgo absolution," I said. "But he'd like me to read him a few psalms."

"Allison," Manko said earnestly, "loves poetry."

I slipped the Bible from my suit pocket and began to read as we started down the corridor, walking side by side.

# The Rough Boys

## HARLAN ELLISON

## Harlan Ellison's Introduction:

*It's common knowledge, or at worst common urban legend, that Ernest Heming-way tossed the only manuscript of his first novel into the Atlantic Ocean midway between France and the United States. Not* The Torrents of Spring *and not* The Sun Also Rises. *The one before those. The one he'd labored over in Paris after his collection,* In Our Time, *became a cause célèbre in 1925.*

*No amount of blandishments or coercion could get him to reconstruct it, or encapsulate the plot of it for interviewers, or so much as repeat the title, save to refer to it as "that thoroughgoing stinker."*

*Doctors are lucky. They get to bury their mistakes.*

*For writers, especially those whose careers have some extended viability, or who may amass a modicum of "celebrity," the first wretched experiments pincered up out of the vats are not interred. They get reprinted, and they get referred to in academic incunabula, and they shamble in out of the misty darkness behind you, like day-players out of Val Lewton's* I Walked with a Zombie.

*Hemingway was nobody's fool. He may have been reckless in many aspects of his life and career, but he knew when to deep-six the sophomoric rodomontade. Chum he knew it to be, and chum it became.*

*Larry Block has asked me for "the first crime story" I ever wrote. In his cover letter of solicitation he adds, "There's some leeway here. Your selection can be your first story written, the first one sold, or the first published—your choice."*

*I wrote my first crime story in 1956. I cannot remember which one it was. It may have been "Riff" or "Johnny Slice's Stoolie" (published as "I Never Squealed!") or "Thrill Kill" (published as "Homicidal Maniac") (ah, them was the days!), but if it was any of those, fuggedahbahtit. You get my drift? Chum. Fish food.*

*And so this fortuitous amnesia, this inability to know for sure if the first one I wrote was "Can Opener" (published tastefully under the lavatorial-sounding "Killer in the Can") or "White Trash Don't Exist" or "The Rough Boys," gives me precisely and conveniently the rat-hole through which I scuttle to bypass the* former quintet of shambling grotesqueries, to select the one of that batch penned in the dim distant beyond that still reads pretty sweetly. "The Rough Boys."

I was living in upper Manhattan at the time, on a street where gang kids hung out. They were hard numbers, those kids; but we got along. And some nights I'd sit out on the stoop of one or another apartment house, and we'd shoot the shit, swap lies, pretend to be iron and lead, when in truth we were mostly just insecure flesh and blood.

And one night I got the idea: what would happen if a brace of professionals met these braggart urchins? What a nice juxtaposition, I thought.

I wrote this one in 1956.

It needn't go over the taffrail to sleep with the fishes.

# The Rough Boys

## HARLAN ELLISON

VINCE AND TERRY HAD to go underground after they'd iced the fink. They had been hired in from Detroit to help Gongo and the outfit. Hired to put the silence on a creep named Robbison; they'd done it; smooth, nice, like always.

Two days after they'd left the 707 at JFK, they'd bushwhacked Robbison in a midtown parking lot and blown him all over a brick wall with .357 Magnum efficiency.

The job was done, but the payment was forthcoming. It wasn't a matter of double-cross—Gongo knew better than that, and he always paid off promptly for a job properly done—but Vince and Terry had gotten word the D.A. was really pissed off about this one: Robbison had been ready to spill. So . . . underground.

Vince and Terry were professionals, they could see the big picture: hot cop breath down Gongo's neck from an anxious D.A. and the cooling had come just in time. So *much* in time, perhaps, that the D.A. saw a beautiful indictment going up in smoke. So the heat was on.

Gongo couldn't take a chance of sending someone over with the payoff, and they couldn't telephone him because the line was probably spooked. So it was a matter of staying here in this greasy Broadway furnished room till the word came through that the heat was off.

It wouldn't be much longer, they knew, but still, being cooped up with just each other—meals being sent in with the papers—was making Vince and Terry jumpy.

"How far'd you get with that MacElhone girl?" Vince said, from the broken-down armchair.

"Far? She wouldn't know from far. A real dummy, that one," Terry answered from the bed. He grinned and waved all thoughts of the girl from his head.

"Far, schmar, I couldn't wish any harder that she was here, locked up with us for a week or so. It'd kill the time a little better than two-handed poker, which is abysmal, and reading these miserable paperback novels." He kicked at a stack of badly-thumbed books on the floor.

They looked alike, in the smooth, efficient way all syndicate assassins looked smooth and efficient.

Vince was tall and slim; dark, wavy hair and an unlined, almost adolescent face. He looked more like a college senior than a hired killer. He wore a charcoal gray, single-breasted Brooks Brothers suit, with a white button-down shirt, conservative gray rep tie, and black shoes.

Terry was darker-complexioned, but his hair was almost blond. He wore turtle-shell glasses, and had a tiny white scar at the corner of his mouth. He had gotten it in Nam, shortly before he'd cut away seven men in a bunker with a flame thrower. He had won a medal for that. He wore a charcoal gray, single-breasted Brooks Brothers suit, with a white button-down shirt, conservative blue challis tie, and black shoes.

Neither one looked like what he was. A paid killer. But they earned their money, and had been doing so, in Vince's case for eight years, and in Terry's for five. They were the top rough boys in the syndicate's stable, and they knew it.

There wasn't anyone in the organization who would dispute it. For this reason, they wore their handsome composures as they wore their suits: almost as if they had been born with them; pressed, sharp, and casual.

Vince sighed deeply, smacked his lips loudly. "Want to take a chance on seeing a movie?" He looked over at Terry on the bed.

Terry bit the inside of his cheek, swung his legs off the bed, and sat up. "Don't know," he said slowly, thoughtfully. "Might not be a bad idea. Take the edge off us, at any rate. Anything good in the neighborhood?"

"We can always hop the subway to Times Square if there isn't," Vince reminded, turning to the movie pages of the *Daily News*. He caught Terry's shake of the head with the corner of his eye.

"Uh-uh," said Terry, reaching over to the bureau for his cigarettes. "No sense fouling it up now. We can wait. If there's anything good up the block, we'll take it in. If not—" he waved his hand in resignation, "—then it's another night of playing ostrich."

Vince agreed in silence. "Here's a John Wayne flick at Loews 83rd.

That's just up in the next block. Supposed to be a pretty fair piece of work, cops and robbers thing, not a western."

Terry shook his head, blowing a thin plume of smoke at the floor between his feet. "Saw it in Detroit. Lousy picture."

Vince nodded understanding, turned his attention back to the newspaper. A minute later he said, "Place called the Thalia on 95th off Broadway. They've got Fernandel in *The Sheep Has Five Legs* and something else with Trintignant. I suppose this is one of those little art theaters where they serve black coffee in the lobby.

"I'd like to take those in. I'm getting sick of shoot'em-ups."

Terry looked up with frank amusement on his face. "Violence doesn't agree with you, right?"

Vince smiled, tossing a mock blow at his companion. "Don't push me, friend. You want to go or not? if you're too lowbrow, say so now, and I'll go edjakate myself alone."

Terry chuckled deep in his throat, got off the bed.

They were very literate, these ex-college boys turned professional. Their tastes were very refined.

"Sounds okay to me," said Terry. He walked over to the mirror, began tightening his tie. "What if we get spotted?"

He asked the question absently, bending over to get a clear spot in the mirror. The silver had worn off its back, and leprous spots covered most of the glass.

"What if we get spotted?" he heard Vince repeat. He saw Vince's reflection in the mirror as it dipped a hand to its belt. The reflection came up with a .32 with smoked sights. "Then we get *unspotted*. Like Gongo said the other night, we're real rough boys." He smiled boyishly.

"That clod," Terry replied, grinning back, pulling the knot high between the points of his collar.

"He's not far wrong, though. We are rough," Vince persisted, carrying the gag a bit.

"Well, *bang, bang!*" Terry made the joke, forming a finger gun with his left hand, straightening the tie with his right. "Yeah. Rough. Now will you *please* get your goddam coat on so we can go see some Fernandel?"

On a slab downtown, a guy named Robbison lay caked with his own blood—let out through the eight direct hits in his chest and face.

THEY WALKED SLOWLY DOWN Broadway, back toward 82nd Street. Keeping to the shadows, smoking carelessly, their nubby tweed topcoats collared-up, their heads bare, conversing casually. Typical. Two typical men walking on Broadway.

"Good show," said Terry, lighting a cigarette.

"Mmm," Vince agreed. Then he changed the subject quickly: "Lord, but I'm hungry. Want to stop in at Schrafft's?"

Terry shot him a quick glance, the smoke from his cigarette blowing back in a fine, vaporous trail. "You must be losing your mind. That's the second time tonight you've suggested something as ridiculous as that. Why don't we just walk into the 20th Precinct station and turn ourselves—"

"Okay, okay!" Vince cut him off with a smile. "Sorry, my stomach blocks off my brain sometimes.

"But listen, it's too late for anyone at that flea circus to go out for us. They all go off at ten. We'll have to wait till tomorrow morning, and frankly, friend, you know what a splitting headache I get when I'm hungry. In fact," he said, licking his lips in seriousness, "I'm starting to throb a little right now."

They turned into a crosstown street, 88th, it was—toward Amsterdam. As if the talk about being spotted had driven them off the main artery.

The streets were almost pitch black, with the feeble yellow of a distant lamppost casting a watery pool of light on the front of a tenement halfway up the block.

The wind had risen off the Hudson, was whispering up the hill into the crosstown streets. Vince and Terry hunched lower in their topcoats. A young boy was sitting on the tenement's steps, leaning far forward, toying with an identification bracelet on his right wrist, his hands down between his legs.

The boy looked in their direction, and his head came up abruptly. He stared at the two men as they approached. Terry nudged Vince with an elbow. "There's our gofer," he said.

"Should have thought of that myself." Vince grinned back. They walked toward the boy.

He seemed to be about seventeen, short for his age, with a face full of blemishes. His cheekbones were hardly noticeable, and his mouth was a tight, thin line. His hair was black and long. He slouched easily in the tight-fitting blue jeans and Ike jacket, and continued to finger the chain bracelet on his wrist.

He watched them carefully as they moved in on him.

"Want to earn yourself five bucks?" Terry asked, leaning against the stone railing of the stairway. The kid looked up at him with caution in his eyes.

"On the up-and-up," Vince added, moving closer. "All we want is for you to pick us up some food."

"Maybe," the kid said.

"Okay," Terry said, sitting down next to the boy. He took a long, thin leather wallet from an inside jacket pocket, and drew a pen from the holder within. He scribbled something on a piece of paper. "Here's the address."

He handed the paper to the boy; the kid took it without hardly noticing it. The boy stuck out his hand. "Dough," he said. Terry looked at Vince; this kid was a quiet one.

Terry fished out a five-dollar note, tore it neatly in half. He stuck one half back in the wallet, gave the other to the boy. "You got any money of your own?" he asked the kid.

"A couple bucks," the kid said warily.

Terry gave him three dollars more. "Use your two bucks, and these, and you get the other half of that fiver when you show. We only gave you three, so it's worth your while to bring the stuff—that way you make two more on the deal."

"What if it runs more than three bucks?" the kid asked.

"Pay for the balance out of your money. Bring along a copy of the check, and we'll give you the difference—plus the other half of the five. Okay?"

The kid nodded. "Okay. What do you want?"

They gave the boy the order—a couple of grilled cheeses, two coffees black, two bottles of beer, slaw—and moved on. They looked back as they turned the corner onto Amsterdam. The kid was already gone. The steps were empty.

TIME SEEMED TO HAVE contracted. They were back in the dismal room, brown stains on the wallpaper near the ceiling, from someone's radiator on the floor above. They were back in the same positions they had been in hours ago.

Terry was in his stocking feet, stretched out on the bed with eyes closed and a curling pillar of smoke rising from his cigarette.

Vince slouched in the ratty, overstuffed armchair, one leg thrown over its worn and padded arm; he was still reading the *News*. "We should have bought the *Times*," he said to the room in general.

Sounds of cars passing in the street below floated to their ears. The shades were pulled down, and because of the stiff spring breeze from the river, the windows were tightly closed.

Signs of previous meals were scattered about the room in the form of paper cups and plates.

"Kid's late," Terry remarked, around the cigarette. His voice was a toneless statement. He didn't bother opening his eyes.

"Yeah, I know," Vince replied, letting the paper fold itself onto the floor. He sat up in the chair. "Well, looks like you're out a fiver—"

The sentence was left hanging. The knock came twice, softly. Terry snapped upright, his .32 in his hand, the cigarette dumping ashes on his pants.

Vince was out of the chair, back flattened against the wall next to the door, pistol ready. The knock came again, more urgently this time. They waited. If it was anyone that they wanted in the room, well, let *them* make the first move.

"Hey!" It was the kid's voice. "Hey! Better open up. This crap is gettin' cold!" Vince tossed a smile over his shoulder, shoved the .32 into his belt, moved to unbolt the door.

"Guess we misjudged the kid," he said.

He turned the key, threw the bolt, and let the door open on its own. The kid appeared in the doorway, holding a paper bag at an awkward angle. "Hot," he explained, starting to come in.

He shoved the door open completely with his foot, took three quick steps that brought him next to Terry, and suddenly there were six boys in the room.

They stepped in quickly, all of them, as though they were on strings. Another instant and the door was closed, locked, bolted. They stood in a row, backs to the door.

Terry had started to bring the gun up as they stepped into the room. As the revolver rose, the kid with the bag dropped it on Terry's hand. The coffee was scalding—he screamed with the pain.

The kid chopped down with his free hand, and the gun dropped to the rug. The boy scooped it up, took a step back, and made a queer shaking movement with his arm. He shook the arm toward the floor.

A knife dropped into his hand. An instant later the blade was switched open, the tip slightly denting the smooth skin of Terry's neck. "Don't like guns," he explained. "They wake people." The knife hand was steady and rigid.

Vince stood petrified, so suddenly had it all happened. Now abruptly he was galvanized into action. His hand yanked the .32 from his waistband, and the gun swung in an arc. "Get away from him!" He used the flat, cold, dangerous voice, pointing the revolver at the kid's head.

"So shoot, wise guy," the kid said, leaning a bit toward Terry. The knife dented the skin even more; an angry spot of red appeared beneath the point. "So shoot, and your *compañero* gets my steel in his windpipe." His blemished face broke into a thin sneer.

The other five boys laughed. Vince started to swivel the gun in their direction, but a boy wearing an ornate poncho stepped out of the line and brought a bottle down across his wrist.

The gun hit the floor, and another boy scooped it up, shoving it into his pocket. The click of its opening was clear in the room.

"Whatta ya think, Rafe? They holding?" The boy addressed the question to the blemish-faced kid holding his knife at Terry's throat.

"What do you want?" Terry gasped, his face dead white, his body leaning away from the first boy's knife.

"Man," said Rafe, "when I saw that wad you was toting, I knew you was the ripest ever. I don't know what you two dudes got hiding in here, but I know you got enough chips to keep us happy for a long while. Cough!"

Terry looked across at Vince. He knew the message the other man's eyes were screaming: *What the hell is going on here? We're grown men—we're paid to handle people—and these are a bunch of kids. We're supposed to be rough boys, so why the hell are we letting them do this to us?*

"Okay, kids," said Terry, starting to rise. "This is it. Pile out of here before we sic the cops on you, or tan your tails ourselves."

The first boy placed his hand against Terry's chest, shoved hard. Terry fell over onto the bed. "Sit down, hard rock. We'll tell you when to talk."

"Hey, Rafe," said one of the boys, from the clothes closet. "I think I found this one's roll." He came out of the closet, carrying Vince's wallet. He opened it before the rest of the gang, took out a sheaf of bills.

Rafe whistled. "Nice, nice! How much there?"

The other boy continued counting. In a moment he looked up. "Seems to be eight hundred bucks."

The other four boys whistled, almost in unison.

One of them advanced on Vince, backing him against the wall. "Who *are* you, buddy? What're you doing holed up in here?"

Vince shot a sharp look at Terry. It didn't seem real, this entire scene. Here they were, the two top men in the syndicate kill-squad, held at bay by a half-dozen street punks.

"What makes you think we're holed up, you little snotnosed . . ."

The kid's hand came up, arced across, and caught Vince a vicious crack under the eye. Vince slid along the wall, came into contact with the radiator, and straightened up quickly, his face flame red.

"You lousy little bastard!" he yelled, reaching for the boy.

Before he could reach the kid, two of the others were on him. In a minute—a minute of leather gloves filled with coins and the sharp edge of flattened hands—Vince was stretched on the dirty carpet, his head bleeding.

Rafe stepped away from the bed, gave Vince a kick in the side of the head. He rolled, and the bleeding got worse.

"Real rough character," Rafe said. "Real rough."

"Look, kid, what the hell do you want with us? You've got our money, now why don't you beat it?" Terry's face had hardened, the scar at his mouth standing out in sharp white relief.

"We only got *part* of your money, *pocho. You* got a wallet, too. I saw it, remember?" He stepped back to the bed, hand outstretched.

Terry reached into the inner pocket of his jacket, hung on the bed-post, and handed the boy his wallet. "Now scram, will you?"

"Rafe," said one of the other boys, "I don't dig the way this *cabrón* talks to us."

He stepped over and flat-handed Terry across the mouth, twice. The syndicate man's head snapped back and cracked against the bedpost.

Vince made a mewling sound from the floor. He started to sit up. One of the boys moved toward him, stepping carefully, bringing his booted foot back for a vicious kick.

"Nix!" said Rafe. "Let him be."

Vince got up, clutching his bleeding face, staggered to the big chair and fell into it. "Now," said Rafe, "how about telling us who you are."

Terry looked at Vince. The other assassin was doubled over in the chair, trying to stop the flow of blood with an initialed handkerchief. "We-we're two buyers from a company in Detroit—" he began, but Rafe cut him off.

"With guns? Nah, that don't figure—not even a little bit."

Bubbling sounds came from Vince. "We're rough boys from the Outfit, Syndicate," he mumbled, with sarcasm still coming through.

One of the other boys stumbled back against the closet door, clutching himself as he shook with laughter. "Oh, *no*! Dig *them*, will ya!" The others all laughed.

Abruptly, Terry felt the fear and humiliation that had come with these kids mount to a frenzy point. He had never been held down like this—not since he was a kid himself. And it wasn't going to happen now.

With one fluid movement he was off the bed, slamming into Rafe as hard as he could. The knife went into the air and he caught it on the fly, stepping back and dragging the boy in front of him.

It was a calculated move, and one that would have worked had Rafe not brought his booted foot down as hard as he could on Terry's instep.

The assassin howled, and Rafe spun around quickly, his hand darting out. Two straightened, stiff fingers, close together, went into Terry's windpipe, and the syndicate man's eyes went glazed.

He started to fall back, clawing at the air.

Rafe chopped again, and the knife dropped to the floor.

"You little punks!" Vince screamed, and was out of the chair, fists doubled, about to strike.

A boy moved in swiftly, tripped Vince as he started toward Rafe. Rafe picked up the knife.

Another boy whipped Vince's gun out of his pocket, leveled it. "You're more trouble than you're worth," he said evenly. "Who gives a damn *who* you are!"

He fired once, carefully. The bullet caught Vince just below the collarbone, spun him hard. He dropped to his knees, and the boy fired again. The second bullet shattered Vince's right cheek. Rafe watched silently.

Vince spat twice, blood spilling down the front of his white button-down shirt. He moaned off-key, and pitched onto his face, twitching.

The boy fired again.

"You're making a helluva racket," Rafe said slowly.

"Yeah, loud, ain't it?" the other boy answered.

"Now we'll have to check out," Rafe said resignedly.

Terry stepped toward them, his eyes wide. "Vince . . ." he began. Rafe turned carefully, and thrust the knife into Terry's stomach.

The syndicate man settled onto the blade, then pitched sidewise with a muffled shriek. He slid off the blade, clutching his stomach, fell into a heap next to Vince.

"Like *that*, you should waste them," Rafe explained to the boy with the gun.

"Not noisy like you done." The other boy nodded his head solemnly.

They heard doors opening in the building, down the hall.

"Fire escape here," one of the boys announced, opening a window. "Let's go!"

They began piling out the window, clanking down the fire escape and vanishing in the night. Rafe was the last to leave, the captain remaining on the bridge till the last moment. He thrust one leg over the sill, then stopped.

He turned his head and looked back into the room, at the carnage. It was starting to smell warm and nasty, like old, bad beer. There was a thumping from the hall and then something hit the door, bowed it slightly as someone tried to break in.

Rafe grinned down at the two bodies. Terry's eyes were open, staring past Rafe at the ceiling. The boy snapped the lock on his knife, breaking it smoothly and almost in the same motion sliding it back up his sleeve where a leather thong snugged it against his forearm.

"If I'd known you were so tough, I never woulda fucked with you," he said, stepping out onto the fire escape and carefully closing the window.

# Tole My Cap'n

JOE GORES

## Joe Gores's Introduction:

*Three elements.*

*One. When I was still in high school, I saw a painting in an art book of a hulking, mournful black prisoner sitting on the floor of his cell wearing black-and-white-striped convict clothing. I knew the painting was trying to tell me a story. I just didn't know what the story was.*

*Two. Skip ahead four years. By then I knew I wanted to be a writer and tell my own stories, and spending the summer between my junior and senior years at Notre Dame riding freight trains around the country seemed like a good way to start. When I got vagged in south Georgia, I spent a month on a road gang, cutting brush and shovelling dirt.*

*Three. When I heard a Harry Belafonte song called "Tole My Cap'n" about two buddies on a chain gang, I knew instantly that the black guy in the song just had to be the black guy in the painting I had loved back in high school.*

"I raise my han'
To wipe the sweat off my head,
Cap'n got mad, Lord,
Shot my buddy dead."

*Three elements. But somehow I couldn't put them together in my mind; I kept trying to use only two of them. I tried to write the story of the two buddies on the chain gang, but it refused to be told. I filed it and forgot it.*

*Becoming a private detective in San Francisco in the early 1950s gave me stories, but I was telling them as reports instead of fiction. I loved the life but I still wanted to be a writer in the worst way. Then in January 1957 a friend told me he was going to Tahiti for a year. I told him, "Oh, hell, Earl, I'll go with you." I saw it as a chance to have South Seas adventures, and, free of interruptions, take my best shot at being a writer.*

*We spent two weeks on a slow New Zealand freighter called the Wairuna. In Tahiti, we rented a little thatch house for twenty-five dollars a month in* the Arue District five miles north of Papeete, and we rode our bicycles to and from town. I developed work habits that have lasted a lifetime. Up at four each morning, write until noon, then skin-dive along the reef until dark. I kept a daily journal—and I wrote stories. Dozens of stories.

One of them was based on the Belafonte song. I realized the missing element lay in my own experiences on that road gang in Georgia five years before. When I put them into the failed fragment of story I had written earlier, it worked. The black man's buddy became a white man—me, I guess. The rather decent captain of my work crew became the murderous captain of Belafonte's chain gang.

I called it "Tole My Cap'n" and in May 1957 I sent it to Manhunt magazine. They bought it for sixty-five dollars and published it in their December issue as "Chain Gang." It was my first sale and my first published story.

In 1958 I returned to the States from Tahiti to serve two draftee years in the army. Later, back in San Francisco, I reentered the detective business and eventually became a partner in the firm. It took me twelve years as a P.I. to finally find the guts to quit and try it as a writer full-time. My first novel, A Time of Predators, was published three years later.

I expanded and revised "Chain Gang" in 1999 as the first section of my novel, Cases. Apart from these two appearances, in Manhunt and Cases, the story has never appeared anywhere else. It's very gratifying to have it reprinted here in its original form for five times the amount of money I got for it originally.

# Tole My Cap'n

## JOE GORES

At first there were only three of them, attracted by the scent of blood. They were large, fat flies, with very shiny green bodies; the sort that feed on garbage and buzz loudly like a radio warming up. There would be more of them.

The Negro boy sat hunched over as if a pain in his body was dragging him down in unbearable agony. But his pain was of the spirit: It showed in the dark eyes, glazed with grief. A tear had furrowed the dust that caked one cheek. He cradled his buddy's dark broken head in his lap; blood from the exit wound in the back of the skull, black among the tight brown curls, had smeared across his blunt hands, had splashed his arms, had impregnated the thin denim of his trousers. A large number was stenciled across the back of his faded blue cotton shirt. On his right ankle was an iron shackle; around it the flesh was raw and broken, like meat left too long in the sun. A chain, starting from a staple welded to the iron, connected him with a similar staple on a similar iron on the leg of the corpse. As the Negro boy rocked back and forth the chain links ticked together with a faint, melodious sound.

"Why fo he have to shoot him?" he moaned. The four other men in the gang remained silent. He looked up with ravaged, unseeing eyes that accused everything still living. "Why did he have to shoot him in the head? All he did was to stop and wipe his face; he just raise his hand to wipe his face. Why fo he shoot my buddy, why?"

The medium-sized, heavy-bodied man known only as Captain Hent slowly returned his revolver to a stained and shiny holster worn low on his hip. A heavy leather belt encircled his waist, which was thick without being fat. His strong jaws looked as if they needed a shave, and he smelled of sweat, though not so much as the prisoners, not nearly so much.

*"Leave him be." His voice was heavy, ugly. "Leave him be, but—" here a movement of the cold blue eyes included all of them—"remember him. Remember he raised his hand to me."*

*Chained in pairs the men began to move. The Negro bent and buried his face in the taut neck of his buddy. In a whisper he said, against the strong dead throat: "That Cap'n is bound to die." Then he slid the body off his lap. Blood smeared down across the knees of his trousers, and the dead boy's left hand struck the dirt as softly as a girl's breath stirring a window curtain. The hand looked white and still against the dark earth.*

THEY HAD DROPPED OFF a rattler five weeks before, when it slowed for the grade half a mile this side of town. Their heavy shoes struck the embankment running and sank into the soft grade fill, sending out rattling showers of wet pebbles. One of them, missing his footing in the dark, rolled over and over down the slope until the long grass beside the right of way stopped him. Sniffing the half-acrid scent of dirt newly wet down, he laughed.

"Hey, man, old brakeman never catch us now."

"I'd have whipped that bastard flat if you hadn't stopped me."

A moving shadow trudged back, slid down the embankment on its heels, lit a cigarette, and became a man. The cupped match flame revealed a young, hard face with deep-welled blue eyes and a square, cleft chin. His hair was brown and curled tightly against his skull by the rain.

The Negro, taller, rose and brushed off his brown cord trousers. Slanting rain popped on his leather jacket and slid off, glistening. A dirty plaid cap hid his kinky hair. His name was Larkie and he was light-colored for a Haitian Negro.

"I still got two bits and a dime," he said. "Come on, let's go into town and get us something to eat. You got any loot?"

"Just half a pack of butts. God, could I use a drink. I'm wet and cold clean through."

"No whiskey. Won't no one serve a white man and a colored man anyway."

"If we weren't broke—"

"We are, though."

"Okay. Soup it is."

They waded through the sodden whip-grass and smart weed that choked the ditch. A quail exploded ahead of them and squeaked away into the darkness. Beyond the tracks was a shallowly rutted road of muddy sand: they turned toward the fitful yellow pocks that marked the town through the rain. Far ahead, the freight train dropped its pressure with a great sigh. Dim bushes to their left, blessed by the rain, smelled fresh and sweet.

The dirt road became a dirt side street over which two street lights bounced like buttons on a string. Through their dim glow the rain seemed to drift, yet it drummed the wooden walk like running feet and splattered brown geysers from the muddy puddles. A big man came from an all-night diner and stopped to pick his teeth in its light. Yellow highlights gleamed on his black slicker as he moved down to the corner.

Looking in the diner window, the boys saw that a counter, topped with red linoleum, ran the length; its wooden edging had been chipped and carved by generations of pocket knives. Most of the stools had rips in their imitation leather seats. The homely waitress was alone, washing fountain glasses in gray, soapy water.

"What you think, Dale?"

"She's got a kind face. And I got to get something in my gut."

"Okay, Dale. In we go."

They stopped just inside the door to drip water on the floor. The girl looked at them uncertainly, finally came down the counter drying her hands on the towel wrapped around her middle. Her hair was the color and texture of straw, and nearly as straight. She wore no makeup.

"Yes?"

"Look, miss," said Larkie. His hands moved like instruments measuring her credulity. "We got us thirty-five cents. It's cold and wet out, and we just passing through. What that money buy us?"

She bit her lip, looking from one to the other, finally said:

"Well—I'll let you have two bowls of soup and two coffees, if you promise to eat fast. It should be forty cents but I'm on alone tonight. I'm not supposed to serve—" she stopped abruptly, blushing.

Perched on the end stools, they guzzled hot soup and drank steaming coffee as fast as their mouths could stand it, and ate the whole bowl of crackers she brought.

"Any work around here?" asked Dale. Under the light he was too big-boned for his size; though his hands were large and powerful his wrists made them seem small.

The girl shook her head. She looked around the empty diner, then leaned across the counter. Her hair smelled of dime-store perfume.

"No work in the state, I don't think. Listen, where are you fellows from?"

"Up no'th," said Larkie.

She nodded. "You'd—they're sort of funny about Negroes and whites around here. You'd do better to either split up or else go back up north again. You don't know how it is in this state."

"We're learning," said Dale. "Me and Larkie have—"

"Much obliged for the food, ma'am," said Larkie. "Come on, white boy, let's blow."

The big man in the black slicker was standing on the boardwalk, looking at the display of women's hats in a small store next to the diner. He looked like the sort of man who would find women's hats very uninteresting. Without seeming to, he blocked their way.

"Just a minute, 'bos."

Larkie said: "Oh-oh." Dale skipped sideways like a monkey, his hand whipping toward his trouser pocket. Moving with amazing speed for his size, the Negro shot out a long arm and locked the white boy's wrist with strong fingers.

"Easy on, Dale," he said.

The big man hadn't moved except to put his right hand under the shiny slicker. His straight brown hair, touched with grey at the temples, was combed severely back from his high forehead, and he wore a large moustache.

"You got a head, black boy," he said. "Just passing through?"

"You the Law?"

"That's me."

"Just passing through."

The big man shook his head slowly. A drop of rainwater fell from the tip of his nose.

"Looks like maybe you were waiting around to do a little business at the diner here, after a while. The brakeman off the train told me about you two 'bos. Said to keep an eye on you, white boy." He extended a long finger.

Dale stepped back, blinking his eyes against the water running down from his tight curls. His face was deeply tanned and he wore a heavy blue navy watch sweater that smelled wetly of wool.

"We ain't done anything in your town, mister. We ain't been near the railroad yards." His voice was low and sullen.

"Not the yards, that I believe," said the Sheriff. "Riding the rattlers, bumming meals in white restaurants where Negroes ain't allowed. . . . Know what that means, 'bos? Vag, that's what it means. Lots of road going through here, and the state's poor. Needs cheap labor." He took Larkie's arm in one big paw. "Let's take a walk."

They started down the main street of town. "Walk in front of us, 'bo," he said to Dale. "And keep your hand out of that pocket."

Larkie pulled his cap down against the rain and said politely:

"Nice little town you got here, Sheriff."

"It grows on you, 'bo. It grows on you."

THERE HAD BEEN NO rain since the night of their arrest. The ground was hard and dry; the men had to stamp on their shovels to make them bite at the earth, and reddish dust drifted from each shovelful of clods that went into the wheelbarrows. The backs of their necks were red and sore from the sun, their horny palms cracked from the sweat-slick shovel handles. Two pairs of men shoveled while the other two men, unchained, wheeled the barrows.

"Cap'n." Larkie's shovel did not pause in its rhythm.

"What is it, black boy?"

Captain Hent stood in the dry grass under a drooping, scrubby willow, thick arms crossed on his chest, hips slung forward in a comfortable slouch. His shirt was black with sweat. By his right foot was a water jug, its sides beaded with moisture.

"How about a drink of the water?"

"You know better than that, black boy. Ten minutes yet." His voice was heavy, like the baying of an old hound that has grown mean.

The only sounds were the grunts of the men, the rattle of earth in the barrows. Each time they bent to shovel, whole beads of hot sweat rained from their foreheads onto their hands and wrists. A heat-haze enveloped the sun.

"Cap'n."

"What, black boy?"

"How about giving me my time, Cap'n? I figure on quitting."

Whites and Negroes stopped shovelling, watched, listened. One of them snickered. The Captain's face reddened, and he stepped closer to Larkie, unfolded his arms.

"You making fun of me, boy?" he asked softly.

Larkie's eyes widened with surprise. They became almost wide enough to be too wide for real surprise.

"No, Cap'n, I sure ain't. We out here expiating, sure ain't gonna draw no time."

"Aw, shut up, for God's sake," snarled Dale suddenly, straightening up and holding a hand to the small of his back. "Why argue with that . . . *Captain*? All he's got's a gun makes him feel like God Almighty."

"Cap'n just doing his duty, Dale." Larkie bent over his shovel again.

Captain Hent brought his face inches from Dale's. They stared at each other with eyes bloodshot from the heat. The Captain's fists were dumb clubs; Dale's shovel came up slowly across his body like a staff. It was some time before the Captain relaxed. He said intensely:

"All I need's a gun, 'bo. Maybe tonight at the compound we'll see how tough you are. Tonight on your own time."

As Dale attacked the red earth, he muttered, "If you're there—*Captain*."

Captain Hent watched him shovel for some time, his pale killer's eyes thoughtful. He seemed to derive a physical pleasure from the heavy straining muscles etched sharply beneath the thin blue shirt.

For noon they ate bread and sat under the trees for half an hour. Larkie leaned back and shut his eyes wearily: men had been booked for vagrancy and had spent years in the chain gangs, forgotten by the courts. He wondered if the judge who had sentenced them to *six months hard* would forget. There had been egg on his tie and he hadn't shaved before coming to court. Rimless glasses had made his eyes benevolent, but he had allowed them no word of defense. Was it such a sin to be out of work? Did the good Lord make a man to wear a shackle around his ankle until the worms got into the raw flesh underneath and maimed him for life?

Beside him Dale said, "I can't take no more of this, Larkie."

"Got to take it, Dale—ain't nothing else to do."

"We could get him down, take his gun away."

"Chained together? Man, you crazy."

"We could do it, I tell you. What if he has me whipped or something tonight?"

Larkie opened his eyes and turned to look at Dale. Dale stared straight ahead, upturned nose red and peeling, stubbled jaw thrust out with the old obstinacy Larkie had grown to know so well.

"You hear me now, man. We got us plenty of country to cover once we's out of *this* bind. Ain't no six months going to last forever."

"You think of something, Larkie: you think of something good, 'cause I can't stand it no more. I remember when I was a kid we lived in a big white house with a white fence around it and a red pump out in back higher than I was. I'd stick my head under there, hot days, and my brother would pump cold water on me." When he finally turned to Larkie his blue eyes burned. "I came from a good family, Larkie—I remember things like that, and I know I can't take this no more."

"Okay, Dale. I'll think of something. You promise me you won't do nothing till I say."

Captain Hent blew a little whistle that ended the noon break. As they got painfully to their feet, Dale said, "Okay—promise."

THAT AFTERNOON CAPTAIN HENT shot him dead.

The Captain put one .44 slug in his head just under his right eye, firing from a crouch with body turned and gun arm extended in the approved police manual method. The gun was swept from its holster with a fluid movement that denoted long hours of practice before a mirror. His eyes became very hot and excited, as if he were making love to a woman; his face bore an elated and transported expression. The back of Dale's head split outward like a melon; he dropped his shovel and fell face forward across it. His nose broke against the pink earth.

"Good Christ in Heaven!" cried Larkie. He fell to his knees beside the corpse, heavily, breathing like a man who has just been kicked in the groin.

Captain Hent looked around at the expressionless, embittered faces; at the eyes that had not seen, the lips that would not speak.

"He was going to hit me with that shovel," he stated. "You all saw that. When the warden comes around to find out what happened, you'll tell how he raised that shovel. He's been laying for me for a week."

After a long time, Anderson, who was up for attempted rape, said:

"We'll all say that, Captain. But we'll all know he was just wiping his face."

In order that the warden could evaluate the manner of death, the corpse was left where it had fallen, and the men were returned to work. Flies were busy before evening and buzzards had clustered the trees darkly in silent speculation.

*AT NIGHT THEY WERE fastened to their beds like beasts in a kennel. A long chain, threaded through the staples of their leg irons, was passed down each row of cots. There was to be no talking after the lights were cut, but that night the electric word roved among the bleak lines of beds like an unleashed voltage of hate. Final sentence is not always pronounced by a judge: sometimes it is spoken soundlessly in the human heart. There are many ways o f carrying out an execution.*

*The next day was Friday. Captain Hent's gang was a man short, but Larkie, the big Negro, was able to handle the barrow work alone. The Captain was in high spirits, free from the petty manifestations of frustration: when one of the men swung his shovel carelessly and sliced a long sliver of flesh from his partner's leg, the Captain did not even curse. He merely came over to unchain the fallen man before he bled to death.*

*As the Captain bent over, fumbling for his keys, shovel-strengthened fingers suddenly closed over his hand, pinioning it in his pocket. His left arm was jerked so the scatter gun fell, unfired, to the ground. The injured man's legs flailed and the Captain sprawled on his belly in the dust. When he opened his mouth to shout, a torn shirt, foul with brine, was stuffed between his teeth. Sharp clods scarred his back; his clothes were plucked away like feathers from a chicken. Despite the warm sun a chill ran through him when his trousers were yanked down, and his naked white flanks exposed.*

*By twisting his head the Captain was able to see Larkie set aside his barrow and bring out a switchblade knife. The Captain, belatedly, remembered many things: after the kill, the men had been too silent; Larkie had wept over Dale too long. He remembered that Larkie was supposed to be from Haiti, and that Haitian Negroes are often very clever with knives.*

*Captain Hent was given no reason to doubt his memory, though he lived much longer than he cared to live. Fifty yards down the road, the next guard did not hear a sound or notice the stained earth being hurriedly wheeled by to serve as fill for the highway; the river half a mile away was deep and brown, its current swift enough to carry a new corpse a hundred miles before it surfaced. On the banks, bloodhounds lost Larkie's scent. It was assumed that he had drowned.*

*With so many men bumming on the trains that passed beyond the river, it was easy for a big light-colored Negro with cunning, careful eyes and fresh shackle scars to pass unnoticed. Three days later he was out of the state. In his heart he bore the serene realization that a death had paid for a death.*

# Layover

ED GORMAN

## Ed Gorman's Introduction:

*Back in the early sixties, before I'd quite turned twenty-one, a used bookstore owner who knew how desperate I was to sell a short story said, "You should try one of those girlie mags they put out in Chicago."*

*I wasn't sure what he was talking about. The only Chicago girlie mag available locally was Playboy. The distributor wouldn't handle any others. He'd gotten too much grief from religious groups.*

*So I didn't know what magazines Stan had in mind. "These," he said, and hefted a cardboard box up on his checkout counter. Remember, these were the days when some publishers were being put in prison for selling photos you can see in Cosmo today.*

*This was my introduction to what one might call downscale girlie magazines. Gone the colorful healthy splendor of Playboy girls. Gone the high-tone ads and the celebrity interviews and the interminable self-promotion of Mr. Hefner.*

*These were all black-and-white pages except for two-color covers, printed on the pulpiest of pulp, and featuring girls who looked as if they'd recently spent time in prison.*

*"Guy I know sells to these magazines all the time," he said. "And you're a lot better writer than he is."*

*Stan had read all the Bradbury imitations I'd written for science fiction fanzines that included the likes of Roger Ebert, Greg Benford, and a young Marion Zimmer Bradley.*

*"No reason you can't sell to them."*

*When you grew up in the Iowa of the fifties, you never had a chance to meet writers. So the idea that Stan actually knew somebody from around here who was selling actual stories for actual money . . . and who could walk around boasting, "Yes, I am a professional writer". . . no drug in the world could have stoned me the way Stan's words did that day.*

*I bought the three most recent issues of the magazines and took them home and read them. I had a new experience. Whenever I read people like Ray Bradbury or Robert Silverberg or John D. MacDonald, I was always happy and depressed* at the same time. Happy because their words gave me such pleasure. Depressed because I knew I'd never be a third as good as these guys.

But the writers I discovered in these downscale girlie magazines . . . I'd finally found writers who were worse than I was.

One of the things I noticed was that each issue featured a "sexology" article written by guys who had PhDs at the ends of their names. And that the editor always featured one or two short stories based on the premise of the article. Most of the sexology stuff concerned, as I recall, keeping your girlfriend and/or wife chained in the basement (werewolf style) before she gave into her screaming natural need to become a NYMPHO (NYMPHO was almost always in caps.) Apparently, in every state but Iowa, nymphomania was such a problem that the governors were considering calling the army in, the way they did in the final acts of all those Big Bug movies of the sci-fi fifties. You know, the big guns that only the Pentagon could supply? Apparently, the nationwide (except for Iowa) NYMPHO problem was that bad.

Well, the most recent of the copies I had described a sexology article that would be in the very next issue, along with all those sullen-looking nude models they used. The premise of this article was that there were some women (NYMPHOS, in fact) who just couldn't get enough sex and so went looking for it in dangerous places.

Now, I have to say that this didn't make any sense to me. There was a neighbor lady of ours who'd been raped and her life was sad ever after. She was a nice lady and my dad always said he'd like to kill the man (never caught) who'd done it.

So I didn't see anything funny about rape at all.

But I decided to go along with the gag (even then, naive as I was, I figured the PhD routine was a scam). I decided to write a story about a NYMPHO who just couldn't get enough sex and who thus took buses around Chicago to bad neighborhoods, where the rapists gave her all the sex she can handle.

Stan was ready to send my masterpiece to the Nobel committee. But since he didn't have their address, he showed it to his writing buddy and the guy said this was a sure sale.

During this time, I was also bombarding science fiction and mystery magazines with dozens of stories. But I knew, if forced to tell the truth, that I wasn't ready for those markets yet. But these downscale girlie mags . . .

Weeks went by. Stan was encouraging at first—they probably get a lot of stories, Ed, and they're just busy—but then even he lost hope. Well, maybe not this time, kiddo. But maybe the next one . . .

The story came back in the stamped, self-addressed manila envelope I'd enclosed with the masterpiece. I opened it up and saw paper-clipped to the top of the story the standard-form rejection. But at the bottom of the slip was written in smudgy blue ballpoint the single word "Over."

I removed slip from clip and turned it over and quickly read the most glorious words my eyes had ever gazed upon: "You've got three rapes in this story. If you can work in one more, we'll pay you fifteen dollars."

This was a much higher-class publication than even I had realized. You bet I added that rape.

And thus my illustrious career was born.

Larry Block not only asked me to write about the story, he asked if there was any way we could include the story in this book. Yeah, right.

Fortunately, the story was lost the last time we moved. The van company lost twenty years of my writing. Very little of it was worth saving, a lot of inconsequential stories for inconsequential literary magazines, and a lot of men's magazine bilge not quite as crude as my first sale.

Looking back, and having lived for a few years in the seventies with a woman who was raped in her teens, the story is not only crude but offensive. And I'm glad I don't have a copy of it anymore.

Here's another very early story that was lost in the aforementioned move. I rewrote it many years later from memory and sold it first to Ellery Queen. It's been reprinted three times, and I now think of it as my first official crime story. It has that rough-edged men's magazine quality but at least it doesn't have any NYMPHOS. I'm pretty sure it doesn't, anyway.

# Layover

## ED GORMAN

IN THE DARKNESS, THE girl said, "Are you all right?"

"Huh?"

"I woke you up because you sounded so bad. You must have been having a nightmare."

"Oh, yeah. Right." I tried to laugh, but the sound just came out strangled and harsh.

Cold midnight. Deep Midwest. A Greyhound bus filled with old folks and runaway kids and derelicts of every kind. Anybody can afford a Greyhound ticket these days, that's why you find so many geeks and freaks aboard. I was probably the only guy on the bus who had a real purpose in life. And if I needed a reminder of that purpose, all I had to do was shove my hand into the pocket of my peacoat and touch the chill blue metal of the .38. I had a purpose all right.

The girl had gotten on a day before, during a dinner stop. She wasn't what you'd call pretty, but then neither was I. We talked, of course, the way you do when you travel; dull grinding social chatter at first, but eventually you get more honest. She told me she'd just been dumped by a guy named Mike, a used-car salesman at Belaski Motors in a little town named Burnside. She was headed to Chicago where she'd find a job and show Mike that she was capable of going on without him. Come to think of it, I guess Polly here had a goal, too, and in a certain way our goals were similar. We both wanted to pay people back for hurting us.

Sometime around ten, when the driver turned off the tiny overhead lights and people started falling asleep, I heard her start crying. It wasn't loud and it wasn't hard, but it was genuine. There was a lot of pain there.

I don't know why—I'm not the type of guy to get involved—but I put my hand on her lap. She took it in both of her hands and held it tightly. "Thanks," she said, and leaned over and kissed me with wet cheeks and a trembling hot little mouth.

"You're welcome," I said, and that's when I drifted off to sleep, the wheels of the Greyhound thrumming down the highway, the dark coffin inside filled with people snoring, coughing, and whispering.

According to the luminous hands on my wristwatch, it was forty-five minutes later when Polly woke me up to tell me I'd been having a nightmare.

The lights were still off overhead. The only illumination was the soft silver of moonlight through the tinted window. We were in the backseat on the left-hand side of the back aisle. The only thing behind us was the john, which almost nobody seemed to use. The seats across from her were empty.

After telling me about how sorry she felt for me having nightmares like that, she leaned over and whispered, "Who's Kenny?"

"Kenny?"

"That's the name you kept saying in your nightmare."

"Oh."

"You're not going to tell me, huh?"

"Doesn't matter. Really."

I leaned back and closed my eyes. There was just darkness and the turning of the wheels and the winter air whistling through the windows. You could smell the faint exhaust.

"You know what I keep thinking?" she said.

"No. What?" I didn't open my eyes.

"I keep thinking we're the only two people in the world, you and I, and we're on this fabulous boat and we're journeying to someplace beautiful."

I had to laugh at that. She sounded so naive, yet desperate, too. "Someplace beautiful, huh?"

"Just the two of us."

And she gave my hand a little squeeze. "I'm sorry I'm so corny," she said.

And that's when it happened. I started to turn around in my seat and felt something fall out of my pocket and hit the floor, going *thunk*. I didn't have to wonder what it was.

Before I could reach it, she bent over, her long blonde hair silver in the moonlight, and got it for me.

She looked at it in her hand and said, "Why would you carry a gun?"

"Long story."

She looked as if she wanted to take the gun and throw it out the window. She shook her head. "You're going to do something with this, aren't you?"

I sighed and reached over and took the gun from her. "I'd like to try and catch a little nap if you don't mind."

"But—"

And I promptly turned over so that three-fourths of my body was pressed against the chill wall of the bus. I pretended to go to sleep, resting there and smelling diesel fuel and feeling the vibration of the motor.

The bus roared on into the night. It wouldn't be long before I'd be seeing Dawn and Kenny again. I touched the .38 in my pocket. No, not long at all.

IF YOU'VE TAKEN MANY Greyhounds, then you know about layovers. You spend an hour and a half gulping down greasy food and going into the bathroom in a john that reeks like a city dump on a hot day and staring at people in the waiting area who seem to be deformed in every way imaginable. Or that's how they look at 2:26 A.M., anyway.

This layover was going to be different. At least for me. I had plans.

As the bus pulled into a small brick depot that looked as if it had been built back during the depression, Polly said, "You're going to do it here, aren't you?"

"Do what?"

"Shoot somebody."

"Why would you say that?"

"I've just got a feeling is all. My mom always says I have ESP."

She started to say something else, but then the driver lifted the microphone and gave us his spiel about how the layover would be a full hour and how there was good food to be had in the restaurant and how he'd enjoyed serving us. There'd be a new driver for the next six hours of our journey, he said.

There weren't many lights on in the depot. Passengers stood outside for a while stretching and letting the cold air wake them up.

I followed Polly off the bus and immediately started walking away. An hour wasn't a long time.

Before I got two steps, she snagged my arm. "I was hoping we could be friends. You know, I mean, we're a lot alike." In the shadowy light of the depot, she looked younger than ever. Young and well scrubbed and sad. "I don't want you to get into trouble. Whatever it is, you've got your whole life ahead of you. It won't be worth it. Honest."

"Take care of yourself," I said, and leaned over and kissed her.

She grabbed me again and pulled me close and said, "I got in a little trouble once myself. It's no fun. Believe me."

I touched her cheek gently and then I set off, walking quickly into the darkness.

Armstrong was a pretty typical midwestern town, four blocks of retail area, fading brick grade school and junior high, a small public library with a white stone edifice, a courthouse, a Chevrolet dealership, and many blocks of small white frame houses that all looked pretty much the same in the early morning gloom. You could see frost rimed on the windows and lonely gray smoke twisting up from the chimneys. As I walked, my heels crunched ice. Faint streetlight threw everything into deep shadow. My breath was silver.

A dog joined me for a few blocks and then fell away. Then I spotted a police cruiser moving slowly down the block. I jumped behind a huge oak tree, flattening myself against the rough bark so the cops couldn't see me. They drove right on past, not even glancing in my direction.

The address I wanted was a ranch house that sprawled over the west end of a cul-de-sac. A sweet little red BMW was parked in front of the two-stall garage and a huge satellite-dish antenna was discreetly hidden behind some fir trees. No lights shone anywhere.

I went around back and worked on the door. It didn't take me long to figure out that Kenny had gotten himself one of those infrared security devices. I tugged on my gloves, cut a fist-sized hole in the back-door window, reached in, and unlocked the deadbolt, and then pushed the door open. I could see one of the small round infrared sensors pointing down from the ceiling. Most fool burglars wouldn't even think to look for it, and they'd pass right through the beam and the alarm would go off instantly.

I got down on my haunches and half crawled until I was well past the eye of the infrared. No alarm had sounded. I went up three steps and into the house.

The dark kitchen smelled of spices, paprika, and cinnamon and thyme. Dawn had always been a good and careful cook.

The rest of the house was about what I'd expected. Nice but not expensive furnishing, lots of records and videotapes, and even a small bumper-pool table in a spare room that doubled as a den. Nice, sure, but nothing that would attract attention. Nothing that would appear to have been financed by six hundred thousand dollars in bank robbery money.

And then the lights came on.

At first I didn't recognize the woman. She stood at the head of a dark narrow hallway wearing a loose cotton robe designed to conceal her weight.

The flowing dark hair is what misled me. Dawn had always been a blonde. But dye and a gain of maybe fifteen pounds had changed her appearance considerably. And so had time. It hadn't been a friend to her.

She said, "I knew you'd show up someday, Chet."

"Where's Kenny?"

"You want some coffee?"

"You didn't answer my question."

She smiled her slow, shy smile. "You didn't answer mine, either."

She led us into the kitchen where a pot of black stuff stayed warm in a Mr. Coffee. She poured two cups and handed me one of them.

"You came here to kill us, didn't you?" she said.

"You were my wife. And we were supposed to split everything three ways. But Kenny got everything—you and all the money. And I did six years in prison."

"You could have turned us in."

I shook my head. "I have my own way of settling things."

She stared at me. "You look great, Chet. Prison must have agreed with you."

"I just kept thinking of this night. Waiting."

Her mouth tightened and for the first time her blue eyes showed traces of fear. Softly, she said, "Why don't we go in the living room and talk about it."

I glanced at my wristwatch. "I want to see Kenny."

"You will. Come on now."

So I followed her into the living room. I had a lot ahead of me. I wanted to kill them and then get back on the bus. While I'd be eating up the miles on a Greyhound, the local cops would be looking for a local killer. If only my gun hadn't dropped out and Polly seen it. But I'd have to worry about that later.

We sat on the couch. I started to say something but then she took my cup from me and set it on the glass table and came into my arms.

She opened her mouth and kissed me dramatically.

But good sense overtook me. I held her away and said, "So while we're making out, Kenny walks in and shoots me. Is that it?"

"Don't worry about Kenny. Believe me."

And then we were kissing again. I was embracing ghosts, ancient words whispered in the backseats of cars when we were in high school, tender promises made just before I left for Nam. Loving this woman had always been punishment because you could never believe her, never trust her, but I'd loved her anyway.

I'd just started to pull away when I heard the floor creak behind me and I saw Kenny. Even given how much I hated him—and how many long nights I'd lain on my prison bunk dreaming of vengeance—I had to feel embarrassed. If Kenny had been his old self, I would have relished the moment. But Kenny was different now. He was in a wheelchair and his entire body was twisted and crippled up like a cerebral palsy victim. A small plaid blanket was thrown across his legs.

He surprised me by smiling. "Don't worry, Chet. I've seen Dawn entertain a lot of men out here in the living room before."

"Spare him the details," she said. "And spare me, too, while you're at it."

He whispered a dirty word loud enough for us to hear.

He wheeled himself into the living room. The chair's electric motor whirred faintly as he angled over to the fireplace. On his way, he said, "You didn't wait long, Chet. You've only been out two weeks. You never did have much patience."

You could see the pain in his face when he moved.

I tried to say something, but I just kept staring at this man who was now a cripple. I didn't know what to say.

"Nice setup, huh?" Kenny said as he struck a stick match on the stone of the fireplace. With his hands twisted and gimped the way they were, it wasn't easy. He got his smoke going and said, "She tell you what happened to me?"

I looked at Dawn. She dropped her gaze. "No," I said.

He snorted. The sound was bitter. "She was doin' it to me just the way she did it to you. Right?" he said, and called her another dirty name.

She sighed, then lighted her own cigarette. "About six months after we ran out on you with all the money, I grabbed the strongbox and took off."

Kenny smirked. "She met a sailor. A goddamn sailor, if you can believe it."

"His name was Fred," she said. "Anyway, me and Fred had all the bank robbery money—there was still a couple hundred thousand left—when Kenny here came after us in that red Corvette he always wanted. He got right up behind us, but it was pouring rain and he skidded out of control and slammed into a tree."

He finished the story for me. "There was just one problem, right, Dawn? You had the strongbox, but you didn't know what was inside. Her and the sailor were going to have somebody use tools on the lock I'd put on it. They saw me pile up my 'vette but they kept on going. But later that night when they blew open the strongbox and found out that I'd stuffed it with old newspapers, the sailor beat her up and threw her out. So she came back to me 'cause she just couldn't stand to be away from 'our' money. And this is where she's been all the time you were in the slam. Right here waitin' for poor pitiful me to finally tell her where I hid the loot. Or die. They don't give me much longer. That's what keeps her here."

"Pretty pathetic story, huh?" she said. She got up and went over to the small wet bar. She poured three drinks of pure Jim Beam and brought them over to us. She gunned hers in a single gulp and went right back for another.

"So she invites half the town in so she can have her fun while I vegetate in my wheelchair." Now it was his turn to down his whiskey. He hurled the glass into the fireplace. A long, uneasy silence followed.

I tried to remember the easy friendship the three of us had enjoyed back when we were in high school, before Kenny and I'd been in Nam, and before the three of us had taken up bank robbery for a living. Hard to believe we'd ever liked each other at all.

Kenny's head dropped down then. At first I thought he might have passed out, but then the choking sound of dry sobs filled the room and I realized he was crying.

"You're such a wimp," she said.

And then it was her turn to smash her glass into the fireplace.

I'd never heard two people go at each other this way. It was degrading.

He looked up at me. "You stick around here long enough, Chet, she'll make a deal with you. She'll give you half the money if you beat me up and make me tell you where it is."

I looked over at her. I knew what he said was true.

"She doesn't look as good as she used to—she's kind of a used car now instead of a brand-new Caddy—but she's still got some miles left on her. You should hear her and some of her boyfriends out here on the couch when they get goin'."

She started to say something but then she heard me start to laugh.

"What the hell's so funny?"

I stood up and looked at my watch. I had only ten minutes left to get back to the depot.

Kenny glanced up from his wheelchair. "Yeah, Chet, what's so funny?"

I looked at them both and just shook my head. "It'll come to you. One of these days. Believe me."

And with that, I left.

She made a play for my arm and Kenny sat there glowering at me, but I just kept on walking. I had to hurry.

The cold, clean air not only revived me, it seemed to purify me in some way. I felt good again, whole and happy now that I was outdoors.

The bus was dark and warm. Polly had brought a bag of popcorn along. "You almost didn't make it," she said as the bus pulled away from the depot.

In five minutes we were rolling into countryside again. In farmhouses lights were coming on. In another hour, it would be dawn.

"You took it, didn't you?" I said.

"Huh?"

"You took it. My gun."

"Oh. Yes. I guess I did. I didn't want you to do anything crazy."

Back there at Kenny's I'd reached into my jacket pocket for the .38 and found it gone. "How'd you do it? You were pretty slick."

"Remember I told you I'd gotten into a little trouble? Well, an uncle of mine taught me how to be a pickpocket and so for a few months I followed in his footsteps. Till Sheriff Baines arrested me one day."

"I'm glad you took it."

She looked over at me in the darkness of the bus and grinned. She looked like a kid. "You really didn't want to do it, did you?"

"No," I said, staring out the window at the midwestern night. I thought of them back there in the house, in a prison cell they wouldn't escape till death. No, I hadn't wanted to shoot anybody at all. And, as things turned out, I hadn't had to either. Their punishment was each other.

"We're really lucky we met each other, Chet."

"Yeah," I said, thinking of Dawn and Kenny again. "You don't know how lucky we are."

# A Bunch of
# Mumbo-Jumbo

JAN GRAPE

## Jan Grape's Introduction:

*The year was 1990 and I'd been trying to complete my first novel and open* Mysteries & More *bookstore. I also had been writing a column for* Mystery Scene *magazine, titled "Southwest Scenes," for a little over two years, and during one of my periodic conversations with editor Ed Gorman, he asked if I happened to have a short story for an anthology he was editing.*

*"I have one in the works," I lied. "Send it along," Ed said. A short time later I sent him an earlier draft of "Mumbo-Jumbo."*

*During this same time period, Robert J. Randisi was editing an anthology titled* Deadly Allies, *a joint venture between the Private-Eye Writers of America and Sisters-in-Crime. Bob said there were a couple of slots for new authors if I wanted to submit a story for it, so I wrote a P.I. story and sent it to Bob. Now I had two short stories being considered.*

*Ed Gorman called one day and said if I could change my story just enough to fit the format for the* Invitation to Murder *anthology, then he thought he could use it. The slots in the earlier anthology had been filled already. The theme for* Invitation *was that each author would use the same idea of "a young woman was found dead on her apartment floor." My story "Mumbo-Jumbo" didn't quite fit that format, but I could incorporate the theme idea into my story without a huge rewrite. I sent the revised story in and kept my fingers crossed.*

*Within a couple of days of each other that December, I got my responses, although I don't actually remember which came first, the call from Ed Gorman or the one from Bob Randisi. Both stories had been accepted and both stories would be published—a dream come true. I believe the check from Ed Gorman came first, but even that certainty is shrouded in the mental mist. However, I do know that "Mumbo-Jumbo" in* Invitation to Murder *was published first in 1991.*

*The excitement of having sold a short story only intensified when I finally held that anthology in my hands and saw my name on the back of the book along*

with some of the biggest names in the mystery business: Bill Pronzini, Nancy Pick-
ard, John Lutz, Carolyn G. Hart, Joan Hess, Loren D. Estelman, Barbara Paul,
Judith Kelman, Teri White, Andrew Vachss. It was the thrill of a lifetime and a
never-to-be-forgotten feeling.

I do hope you enjoy "Mumbo-Jumbo."

# A Bunch of Mumbo-Jumbo

## JAN GRAPE

NATHAN FOSTER WALKED BACK from the bathroom just as his wife Sara awoke. He'd heard her moans and saw her threshing when he walked through their bedroom, but hoped the nightmare would quickly subside and she'd slip back into a deeper sleep. It was not to be, he saw, when he reached the bedside, for she was staring wide-eyed at him, perspiration causing her pale brown hair to curl around her face. The sheet and bedspread were tangled around Sara's left arm and both legs.

"Sara?" he asked, "are you all right? You must have had a bad dream. Your cries woke me up." Nathan was lying; he'd only walked into their house a few minutes ago. He slipped quickly onto the bed, beside his wife of twenty-four years, and hoped Sara wasn't awake enough to realize he'd not been there before.

"Oh, God. Nathan. It was horrible."

Sara turned to him for comfort, and he put his hand on her shoulder, patting clumsily a moment before removing his hand. "Sara, was it about your mother again?" He felt a small pang of guilt because he really didn't care about hearing her answer.

*If she hadn't been so wrapped up in all that metaphysical stuff,* he thought, *none of this would have happened.* Damnit all. . . she'd even taken to wearing crystals, some of them two and three inches long and talking with some "entity" she claimed had been her mentor and teacher for the past two thousand years. Channeling she called it.

Nathan's world focused on mathematics; numbers were so precise and absolute. He had great difficulty understanding Sara's psychic leanings.

Nathan, born during the depression years into a family fathered by an alcoholic, remembered being five years old and going to bed hungry. He swore an oath that he'd have all he wanted to eat when he grew up. There would be no help from anyone; he'd have to depend solely on himself.

In junior high school, his aptitude for mathematics was noted by a conscientious teacher, and he soon excelled. He learned to set goals based on the application of numbers and figures. Step by step, he attained his goals and now owned a highly successful CPA firm in Houston, Texas. The exact science of dealing with numbers was so far removed from Sara's ESP that his mind could never grasp her clairvoyance.

His wife, Sara, was a warm, caring person and a good mother to their only child, Kimberly, now twenty-two. Yet her "gift" as she called it, a strong ability for ESP and predictions, set her apart from other people, even Nathan. When she was small, she had "movies" that played in her head of events that would happen later. More than once she had "seen" a friend or family member lying in a casket and invariably, that person had died. Throughout their marriage, Nathan had laughingly called Sara's gift: *mumbo-jumbo*.

Nathan yawned and closed his eyes, but Sara insisted on telling him all about her dream. "Nathan, I don't know what's happening. Ishtar says I'm only going through a growth change, brought about by Mother's death, but it's so . . . so horrible. The dreams are getting more . . . well, violent and bloody, and this nightmare seemed so real."

Ishtar was the name of Sara's spirit guide and she claimed to believe all he told her, but sometimes she was frustrated by what "he" said.

Nathan sighed and didn't speak, knowing all the time Sara would continue even if he feigned sleep.

"Mother and I were at her house, sitting on her sofa and talking. A man wearing a ski stocking mask and carrying a baseball bat broke in; and before I could stop him, he started beating her on the head. It was awful. Bone cracked and blood was everywhere, and I ran at him to stop him. I was beating him with my fists and Mother was lying on the floor. Blood was pumping out of her and covering my feet and legs, but somehow I . . . uh . . . I was able to get my fingers under the bottom part of the mask. Before I could put it off though, I woke up. I want to know who that man was, I've got to know."

"Sara, you shouldn't talk like this."

"But he murdered my mother. I know it was Jack who killed her. I didn't see his face, but I know it was him. And I'm in danger now, too."

"Sara, it's just a dream you're talking about. Jack didn't kill Maudi. Her death was an accident." Sara's mother had died in a fall while on her honeymoon in the Greek Islands. "You know Maudi wouldn't want you acting like this."

While it was true Maudi's skull had been crushed, the police said the older woman had sustained the type of injury you'd expect from falling down a steep staircase.

"Stop thinking about the nightmare, Sara. Try to go back to sleep if you can."

His wife's visions and dreams had intensified after Maudi's death. Nathan was sure it was only the grief causing her to have nightmares and behave like a woman obsessed. Sara used all of her energy to try and convince people that Maudi had been murdered.

Murdered by her new husband. The motive? Money.

Sara's father had made a fortune, running whiskey into Galveston during prohibition. He'd invested in real estate and in the 1940s and 50s had made another fortune when oil had been found on much of his West Texas land. When he died fifteen years ago, his estate had been worth an estimated ten million dollars.

Sara closed her eyes and breathed deeply, hypnotically. Nathan turned away from her abruptly as he felt the flush coming over him. Thinking of Maudi's death had reminded him of Allison. Strange how Maudi's death had led to new life for him.

Allison Neely. Three weeks ago, Nathan's whole world changed when the beautiful young woman touched his arm in a gesture of sympathy over his mother-in-law's death and seared herself into his soul.

She'd been working in his office for three months, and, although he'd noticed her, he'd not really seen her. Allison, the most beautiful, voluptuous woman he'd ever encountered, with raven-colored hair and sparkling green eyes, had taken him into her bed that same night and he'd been with her every day or night since.

Every moment he could snatch from work and home, Nathan would take, and take Allison and spend hours, lost in the scent and taste and the flesh of her. He had been with Allison again tonight and the memories of what had happened in her bed with her wiped out Sara's nightmare and even erased the realization that Sara was now lying beside him, unable to return to sleep. Nathan's sleep and dreams were filled only of Allison Neely.

The next morning, Sara bustled around fixing breakfast, but it was obvious she wanted to talk about her mother's death again. "Nathan, it's quite clear you and everyone else thinks I'm losing it, that I'm crazy or heading that way, but I know Jack had something to do with Mother's accident. That courtship and marriage was entirely too quick. Remember when she called to tell us they were getting married—how giddy she sounded. Like she was on a champagne drunk."

Sara's mother had met Jack Clifford while on a trip to Europe. Two weeks later they were married, and three weeks later Maudi was dead. Maudi had never returned home. According to instructions in her new will, Jack had her cremated and her ashes sprinkled around the Greek Isles where they met.

"Honestly, Nathan. Mother was mesmerized by that man and didn't realize her danger. She sounded worse than some sixteen-year-old. In fact, our Kimberly never was that giddy over any boy." Sara sat down, but didn't touch her food.

Nathan was weary of the whole discussion, but he tried to reach Sara once again—to make her see how wrong she was. He even tried to reach her intuitive nature. "Maybe Maudi knew she didn't have much time left. Maybe she only wanted to grab a little bit of happiness. Can you really blame her?"

"Noo-o-o. I guess not. But I didn't get to see her or be with her. The happiest weeks of her life in years, and I didn't get to share in them. That hurts.

"And we never got to meet Jack either. That's a real puzzle—him not showing up for the memorial service we held. No one has heard from him since either. Isn't that proof of his . . ."

"It is odd, but not exactly sinister."

"Well, it is to me. After all, she did leave him a million dollars. . . ."

"Yes. And the other nine million to you and Kimberly, but that doesn't mean that you or I killed Maudi."

"Well, he got her to change her will, but I'll bet he didn't know she made one more change the day before she died. I'll bet he thought he was going to get it all."

Nathan drained his coffee, eager to be on his way. Eager to see Allison. "Sara. You've got to put all this behind you. And you've got to stop thinking this non—"

"Nathan? Do you have to go? I wanted to tell you my other dream. The one after my nightmare. It was a bad dream, too. I can't remember exact details, but you and I were in extreme danger. There was water all around me and . . ."

"Sara, I've told you and Dr. Simms has told you. You're letting grief cloud your judgment about everything." He started to get up when he thought of one more new argument to try to get through to her. "Listen, you've never had dreams like this before, have you? I mean, all these years you've always been wide awake when you see whatever it is that you see?"

"Yes, but . . ."

"That should prove to you that what you're dreaming is something grief-induced."

Sara's anguished look made him guiltily think he should stay home with her a few minutes longer, but then Allison filled his mind and the guilty thought vanished. He got up and picked up his briefcase from the kitchen counter.

"Even if you're right about Jack, there's nothing you or anyone can do about it now." He turned and left.

Nathan discovered later that Sara's obsession was stronger than even he'd imagined. She hired a private investigator, sent the man to Europe, all expenses paid, in an effort to determine what really had happened to Maudi.

Sara reported the P.I. could find no evidence of foul play, and two witnesses placed Jack at a hotel bar a mile away when Maudi's accident occurred.

Nathan, who was totally wrapped up in *his* new obsession, in the form of Allison, stopped listening to Sara's news or lack of it.

Once, just before he moved out of the house, Nathan did listen to Sara complaining that the P.I. was making little progress in locating Jack. He tried to make Sara see the investigator was taking advantage of her. "He's milking you for thousands, Sara."

"I don't care. It's my money, to spend as I please."

Nathan didn't answer. Nothing of his old life mattered anymore. His daughter, Kim, was the only thing from his past to linger in the back of his mind, and thoughts of her were brief. Nothing else was important. Not Sara with her metaphysics nor Maudi nor the missing Jack Clifford.

Nathan's every waking thought was filled with thoughts of smoothing Allison's dark silky hair away from her eyes and kissing her warm, sensitive mouth.

Allison was totally intoxicating; she never seemed to have enough of him nor was his desire for her ever satiated. Her slightest touch electrified him and turned his legs to rubber. And each time he crawled into her bed and pulled her fabulous body up close to sear his flesh each place they touched, Nathan felt certain he knew what paradise was like.

Allison was like having champagne and lobster every night, a new sports car every day, and she was as addictive as heroin; he knew he could not rest until she would be with him every moment, in his life and in his home as his wife.

Sara did not protest when Nathan moved out. She was in a mostly unresponsive world of her own, filled with "entities and ethereal planes." When Nathan asked for a divorce, she quickly signed the papers and all of Sara's dreams and visions and mumbo-jumbo faded from Nathan's mind.

The day after his divorce was final, Nathan and Allison were wed in Las Vegas.

To the newlyweds' surprise, Sara remarried also, a month after their wedding, but two weeks later she was found dead, floating facedown in her newly installed swimming pool.

ALLISON FOLLOWED NATHAN INTO the living room. "That was such a nice send-off Clifton gave Sara, don't you think, dear?"

Nathan didn't answer as he loosened his tie, slid out of his jacket, throwing it across the back of the sofa, then headed to the liquor cabinet and mixed a pitcher of martinis. *Psychics and ESP*, he was thinking. *Was it all really a bunch of hogwash?*

From the minute he'd heard of Sara's death, all of her gloomy predictions—all of her mumbo-jumbo warnings of danger—came swirling and rushing back to him as quickly as a Gulf Coast hurricane. He still couldn't believe Sara was gone. He had seen her body—lying in the bronzed casket, but even so, the actual thought of Sara dead made him queasy and nauseated.

He took a slow, deep breath to clear his head and walked slowly to the sofa and sat, leaning back into its softness. Nathan lifted the glass and drank half of the gin and vermouth, feeling the warmth spread through his abdomen. God. What a nightmare. Sara's funeral. His first thought had been to not go, but he felt obligated for Kim's sake. How would it have looked to his daughter if her father didn't attend her mother's funeral? Besides, Sara's ghost probably would have come back to haunt him.

"Wonder if Sara had a premonition of how or when she'd die?"

"What dear?"

Allison wasn't paying attention, he thought. We don't communicate anymore except in bed. The emptiness in her head somehow makes our twenty-year age difference seem greater. "Never mind," he said.

Beautiful Allison, sexy and voluptuous, but oh, so selfish and greedy. If he wasn't talking about money or giving her money or telling her to go spend money, she wasn't interested in what Nathan said.

She spent as if she thought he was churning money out in the basement. Nathan deplored waste. Allison never understood and when he tried to talk to her about cutting back, she would laugh and call him "Old Scrooge."

Sara, on the other hand, had always understood about being careful with a dollar, even though she had been born into money. They had lived on his salary, and in the early years and later, when he made a good six-figure income, she would account for every dollar. Right up until they divorced, at least, Sara's only splurge had been hiring that private detective, and she had paid for him out of her inheritance.

But Sara had changed, too. After her marriage to Clifton, she changed completely. She'd bought her new husband an expensive sports car and new clothes and that fancy house where she built that damned swimming pool.

Thinking of the pool reminded him of what had happened. Sighing, he got up and poured another martini. If Sara could actually have foretold her own death, why, then, did she go swimming at night when she was all alone? Could she have been right about being in danger? The idea made Nathan's head roar like a jackhammer digging out concrete.

Allison kept flitting around the room, her mind obviously on money. Eventually, she lit beside Nathan on the sofa. "I don't understand why I couldn't buy a new dress to wear to Sara's funeral."

"A funeral is not a fashion parade. Honestly, Allison, sometimes I think you're sick . . ."

"Just because I wanted a new outfit?"

"You have a closet full of clothes. Anyone who's a compulsive shopper, like you are, is definitely sick."

"Speaking of money," Allison said, turning the conversation from her herself, but staying on her favorite subject, "I'll bet old Clifton spent plenty on that funeral."

Nathan ignored her.

"He couldn't afford not to, of course. Not after getting all of Sara's money. His fancy friends would have laughed at him behind his back if he'd been stingy."

Nathan shook his head, "Mr. Jackson did not inherit all of Sara's money. Oh, Sara left him a tidy lump sum, but Kimberly gets the majority."

"But I . . . I thought Sara left him everything or gave him control or something. Isn't Kimmy too young to handle that much money on her own?"

"Sara rewrote her will, the day before her death. The money will be in a special account until Kim reaches twenty-five. I'm her trustee and Sara's executor."

Allison was listening intently, but Nathan didn't notice. "I didn't know Sara changed her will, did you know? And what does being the trustee mean? Do you have actual control?"

"It wasn't something Sara would discuss. And no. She didn't talk to me about it. She just went to Poindexter's office and had him make the changes. And yes, the trustee has some control and also gets a salary for taking care of things."

"I see." Allison tapped a fingernail against her front tooth. "Sara always was a suspicious person, wasn't she? She always thought all those awful things about me, and now it looks like she didn't trust her new husband either."

"Maybe she suddenly came to her senses and wondered where in the hell Clifton came from."

"Ooooh! Who would really care? A sexy hunk like that. He's athletic, plays golf, tennis, sails, rides horses, flies airplanes and gliders—the man does everything well—and I adore his British accent. He's so handsome, so dashing."

"So gigoloish, if you ask me. He'd do anything for money."

"Speaking of money, Nathan. What happens if you should die before Kim reaches twenty-five? She'd be . . . I'm sure I . . . I mean, would I lose . . ."

"Don't worry Allison. You'll be well cared for."

Allison slid across the cushions, closer to Nathan, and pulled his head into her lap. She snaked her arm around his neck, smoothing his salt and pepper gray hair back from his forehead. "Let's not talk about Clifton or Kim or anything else tonight, okay?" she said, and began putting teasing, little kisses onto his eyelids and face and mouth.

Nathan couldn't deny the desire that arose—how his blood pounded—as he automatically began caressing her warm, firm breast with his right hand. Instantly, he felt the response of her nipple underneath his fingers.

NATHAN SHOOK HIS HEAD to clear away the grogginess of sleep and answered the ringing telephone.

"Daddy?"

"Kim? What's wrong, Baby? Why are you crying?"

"I'm sorry, but I . . ."

"Honey, what is it? What's wrong?"

"I, uh . . . I got a letter from Mother, written before she died. Mr. Poindexter was to send it if anything strange happened."

"What does it say?"

Kim snubbed and blew her nose. "I can't read it over the phone. Can you meet me for brunch?"

Nathan reached the Glass Hut in a little over an hour. The hostess led him to a corner table in the back where Kimberly was already seated. He was shocked by his daughter's appearance. Her face was devoid of makeup and her hair had been hastily pulled back into a ponytail, giving her such a vulnerable little-girl look that his heart tightened in his chest. He remembered how she'd worshiped him, looking to him for every answer.

Kim could barely wait until he sat and the hostess left. "Daddy, I'm so afraid!" Fear clouded her eyes.

*When did he lose Kim?* he wondered. She was part of him—part of his own flesh and blood. "Honey, what on earth? What did Sara say?"

"Mother said she'd had this dream."

"Oh, hell. You know your mother and her ESP. It's all a bunch of malarkey. Is that all?"

"Look. I happen to believe Mother was psychic." Kim jumped up, anger tightening her face and forcing her words out through clenched teeth. "I should have known better than . . ."

Nathan was overwhelmed by his feelings of love for his child. If he turned her down now, she might be lost to him forever. He reached out his hand, gently taking his daughter's arm. "I'm sorry, Kim. Let's not argue. Sit back down. We'll eat, and then you can tell me what your mother said that frightens you."

Kimberly hesitated, but only for a second, then sat. They made small talk until their food came and they had eaten.

"Now," said Nathan. "Tell me about your mother's letter."

"Mother said for us to be *very* careful. You and me. Something terrible is going to happen. That it was too late to save her, but not us."

"She saw something about her own death?"

Kimberly nodded her head, slowly. "She dreamed Clifton hit her in the head with a hammer." The girl stopped, biting her lip and fighting back her tears. "She saw herself falling . . ." Kim sobbed. "Falling into water and sinking like a rock." The tears rolled down the girl's cheeks and dripped onto the table.

"Kim, honey, Clifton was in Dallas, uh . . . when your mother, uh—the coroner said Sara hit her head on the diving board." Nathan pulled his chair closer and put his arm around his daughter's slim shoulders. "I do wish Sara had kept all this psycho stuff to herself. You know the police found nothing suspicious. I believe it was a horrible accident."

"But Daddy. There's something else. That's why I'm so afraid. Look at this newspaper clipping."

Nathan took the clipping from his daughter and read:

### BEAUTY BLUDGEONED TO DEATH
#### Twenty-two-year-old

Kimmie Foster was found dead yesterday in her apartment near Rice University. Houston homicide detectives have no suspects and no clues. When questioned they also had "no comment."

"But Kim, this newspaper is from the 1960s, this isn't you."

"No. But mother's letter said that's how I died before and if I'm not careful it would happen again. The exact same way."

How ridiculous. Kim living before, with the same name—and being murdered? Nathan could not take it seriously. He almost laughed, but one look at Kim's face sobered him. "Honey, it's just a coincidence." Yet, suddenly, something felt almost spooky about the situation.

"But wait; let me tell you what she said about you. She dreamed she saw Allison pushing you out of a boat." Kimberly buried her face into her hands.

Nathan stared at the top of Kimberly's head. Migod. Just last night, Allison *begged* to be taken on a Caribbean cruise. He'd objected strenuously, not really knowing why, but finally had put his foot down and had eventually talked Allison into a trip to the Grand Canyon. *No*, he thought, *that's utter nonsense.*

Logical, practical Nathan, with a new awareness of the trust Kim always had in him, was determined to calm her fears. He mentally shrugged off his uneasiness, but it *was* weird. "Believe me. None of this is going to happen, Kim. Your mother's dreams were unusual, but they're not real life."

It took some talking to calm her, but Nathan eventually saw Kim's composure return. Before parting, he mentioned the trip he and Allison were planning. "No boats there," he teased, "but your old Dad will stay on his toes." Her trusting smile warmed him.

NATHAN SUPERVISED THE LOADING of the luggage while Allison checked to make sure all the doors were locked.

The telephone rang and was quickly answered.

"Is everything set?" the caller asked.

"Signed, sealed and delivered."

The couple climbed into the limousine for the hour-long ride to the airport.

"Who was it?'

"Clifton. Calling to wish us a pleasant trip."

Two days later in a remote forested section of the north rim of the Grand Canyon—and after a brief struggle—Nathan pushed Allison out of the single-engine Cessna. He turned and tapped the helmeted pilot on the shoulder. "Okay, that's one million dollars I owe you, Clifton Jackson. Aren't you glad you decided to deal with me instead of my wife?"

"Shit, yes. You pay a lot better. Besides, that damned Allison was one greedy bitch. She was going to be more trouble than Maudi or Sara put together. The best part? This time, I don't have to split the take with anyone."

Clifton had told Nathan how Allison had figured out his scheme of marrying rich women and then killing them. She convinced him to work with her. Together, the two had planned Nathan's demise, hoping for a bigger prize.

Nathan smiled as they headed back to the airport in Flagstaff. Of course, it was too late for Sara and her mother, but he'd managed to outfox the murdering schemes of Allison and her hired killer. And more importantly, both he and Kim would be safe.

Clifton would never be as greedy as Allison. Especially after he turned the man over to the police. That private investigator Sara had hired finally came through. The P.I. had turned up two previous women in Clifton's background who had also died mysteriously—murdered for their money.

Nathan's testimony of how Clifton and Allison had schemed to murder him and how she'd fallen from the plane during a struggle to push him out would be believed. He couldn't help mumbling aloud the thought which deepened his smile. "I always told Sara her psychic abilities were just a bunch of mumbo-jumbo."

# The Cure

## DAVID HANDLER

## David Handler's Introduction:

*I got the idea for "The Cure" when I was riding the Metro-North commuter train into New York City one morning from my house in Connecticut. It was, for reasons that will quickly become apparent to you, a story I absolutely had to write. It was either that or commit a murder.*

*You will also note that this story is of a very recent vintage. I had never published a short story before "The Cure," even though I was well into my forties and the author of a dozen novels. In fact, I have only recently discovered the joys of writing short fiction. For crime writers of previous generations, many of whom earned their stripes and their rent money by cranking out magazine fiction, this would have been unthinkable. They learned their trade by writing short stories. But that market was pretty much gone by the time baby boomers like me came along. I was schooled as a journalist, and I served my storytelling apprenticeship by cranking out television and film scripts.*

*Throughout my career, one editor after another has urged me to Think Big. And I've tried to. But I've reached a point in my life where I'm also discovering just how important it is to Have Fun. And short stories are fun—spontaneous, fresh, and full of surprises. Putting this one down on paper reminded me why I wanted to become a writer in the first place.*

*I don't know what else to say, except that I'm really glad I decided to take the train that day.*

# The Cure

## DAVID HANDLER

*"HI, IT'S ME . . . DON'T say a word. Just tell me yes or no—are you still in bed?"*

Julian Embry, a trimly built, meticulous man of fifty-two with thinning, mouse-colored hair and a resting pulse rate of 108, had just settled into his usual seat on the 7:42 train to Grand Central when the cell phone junkie in the seat behind him started in like he did every morning.

*"You are? What are you wearing? . . . Rita, you are killing me here. I'm not going to be able to think about anything else all day."*

This man, whose name was Barry Ackerman, was no taller than five feet six and no older than thirty. He had a goatee, great bunches of fitness center muscles, and a seemingly endless collection of Armani suits. Barry Ackerman had invaded Julian's life about three months earlier. Always, he waited for the same train at the Willoughby station as Julian. Always, he sat right near Julian, reeking of cologne and self-importance. Always, he called his mistress just as soon as he got settled. Always, he was loud. Very, very loud.

*"Rita, I have got to go. I'll be there at five. You know I'll be there. . . ."*

Next came the unending stream of business calls. Julian wasn't exactly sure what Barry Ackerman did for a living. He was some variety of dot-com entrepreneur involved in web hosting centers, B-to-B service providers, and other revolutionary forms of instant communication that were of even less interest to Julian than what, if anything, Rita was wearing.

*"Hi, it's me. My train gets in at 8:36. Will you tell Marcie I've got a truly tasty broadband idea I want to talk over with her? Great. . . . Hi, it's me. Are we still on for lunch? Great. I'll call you. . . . Hi, it's me. . . ."*

All Julian knew was that Barry Ackerman was ruining his life.

Julian was a polite, soft-spoken man who placed a great deal of emphasis on precision and order. Every weekday morning for the past sixteen years

159

he had caught this same 7:42 train. *His* train. He parked in the same parking space. *His* space. He sat in the same seat. *His* seat. He would take off his jacket, fold it neatly, and place it in the rack overhead. He would open his briefcase and pull out his work and four needle-sharp No. 2 pencils. Then, for the next fifty-four minutes, Julian Embry would focus all of his intense powers of concentration on the pages before him. For Julian, his morning commute was precious work time, the one private interlude in his day when there were no interruptions, no distractions, and—above all—no phone calls.

But, lately, all of that had changed.

"Hi, it's me. . . . *Would you get me everything you can on Dynelectron? Great. . . . Hi, it's me. . . .*"

First, Julian had tried moving to a different car on the same train. But since the 7:42 originated out in Fairfield, the only seats that were still empty by the time it got to Willoughby were in the first car. *His* car. Next Julian had tried taking the 7:28, but it was a local that actually ended up lurching in sixteen minutes later than the 7:42. He'd even considered driving thirty minutes in the wrong direction to Fairfield and catching the train there, but that would mean he would have to leave the house an hour earlier every day and get home an hour later. Plus his monthly commute would cost him an extra forty dollars.

"*Hi, it's Barry Ackerman. Would you have Lew call me just as soon as possible? The toilet in one of our guest bedrooms is stopped up, and it needs fixing right away. Thank you very, very much.*"

Julian could not believe it. This man was so windy and self-important that he actually thought everyone else in the car wanted to hear him talk to a plumber about his toilet. If Julian had been a different sort of a person, a confrontational loudmouth who had been raised by the same set of boors who'd raised Barry Ackerman, he would have spun right around in his seat and told the smug little bastard to either shut up or risk being hurled bodily from the moving train.

But Julian had not been brought up that way. He was brought up to be civil. Therefore, he stewed, his heart racing faster and faster as he tried to concentrate on his work.

After he got out of Princeton, Julian had spent three years as a fact checker at *The New Yorker*, where he'd dreamt of being the next J. D. Salinger and he'd met Sylvia. Their twin boys, Jason and Jeremy, were now at Princeton themselves. Sylvia's inheritance was bankrolling it. She ended up as a school librarian in Westport. He ended up at Seagrove Press, first as a copy editor, then as an editor. For the past fourteen years he had been a senior editor.

Along the way he published one slim collection of literate, moody short stories, *The Song of the Piping Plover*, which was politely reviewed and sold 1,648 copies.

While his own personal reading taste ran more toward the elegantly crafted short fiction of O'Hara and Cheever, Julian's strength as an editor was fine-tuning complex, nail-biting thrillers. When it came to plotting, Julian was a dogged and demanding master surgeon who believed that a properly constructed plot possessed all of the inner beauty and precision of a fine Swiss watch. Above all, it should work. Whenever one of Seagrove's authors turned in a manuscript that didn't, and no one in the house could figure out why, they passed it to Julian. There was no editor in all of publishing better than Julian Embry at the fine and increasingly rare art of diagnosing where a plot had jumped its tracks and how to coax it back onto them. Through the years he had rescued dozens of brand-name writers. So prized were his skills that authors who had moved on to lucrative deals with other houses still sought out his input.

*"Hi, it's me. Honey, I forgot to take my blue suit to the cleaner's. . . . Will you? Thanks. Yeah, yeah, I called Lew about it. He hasn't gotten back to me yet. I'll let you know. . . ."*

Right now, Julian was trying to shepherd along *Skid*, a first novel about a pilot of commercial jumbo jets who is also a multinational serial killer. Seagrove had paid $2.5 million for it on the strength of a great first chapter and a sexy heroine who had Julia Roberts written all over her. The author was a San Francisco criminal defense attorney with blonde hair down to her butt who had the top literary agent in New York, Libby Gotbaum, and three film studios panting for a first look. She had everything but the book. Her first draft, in Julian's opinion, was nothing more than three hundred pages of warmed-over Farina sporadically livened with kinky sex, brutal violence, and gaping lapses in logic and credibility. An amateurish mess, in other words.

In Julian's most private moments, such as when he lay awake at two in the morning with his heart racing and Sylvia fast asleep beside him, he wished he could come up with just such a can't-miss, seven-figure thriller idea—for *himself* to write. *He* was a professional. *He* knew craft—every trick there was going all the way back to John Buchan and Sax Rohmer. *He* should be the one to make the fortune, not some telegenic amateur. And then he'd never have to ride the 7:42 with Barry Ackerman again. He could stay home and work on another collection of his literate, moody short stories. Possibly edit a select few authors on a freelance basis if he felt like it. The trouble was, Julian had never come up with a can't-miss commercial idea in his life. Not ever. His mind just didn't work that way. If only it did. If only life was fair. If only . . .

Now Barry Ackerman's cell phone was ringing. Once, twice, three times. Why the devil didn't he answer it? He was sitting *right* there.

*"Hello? . . . Oh, hi, Lew. I don't know, it's just like totally plugged up. . . . Yeah, yeah, I tried a plunger. . . . Today is impossible? Are you sure? . . . Yeah, I guess noon tomorrow will have to do. No, wait, Darla won't be around. She helps out over at the Shoreline Soup Kitchen on Thursdays."*

From this man's lips even charity work sounded boastful. Julian could feel his face beginning to flush. He was now totally unable to concentrate on his manuscript. All he could think about was diving over the seat and strangling Barry Ackerman with his bare hands.

*"Yeah, she's there from ten until three. How about after three? . . . No way, we can't wait until the weekend. You know what, Lew? Tomorrow's not a problem. I'll just leave the kitchen door open for you. Yeah, yeah, I'll turn the system off. Yeah, yeah. I promise. You remember where we are, right? Good, good. You're the best, Lew. . . ."*

Incredibly, none of Julian's fellow passengers seemed bothered by Barry Ackerman. No one rolled their eyes. No one shot dirty looks at him. It was strictly Julian who was bugged by this self-important, philandering little loudmouth. For Julian, it was if his whole world had shrunk to this car and there was only enough room on board for one of them. This could not continue. One of them, to put it simply, would have to go.

Julian knew he was letting Barry Ackerman bother him more than he should. But this was how he felt. As the train began to slow to a stop at 125th Street, he wondered if he was on the verge of a nervous breakdown.

The offices of Seagrove Press had been situated a short walk from Grand Central on Fifth Avenue until earlier that year, when Seagrove's parent conglomerate merged with another, larger conglomerate. Now Julian had to take the shuttle over to Times Square, where Seagrove shared sparkling new high-rise office space with several other hardcover publishers, two mass market paperback empires, a record label, a cable channel, and a stable of monthly magazines. It wasn't the additional shuttle trip Julian minded so much as it was the presence of the MTV studio next door. This meant that every morning he had to fight his way through a mob of screaming teenaged girls who had cut school and were lined up in the street in hopes of getting on *Total Request Live.*

He arrived before his secretary and discovered he had an urgent message on his voice mail from Roger Parkman, the twenty-eight-year-old British wunderkind who was the latest in a long line of editorial chiefs under whom Julian had served. The conglomerate had recently promoted Roger to the top slot at Seagrove after a year of seasoning in Hollywood, where he had distinguished himself as a cutting-edge visionary in the new world order of multimedia synergy.

Roger wanted to see him as soon as he got in.

Julian found him in his corner office slouched at his desk with his morning tea and a stack of sales printouts. Mr. Jones was dozing on the sofa next to a stack of manuscripts. "I've gotten a wake-up call from Libby Gotbaum this morning, Julian," he said glumly. "She didn't stop screaming at me for twenty minutes. Do you have any idea what it's like to be screamed at by Libby Gotbaum for twenty minutes?"

"I can guess. Last night she screamed at me for ten."

Roger sat back in his chair, sighing. He was a lanky young man with a huge Adam's apple, an unruly mop of reddish hair, and a silver nose stud. His concave chest and Buddy Holly eyeglasses gave him the aura of a cyber-geek, but he was always fashionably turned out in black designer suits and matching black silk shirts—even though it meant he was invariably covered with cat hair. Roger insisted on lugging his cat, Mr. Jones, to work with him every day. Anyone who came into Roger's office was expected not only to make a huge fuss over Mr. Jones, an utterly unremarkable tabby with no discernible personality, but also to overlook the odor that emanated from the overflowing litter box on the floor behind Roger's desk. The building's cleaning staff refused to go near it, and Roger himself did not seem to notice the smell.

"Libby is not fun when she is riled, Julian. Root canal with a complete absence of Novocain is more fun. What exactly did you *do* to her?"

"She wanted to know how I was making out with *Skid*."

"And . . . ?"

"The book still needs a lot of work," Julian informed him. "Her author keeps changing the rules as she goes along. She flashes backward and forward, switches points of view, verb tenses, voices. She gets herself so bollixed up that her villain ends up killing two different people on two different continents at virtually the same time. There's no way any of it can happen. And no way the reader can follow it."

"Well, that's the point, isn't it?" Roger said offhandedly. "It *is* a thriller."

"I'm not sure I understand what you mean," Julian said, frowning at Roger.

"I mean there *are* no rules. One's goal is simply to keep the reader off-balance."

"But it has to be credible and real. Otherwise the reader is being cheated."

"You see, I don't agree. When it comes to a thriller, there is no such thing as cheating. You're living in the past, Julian. We're not going up against Le Carre anymore. Our competition now is *WWF Smackdown* and Nintendo. I've been out there in our brave new world, Julian. I've drunk the Kool-Aid. And, believe me, what our readers want is thrilling moments. *Spielberg* moments." Roger jumped to his feet and began to pace around the office, bursting with the cocky certainty of a privileged youth who had his parents' world by the tail and knew it and loved it. Julian himself had never been so certain of anything, or so young. "I did not buy this book because I thought it was well written or ever *would* be well written," Roger went on, lecturing him now. "I bought it because it has a truly great aerial chase scene between two jumbo jets. That's fantastic stuff. That's what readers want. Give them a half-dozen scenes like that and you've got a break-out winner. And to hell with the connective tissue. Most of them don't even bother to read it anymore. They just race right on by, same as they surf by the commercials on the telly."

Mr. Jones stirred now and padded over toward the window and jumped up onto the sill, where a number of plants grew in pots.

Roger watched his cat for a moment, a beneficent smile on his face, before he turned back to Julian. "Readers want to have fun. They *like* to have fun. I'm not entirely sure you understand that, Julian. The concept of fun, I mean."

Julian stood there in silence, not quite sure how to respond.

Roger broke it with a boyish whoop of laughter. "God, listen to me. I sound like the worst sort of armchair shrink. Please forget I said that, will you? Because this isn't personal. We simply have a great deal of money tied up in this author."

"I do realize that. That's why I'm—"

"I'm taking you off of this book, Julian," Roger cut in brusquely. "I'm giving it to Glynis."

Julian drew in his breath, staggered. For the very first time it hit him—he had no future at Seagrove or anywhere else in publishing. Everything he knew and cared about was obsolete. *He* was obsolete, an old-time nuts and bolts repairman with grease-stained hands in a new age in which everything, including literature, was merely something to be used up and thrown away like a piece of Kleenex.

Briefly, Julian Embry felt as if he might pass out and have to be taken downstairs on a stretcher.

"Glynis does cookbooks, Roger," he finally managed to get out hoarsely. "She's never done a thriller. I'm not even sure she's read one."

"I know that," Roger said easily. "But she'll take the author to good restaurants and stroke her and make her purr. Besides, it isn't about *this* book. It's about Libby Gotbaum. She has the top client list in New York. If she decides we're the sort who'll make her authors jump through flaming hoops then she'll take them somewhere else. And then where will we be? Out of business, that's where. You're a highly competent editor, Julian, but you have a mid-list mentality. If a book is well reviewed and it earns a nice little profit then you're satisfied. I'm not. My mission, and I *have* chosen to accept it, is to eliminate our mid-list entirely. We need fewer books and bigger books. Nothing but big books."

A steady chewing noise began to compete with him from over by the window. Mr. Jones was busy gnawing on a plant and swallowing it. Soon, he would *gaack* it back up.

"Mr. Jones, what *are* you doing?" Roger exclaimed brightly. "Tell me, Julian, isn't that the cutest cat you've ever seen?"

"You're absolutely right, Roger. I have never seen a cuter cat."

"HAVE YOU TAKEN A vacation lately?"

Now Julian was seated in Dr. Theodore Goldman's small, paneled private office on the ground floor of a doorman building on Park Avenue, his clothing and his dignity restored. Julian had made the appointment a week earlier out of concern for his rapid heartbeat and how it kept waking him in the night. Sylvia knew nothing about any of this.

"We went abroad in April," he replied. "A week in London, another in Tuscany."

"And how was that?"

"Stimulating. Fattening. Wonderful. Why?"

Dr. Goldman had given him an electrocardiogram and stress test, both of which showed that Julian's heart was healthy. He'd also extracted an array of Julian's bodily fluids and subjected him to that special examination procedure which is reserved for suspected international drug mules and perfectly law-abiding men over the age of forty.

"Julian, I think what you've got is a mild case of anxiety. I'm going to give you a prescription for Valium. Take it if you need it. Don't take it if you don't." He handed the prescription slip across the desk to Julian, then sat back with his hands folded across his ample tummy. Theodore Goldman had been Julian's doctor for almost thirty years. He was an old-school physician who liked to chat and liked to listen. Julian, for his part, enjoyed their talks. Teddy Goldman was one of the only people he came in contact with anymore who was older than he was. "Has something been bothering you lately? Money?"

"Not really, no."

"How are things at home? You aren't having an affair, are you?"

"No, no. God, no. I just . . ." Julian trailed off, struggling for the words.

"Don't hold back, Julian," Dr. Goldman urged him. "Tell me what's on your mind. Otherwise, I can't help you."

"I was brought up to live in a different world, that's all," he began slowly. "A world where people valued civility and integrity, where they cared about quality. All anyone cares about anymore is grabbing what they can for themselves, right now, and to hell with everyone else."

"The world is changing. And not for the better."

"Well, it's getting to me. People . . . cocksure kids, loud-mouthed jerks with cell phones . . . they bother me more than they ought to."

"Bother you how?"

"They make me angry. And that scares me. Because there's only one world. And there's only one me. And I . . ." Julian broke off, running a hand through his hair. "Should I go see a shrink or something?"

"Possibly," Dr. Goldman conceded. "But before we go down that road, may I suggest a different cure? Because I know exactly how you feel. I was there myself once. And this worked for me."

Julian leaned forward anxiously. "What is it?"

"Confront your fear."

"Confront it how?"

"Have you ever gone scuba diving?"

Julian stared at him with his mouth open. "Scuba diving? No, I haven't."

"I did. And let me tell you something—a tremendous fear hits you when you're twenty feet underwater, Julian. All of that water pressure is bearing down on you. And the only thing keeping you alive is the oxygen in that tank on your back. Unless you relax, breathe slowly and evenly, you're never going to make it. But you *can* make it. You *do* make it. And when you do, a tremendous calm comes over you. Because you've proven to yourself that you still have control over your own emotions and your own body. Go scuba diving, Julian. Go white-water rafting. Go rock climbing. Show yourself that you've still got what it takes. That you're still standing on your own two feet. We all need to do that when we reach a certain age. *Your* age. Am I making any sense?"

Julian Embry smiled at him. "A great deal of sense. In fact, I think I feel better already."

JULIAN SPENT FORTY-FIVE minutes the following morning cutting up old magazines in his den.

Sylvia had already left for the library by then. He told her he had picked up a flu bug and would be working at home that day. She told him to make sure he drank plenty of fluids.

Home was a snug, weathered, four-bedroom cape on Johnny Cake Hill Road, a winding country lane lined with mature, leafy oaks. Most of the houses on Johnny Cake had been built in the fifties. It was a transitional street by Willoughby standards, a street for folks on their way up, folks on their way down, or, in the case of the Embrys, folks who were not going anywhere at all.

Julian had not said a word to Sylvia about being unceremoniously yanked off of *Skid* by Roger. Or about his appointment with Dr. Goldman. They had spent a quiet evening at home watching a tape of an old Falcon movie starring George Sanders, an actor they both liked.

At 9:30 A.M., he climbed into the green workman's coveralls he'd bought when he was redoing the attic insulation. Then he grabbed his toolbox from out of the garage and hopped into the twins' truck. Before they went away to Princeton, Julian had gone in with them on a three-year-old Toyota Tacoma with four-wheel drive. When they were home, it was theirs for toodling around. When they weren't, Julian used it for hauling brush to the dump and negotiating the trip to the Willoughby train station in bad weather.

Julian headed over to West Avenue and around Willoughby's historic town green, with its gazebo and benches and war memorials. The steepled white Congregational church overlooked the green, which had been voted

Connecticut's prettiest many times. Willoughby was mostly a commuter town now. But it retained its original small-town flavor thanks largely to its green. Julian turned onto Water Street, which skirted along Long Island Sound past the yacht club and boatyards and eventually intersected with Georgetown Avenue. Georgetown took Julian past the high school and the country club. It was a warm, sticky May morning. The sky was the color of dirty dishwater. Julian found himself sweating profusely in his coveralls. Still, he needed them. Just as he needed a new map to find Powderhorn Hill Road. It was a brand new cul-de-sac in a brand new development on the edge of a forest. A herd of deer, eight in all, stood there in the middle of the street in broad daylight. They would not move. He had to inch his way around them.

The house he was searching for, number 50, was one of those gargantuan trophy chateaus that were popping up, shoulder to shoulder, on tiny lots all over town.

He parked the pickup in the driveway and got out. If any of the neighbors noticed him, they would pay him no mind. He was a workman in overalls carrying a toolbox. Around back, he found a sparkling blue swimming pool, a cabana, an apron of manicured lawn. There was a patio with teak furniture and a built-in gas grilling island with a wet bar and refrigerator.

The back porch was well shielded from the neighbors by trees. No one could see him here. He put on the pair of disposable white latex gloves he'd bought at the hardware store so he'd leave no fingerprints behind. He took a deep breath and tried the door. Unlocked. He opened it. No alarms went off. He went inside and closed the door behind him, setting down his toolbox.

Now it was official: Julian Embry, a man who had never once gotten a speeding ticket or lied on his income tax return or raised his voice in public, was already guilty of illegal entry, trespassing, and God knows what else. He could go to jail if he messed up. This realization made Julian's mouth go dry, but his breathing was slow and steady.

*I can do this. I still have what it takes.*

The kitchen was airy and vast with a center island topped with slate gray granite. Copper pots hung from a rack overhead. There was a commercial range with two ovens, a Subzero refrigerator, an antique farmhouse table, and chairs. There was silence, so much silence that Julian's ears rang.

There was a dining room with a chandelier and upholstered walls. The living room was as large as Julian's entire home. In there he found a grand piano topped with photos in silver frames. Mostly, the pictures were of Barry . . . *Hi, it's me* . . . Barry aboard a yacht, grinning. Barry in front of the Eiffel Tower, grinning. There was only one picture of Mrs. Barry, Darla, who had big, bleached hair and big, bleached teeth. There were no pictures of kids or pets. It was just the two of them in this great big designer show house.

One entire wall of the living room was lined with glass-fronted book-cases. Rows and rows of hard-covered books. Books on politics, on history, on philosophy. Julian flipped through random volumes with an expert's eye. The bindings were unbroken. Not one of these books had ever been cracked. They were decor, nothing more.

Standing there in the Ackermans' living room, Julian suddenly felt exhilarated. He hadn't experienced such a rush of pure, sinful elation since those nights when he was ten years old and he'd camp out in a tent in the backyard, reading the Hardy Boys deep into the night by flashlight and munching on Hershey Bars with almonds. He and Sylvia had never gone camping together. In fact, camping out was something Julian hadn't so much as thought about in twenty years. Why was he thinking about it now?

He roamed. There was a game room with a pool table and video arcade games. There was a sound-proofed music room with electric guitars, amplifiers, and a full set of drums. A gym outfitted with gleaming chrome exercise equipment and a sauna. An entertainment room with a giant television, stereo, and a collection of videos as huge as one would find in a neighborhood Blockbuster. Julian marveled at all of the Ackermans' toys. Never in his life had he owned such toys.

Now he went upstairs, humming an old Les McCann tune, "Compared to What," under his breath. The master bedroom suite featured a sitting room with a fireplace. Barry and Darla had their own personal dressing rooms. Barry owned at least two dozen Armani suits and over twenty pairs of Ferragamo loafers. Julian moseyed down the hall toward the guest rooms. There were four of them, each with its own bath. In one of these he found a note taped to the toilet tank: *"Lew, please be careful not to stain the carpet."*

Julian heard a car door close out front. Instantly on alert, he dashed over to a front window and glanced outside. Just a neighbor across the street. Letting out a sigh of relief, he glanced at his watch. Nearly eleven. Quickly, he went back down to the kitchen and returned to the master bedroom carrying a long, sharp, Wusthof carving knife. He turned back the bedspread and removed the note from his pocket, the one he had made out of headlines from old magazines. Julian laid it flat on one of the bed pillows, gazing at it with satisfaction. The note read:

*Barry—stay away from Rita or next time this will be you!*

Now Julian raised the knife over his head and with a swift, vicious downward movement of his right arm plunged it through the note and deep into the pillow, unleashing a small cloud of goose feathers.

His mission accomplished, Julian returned downstairs, retrieved his toolbox, and went back outside the way he came in, leaving the kitchen door unlocked. He removed the latex gloves, pocketed them, and climbed back in the truck, pausing to gaze at himself in the rear-view mirror.

He looked the same, but he did not feel the same. Dr. Goldman had been right—not that Julian had ever doubted him.

Now Julian started up the truck, backed out of the Ackermans' driveway, and went shopping.

THERE WAS NO SIGN of Barry Ackerman on the 7:42 to Grand Central the next morning.

All was quiet in Julian's car. Blissfully so. And Julian could not stop smiling. He had fought back and he had triumphed. Won back his train. Won back his dignity. Won back his life—and he had the resting pulse rate to prove it. In fact, he had even more than that.

He had a can't-miss idea . . .

*A middle-aged, suburban accountant has just lost his buttoned-down shirt on the NASDAQ. The bank is about to seize his house. His marriage is crumbling. One morning on the train he overhears the hot-shot Wall Street operator seated behind him tell a plumber that he'll be leaving his house unlocked so the guy can fix his toilet. Desperate, the accountant lets himself in and robs the guy. While he's there he discovers a briefcase under the bed with $10 million in it. It turns out the operator is actually a money launderer for the Russian mafia. Which the accountant doesn't know. All he knows is that by the time he gets home that night with the briefcase his own house has been ransacked and his wife kidnapped. The operator has tumbled to him and he wants his money back or else. What he doesn't know is that the accountant doesn't particularly want his wife back . . .*

As Julian rode into the city in rich, luxuriant silence, he began to scribble notes, writing as fast as he could.

*What if the operator's beautiful wife walks in on the accountant while he's robbing the place? She demands to know who he is. "I'm Rita's husband," he explains. "Your husband and my wife are having an affair." In response, she actually wants to help him rip off her husband.*

It was all beginning to spread out before Julian, a smorgasbord of choices, each one more exciting than the next. All he had to do was write it. He'd stick it out as long as he could at Seagrove. Meanwhile, he'd channel his time and energy into this.

A big book of his own.

He could do this. He had the talent and the knowledge. What's more, he had the nerve.

*I am still standing on my own two feet.*

When he was done he would place it with a good agent, make $2.5 million dollars, and he would never, ever have to stand in Roger Parkman's office smelling his cat's poop again.

Now Julian dug down into his briefcase and pulled out the new toy he had bought for himself yesterday. He used it to call Sylvia, who didn't leave for the library until nine.

*"Hi, it's me . . . No, I'm on the train . . . Never mind how. Don't say a word. Just tell me yes or no—how would you like to camp out in the backyard tonight?"*

# Till Tuesday

JEREMIAH HEALY

## Jeremiah Healy's Introduction:

*"Till Tuesday" was my first John Francis Cuddy short story, and, at that, it almost never came into being.*

*In 1984, the debut Cuddy novel, Blunt Darts, was published. I painted the main character as a Vietnam vet who survived the Tet Offensive in Saigon only to return home and lose his young wife, Beth, to cancer. In that first book, Cuddy visits her grave site several times, an idiosyncrasy that was to become, by the third novel in the series (So Like Sleep), his subliminal signature. Accordingly, since I had no confidence I could keep reproducing such "Beth" scenes freshly, I decided that I wouldn't do any short stories about him. Also, as a full-time professor at New England School of Law, I didn't think I had the time to write anything but novels.*

*Then, at an Edgar Awards cocktail party in New York City, I was approached by a sharp, polite young woman who identified herself as Lois Adams, managing editor at Alfred Hitchcock's Mystery Magazine. Lois told me she'd enjoyed the Cuddy novels, and she hoped I'd send her a Cuddy short story. Frankly flattered, I kind of said yes, then—as with many honorable mentions and good intentions—I forgot to do so.*

*Well, at the next Edgars a year later, I ran into Lois again. This time she was visibly pregnant. She said, "I'm going to be going on maternity leave soon, and I'd really like that story beforehand." Of course, I agreed, then went right back to Boston and, on the train, the idea for "Till Tuesday" just came to me.*

*I hope you enjoy reading the product of my professional embarrassment.*

# Till Tuesday

## JEREMIAH HEALY

### 1

CAMBRIDGE, MASSACHUSETTS, IS HOME to Harvard University, boutique restaurants, and people who believe that Anthony Lewis editorials really make a difference. The two men sitting across from me lived there, but I pictured them more as *Wall Street Journal* than *New York Times*.

The one on the right was an architect, Michael Atlee. Atlee was lanky and angular; his brown hair showed licks of white at the temples. He fit poorly into an expensive blue tweed sports jacket and red rooster tie over slacks a little too pale to contrast correctly with his coat. Atlee held a pipe by its bowl in his hand but made no effort to light it.

The man next to him spelled and smelled lawyer through and through. Thayer Lane, Esq., was on his business card, followed by his firm's four named partners and an upscale address. Slim, with black hair, Lane wore a charcoal pinstriped uniform of power and a muted paisley tie.

I guessed both men to be perched on the far side of forty-five. Neither seemed especially comfortable having a conference on the Wednesday after Labor Day in a one-room office with JOHN FRANCIS CUDDY, CONFIDENTIAL INVESTIGATIONS on the door.

After the introductions Lane said, "Mr. Cuddy, we are here on a matter which cannot be discussed with the police. You come highly recommended, especially in the categories of loyalty and discretion."

"Thank you."

"I should say that while Mr. Atlee will be your client in this regard, he is uncomfortable with speaking at length. Hence, he asked me to accompany him here today."

I looked at Atlee. "What seems to be the problem?"

176

Atlee said, "Thayer?"

Lane took his cue. "Mr. Atlee—Michael—is a designer of buildings. Perhaps you're familiar with some of his works?"

Lane ticked off five recent commercial towers. I recognized two of them. I thought they looked like I-beams wearing Tina Turner dresses, but I kept it to myself. "Is the difficulty related to one of the buildings?"

"No, Mr. Cuddy," said Lane. "Let me try to outline the situation for you."

"Go ahead. And please call me John."

"John." Lane spoke as if he might otherwise forget the name. "John, are you married?"

"Widower."

"Ah, sorry. Well . . ." Lane took a deep breath. "Michael is married. However, he has been engaged in an affair for three years with a woman, Gina Fiore. Michael believes that Ms.—Gina has disappeared, and he would like you to find her."

I looked over to Atlee, who sucked on his unlit pipe and blew imaginary smoke at me. His facial movements masked any emotion.

"How long has she been missing?"

"That's uncertain. Michael last saw her this past Thursday but couldn't reach her yesterday."

Atlee said, "Tell him all of it."

Lane glanced at Atlee and sighed. "Every Labor Day Michael hosts a family retreat at his summer home on Parker Pond in Maine. We all go up on Thursday night, scour and spruce the place up with paint and so forth against the elements, then relax and shoot skeet Sunday and Monday."

"You shoot skeet on a lake on Labor Day weekend?"

Atlee said, "I've got ten acres. It's private enough."

I said to Atlee, "So she could be gone for as long as six days."

"Right."

"Or as little as twenty hours."

Lane stuck in, "My point precisely."

Atlee said, "Doesn't matter. She's gone."

"Where does Gina live?"

Atlee nodded to Lane, who took over again. "Gina lives in a condominium on Revere Beach that Michael purchased as an investment. Part of their, ah, arrangement is that she is to be available at all times. By telephone and in person."

Lovely. I said to Lane, "A few minutes ago you said 'we'?"

"I'm sorry?"

"You were talking about the lake thing being a family event but you said, 'We all went up to the summer place.' "

"Oh, quite. Michael is a client of my firm, but we're also best friends. Roomed together at Harvard and prepped at Choate before that. My wife and I are like family to Michael and Winnie, and Seth's my godson."

I said to Atlee, "Winnie's your wife and Seth's your son?"

He nodded and bit down on the pipe stem.

"Any reason for Gina to take off?"

"None." Decisively.

"Who else knows about your relationship with Gina?"

Lane said, "A woman named Marla—I'm afraid we don't have her last name—lives in the next unit in Gina's building and is aware of, ah . . ."

"Anybody else?"

Atlee fidgeted in his chair, I thought at first from impatience. Then he said, "Seth knows, or suspects. Same damned thing, I guess. Saw us once together a couple of years ago in a bar over there. Slumming with one of his swim-team chums. Damned bad luck, but there it is."

I had the impression I'd been treated to Atlee's longest speech of the decade. "Any point in my talking with him?"

"No." Case closed.

Lane said, "That would be rather difficult anyway, John."

"Why is that?"

"You see, Seth is a junior at Stanford this year, and he always leaves the morning after Labor Day to head out there."

Atlee said, "Damned fool has to drive his Jeep three thousand miles. Can't take the plane like a normal person."

"In any case," said Lane, "I had a call from him last night. He was near Pittsburgh and wasn't sure of his next destination."

I said, "He called you?"

Lane seemed affronted. "I am his godfather."

"All right. I'll need a photo of Gina and her address over in Revere."

Atlee said, "Don't have a photo."

"I'm sure you understand," said Lane.

Before I could reply, Atlee leaned forward, tapping his pipe on my desk for emphasis. "Just understand this. I really care for that girl. I may not show it, but I do. And I want you to find her."

2

REVERE BEACH IS AN incongruous strip of old clam-shacks and new high-rise towers along a slightly polluted stretch of sand and ocean about ten miles north of Boston. I flashed the key Atlee had given me at the security guard, who smiled deferentially and used his magazine to wave me into the lobby. I took an elevator to the ninth floor.

Unit 9A was at the end of the hall. I had a little trouble with the lock, rattled it and the knob twice before the tumbler would turn. Inside, the apartment was airy, with a striking view of the Atlantic through sliding glass doors to a narrow balcony. Versatile sectional furniture for couch and chairs. Track lighting overhead, a wall unit with stereo, color TV, and even a few books.

I entered the bedroom and had been drawn toward some framed photos on the bureau when I thought I heard the snap and creak of a quick entry at the front door. I managed two steps before a perfectly tanned woman in a European string bikini appeared in the doorway to the living room. She leveled a tiny automatic at me and said, "My boyfriend told me to just keep firing until the guy falls."

I got the hint.

"GINA AND ME WATCH each other's places, you know?"

"Good system."

"Look, at least I can make you a drink or something, huh?"

She was trying hard, a little too hard, to make up for the gun scene. My investigator's I.D. had convinced her I wasn't a "real" burglar, and she was pleased to introduce herself as Marla, the girl next door. I'd seen everything except the bedroom closet with nothing to show for it. Now she was watching me rummage through Gina's dresses, slacks, and shoes.

"So Mikey figures Gina's flown on him, huh?"

I liked her using "Mikey." I said over my shoulder, "That the way you see it?"

"Without telling me? And leaving all her stuff like this?" She paused. "Hard to say for sure, though. Gina's been a little restless lately."

I stopped searching and turned around. "Restless?"

"Yeah, well, it's not so easy being somebody's sweet harbor, you know? Waiting for a phone call, planning your life around a lunch here or there

179

and some afternoon delight."

Somehow the phrase sounded sweeter in the song. "Would she have left on her own?"

"Not likely. Gina enjoyed being took care of, even by a creep like Mikey."

"How do you mean?"

"Aw, we double dated a coupla months ago. Her and Mikey and this guy called himself 'Jim.' We drove up to Swampscott to go sailing, like they was afraid to do the class thing and go all the way to Marblehead; maybe one of their bigshot friends sees them there with two bimbettes from Revere."

"You ever see this Jim again?"

"No, but like I said, that wasn't his real name. Stupid guy, he drives us all up there in this big green Mercedes, like we're too dumb to know how to run a plate at the registry."

"You ran his license plate?"

"Yeah. Turns out he's another Cambridge high roller with, get this, the name 'Thayer Lane.' "

Ah, Mr. Lane. "This Lane seem interested in Gina?"

"Coulda been. I kept him pretty interested that day, I'll tell you. Never did hear back from him, though. Good old 'Jim.' "

"Gina ever mention Atlee's son?"

"Not really. Just that the father and him didn't get along too well."

"Some families are like that."

"Boy, you got that right." Her tone changed. "You got any pressing commitments after this here?"

I stuck my head back into the closet. There were three matching pieces of luggage; the size just up from the smallest seemed to be missing.

"Well, do you?"

"Marla," I said, pointing, "does Gina have a full set of these bags?"

She came over, pressing and rubbing more than my request required. "Uh-huh. Gina uses the other one for dayhops." She was wearing some kind of coconut-scented lotion.

"Meaning not overnight?"

Marla stepped back without answering. She kept going until her calves touched the bed, then sat back and onto her elbows, in one languid motion. She hooded her eyes. "Doesn't have to take all night, sugar."

Walking to the bureau, I picked up one of the photos. A girl about Marla's age, long frosted curls, winking at the lens.

"This Gina?"
She licked her lips. "Uh-huh."
"Recent?"
"Hair's a little shorter now. Let's talk about you. And me."
I think she was laughing as I went through the front door.

I STOOD UP, PUT my hands in my pockets. "Mrs. Feeney told me what they were, but it was some Latin name, and I forget it."

*What happened to that elaborate altar boy training?*

I looked at the purplish flowers with yellowish petals, then at her stone. Elizabeth Mary Devlin Cuddy. "Won't help me much with this one, Beth."

*What's the problem?*

I told her.

*An architect's mistress. Sordid.*

"It's about to get worse."

*How?*

"Tomorrow I intend to see his wife about their son."

3

THE NEXT MORNING I stopped at the office to hoke up a manila file folder and some documents, then took Memorial Drive to Cambridge. The Atlees' home was on one of those short streets off Brattle. An aggressively traditional mini-manse, it was surrounded by an outside fence nearly as tall as the trees behind it. I tapped a button on the intercom at the wrought-iron entrance and a minute later received a metallic, female "Yes?"

"Mrs. Atlee?"

"Yes?"

"My name is John Cuddy. I'm a private investigator, and I'm here about your son."

"My son? Is there some kind of problem?"

"No, no, ma'am. It's just that, well, it would be easier if I could show you the file."

Hesitation, then the grating buzz and click that tell you to push on the gate.

"AND YOU SAY MY son witnessed an accident?"

"Yes, ma'am." I slid the folder over to her, holding my index finger on the document in the middle of the Acco-clipped bunch till she held the place for herself and began reading it.

She was about Atlee's age, with strawberry-blonde hair pulled severely behind her head. A peasant dress heightened the sense of bony strength about her. Striking, not beautiful, she probably sat an English saddle well, given some of the bronzed trophies on shelves in the den. The other statuettes looked like awards for swimming and shooting.

"But this isn't even my son's handwriting."

"No, ma'am. That's the handwriting of our Mr. Green, who's no longer our Mr. Green because he fouled up so much, like here when he took down your son's statement then forgot to have him date or sign it over . . . there."

She shook her head and handed me back the file. "Well, I'm sure if Seth were here he'd be glad to help you, but he left for California on Tuesday."

I let my face fall. "Gee, Mrs. Atlee, this case is coming up for trial and all. Do you have a number where I can reach him?"

"Yes. Well, no. Not for a few more days. You see, he drives there, to return to Stanford, and he rather dawdles really, taking roads that interest him and stopping wherever."

"Does he call you?"

"Sometimes. Other times no. If we hear from him, we could ask him to call you, but it would probably be late at night and perhaps not at all."

"Is there anyone else he might call?"

She considered it. "Yes. His friend Doug Cather. Seth and Doug were on the swim team together at prep school. Doug's at Harvard now."

I looked past her to a photo on the mantel. A family portrait of a younger Atlee and wife behind a seated teenager.

"Is that Seth?"

She twisted around and looked back at me. "Yes." She darkened. "Is there something else?"

"No, no. He looks like a fine boy."

Doug Cather lived in Kirkland House, part of the not-quite-quadrangle of more-than-dorms nestled near the Charles River. He was tall, broad-shouldered, and completely hairless.

"We shave our heads."

"Why?"

"For swimming. Cuts down on the drag effect in the water."

Anything for dear old Harvard, I guess. Cather accepted my bogus accident story.

"No, I haven't heard from Seth, which is kind of funny."

"You two stay in touch that closely?"

"Not really. It's just that he always calls me when he leaves for school, and I kind of waited around for it yesterday morning. Cut classes and all."

"Wait a minute. I thought Seth left for California on Tuesday. Yesterday was Wednesday."

Cather's face clouded over.

I said, "There's something you're not telling me."

"There's something I don't think is any of your business."

"Something about Seth?"

"Yeah."

"Look, I'm not going to give you a long song and dance about confidentiality. You don't know me at all, so you don't know if you can trust me."

"That's right."

"Okay. Here's my problem. I've got to find your friend. You can help me, or I can do it the hard way. Go see other people, his dad, whoever. That might mean I find out worse things than I need to know. All I can say is if you tell me what's going on, I'll try to keep it to myself."

Cather didn't speak.

"We want Seth as a witness for us on this collision. I'm not about to spread rumors that would make him look bad."

"It's not . . ." He seemed to search inside for a moment. "I want your promise anyway. You won't tell anybody?"

"Promise."

He blew out a breath. "Okay, it's like this. After we graduated from Choate, Seth and I bounced around for the summer. One day we decide to go to Revere Beach, kind of scope out the other half, you know? Well, we dare each other to go into this bar. I mean, we're way underage and nobody's ever gonna serve us without I.D., but we try it anyway. Right off, I spot Seth's father in one of the booths, with a real tough . . . a really sharp-looking chick just a couple of years older than us. So I start to say something, and Seth sees them and gets all uptight. He's kind of impulsive anyhow, and he bolts out of there and like won't even talk with me all the way home."

"What's that got to do with his driving to California?"

"Well, it didn't take a genius to see what his dad was doing there, and I guess Seth and him had a real blowup over it. Anyway, Seth decides not to go out for swimming at Stanford, like to punish his dad, I guess. But every year his family has this Labor Day thing to please his mom. So, okay, after Seth gets home from the weekend each year, he goes back up there."

"Seth goes back?"

"Right. He tells his parents he's leaving for school, and he does, sort of, but first he drives up to Parker Pond and does the swim."

"The swim."

"Yeah. He swims out from their property to this little island and back. It's like a ritual, I guess, to prove he can still go the distance. And maybe to think about when he was younger and he didn't, well, know about his dad."

"Would Seth sleep over in Maine on that Tuesday night?"

"Definitely. It's almost four hours to get there, and he probably wouldn't leave his parents in Cambridge much before lunchtime."

"You ever been to this Parker Pond house?"

"Sure. Lots of times."

"Can you draw me a map?"

4

EVEN WITH DOUG CATHER'S sketch, I had to stop at an inn on the main road for supplemental directions. A turnoff went from paved to gravel to hard-packed dirt. Then I saw rutted tracks curve off the road, a primitive driveway running under a white tollgate. Leaving the car, I walked up to the gate. A single horizontal bar, very freshly painted, was hinged on one of two posts and swung inward freely.

The day was warm, the only sounds the wind in the trees and a woodpecker pocking away nearby. I decided to approach more quietly than my old Fiat would allow. I tossed my sport coat into the front seat and switched on the hazard lights. Ducking under the gate bar, I started walking.

The driveway doglegged right to insure privacy and squiggled here and there to avoid particularly substantial pines. Passing the last big tree, I spotted the back of the house.

A black Jeep Wrangler was parked at the mouth of an adjoining shed.

I moved through the underbrush and approached the shed, keeping it between me and the large chalet-style house behind it. I stopped at the side of the shed to listen. No noise from inside.

Edging toward the front, I looked through the webby pane at the shed's door. Paint buckets, rake and lawn mower, gasoline can, etc. The Jeep was stuffed to the roof with the odd-lot cartons and containers students use to return to college.

I circled around the house. Every door and window seemed sealed tight. The wind was really howling lakeside, kicking whitecaps against the shoreline.

At the back door, I knocked, waited, and knocked again louder. Inside I could see the kitchen area. Using a rock to break the glass, I was hit with the stench as I opened the door itself. I gagged and tried to close off my nasal passages with the back of my tongue. Grabbing a dish rag off the rack over the sink, I took it to the shed and doused it with gasoline. I held the rag to my face and went back inside.

He was lying on the floor of the great room, cathedral ceiling above him. A dry pair of swim trunks and a beach towel lay on a chair next to him. At his side, a carefully carved and scrolled double-barreled shotgun, one hand around the trigger mechanism. His face was bloated, the head connected only by the few tendons the blast had left of his neck. Seth Atlee, a marionette past all mending.

Gina was on the open, slatted staircase leading to the upper level. Naked, she'd taken the other barrel between the shoulder blades and would have been dead before her nose struck the tenth step.

The house was twenty degrees hotter than the ambient temperature outside. I didn't think my gasoline filter would support a telephone call indoors.

I pulled the door closed and walked slowly down the driveway. At the gate, I noticed what seemed to be a grass stain on the house side of the swing bar, stark against the gleaming white. Like someone had scraped the inner edge of the bar against a car.

I started the Fiat and drove to the inn to learn about law enforcement in Maine.

5

THE FUNERAL WAS SCHEDULED for Saturday afternoon, beginning from a mortuary on Massachusetts Avenue in Cambridge. I got there early and parked a block away. Even announced murder-suicides draw large numbers of sincere mourners these days. I watched the arrivals of Michael and Winnie Atlee, Doug Cather, and Thayer Lane with a woman I took to be his wife.

Forty minutes later the crowd came back out, repairing to private cars to form the procession. I left the Fiat. Pausing at Lane's Mercedes, I could see the lawyer on the porch of the funeral home, bending slightly at the waist and using both hands to shake hands gently with a short, elderly woman. I caught his eye. He glared at me. I smiled and beckoned. He excused himself, moving stiff-legged over to me.

"Counselor."

"Mr. Cuddy, don't you think it a bit tasteless for you to appear here?"

"What I think is that Seth didn't kill Gina or himself."

Lane stopped fussing.

I said, "How long did you figure it'd take before they were found?"

"I beg your pardon?"

"The bodies. Buttoned up in the house and all. Seth would be reported missing by his college after a while, but who would think to check the lake place?"

"What in the world kind of question is that?"

"You see, the longer the wait, the tougher to peg time of death. After a couple of weeks, no one would swear to anything shorter than a few bracketed days."

"Mr. Cuddy, I really must get back."

"You didn't want me searching for Gina so quickly after Atlee couldn't raise her. You double dated with him, Gina, and Marla once. Gina was restless, maybe you caught each other's fancy."

"Preposterous."

"But Atlee's a big client and an old friend. So you needed a safe place to try your luck. None safer than the summer home you helped close up the day before."

"I'm not going to—"

"Listen any more? You've listened too much as it is, Lane. An innocent man would have walked already."

He clenched his teeth. "Finish it then."

"You didn't know about Seth's ritual swim. I'm guessing you were in the sack with Gina when Seth burst in downstairs. He would have seen your car. Did he call out to you? 'Hey, Uncle Thayer, you upstairs?' "

Lane looked clammy, unsteady.

"You jump out of bed, try to pull some clothes on. Seth's in good shape, though, takes the steps two at a time. Sees you in the nearly altogether with the woman he recognizes as his dad's mistress. He goes nuts, runs back downstairs, gets a skeet gun. He loads it and comes back, back to purge the stain from the one place he still thought was family inviolate."

"No, no."

"You try to reason with him in the great room, Gina following you down the stairs. A struggle, the gun wavers toward Seth as somebody hits the trigger. Seth goes down, Gina yells, 'You murdered him!' Or maybe she just starts screaming, screaming till you lock onto her as a target and she—"

"You can't prove a word of this!"

"No?" I gestured toward the hood of his Mercedes. "Those gouge marks. You put them there when you swung the gate in to leave the place on Tuesday."

He blinked, trying to make the scratches go away. "They . . . they . . ."

"Freshly painted gate, two days before. If you'd taken a piece out of the car driving back Monday, the missus would remember it. The kind of thing that would spoil the whole weekend."

"Seth, he called me . . ."

I shook my head. "Nobody called you Tuesday night, because Seth didn't call his friend Wednesday morning. I'm betting the medical examiner saw the bodies soon enough to place both deaths on Tuesday afternoon. The phone alibi would have been perfect in a few more weeks. Now it's going to hang you."

"Thayer? Thayer!"

We both turned.

Michael Atlee was chopping his hand toward the lead limousine. For the godfather.

Lane whispered. "What are you . . ."

"Going to do? I'm going to give you a chance here, Thayer. Mikey there is your best friend, right?"

"I . . . yes he is, but—"

"Then sometime in the next two days you're going to tell him all about it."

"Money. You want money."

"I don't want money, Thayer. I was hired to find Gina Fiore. I found her and was paid. Now you're going to do your job. You're going to be the first to tell your best friend how his mistress and son really died."

"Thayer!" called Atlee, striding determinedly toward us.

Lane said, "But for God's sake, Cuddy, that's not how it happened! The way you said, it wasn't like that."

"Maybe not. You've got till Tuesday to come up with a better version."

I walked back to my car.

# Village of
# the Dead

### EDWARD D. HOCH

## Edward D. Hoch's Introduction:

*"Village of the Dead" was the first story I ever published. It appeared in the December 1955 issue of* Famous Detective Stories, *one of the last of the old pulp magazines. I was twenty-five years old at the time and had collected scores of rejection slips since I began writing in high school.*

*The origin of the plot is still fresh in my memory, though it took shape nearly a half-century ago. During the summer of 1953, I was at an amusement park in Rye, New York, and excursion boats came across Long Island Sound to deposit visitors for the day. In the late afternoon I noticed hundreds of people making their way onto a long pier even though there was no boat in sight. It seemed as if they were marching lemming-like to their deaths. The boat appeared soon after, of course, and no one jumped off the pier, but the image stuck in my mind. The pier became a cliff when research uncovered the ancient North African cult of the Circumcellions, whose followers sometimes cast themselves off cliffs.*

*For a plot like this I knew at once that I needed an unusual, almost mystical, protagonist. I chose Simon Ark, a character I'd tried unsuccessfully before. This time I gave him a nameless Watson figure as narrator. The story made the rounds of the mystery magazines without immediate success. In those days, long before the horror of Jonestown, the idea of a modern cult leader forcing his followers to commit mass suicide struck most editors as unbelievably bizarre. Happily, the story finally reached the desk of Robert A. W. Lowndes, then editing* Famous Detective Stories *and several other magazines for Columbia Publications. Lowndes was a longtime admirer of psychic detectives and perhaps he saw something in Simon Ark that reminded him of earlier sleuths. The story was featured on the magazine's cover and Lowndes bought several more of my stories in quick succession. My career as a mystery writer was launched.*

# Village of the Dead

## EDWARD D. HOCH

PERHAPS, IF YOU'RE OLD enough, you remember the Gidaz Horror. At least that was the name the newspapers gave it during those early days when the story shocked the world.

I was near Gidaz when the thing happened, and I suppose I was one of the first to reach the village. I went without sleep for forty-eight hours to get the story and then I never could use it. All these years I've thought about it, and I guess sooner or later I just had to tell someone.

So this is the way it happened, that day in Gidaz. . . .

I WAS AT THE state capitol, covering a political story, when the flash came in. We crowded around the teletype in the press room and watched the words as they formed on the yellow paper: . . . THE TINY VILLAGE OF GIDAZ, IN THE SOUTHERN PART OF THE STATE, WAS THE SCENE TODAY OF AN APPARENT MASS SUICIDE. A MAIL TRUCK, ARRIVING IN THE VILLAGE THIS MORNING, FOUND THE HOUSES DESERTED, AND, AT THE BASE OF A HUNDRED-FOOT CLIFF NEARBY, SCORES OF BODIES WERE FOUND AMONG THE ROCKS. . . .

That was all. There was more to follow, but none of us wanted to see it. Ten minutes later we were in a car heading south, toward the village of Gidaz, eighty miles away.

It was almost evening when we arrived, but there were no lights in the village. The streets and the few dozen houses that clustered around them were dark and silent. It was as if the entire population had suddenly vanished.

And in a way it had.

We found people and cars at the edge of the village, but the people were not toiling silently, as at the scene of a train wreck or a fire. They only stood at the edge of the cliff and looked down at the rocks below.

We joined them at the edge, and I saw it, too. In the reflected glare of a dozen headlights and in the dying glow of the setting sun, I saw the bodies on the rocks below. There must have been nearly a hundred of them; men, women, and children. I could almost imagine a giant hand sweeping them over the edge to their death.

Presently we made our way down the steep path to the bottom, and men began to set up floodlights for the long job ahead. They were piled on top of each other, among the pointed rocks that stretched upward toward the sky.

"Think any of them could be alive?" I heard myself asking.

"Not a chance. A hundred feet is a long way to fall, especially with rocks like these at the bottom."

"Yeah. . . ."

And they began moving the bodies. An old man with his skull shattered by the fall, a girl with her neck broken. . . .

They carried them from the rocks and laid the bodies in neat rows on the ground. Soon there were only the red-stained rocks remaining. And I counted the bodies, along with the others. "Seventy-three."

"Seventy-three . . ."

A state trooper joined the group at the foot of the cliff. "We've gone through every house in the village; there's not a living thing up there. . . ."

"The entire village walked over the edge of that cliff sometime last night. . . ."

After that, the deserted village of Gidaz was alive with reporters and photographers from all over the country. They wrote a million words about the Gidaz Horror. Seventy-three people, the entire population of the village of Gidaz, had committed suicide by walking off the edge of a cliff. Why? What had driven them to it? That was the question we all wanted to answer.

But there was no answer.

A New York paper compared it to an incident during the Napoleonic Wars, when a charging cavalry had ridden over the edge of a cliff before they realized their error. A national magazine brought up the legend of the Pied Piper, and suggested that some supernatural force had lured them to their death.

But still there was no answer.

The houses were searched for clues but yielded nothing. In some places, food was still on the table. In others, people had been preparing for bed. It must have been around eight o'clock when something brought them from their houses. There were no notes or messages remaining. Apparently, they had planned to return when they left their houses for the last time.

But they had not returned. . . .

I WAS THE FIRST one to think of digging into the background of the town, and I spent most of the first night in the deserted building that had once held town meetings. There were records here—records and memories of days past, when Gidaz had been founded by a group of settlers pushing westward. It had been named after one of them and had grown rapidly after the discovery of gold nearby.

I studied one of the old maps I found and decided that the gold mines must have been almost at the spot where those seventy-three persons had plunged over the cliff to their deaths.

It was while I was looking at the map that I suddenly became aware that I was not alone in the old building. I turned and pointed my flashlight at a dark corner, and a tall man stepped out of the shadows. "Good evening," he said quietly.

"Who are you?"

"My name is not important, but you may call me Simon Ark if you wish."

"Simon Ark?"

"That is correct," the stranger replied. "And now may I ask who you are?"

"I'm a reporter, a newspaper reporter. I came down from the state capitol to cover the story."

"Ah, and you thought you might find something in the old records of the village? I also had a similar thought."

The man called Simon Ark had advanced closer now, and I could make out his features clearly in the light from my flash. He was not old, and yet his face had tiny lines of age to be seen if one looked closely enough. In a way he was perhaps a very handsome man, and yet I somehow could not imagine women ever being attracted to him.

"Are you a writer or something?" I asked him.

"No, I am simply an investigator; I make a hobby of investigating any strange or unexplained happenings in the world."

"How did you manage to get here so quickly?"

"I was in the area, just across the state line, on another mission. I would have been here sooner, but it is very difficult to reach Gidaz by road."

"It certainly is. The village is almost completely cut off from the rest of the town. Ever since the gold mines died out, the place has been almost a ghost town."

"And yet," Simon Ark said quietly, "there were seventy-three people remaining here. Why did they remain, I wonder. Why didn't they leave this dying village?"

"They've left it now," I said; "they left it last night when they walked over that cliff."

"Yes. . . ." And the man called Simon Ark left the ancient building. I followed him outside to see where he would go.

He was a strange man, strange in many ways. He seemed almost to be from another world or another time as he walked slowly along the dirt road that led through the center of the dead village.

The reporters and the police had already searched the houses, but he seemed to be looking for something more. . . .

SOON, HE HAD ALMOST disappeared in the darkness, and I hurried after him. When I finally reached him, he was bending over a dark spot on the ground. I could see only by the light of the moon overhead, but he seemed excited by what he had found.

"There has been a fire here recently," he said, almost to himself. He pulled something from the ashes and attempted to brush it off. It looked as if it had once been a book, but in the dim light it was impossible to tell more.

I had not realized the utter silence of the night around us until that moment, when it was suddenly shattered by the distant sound of an approaching car.

"Someone's coming," I said.

"Odd. . . ." And a strange expression passed quickly over the face of Simon Ark.

He pushed the remains of the charred book into his topcoat pocket and walked back toward the dirt road.

Somewhere above, a cloud passed over the moon, and for the moment all was darkness. Then the night was broken by the gleam of two headlights moving slowly along the road.

Simon Ark stepped in front of the car and held up both hands, like some ancient high priest calling upon the gods above. A chill ran down my spine as I watched him.

The car, a light green convertible, came to an abrupt halt, and a girl climbed out from behind the wheel. "Are you the police?" she asked him.

"No, only an investigator. This other gentleman is a reporter." She noticed me then for the first time, and the tense look on her face softened.

"I'm Shelly Constance," she said. "I . . . I used to live here."

Simon Ark introduced himself. "You had a family still living here in Gidaz?" he asked quietly.

"Yes. . . . My father and brother . . . I . . . I heard on the radio what happened last night. I came as soon as I could. . . ."

"It would have been wiser to stay away," Simon Ark told her. "Your father and brother are beyond all worldly aid now, and the evil of Gidaz still fills the air, mingled now with the odor of death."

"I . . . I must see them," she said. "Where did it happen?"

Simon Ark motioned toward the distant cliff and led the way through the darkness. "The bodies have been covered with canvas for the night," he told her. "I believe the plans are to bury them tomorrow in a mass grave at the bottom of the cliff. Most of them, of course, have no living relatives."

We reached the edge, and I played my flashlight down on the rocks below, but nothing could be seen from that far up. In the light of the flash, however, I got my first good look at the girl by my side. She was young and tall and pretty in a casual sort of way. Her blonde hair hung to her shoulders, and helped to set off the lines of her face.

"Tell me," I asked, as we walked back to her car, "why did you ever leave Gidaz?"

"That is a long story," she said, "but perhaps it has something to do with this horrible thing. Come, come into my . . . house over here for a few minutes, and I'll try to tell you about it."

SIMON ARK AND I followed her in silence to one of the houses just off the main road. It seemed strange entering this house that no longer belonged to the living. There were things, dishes and books and clothing and cigarettes and food, that were reminders of the people who had lived here. On the wall was a map of the gold mining area, where some of these people had continued to work until yesterday, in the futile hope of recovering the village's lost greatness.

It was then, as the girl entered this dead house that had once been home, that she seemed to go to pieces. She began sobbing and threw herself into a big armchair to cover her face. I remained where I was and let her cry. There was no way to comfort this girl who was almost a stranger to me.

I noticed that Simon Ark also left her to her sorrow and moved over to inspect the small bookcase in the dining room. After a moment's hesitation I joined him and glanced at the titles on the shelves. They were mostly children's books, with a few others that had probably served as college textbooks. One, an ancient history book, was stamped State University.

This seemed to remind Simon Ark of the charred remains of the book he had found earlier. He removed it from his pocket and carefully examined it. A few charred pieces drifted to the floor.

"It seems to be . . ." Simon Ark began, and then fell silent.

"What?"

"Ah, yes, *The Confessions of Saint Augustine*. A truly remarkable book. Did you ever read it?"

"No, I'm not a Catholic," I replied.

"Augustine wrote for all men," Simon Ark said slowly. "This is a very interesting discovery."

"Why should anyone want to burn it?"

"I am beginning to fear that I know the answer to that," he told me, and there was something in his voice that scared even me.

He returned the remains of the book to his pocket as the girl joined us again. "I'm sorry," she said. "Please forgive me."

"Certainly," I told her. "We understand."

"I'll see if I can fix us coffee or something," and she disappeared into the kitchen.

Presently she returned, with three steaming cups, and as we drank she told us of her early life in Gidaz. . . .

". . . I suppose it was about five years ago when I left to attend college. Of course, I was home for the summers, but for the first two years things seemed the same as they had always been in Gidaz. Then, in the summer following my third year at the University, I returned home to find things had changed slightly."

"In what way?"

"Well, I suppose it would be hard for you to understand, because it was really nothing I could put my finger on. It seemed to be just a change in attitude at first. They talked of a man who had come to Gidaz—a man named Axidus, who seemed to have a great influence on their lives from then on. Of course, you must realize that Gidaz is so remote from other cities that these seventy-three people were forced to live entirely among themselves. My father and brother usually got into town about once every month or two. To them, the village was everything, even though it was slowly dying. A few of the men kept working in the mines, finding just enough gold to keep them alive. Others worked small farms in the valley. But they were happy here, probably because they had never known anything better."

"But you were not satisfied with it?"

"I wasn't the only one. Many of the young people like me left Gidaz, especially after the coming of this man Axidus."

SIMON ARK'S FACE HAD grown dark while she talked. "You say his name was Axidus?"

"Yes, do you know him?"

"I may have met him once, long ago. . . ."

"Well, he was the cause of all the trouble, and I saw that right away. When I came home for Christmas that year, it was as if a madness had seized the people. They talked of nothing but Axidus, and how he was going to help them save themselves. He seemed to have some kind of new religion. . . ."

I glanced at him, but his face was like stone. Once again I seemed to feel a shiver run down my spine.

"It really scared me, the way they all believed in him so completely," she continued. "Once each week he held a meeting in the old town hall, and everyone would go to hear him—even the children. It was uncanny, the way he seemed to know everything that happened in the village. He would tell people secret facts that no one else could possibly have known. When I was away at school, he would tell my father everything I was doing. Of course, people like this have always been attracted by fortune-tellers and the like, and a person like this knew exactly how to get them in his power. I went to see him just once, and I must admit I found something strangely haunting about this man Axidus."

"What did he look like?" I asked.

"He was fairly tall, with a white beard that hung to his chest. His hair was long and white, too, and he wore a white robe. He would come out on the small platform at one end of the hall and begin talking without any introduction. Afterward, he just seemed to disappear. Sometimes people would see him around the village during the week, too, but always in this white robe. No one knew where or how he lived."

"It's fantastic," I said; "it sounds like something out of the dark past."

Simon Ark frowned. "It is dark, and it is certainly from the past. My only wish is that I had heard all this before it was too late. . . ."

There was a wind coming up outside, and from somewhere up in the hills came the cry of a lonesome timber wolf. I glanced at my watch and was surprised to see it was already past midnight.

"What do you mean . . . ?" the girl started to ask, but she never completed the sentence.

Suddenly, Simon Ark was out of his chair, and he was pulling open the front door of the house. I ran to his side, and then I saw it, too. . . .

A figure, or a thing, all in white, running with the wind toward the cliff where Death slept in the darkness. . . .

WE FOLLOWED, THROUGH THE night, with the gathering breeze whistling through the trees around us. The girl started to follow, but I waved her back inside. Whatever was out here, it was not for her to see. . . .

In the distance a sudden streak and rumble of thunder followed. It would be raining back in the hills, but with luck the storm would miss us.

The wind was picking up, though, and by the time we reached the edge of the cliff it was close to being a gale. I wondered briefly if a strong wind could have blown these people to their death, but that, of course, was fantastic. . . . But perhaps the real reason for their death would be even more fantastic. . . .

"There!" He pointed down the cliff, to the very center of where the seventy-three bodies rested under canvas on the rocks.

And I saw it again.

The moon that had given us light before was hidden now by the threatening clouds of rain, but I could see the blot of white against the blackness of the rocks.

"Axidus?" I breathed.

"Or Satan himself," Simon Ark answered. "Perhaps this is the moment I have waited for." He started down the rocks, and I followed.

But the white form seemed to sense our approach. Suddenly, before our very eyes, it seemed to fade away.

"He must be hiding in the rocks somewhere," I said.

The odor of the corpses was all around us then, and my head swam sickeningly.

"I must find him," Simon Ark said, and he shouted something in a strange language that might have been Greek, but wasn't.

We searched the rocks until the odor was overpowering and forced us to retreat. We found nothing. . . .

On the way back up the cliff, I asked Simon Ark what he'd shouted before.

"It was in Coptic," he said, "which is very much like Egyptian. It was a type of prayer. . . ."

WITH THE COMING OF daylight, the horror that hung thick in the air over Gidaz seemed to lift a little. The girl had slept through the remainder of the night, and I had sat alone in the front room of the house while Simon Ark prowled the night on some further mysterious investigations.

Since I knew sleep was impossible, I spent the time attempting to set down in words just what had happened to me that day, ever since the moment in the early evening when I'd first arrived in Gidaz. But I couldn't do it; I was still living the thing, and the terror that clung to the village was still a very real part of the air I breathed. Maybe later. . . .

Simon Ark returned to the house soon after daybreak, and the sound of our talking awakened the girl. She made breakfast for us from among the remains we found around the house, and by nine o'clock we were ready to leave.

The lack of sleep was beginning to get me then, but the sunlight helped revive me. Simon Ark looked the same as he had the evening before and seemed anxious to leave the village. "I have things that must be done," he said. "In the meantime, if you would desire to help me, there are one or two things you could find out."

"Sure. Anything for a story."

They were interrupted then by the sound of an approaching truck. Down the single road that led to civilization, an ancient mail truck was coming toward them.

"This must be the man who found the bodies yesterday," Simon Ark said.

And it was. A fairly tall, middle-aged man named Joe Harris. "They haven't buried them yet, huh?" he asked us.

"No," I answered. "The bodies are under canvas at the bottom of the cliff, a short distance from the rocks. The funeral is to take place today. I understand they've decided to bury them here in a mass grave rather than try to remove all the bodies to another town."

"Gee," he said, "I near died of shock yesterday morning when I drove up and found them all down there. Why do you think they jumped?"

"I don't know," I said. "It would make a great story if I did."

THERE WERE OTHER TRUCKS and cars coming now, with a gleaming state police car in the lead. There were workers with shovels, who would soon bury the remains of the Gidaz Horror. And there were more photographers and reporters, from all over the country, coming to record forever the strange happening in this forgotten village.

They took pictures of Joe Harris and his battered mail truck; they took pictures of Shelly Constance, and questioned her about her life in the village. She talked to them at length, but she did not mention the strange man, Axidus, again; I suspected that Simon Ark had suggested she keep silent about this part of it.

Simon Ark himself kept in the background during most of the morning, and he went unnoticed in the crowd of curiosity seekers who poured over the scene in growing numbers throughout the early hours of the day.

It was nearly noon before Simon Ark and I could make our escape in my car. I wondered briefly how this strange man had arrived the previous night when he had no car, but the thought passed from my mind as we watched them lowering the last of the seventy-three into the long grave at the base of the cliff.

For a moment, there was silence over the scene, as the last rites of various religions were spoken over the grave. Then, once again, a murmur of voices arose, as I turned my car away from the village.

Simon Ark was in the seat next to me, and I was glad I had managed to avoid the other reporters who'd ridden out to the village with me the previous day. For I had a feeling that the answer to this riddle rested somehow with Simon Ark, and with the white figure we'd seen on the cliff.

I turned into the highway that led north, toward the state capitol. "What did you want me to do?" I asked.

"Do? Oh, I would like you to look up some information in the old newspaper files. I would like you to find out if any priests or ministers have been killed in the Gidaz area within the past few years. . . ."

I thought about that for a while. "All right, I'll get the information for you on one condition. That you tell me just who you are, and just who this Axidus is."

"I am just a man," he answered slowly. "A man from another age. You would not be interested in where I came from or in what my mission is. I need only tell you that I am searching for the ultimate evil—for Satan himself. And perhaps, in Gidaz, I have found him at last."

I sighed softly. "What about Axidus?"

"Axidus is also from the past. I knew him long ago, in North Africa, as Saint Augustine did. . . ."

"Are you crazy? Are you trying to tell me we're dealing with people who've been dead over fifteen hundred years?"

"I do not know," Simon Ark replied. "But I intend to find out tonight, when we return to the village of the dead. . . ."

I LEFT THE STRANGE man near the capitol building an hour later, having agreed to meet him there again at five o'clock. It did not take me long to gather the information Simon Ark had requested, and I was surprised to learn that six months earlier, a Catholic priest had been found beaten to death only a few miles from Gidaz. The crime had never been solved, although police were still investigating. . . .

I could make nothing of the information, but I was certain it would mean something to Simon Ark.

I went next to the public library, to do some investigating on my own. I was determined to solve the mystery of Axidus and the seventy-three deaths, and I felt certain that the answer was hidden somewhere in the ancient pages of history.

I looked first in the *Encyclopædia Britannica*, but there was nothing under AXIDUS. I read the article on Saint Augustine, but it contained no clue. A thick history book likewise offered no leads. A biographical dictionary listed no one named Axidus, and I was beginning to believe such a person had never existed.

I glanced out the library window, at the gleaming golden dome of the state capitol. Somewhere, there must be a clue . . . Axidus, Saint Augustine . . . Augustine was a great Catholic saint, and a Catholic priest had been murdered near Gidaz six months ago. . . .

I walked back to the endless bookshelves that lined the walls and took down the index to the *Catholic Encyclopedia*. . . .

A-X-I-D-U-S. . . . Yes, there it was. . . .

"AXIDUS, leader of Circumcellions" . . . Quickly my fingers found the fifth volume and turned to the indicated page.

And I began to read: The Circumcellions were a branch of the Donatist schism, which had split away from the Catholic Church in the Fourth Century. They seemed to be an insane band of outlaws who roamed about North Africa, killing and robbing Catholic priests and others. Saint Augustine had spent much of his life fighting them, and their leader, Axidus.

The whole fantastic thing was beginning to take shape in my mind now . . . Axidus . . . the burned book . . . the murdered priest . . . .

And then a sentence leaped out at me from the page: "*They frequently sought death, counting suicide as martyrdom. They were especially fond of flinging themselves from precipices. . . . Even women caught the infection, and those who had sinned would cast themselves from the cliffs, to atone for their fault. . . .*"

And further down the page was more: "*When in controversy with Catholics, the Donatist bishops were proud of their supporters. They declared that self-precipitation from a cliff had been forbidden in their councils. Yet the bodies of these suicides were sacrilegiously honoured, and crowds celebrated their anniversaries. . . .*"

So this was it. . . .

Something reaching out from fifteen hundred years ago to bring death to an entire village. . . .

Was it possible?

Was it possible that this man Axidus had convinced seventy-three persons to leap to their deaths?

I left the library and stopped in a bar and fought off the gathering clouds of exhaustion and horror with a couple of stiff drinks. Then I went to meet Simon Ark . . . .

As WE DROVE SOUTH once more, toward the dead village and the darkening night, I told Simon Ark what I had found. I told him about the murdered priest and about the Circumcellions.

"I feared that I was right," he said quietly. "The death of that priest proves that there actually existed in that village the ancient cult of the Circumcellions. . . ."

"But . . . but the whole thing's fantastic. It couldn't happen in the twentieth century."

"Consider the circumstances, though. Here is a village almost completely cut off from the outside world. It is eighty miles from the nearest city, and almost that far from a town of any size. Its people are living completely within themselves, leaving Gidaz only about once a month. Except for the daily mail truck, they see no one else. The road leading to it is a dead end, so there are not even any other cars to pass by. The people, nearly all of them, are living in the past, in a time when the town was great and famous."

"Yes," I said, "I'm beginning to see. . . ."

"And into this town comes a man, a man who is completely evil, who sees the opportunity that the village and its people offer. This man, Axidus, plays on their ignorance and their superstition to get up a new religion. It is an area, I discovered this afternoon, largely neglected by the established churches because of its inaccessibility. A priest will come by every six months or so, but the rest of the time the village is alone."

"And so they listened to Axidus."

"Yes. . . . I imagine he had almost a hypnotic quality in his speech, a quality that, over a period of the last two years, convinced even the most hostile that he was their savior. A few, like Shelly Constance, who were young and intelligent enough to know the truth, simply left the village, rather than stay and fight this demon who had taken control. The priest who visited the place had to die, because he realized the truth. Perhaps others who opposed Axidus died, too. Because he was playing for big stakes and could not afford to lose."

"But . . . just how did he work the mass suicide?"

"In the same way that he, or his namesake, did fifteen hundred years ago. He convinced the people that suicide was a form of martyrdom, and that they should throw themselves from the cliff to repent for their sins. He had probably been leading up to it for a long, long time. But two nights ago, when he called them suddenly from their houses, he told them the time had come. They had no time to think, to consider the fantastic thing they were doing. They actually believed, I am certain, that it was good. And they walked off the cliff in the night, probably thinking that Axidus would join them. But of course he did not."

"You've built up a pretty strong case," I admitted. "I'll agree that over a period of years, a fanatic like that might talk most of those isolated people into killing themselves, especially since they seem to have had nothing to live for anyway. But there must have been at least one or two who would have resisted. What about the children?"

"I imagine," Simon Ark said quietly, "that the children were carried over the cliff in their mothers' arms. Or led over by their fathers."

I FELL SILENT AS the horror of the scene formed a terrifying picture in my mind.

"And," he continued, "Axidus could easily have killed any adults who might have resisted the idea of suicide. He could have killed them and thrown their bodies down with the rest."

"Still, such a thing seems so . . . impossible."

"It seems so impossible and fantastic only because of its setting in time and space. In the twentieth century, in the western United States, it is fantastic. But in the fourth century, in North Africa, it was common. And who is to say that people have changed since then? Times have changed, and places have changed, but the people have remained the same, and they suffer today from exactly the same faults and weaknesses they had fifteen hundred years ago. . . ."

I turned the car into the dirt road that led to the village of the dead. "But why are we coming back here tonight?"

"Because Axidus will return this evening, and this time he must not escape us."

"How do you know he'll return?"

"Because from the beginning Axidus had to be one of two things: either a clever killer whose insane mind had devised this fantastic scheme, or else he really was the long-dead Axidus of Saint Augustine's time. If he is the former, then there's something in Gidaz he wants, possibly the gold, and he'll come for it because we scared him away last night. And," he paused for a moment, "if it's to be the latter explanation, then according to legend and history, he'd return to worship at the grave, just as he did fifteen hundred years ago. . . ."

I turned on my headlights against the thickening night and tried to shake the gathering sleep from my eyes. "Which do you think it is?"

"In a way, I hope it is the latter, because then possibly my long search will be over. But there is still one thing that puzzles me."

"What's that?"

"I am wondering why a mail truck was delivering mail this morning, to a village full of dead people. . . ."

AFTER THAT WE WAITED.

We waited in the rocks of the cliff itself, overlooking the grave in the moonlight. We waited as Augustine might have waited those many years before.

The evening slipped slowly by and nothing happened. Once there came the distant call of a timber wolf, and again the hooting of a nearby owl, but otherwise the night was silent.

The grave below us had been marked with a large temporary cross, until some sort of plaque could list the names of the seventy-three.

For a moment the moon slipped behind a cloud, but then it appeared again, and the edge of the cliff glowed in its light.

Then I saw it.

High above us, on the very edge of the cliff, the girl stood. . . .

"Damn!" I whispered. "I forgot about the girl; she's still here."

But before we could move, we realized she was not alone on the cliff's edge. A tall, bearded man, all in white, had come up behind her.

Simon Ark leaped from his hiding place and shouted one word: "Axidus!"

The figure on the cliff paused, startled, and the girl, seeing him behind her, screamed. . . .

After that, it was a nightmare.

The figure in white was clutching the girl, like a scene from some third-rate movie, as I scrambled up the rocks toward them. But already Simon Ark was ahead of me, shouting something in the language he'd used before.

Axidus released his grip on the girl, and I caught her as she fell.

And then, there on the very edge of the cliff, Simon Ark challenged this creature from another time. He held in his hand an oddly shaped cross, with a loop at the top, and he said, in a voice like thunder, "Back, Axidus, go back to the caverns of the damned from which you came." He raised the cross high above his head. "I command it, in the name of Augustine!"

And suddenly the figure in white seemed to lose his footing on the rocks, and he slipped down over the edge of the cliff, with a scream that echoed through the night. . . .

WE FOUND HIM LATER, at the base of the cliff, which had now claimed its seventy-fourth life. And of course, under the blood and the false white beard, we found Joe Harris, the mail truck driver. . . .

And one can argue, I suppose, that it all had a perfectly sane explanation. As driver of the mail truck, the insane Joe Harris would have known enough about the people to scare them into believing he was a man of supernatural powers. He had been after the remains of the gold in the old mines, and had carefully planned for two years to drive the entire town to suicide.

But of course this did not explain how a man like Joe Harris had ever heard the odd story of Axidus in the first place, nor did it explain why he found it necessary to burn the books of Saint Augustine.

That was why I never published my story. There were too many things that could never be explained. Simon Ark and I worked the rest of the night, burying Joe Harris in the big grave with the other seventy-three. His disappearance caused some further excitement, but in a few weeks it was forgotten.

And likewise the Gidaz Horror itself has been forgotten with the passage of time, except for an occasional feature article in the Sunday newspapers.

Perhaps it is better that way. . . .

As for the others who shared my adventure, the girl, Shelly Constance, and I were married six months later, but that is another story, and a much happier one.

And Simon Ark . . . Well, I never saw him again after that night, but I have a feeling that he's still around somewhere. . . .

# Chalk

EVAN HUNTER

## Evan Hunter's Introduction:

It was sometime in 1943 that I decided I wanted to be a writer. Until then, I had studied art, my idea being to become a famous painter, you see. In high school, I was art editor of the literary-art magazine and cartoonist for the school newspaper. Upon graduation, I won a citywide scholarship to the Art Students League and then was accepted at Cooper Union, one of New York's most prestigious art schools. I was seventeen years old and a war was going on. I enlisted in the Navy just before my eighteenth birthday, and was called up in November.

Shortly before the war ended, I was assigned to a destroyer as a radarman striker. When they learned I'd had art training, they asked me to paint the two forward stacks with the Japanese calligraphy for "The First Shall Be First." That was because we were leaving for Japan, and not only were we part of the First Destroyer Squadron, we were also the first American destroyer squadron to enter Japanese waters. We awed the local fishermen when we steamed grandly into Yokohama. What a show! My smokestack artwork is still remembered there.

On the way to Japan, I also made pencil sketches of the officers and crew to send home to their wives and mothers and girlfriends. I didn't charge a penny for these excellent portraits, not a cent, I promise you. I did serious studies of the torpedo tubes and the depth charges and the gun mounts forward and aft and the radar antennas and the masts and the water everywhere around. There was a lot of water everywhere around. Eventually, I grew weary of the sameness and scarcity of subject matter to be found in the middle of the Pacific Ocean. For some peculiar reason, don't ask me why, I borrowed a typewriter from the radio shack, locked myself in an empty storage compartment, and began writing.

I don't know if "Chalk" was the first story I ever wrote. I know it was among the first stories I wrote, and I know for certain it was the only story of those precious few ever to be published—but not until almost ten years after it was written. Back in 1943, the radiomen's typewriter had only uppercase keys on it. This lent a certain urgency to everything I wrote. All that uppercase screaming made my stories look like frantic bulletins from the front. HER FACE WAS A PIECE OF UGLY PINK CHALK, and so on.

*I showed "Chalk" to my fellow radarmen, and asked for their honest opinions. I have since learned never to ask for anyone's honest opinion on anything I write unless he is going to pay cold hard cash for it. But I was eighteen years old and embarking on a new career (although I didn't yet know it) and I was seeking any encouragement I could get.*

*Their collective opinion was that I was crazy.*

*The story quickly circulated outside the radar gang. Soon fire controlmen and gunner's mates, and coxswains and sonarmen had all read "Chalk" and knew that somebody who'd murdered a young girl was one of the ship's crew members. I told everybody I wasn't crazy, I was merely a writer. And to prove the point, I sent "Chalk" off to the Ladies Home Journal.*

*I was honestly expecting the editors there to take pity on a poor sailor occupying Japan, but the war was over, and memories were short, alas, and they returned the story with regrets, which started the Las Vegas phase of my literary development. This was after I had written three or four other stories, among which were a love story and a fantasy, as I recall, neither of which ever sold—but I'm getting ahead of myself.*

*When it became known aboard ship (and everything is almost immediately known aboard a small ship) that there were other arrows in my quiver, other strings to my bow, when it became bruited about that there was an oeuvre, so to speak, and that I was sending off this growing body of work to various and sundry magazines back home, the ship's postman (a dandy from Chicago) started a lively betting operation wherein anyone foolish enough to believe that one of my stories would actually be accepted for publication could reap odds of twenty-to-one. No one ever won. Not a single one of my stories was ever accepted. But the frenzied interest generated each time the mail arrived was what I still believe kept many of those hapless sailors from dying of sheer boredom.*

*Fade out.*

*Fade in.*

*1953. I was working for the Scott Meredith Literary Agency, and beginning to sell a lot of my own short stories hither and yon. This was before I wrote The Blackboard Jungle, which was published in October of 1954, and before Ed McBain was even a thought; the first 87th Precinct novel wasn't published till May of 1956. If I recall correctly, Scott came out of his inner-sanctum office one afternoon to announce that he'd just had a call from a new mystery magazine named Pursuit, whose editor was looking for material. Was there anything in the ANM file we could send him? (ANM alternately meant either "Awaiting New Markets" or "At No Market.") I fished out some clients' stories that had already made the circuit, simultaneously discovering to my delight and dismay that there* was not a single Evan Hunter story in the batch. This meant all of my current stories had already been sold (delight). It also meant we had nothing of mine to send to a new market (dismay).

Ever alert to opportunity (a trait shared by my friend and fellow writer, Lawrence Block), I went home that night and rummaged through the files, coming upon something that screamed out of the box in uppercase type, HER FACE WAS A PIECE OF UGLY PINK CHALK, and so on. I read it quickly, decided it was good enough for jazz, retyped it in proper upper and lowercase letters, and sent it to Pursuit the very next day.

I don't now recall how much I got paid for the story; all of my old records were lost in the great Brickmeyer Building fire of 1957. My guess is that I got a cent a word. The editor of the magazine, apparently sharing the collective opinion of my shipmates ten years earlier, started his blurb to the story with the words, "I am different from you. There are terrible things hiding beneath the shadows in my mind . . ." In an act of editorial class he also changed my original title—"Chalk"—to the much more elegant "I Killed Jeannie." But since this story was among the first I ever wrote, and certainly the only one of that early batch ever to be published, I think I owe it the dignity of its birth name now. So here's "Chalk."

# Chalk

## EVAN HUNTER

HER FACE WAS A piece of ugly pink chalk, and her eyes were two little brown mud puddles. Her eyes were mud puddles and they did not fit with the pink chalk. The chalk was ugly, and her eyes were mud puddles, and they made the chalk look uglier.

"Your eyes are mud puddles," I said, and she laughed.

I didn't like her to laugh. I was serious. She shouldn't have laughed when I told her something serious like that.

I hit the pink chalk with my fist but it didn't crumble. I wondered why it didn't crumble. I hit it again and water ran out of the mud puddles. I pushed my hand into one of the mud puddles and it turned all red, and it looked prettier with water coming out of it and red.

I tore the beads from her neck and threw them at the chalk. I felt her nails dig into my skin and I didn't like that. I twisted her arm and she struggled and pushed, and her body felt nice and soft up tight against mine. I wanted to squeeze her and when I began squeezing her she screamed, and the noise reminded me of the Third Avenue El when it stops going, and the noise reminded me of babies crying at night when I'm trying to sleep. So I hit her mouth to stop the noise but instead it got louder.

I ripped her dress in the front and I swore at her and told her to stop the noise, but she wouldn't stop so I kicked her in the leg and she fell. She looked soft and white on the floor. All except her face. It was still pink chalk.

*Ugly pink chalk.*

I stepped on it with all my might and the mud puddles closed and red came from her nose.

I stepped on her again and the pink chalk was getting red all over and it looked good and I kept stepping. And the red got thicker and redder, and

214

then she started to twitch and jerk like as if she was sick, and I bent down and asked, "Are you sick, Jeannie?"

She didn't answer except like a moan, and then she made a noise that sounded like the Third Avenue El again, and I had to hit her again to make her stop.

I kept punching her in the face and the noise stopped.

It was very quiet.

Her eyes weren't mud puddles. Why did I think they were mud puddles? They were two shiny glass marbles and they were looking right at me, only they couldn't see me because they were glass and you can't see out of glass.

The pink chalk was all red now except for white patches here and there. Her mouth was open but there was no noise.

Then I heard the ticking.

It was loud, like an axe splitting wood, and I was afraid it was going to wake her up and then she would make the noise all over again, and I would have to tell her to stop and hit her again. I did not want to hit her again because her eyes were only marbles and you can't see out of marbles, and her face was a pretty red and not made of chalk that would not crumble.

So I stepped on the ticking. I stepped on it twice so that I could be sure. Then I took off her clothes and she looked all red and white and quiet when I put her on the bed. I closed the light and then I left her to sleep. I felt sorry for her.

She couldn't see because her eyes were only marbles.

IT WAS COLD IN the night. It shouldn't have been cold because the sky was an oil fire, all billowy and black. Why was it cold?

I saw a man coming and I stopped him because I wanted to know why it was so cold when the sky was burning up. He talked funny and he couldn't walk straight, and he said it was warm and I was crazy if I thought it was cold. I asked him if he was warm.

He said, "I am warm, and don't bother me because I feel wonderful and I don't want to lose this feeling."

I hit him and I took his coat because he was warm and he didn't need it if he was warm.

I ran fast down the street, and then I knew he was right. It *was* warm and I didn't need his coat, so I went back to take it to him because he might be cold now. He wasn't there so I put the coat on the sidewalk in case he came back for it.

Then I ran down the street because it was nice and warm and it felt like springtime and I wanted to run and leap. I got tired and I began to breathe hard so I sat down on the sidewalk. Then I was tired of sitting and I did not want to run anymore, so I began looking at the windows but they were all dark. I did not like them to be dark because I liked to look at the things in the windows and if they were dark I couldn't see them.

Poor Jeannie. Her eyes were marbles and she could not see the things in the store windows. Why did God make my eyes out of white jelly and Jeannie's out of glass? I wondered how she knew me if she couldn't see me.

IT WAS GETTING COLD again and I swore at the man who had talked funny and couldn't walk straight. He had lied to me and made me feel warm when it was really cold all along. I lifted my hand up to the light in the street because it was yellow and warm, but I couldn't reach it and I was still cold.

Then the wet fell out of the sky, and I began to run so it wouldn't touch me. But it was all around me, and the more I ran the more it fell. And the noise in the sky was like a dog growling under his teeth, and the lights that flashed were a pale, scary blue. I ran and ran and I was getting tired of running and the wet was making *me* wet, and the damp was creeping into my head and the dark was behind it the way the dark always was.

The damp pressed on the inside and it pushed outward, and then the dark creeped up and I screamed, and it sounded like the Third Avenue El when it stops going, and I screamed again and it sounded like babies crying, and I punched myself in the face so I would stop the way Jeannie did. But I screamed again and the damp was all in and over my head. The dark was waiting, too.

I screamed because I didn't want the dark to come in, but I could see it was getting closer and I knew the way the damp felt always just before the dark came in. I hit my face again, but the damp was heavy now and it was dripping inside my head, and I knew the dark was coming and I ran away from it.

But it was there, and first it was gray like the ocean and then it got deeper like a dense fog and it turned black and blacker, and the dark came and I knew I was falling, and I couldn't stop because Jeannie's eyes were only marbles.

I AM LYING ON a sidewalk in a strange street.

The sun is just rising and the bustle of the day has not yet begun. There is a severe pain in my head. I know I haven't been drinking, yet where did this terrible pain come from?

I rise and brush off my clothes.

It is then that I notice the blood on my hands and on my shoes. *Blood?*

Have I been fighting? No, no, I don't remember any fighting. I remember—I remember—calling on Jeannie.

She did not feel like going out, so we decided to sit at home and talk. She made coffee, and we were sitting and drinking and talking.

How do I come to be in this strange street? With blood on my body?

I begin to walk.

There are store windows with various forms of merchandise in them. There is a man's overcoat lying in the street, a ragged overcoat lying in a heap. I pass it rapidly.

It is starting to drizzle now. I walk faster. I must see Jeannie. Perhaps she can clear this up for me.

Anyway, the drizzle is turning into a heavy rain.

And I have never liked the darkness or dampness that come with a storm.

# It's a Wise Child
# Who Knows

## STUART KAMINSKY

## Stuart Kaminsky's Introduction:

In the mid-1960s, I wrote three Bollo and Pete Breedlove short stories for the now long-defunct Man From U.N.C.L.E. magazine. "It's A Wise Child Who Knows" was the first story in the series and the first mystery story of mine published. I received thirty-five dollars for the story and went up to fifty dollars for the next two in the series. I went on to write a screenplay based on the characters. Nothing ever happened to the screenplay. As far as I know, there are no copies left of that screenplay. I won't know with certainty unless I attack every box in the garage, a task I have no intention of tackling in the near or distant future.

My first published story, "Drup No. 1," appeared a year before "Wise Child" in the New Mexico Quarterly. It wasn't a mystery. For that one I got no money but ten tear sheets of the story and two copies of the journal.

The first story I wrote at the age of thirteen has never been published. It, too, was not a mystery. It was the attempt of a kid who wanted to be a writer to be deep and literary. It was called "Christ Lives in a Chicago Hotel," and dealt with the second coming of Christ who finds himself rejected, forced to live in a Chicago flophouse, considered a run-of-the-street lunatic. It wasn't bad. It wasn't good. My best friends, twins who lived across the alley from us in Chicago, published a four-sheet mimeographed literary journal that they gave out free to neighbors. My friends rejected that first story of mine with the comment that it "had no literary merit."

"Wise Child" and the other Breedlove stories were shamelessly taken from plots stolen from G. K. Chesterton and S. S. Van Dine. So was the lost screenplay.

My most vivid memory of "Wise Child" was receiving the check. That thirty-five dollars made me accept myself as a writer and in my mind forced others to do the same. A teacher had once told me: You are not a writer when you say you are. You're a writer when someone pays you for writing. Now I was a writer.

I carried copies of that Man From U.N.C.L.E. magazine around with me for a couple of weeks. I was a mystery writer. I was good enough to be published and paid. I needed very little encouragement beyond that.

221

Once in awhile a fan will dig up those old Man from U.N.C.L.E. magazines and ask me if I plan to write more in the series. I don't. The truth is that from the vantage or disadvantage point of thirty-five years, I don't think the stories were particularly good.

When I was asked about a year ago by an audio book company to let them include the three stories in a tape of my collected short stories, I considered telling them I would just as soon leave them out. I told this to my friend, the truly brilliant writer Harlan Ellison, and Harlan said the stories should be included, that a good reader would make them sound great. He proceeded to read "Wise Child" to me. Harlan is not only a great writer. He is a great reader. He actually made the story sound good to me.

I had rejected this first child of mine and had it brought back to me by Harlan.

My conclusion was not that I had written a good story, but that I had written a story that was definitely readable. If Harlan could give it life and enjoy it, I hope you will too.

# It's a Wise Child Who Knows

## STUART KAMINSKY

CHIEF WITT PULLED HIS cap forward and slouched slightly, hoping that he would not be recognized by a passing pedestrian. Delftwood's chief of police did not want even a hint of suspicion to leak out that he was about to consult a twelve-year-old boy about a murder case. Political careers had been ruined by far less.

He shifted his weight and smoothed out a crease in his neatly pressed uniform as he glanced at the hulking, unkempt man at his side who drove quickly and expertly through the dark afternoon rain. "Bollo" Breedlove's ever-present smile broadened as he took his eyes off the road for an instant to look at Witt.

"Sergeant Breedlove, will you please keep your eyes on the street?" Witt pleaded.

"Yes, sir. I'm sure it's important, Chief, or Pete wouldn't have asked you to come to the house. If his leg wasn't broken, he'd come down to headquarters, like he did last year with the Decker case."

"All right, Breedlove. I'm not saying the boy didn't give us a lot of help on that case, but that was different. We've got no problem here. Everyone knows Mike Quell killed the old woman and that's that. Plenty of evidence, motive, everything we need. Will you keep your eyes on the road?"

"Right, Chief," whispered the huge driver, removing one hand from the wheel to reach under his worn police cap and scratch a balding, freckled head.

"And besides," Witt continued, "he's been in bed with a broken leg since she was murdered. How can he have any information that we don't? Who does he think did it if it wasn't Quell?"

"Don't know," Bollo Breedlove chuckled, turning the car into a narrow driveway. "Let's see what he has to say."

"I should have my head examined," Witt muttered, getting out of the parked car and waiting while Breedlove lumbered out to join him. "What could your grandson know about this that we don't?" Breedlove smiled and shrugged. The two men made their way to the front porch of the well-maintained but aged little frame house.

"I'm home," Breedlove said, stepping into the warm living room. Witt walked in behind him, removing his cap and brushing back his neatly combed gray hair.

Witt had been in the house a few times in the five years he had been Delftwood's chief of police, and the atmosphere always made him sleepy. Breedlove, his daughter-in-law, and his grandson lived quietly and comfortably, seldom mentioning Walt Junior, who had died in Korea.

"Chief Witt, it's nice to see you again," said Kate Breedlove, coming into the room with her hand outstretched. "How is your wife and the children?"

"Fine," Witt replied, noticing the tiny blonde's flour-marked hands and apron. "Don't let us keep you. We just stopped by to see Pete."

"Well, he's still in his bed, so you won't have any trouble finding him." She sighed. "I think I'll throw a block party when he gets on his feet and back to school. Did you ever try to keep a bed-bound twelve-year-old boy from getting bored? Don't bother to answer. Would you like a drink, Chief? Walt?"

The two men refused and Kate returned to the kitchen. Breedlove grinned and led the way down a short hall and into the small bedroom. A chubby, blond boy in blue flannel pajamas with white circles paused in his attempt to scratch an itch under the plaster cast and looked up at the two men.

"Hi, Bollo. Hi, Chief. This thing really itches like crazy."

Breedlove cleared a pile of books from the bed and sat down next to the boy, whose hair he ruffled playfully. Witt sat in a straw chair next to the bed and cleared his throat.

"About the murder, Pete," said Witt.

"You mean Miss Quell or the one I figured out last year?" replied the boy, trying again to scratch his covered leg.

"I thought we decided that we worked together last year," said Witt.

"Yeah, I guess we did. Well, with Miss Quell, I know who killed her."

"We all know," added Witt quickly. "It was Mike, her nephew."

"I read that in the *Delftwood News Director*, but that's wrong. Bollo told me about the case, and I—"

"Wait," said Witt. "The facts are simple. Miss Beatrice Quell—"

"Quashy Quell, we called her," mumbled the boy. "Fattest woman in Delftwood."

"Pete, you don't talk that way about the dead," said Breedlove.

"Sorry, Bollo."

"May I continue?" Witt whispered. "Thank you. At exactly nine o'clock Monday night, just as the church tower bell rang, Miss Quell called headquarters, and Officer Lydecker answered the phone. She said, and he recognized her voice, 'This is Beatrice Quell and—' Before she could say more, and while the tower bell was still ringing, Lydecker heard a shot over the phone and that was it.

"Lydecker sent a car over and called me. I immediately had her three nephews picked up. Had them within ten minutes. Meanwhile I got to Miss Quell's house about the same time as the patrol car. Both doors were locked. All windows were locked from the inside. We broke down the back door, went in and found Miss Quell, all two hundred forty pounds of her, on the living room floor with the phone in her hand and a bullet in her heart. All clear so far?"

"Sure," said the boy, who had stopped scratching and was now chewing on his pajamas.

"Fine. We check and find from one of the nephews, Al Quell over at Quell's Drug Store, that the locks at Miss Quell's had been changed that morning and only the three nephews and the old woman had keys. We found hers in her purse.

"We checked with the locksmith and he says no other keys were made, and only those keys could open the doors. The nephews all had their keys on them when we picked them up. No one knows whose idea it was to change the locks, but the old woman was a bit of a nut anyway.

"So, with all the doors locked, the logical conclusion is that someone with a key, one of the three nephews, killed the old lady, locked the door and ran. They all stand to make a lot of money. She was loaded. So we began to check alibis, and—"

"Chief," said the boy, "did you check the locksmith's alibi?"

The chief grinned for the first time.

"Yes, we checked him for nine o'clock. He was at an Elks meeting; plenty of witnesses. We also checked the possibility of a duplicate key being made. It's a tricky lock and it would have taken a few days to get the right matrix from Chicago. So, excluding the possibility that one of the nephews had an accomplice, we started to check their alibis for nine o'clock."

"I know why it couldn't be an accomplice," the boy said brightly. "Because if the nephews had the keys on them just a little after the murder, someone would have had to give it to them if that someone were the murderer, and except for Mike, the others were too far away from the house a few minutes later, and no accomplice would have had time to meet them."

"Very clever," said Witt.

"Sure is," agreed Breedlove.

"To continue," Witt went on, "at nine o'clock Al Quell was locking his drug store a mile away. Plenty of people around. Steven Quell—"

"Skinny Minnie Quell," mumbled the boy.

"Steven Quell," Witt went on, "was walking down Center Street and saw his brother locking his store. He remembers seeing who was with him. Half a block further down Center Street he saw the Collins twins in front of the Fox Theater. Both twins remember that it was exactly nine, because the—"

"Church bell was ringing," said Pete Breedlove.

"Right," continued Witt with a frown, "and they were just in time for the feature, which started at a minute after nine. Not only that, but Steve Quell saw Officer Jack Meany giving a ticket to a short, fat man, and Meany's report for the night shows that at exactly nine o'clock he stopped under a street light at First and Center to give a ticket to a Mr. Katz, a short, fat man who had smashed his car into a light pole. I think that is sufficient alibi for Steve Quell."

"He used to be a bird watcher," Pete replied, reaching over the side of his bed and pulling up an old notebook.

"Yes, but it has nothing to do with the case." Witt shifted slightly. "Well, to continue. Mike Quell, a surly ba—son of a gun, has less than an alibi. Claims someone called him and told him to get down to the old boathouse in Cove Woods, behind Miss Quell's house. This so-called caller said they or he'd found something valuable belonging to Mike.

"So, according to a half-sober Mike Quell, at exactly nine he was alone, about one hundred yards from the scene of the murder. Item two, Mike Quell admits owning a thirty-eight automatic, which is now missing. Miss Quell was killed with a thirty-eight. Item three, all the nephews knew they would share the old woman's estate when she went, but Mike is the one who seems most anxious to get his hands on it.

"Add to this the public knowledge that Miss Quell had been threatening to cut him out of her will unless he stopped drinking, and you've got a pretty good motive."

"Mike Quell is the best shortstop Delftwood High ever had," said Pete, looking absently through the notebook.

"That doesn't make him innocent," Witt added quickly.

"He didn't do it," said the boy. "Did he, Bollo?"

The fat man scratched his head and shrugged.

"If I show someone else could have done it, will you get me a new baseball glove?" said the boy slyly.

Kate Breedlove walked into the room with coffee for the men and a glass of chocolate milk for Pete, who downed it in two long gulps before Kate had stepped out of the room.

"If you show that someone else did it, or could have done it, I'll give you a new baseball glove," said Witt, sipping at the welcomed coffee which might help to hold off the migraine he feared was on the way.

"That's a deal, Chief. You heard it, Bollo."

"Yup, but wipe the milk off your mouth."

"Well," the boy beamed, looking down at his notebook, "there are a couple of things to get straight first. Miss Quell's house is way up on Cove Hill over Delftwood. The living room where she was found faces out into the woods away from town."

"This is not new information," said Witt, spying with some distaste a still existent chocolate mustache on the boy's upper lip.

"I know, but listen. Nobody heard the shot, Bollo says, because it's a pretty thick old house and there aren't any neighbors nearby."

"Wait," Witt said. "Officer Lydecker heard the shot over the phone."

"Sure, but—" Pete's excited arms were in the air. "Just listen. When Bollo told me about the murder, some things hit me as pretty funny. Like the murder taking place at exactly nine and the murderer letting her use the phone, and the locks being changed that morning and the murderer locking the door behind him."

"Coincidence," Witt sighed, finishing his coffee. "Locking the door was Mike Quell's mistake. If he had left it open, we'd never have been able to narrow it down to the nephews. It happens all the time. Mike had a fight with the old lady. She got mad when he pulled out a gun and started a fuss. She called the police. He shot her, panicked, locked the door, ran into the woods and threw the gun away. He couldn't even come up with a decent story."

"But," said the boy, reading from his notes, "if Mike is telling the truth, then someone has done a good job of making it look like he's the murderer. Now who would do that but one of the other nephews? With Mike gone they would split the old lady's money only two ways."

"Is that what kids do now?" Witt addressed Breedlove. "Sit around thinking about murder?"

"Chief," the boy said. "So maybe one of the others wanted it to look like Mike did it. Maybe the one who did it wanted everyone to know she was killed at exactly nine, when Mike was in the woods at the boathouse. If that's true, then the killer must have set up an alibi for nine to cover himself."

"I'd say both of the others have perfect alibis," Witt said, placing his empty cup on the floor.

"That's it, that's it!" shouted Pete Breedlove. "They both don't have perfect alibis. At nine Al Quell was closing his drug store. A customer saw him and Skinny Minnie, I mean Steve Quell, saw him, too. But who saw Steve Quell?"

Witt tried to hide the look of disgust as he vowed to tell Bollo Breedlove to stop discussing cases with the boy.

"Look," Witt said, lifting his right hand and counting off the fingers, "Steve was on Center Street, a mile from the murder. He saw his brother close his store at exactly nine. He saw the Collins twins in front of the Fox Theater at exactly nine. He saw Officer Meany giving this guy Katz a ticket at exactly nine."

"That's what I mean," said the boy, laying his notes aside and gritting his teeth for another assault on his itching leg. "He saw them all at exactly nine. The Fox Theater is a block away from the drug store. Meany, according to Bollo, was another block down. At exactly nine, Steve Quell saw three things taking place about two and a half blocks from each other."

"Wait a minute!" Witt grinned and put up a hand. "Al Quell might have closed a minute or two early. Meany might have been a minute or two off. The twins were sure of the time, but—"

"But nobody saw Steve Quell," Pete insisted. "To see all that he would probably have to hurry down the street, but no one saw him, and how come he didn't say anything about seeing that guy Katz's car against the pole? Bollo says it was where he would have to pass at about nine."

"He forgot," said Witt.

"Maybe," said the boy. "But Bollo checked and Steve says he might have seen the wreck, but didn't pay any attention. That seems pretty funny unless he didn't see the wreck at all. So I had an idea. Bollo went up to Miss Quell's last night to see if there's a room in back of the house where you can see Center Street."

"Breedlove," Witt whispered grimly, feeling the headache coming. "Did you go up there without telling me?"

"Well, Chief, you see—"

"We'll talk about it later."

"So," said the boy, "Bollo did find one room. With a pair of binoculars, he could see some good lighted—"

"Well lighted," Breedlove interrupted.

"Yeah, well-lighted places on the right side of Center Street like the drug store, the front of the Fox, and under the light where Meany gave the ticket. But he couldn't see the left side, where the wreck would have been."

"Hold on!" Witt shouted and stood up. "Where was this room?"

"Top floor," said Breedlove. "In back."

"Right," said Witt with a smile. "How could he be on the fourth floor in the back establishing an alibi at exactly nine, while he was murdering his aunt in the living room? And don't tell me he killed her up there and dragged her down to the living room. She weighed a good two hundred forty, compared to his soaking wet one hundred thirty or one hundred forty.

"By the time he got the body down, we would have been there. Besides, there wasn't a mark on her to show she had been bumped or dragged. Even if he could have lifted her, it would have taken him five or six minutes to get her to the living room."

"It would have taken at least ten minutes to get her down," Breedlove whispered. "Pete had me take a keg of nails down from there."

"Yes," said Pete, "and Bollo's strong and the nails only weighed one hundred fifty pounds."

"Well, I'm not all that strong," said Breedlove, blushing.

"Save the family compliments for some other time," Witt shouted, placing a hand on his forehead. "You admit he couldn't have got her down."

"Oh, yes sir," said the boy. "But there is a telephone in that room."

"So?"

Pete Breedlove leaned forward and spoke softly.

"Suppose he shot her in the living room before nine, and then went up to the back room on the fourth floor. Then suppose he had a tape recorder with a tape of her voice saying 'This is Beatrice Quell.' That wouldn't be hard for him to get. So he stood at the window with his binoculars, dialed police headquarters, and when he heard Lydecker, turned on her voice and the prerecorded shot that he could have got any time.

"While Lydecker was listening, Steve Quell was looking down at Center Street. Then he hung up the phone, ran down the stairs, took the living room phone off the hook, locked the door, and left."

"No, wait a minute," cried Witt. "This is—where would he get binoculars and a tape recorder? Why?"

"He's a bird watcher," said Pete Breedlove. "He watches birds, records them in Cove Woods."

Witt's eyes wandered around the room as his headache swelled. A University of Illinois pennant danced over the quilted bed. Autographed photos of ball players surrounded him.

"But," Witt gasped, "the gun. We picked him up just a few minutes after nine. Officers Meany and Carl picked him up and he had no gun."

"Threw it in Cove Woods. Probably stole it from Mike."

"The binoculars and tape recorder," Witt muttered, sitting down again. "He couldn't throw them away. We might find them, trace them to him."

"Easy," said the boy. "He could erase the tape on his way downtown. He wanted to get to Center Street fast. Was he carrying anything when Meany and Carl found him?"

"Yes," said Bollo proudly. "I told you yesterday, Pete."

"But," said Witt, "he didn't have binoculars or a tape recorder in his briefcase."

"Are you sure?" asked Pete. "Or did you just ask them to search him for a gun?"

Witt pulled himself together and stood again. "We can settle it easily enough. I'll just call Meany." He went to the phone next to the boy's bed and dialed a number.

"This is Chief Witt. Is your father there? Hello, Meany. Listen. You and Carl searched Steve Quell the night of the murder. I know he had no gun, but did he have a small tape recorder and a pair of binoculars in his briefcase? I see. No. I'll see you in the morning." He hung up and turned to the two Breedloves, who looked up at him with wide eyes.

"Tape recorder, yes. Binoculars, no," mumbled Witt.

"No binoculars?" the boy sighed.

"No," said Witt, fumbling in his pocket for a migraine pill. "But he did happen to have a collapsible telescope."

"Should I pick up Steve Quell, Chief?" Breedlove said with a wide smile and proud glance at his scratching grandson.

"Yes," said Witt. "We'll question him in my office. And Breedlove, let's just keep quiet for the time being about Pete's part in this."

"Right, Chief." Breedlove rose and shook his grandson's pudgy hand.

"Okay with you, Pete?" said the fat man.

"Sure. I think I'd like a Maury Wills model."

"What?" said the chief.

"Maury Wills model baseball glove," explained Bollo Breedlove on his way out.

"Of course," Witt sighed, and stood up to follow the sergeant.

As Witt turned to the door, a chubby, blond, twelve-year-old boy reached under his pillow for a stack of baseball cards. The top card was a full-color reproduction of Maury Wills.

# Who Killed Cock Robin?

## H. R. F. KEATING

## H. R. F. Keating's Introduction:

*"The Justice Boy" was the first crime short story I ever wrote. I embarked on it, some time in early 1967, in response to* Ellery Queen's Mystery Magazine's *setting up a competition confined, most generously, to Brits who were members of the Crime Writers Association. I wrote it. I sent it off. And then . . . then I got a letter, handwritten, from no lesser person than half of that legendary writer "Ellery Queen." It was signed Frederic Dannay, though in the next stage of our correspondence that swiftly became Fred. Imagine getting a letter from the Archangel Gabriel with the signature rapidly descending to a friendly "Gabe," and a letter, too, saying, "I want to compliment you on the honesty and integrity of your story."*

*And, needless to remind any writer who contributed in those days to EQMM, Fred Dannay wanted to change the title. He wanted to change the titles of almost all the stories submitted to him, or so it used to seem. And, in my case certainly, that was a mark of good editing. I had called my story, which was about the murder of a pet bird in a 1930s British boarding school, "Who Killed Cock Robin?" My title, Fred said in that first letter, "has a humorous connotation over here." But was he saying, very tactfully, that cock was not a word he wanted to see in his chaste pages? Remember all this was a long, long time ago. But there were, too, a good many instances in that first letter of sharp editing. For example, "What exactly," Fred asked, "is the boot-hole?" I cannot remember how I explained that schoolboy term, but I see that boot-hole is there without any paraphrase in the printed version. So I must have convinced Fred the word—it means a room where football boots are kept—did not need any spelling out.*

*A later instance of Fred's editing perhaps confirms me in my guess about that word cock in my first story's title. In a story I sent him a year or two later, I had an English gentleman in the 1930s—I seem to have liked writing about that period then—killing his young wife because she had a lover who was a Rajah, and therefore "a cad." And Fred didn't think his readers would like the thought of a white lady having a black lover. However, I couldn't see my story having its proper impact unless the lover was that cad. Back and forth across the Atlantic* letters were exchanged—no fax then, no e-mail—and at last a compromise was reached. The lover in the printed version is Spanish, sallow complexion enough to meet my terms, cheeks light enough to assuage Fred's fears. Oh, and, yes, Fred changed the title. Referring to the murder weapon, I had called my story "A Bloody Shovel." Fred changed that to the nickname of its cunning long-serving detective, "The Old Haddock."

But what about the actual writing of that very first story of mine? I can recall clearly the circumstances. In those days, although I had had eight or nine crime novels published, as a full-time writer I was by no means rich. (We had also produced four children.) So we had an arrangement with some of the families in the street we lived on—and still do—to cut the cost of a baby-sitter by sending across either husband or wife to spend the evening at a neighbor's in the absence of the parents.

Thus it came about it was over at No. 19, the Smiths, that I set out to explore for the first time the unknown territory of the crime short story.

I thought I knew by then how to write, more or less. But how could I, I asked myself, get into the competition's stipulated length, a maximum of five thousand words, everything I had learnt to do in a book, to tell a story, to unravel a mystery plot, and, at the same time, to say something about some aspect of the human condition? I suppose I must, before I crossed the road to the Smiths, have hit at least on the notion of scaling-down, as it were, a story about adults and real murder into a tale of schoolboys and a pet bird's lesser death. Because as far as I remember, as soon as I had crept upstairs and taken a cautious peep at the little sleeping Smiths, I settled myself at Roger's flap-down bureau and got to work. And what I did was just to compress and compress until at last I had got it all down and in less, a very few less, than that five-thousand-word limit.

Can it really be that before Roger and Anne Smith returned from the theatre I had got to the end? I think I had. By God, I was young and full of energy in those days. And, as I had written it all by hand, I had plenty of opportunity while typing it out at home—Remember typewriters?—to revise and revise until I had got it as right as I could.

So that's how "Who Killed Cock Robin?" became "The Justice Boy" and was eventually awarded second prize, after a tale by that seasoned storyteller, Christianna Brand.

# Who Killed Cock Robin?

## H. R. F. KEATING

SHIVERING UNCONTROLLABLY, THE BOY in the blue-striped pajamas forced back his tears. He put his head round the corner and peered frightenedly into the Long Corridor. No one was in sight. The wide stretch of bumpy, polished brown linoleum shone bleakly under the unshaded lamps between its high walls, glossy dark green at the foot and buff-distempered above.

The air on this November evening at Seacombe Court Preparatory School for Boys was damp and chill. The cold seeped in with the wind that blew relentlessly off the dark waters of the Straits of Dover, past the empty board-inghouses, over the muddy, waterlogged stretch of the school playing field and in through every chink in the red-brick, creeper-covered walls of the building.

At the sight of the empty corridor, the boy gave a little moan, half of relief, half of misery. He wiped his eyes with the back of a rather pudgy hand. A new smear was left running across his right cheek. Both his ears stood out from his head and were even redder now than usual. But they always invited the sudden, sharp, tormentingly painful tweak. And the boy knew it.

Then, as if nothing that lay ahead could be worse than what was with him now, he darted abruptly forward and set out along the corridor. Slipping and scurrying in his bare feet, he shot past the brightly colored print of *H.M.S. Victory* at the Battle of Trafalgar—"England Expects Every Man To Do His Duty"—on past the place where three terms before a paper pellet soaked in ink had missed its target and had left its mark on the buff distemper, past the tall, brown-painted, locked doors of the Stationery Cupboard to reach at last the corner at the far end.

Here he stood still again and choked back a last sob. Then cautiously he peered round. The stairs ahead were clear. Only one more sharp dash was needed now.

And suddenly a renewed storm of weeping swept over him, breaking down the frail barrier of purposefulness that had driven him this far. He stayed where he was at the foot of the stairs—their treads covered with the same brown linoleum and with a gray rubber protector on each edge—and let the tears roll down his large, oval-shaped, unformed face.

But at last he recovered. He peered up the stairs shortsightedly and, clutching the wide, rounded rail of the stout white banisters as if he needed to pull himself up by main force, he began to climb. Up the first broad flight to the landing where the School Bell hung. Then, with one imploring look at the closed green baize door beside the waiting bell, on up the second broad flight. And all the while shivering and shivering in the dank chill . . .

ON THE OTHER SIDE of the green baize door, Alwyn Emanuel Prys-Jones, M.A., sat in his living room in a wing-backed armchair. His feet, which were small for a man of his size, were in slippers. The soles of the slippers were presented to a neat coal fire which sputtered cheerfully every now and again as a dart of white flame popped from the solid red glow at its heart.

Opposite Mr. Prys-Jones sat Mrs. Prys-Jones. She was not idle. Her fingers—only a little affected by the onset of arthritis—were busy mending a sock belonging to Bainbridge, Head Boy of the school. For Mrs. Prys-Jones concerned herself with every aspect of the running of the establishment. It said so in the prospectus sent to every inquiring parent, adding that the school took boys from eight to thirteen, and the fees were eighty-five guineas a term, laundry and music extra.

Mrs. Prys-Jones sent a last thread of gray wool snaking methodically in and out of the warp of her darning and then laid down her burden. Mr. Prys-Jones reached out one large pink hand and took between two thick fingers and a thumb a fine-stemmed glass engraved with a pattern of wheat ears. It contained a full measure of a dry and remarkably delicate sherry. Mr. Prys-Jones conveyed the glass to his lips and sipped . . .

OUT IN THE REAL world where people get hurt and suffer and see no way out of intolerable situations, the boy in the blue-striped pajamas, sobbing and shivering as hard as ever, had reached the top of the stairs. Ahead of him now stretched the Top Corridor, as long and as cold, as green-painted and buff-distempered as the corridor beneath it. On each side there were big white-painted doors, each with a number on it in black. On the left were numbers one, three, and five. On the right were numbers two and four with an unnumbered door at present just a little ajar.

The boy crept up to it and listened. The only sound was the steady dripping of a tap. He risked one hurried glance in at the row of eight wash-basins, each with its liquid soap dispenser, and the four bath cubicles divided from each other by white-tiled partitions reaching not quite up to the ceiling. Then he scuttled on.

The heavy white porcelain knob of the door marked 5 slipped under his chilled fingers. And then mercifully it turned and the big heavy door swung open.

"Who's that?" whispered a voice in the darkness.

"Who do you think it is, you idiot, McWilliam?" another voice whispered. "It's only Prout Major back from feeding that mingy robin of his."

"Oh, shut up, Forshaw. Think you're so clever," McWilliam whispered back angrily.

But suddenly Prout Major, back in the dark haven he had been making for, broke into a flood of noisy and unchecked tears again.

"Hey, he's blubbing," said Trilling, sitting up in bed.

He felt under his pillow and a moment later a beam of light from his torch picked out the figure of Prout Major standing just inside the door, his face in his hands, his two red ears burning like signal lights in the torch beam, and his whole body heaving with the violence of his sobs.

"Stop that row, Prout," Forshaw said.

"And get into bed," McWilliam added. "Some of us want to get some sleep."

From the bed in the farthest corner, where it was the privilege of the Head Boy to rest from his labors and responsibilities, Bainbridge joined in.

"Prout," he said with precarious dignity, "get into bed and shut up, or I'll have to report you to Mr. Prys-Jones."

At this Prout Major did begin to shuffle toward his empty bed. But he could not stop the tears.

"Listen, Prout," Forshaw said, "if you don't shut up I'll lam you."

And then from the other side of the long room with its two rows of black metal beds Hennessy picked up the chorus, sitting suddenly bolt upright, his dark eyebrows below the stiff, dark hair almost locked together in a line of rigid disapproval.

"Forshaw's right," he said. "If you go on making that racket, Prout, you'll get a double lamming."

Prout Major had reached his bed by now. He sat down on the edge, one bare foot on his little brown mat and one on the patterned linoleum. He continued to cry.

Forshaw slipped out of bed.

"I've got a better way to shut him up than a lamming," he said.

He pulled at the towel hanging in the regulation fashion on the bottom rail of his bed. Holding it by one corner, he sent it flicking sharply outward till at its full extent it gave a crack like a pistol shot.

"Now," he said to the sobbing Prout, "are you going to shut up or am I going to make you jump?"

He advanced a step and cracked the towel once again. But Prout was incapable of stopping now. The sobs jerked him to and fro as if he were on puppet strings. Trilling, crouching on top of his blankets, his pointed face with its rash of freckles alive with glee, held him fixed in the torch beam.

Forshaw came forward, the towel flicking out at every step.

"Listen, you fellows," Bainbridge said from his corner, "it's after lights-out."

"Are you going to stop, Prout?" said Forshaw.

Another gush of tears.

The towel flicked once again and this time there was a sharp yelp of pain from Prout. Most of the others were out of bed now, crowding round in a half circle. Trilling held the flashlight steadily on the victim.

"What are you blubbing for anyway?" McWilliam asked, standing out from the group of onlookers by virtue of wearing pajamas with differently colored top and bottom.

"Yes," said Trilling, "come on, Prouty, what is it? We all want to know."

Trilling wanted to know everything. It was his weakness. He went about like a little vacuum cleaner, sucking up anything that came his way.

Without giving Prout time to answer, Forshaw flicked the towel expertly once again. Its end landed with an even louder crack on Prout's chubby thigh just where the blue-striped pajamas were stretched their tautest. Prout gave a long, whimpering yelp.

Bainbridge, still in bed, interrupted agitatedly.

"If you fellows go on making all this row, Mr. Prys-Jones is bound to come in. And what will he say to me then?"

"Come on, Prout, tell us what you're blubbing for?" little Trilling said, entirely ignoring Bainbridge. "Come on, or I'll let Forshaw give you another."

"I'd like to see you stop me," Forshaw said menacingly, an excited glint in his eyes.

Prout, still racked with heavy sobs, did attempt to say something. But he was altogether too distressed to be coherent.

"Stop that filthy noise and let's hear what you're saying," Hennessy broke in.

"It's my robin," Prout Major managed to gasp out at last. "He's dead. He's dead."

"That's nothing to blub about, a stinking bird," Forshaw said.

"It's been killed," Prout Major wailed. "Somebody's smashed it up."

The tears spurted out even faster. "Stop it," said Forshaw. "Or—"

He began flicking the towel all round Prout's chubby legs, seeing how near he could get without actually hitting him. But no threats could quieten the sobbing now.

"All right," Forshaw said, standing back a little, "I'm really going to let you have it now."

"Wait."

Until this moment Watson had been sleepily content to prop himself up in bed on one elbow and watch what was going on. But now he flung back the blankets and came over.

"Stop it, Forshaw," he said. "If someone really has smashed up Prout's robin then he's got a right to kick up a fuss."

He stepped through the surrounding group, a stocky boy with untidy tow-colored hair, and looked down at Prout.

"Listen," he said, "was that the truth? Or were you making it all up? We can easily go down to the boot-hole and find out, you know."

Prout Major looked up at him. His face was totally tear-blotched and his sticking-out ears were redder than ever.

"It's the truth, Watson," he said. "It really is. My robin was all right when I fed it just after Dorm Four bedtime. And then when I went down to give it a bit of bacon rind I'd hidden under my bed this morning, I found it was dead—all smashed to pieces."

He lifted up his head like a dog to the moon and bayed in utter misery.

Abruptly the door behind them opened.

Outlined in the oblong of golden light from the corridor stood the portly, tweed-suited, sandy-haired Mr. Prys-Jones.

"What on earth is going on here?" he thundered.

There was a rapid scrambling of bare feet on polished linoleum and everybody was in bed, lying warily, blankets up to the nose.

"Please, sir," said Bainbridge, "I tried to stop them, sir."

Except for this, there was silence.

"I asked what was going on," Mr. Prys-Jones thundered again.

Still silence.

"One of you boys was making the most appalling noise," Mr. Prys Jones said. "It even disturbed me downstairs. I want to know who that boy was."

Everybody in the dormitory might have been asleep it was so still. Mr. Prys-Jones heaved a reverberant sigh.

"How often have I spoken to you boys about the importance of owning up in a straightforward, manly way?" Mr. Prys-Jones asked sadly.

He got no answer.

"If I've told you once, I've told you a hundred times," he went on with great weariness. "I had occasion to mention it to the whole school not a week ago. There was that disgraceful incident of the broken window in the pavilion. Someone must have kicked a football at it, but no one owned up. I do not know to this day who did that."

"And, sir," said Hennessy, lying flat still, "there was the person who broke my airplane, too, sir. You promised to ask who'd done that, but you never did."

"Be quiet, Hennessy," Mr. Prys-Jones snapped out, with a sudden change from sorrow to anger. "We are not talking about who happened to break what. We are talking about the fiendish din I heard emanating from this dormitory."

"Yes, sir."

"Did you make it, Hennessy?"

"No, sir."

Mr. Prys-Jones sighed and looked gloomily round. From under the blankets of Prout Major's bed there came a half-suppressed moan. Mr. Prys-Jones investigated.

"What's that? Who was making that peculiar sound?"

There was a moment's silence. It was broken by Watson.

"Please, sir," he said, "it's Prout Major, sir. Someone's gone and smashed up his robin. But nobody knows who, sir."

Three enormous strides took Mr. Prys-Jones over to Prout Major's bed. He bent his large pink-complexioned face toward the heap under the blankets to confirm that this indeed was the source of the trouble. Once sure of his facts, he jerked back the top sheet.

"Prout," he said, with a note of growing triumph, "was it you who was responsible for that appalling din just now?"

"Yes, sir," Prout wailed.

"I thought so," said Mr. Prys-Jones. "Then you can take two minus marks straight away, and there'll be another two for you if I catch you making one single sound more tonight. Understood?"

He flung back the sheet and marched over to the open door. At it he turned and addressed the now totally silent dormitory.

"There is one night in the week," he said, "when there happens to be a program on that appalling television which has some slight merit to it. Some of you may know what I am referring to. *World of Ballet.* Hennessy, you at least should be aware of it. Your own father frequently conducts the music for it, with all his customary passion and power. And all of you should know that I try, I *try,* to watch that one program. It isn't much to ask, once in a whole week. But what happens? I am interrupted by appalling misbehavior from the top dormitory. From the *top* dormitory."

He waited to let the full impact of his words sink in. And then, since he was in full spate, he went on.

"I do not approve of the television, as you well know. The standard of programs in general is simply abysmal. Abysmal! We have to have a Television Room because the parents seem to expect it. But that does not mean I condone. Except *World of Ballet.* And that is the very thing you boys have to go and ruin."

He turned on his heel, speechless with chagrin, and drew the door to sharply behind him.

In the darkness little Trilling ventured a comment.

"Honestly," he said, "Old Prissytoes is a bit too much. Everybody knows that program of his was over three-quarters of an hour ago."

"Sssh," said Bainbridge, in purest agony.

And soon enough they were all asleep, even Prout Major, washed out by grief. Only Watson lay awake a little longer than the others, working through the possibilities in the darkness.

IN THE HURLY-BURLY of the next morning—waking bell 7:15 A.M., getting-up bell 7:30, early gym 7:55, breakfast 8:15, bed-making 8:45—there was not a moment for anyone to mention what had happened. Even Prout Major, hurrying from washbasin to drill square, from breakfast to frenzied smoothing down of the uniform green cotton counterpane, had not an instant to think about his loss.

So it was not until a few minutes before the first period was due to begin for the top form—Saturday, 9:15–10:00, Divinity, Mr. Prys-Jones—that Watson put his first question.

Bainbridge and a few others were sitting and waiting, their books open. Most of the rest, like McWilliam who was busy opening a letter with a colorful Swiss stamp, were perched less conventionally on the lids of their desks ready to jump down at the last moment. Prout Major and Trilling were on the floor with their backs to the sole radiator which, with occasional internal gurglings, did little toward taking the edge off the cold air.

Watson stood in front of Prout.

"What time exactly did you feed your robin last night?" he said.

Prout, who had been despondently regarding his two bare knees, flushed sharply.

"Don't start blubbing now," Watson said. "I asked you something, and I want an answer."

Trilling, who had been deep in a science-fiction book, looked up.

"I say, Watsy, are you going to investigate the Case of the Murdered Robin?" he asked. "Because if so, actually you should let me. I mean, you're Watson, so I could be Sherlock Holmes."

"Come on, Prout," Watson said, taking no notice of Trilling, "just when did you feed it?"

Prout blinked. By day he wore a pair of spectacles with large lenses and a pinky-orange frame. They gave him a slightly owlish look.

"I already said," he answered. "I fed him just after the Dorm Four kids had gone up. If I go along to the boot-hole any earlier, one of them always gets in the way."

"You ought to let them help," Bainbridge said. "Everybody ought to take turns."

"I don't see why I should," Prout replied with unusual heat. "It's my robin. I found him when his leg was broken and I mended it with a matchstick splint and I—"

"You didn't mend it," Hennessy broke in scornfully. "You had to go and ask Mr. Jespe."

Prout Major pushed himself to his feet against the tepid radiator.

"I only had to go to him because he had some proper twine in the carpenter's shop," he said. "If it hadn't been for that, I'd have done everything myself."

Hennessy bounced down from his desk. "Are you cheeking me, Prout?" He doubled up his fists expectantly.

"No. No, Hennessy, honestly!" Prout was obviously terrified.

Watson pushed between them.

"Never mind all that," he said. "The point is: when you went and fed the bird at 6:15 it was all right, and you didn't see it again till you found it smashed up just after our lights-out. Is that right?"

It looked as if Prout Major was going to burst into tears again. But Watson went straight on.

"So the bird must have been killed between 6:15 and 7:30. Right?"

Trilling, who had tugged a notebook out of his bulging jacket pocket, turned to an empty page and began to write furiously.

"Yes, Watson," Prout said miserably.

"Well, nobody's going to break in here from outside at that time of the evening just to go to the boot-hole and kill a bird," Watson said.

There was general agreement.

"And last night was Friday," Watson went on. "And on Fridays Old Prissytoes lets all the other masters have an evening off."

"Quite right," Trilling said, scribbling hard. "They go to the pub, but they can't afford to get drunk because they're not paid enough. I heard them say so."

"So it must have been one of the boys," Watson said.

Again there was a general murmur of agreement.

"Listen," said Forshaw, "this is good. When we find out who did it, I vote we give him a top-form beating. Take him along to the gym, bend him over the horse, and everyone in the top form allowed to give him six of the best. Bags I go first!"

"Bags I last," said Trilling quickly. "When he's nice and tender."

There was an outburst of shouting as places on the torture line were rapidly claimed.

When it had subsided Watson looked at them calmly.

"You realize that the bird wasn't killed till after Dorm Four had gone up to bed," he said. "And from the time they go up till our lights-out, one of the prefects is on bell duty halfway up the stairs."

"Hey, yes," said Bainbridge, losing some of his dignity with excitement, "I was on bell duty last night. No one got past me."

Trilling looked up from his notebook.

"That means it must be someone from this form," he said. "One of us."

"That's precisely what I meant," Watson said. "And it's even fewer than that, if we can work it out, because I for one stayed in this room the whole time from when Prep ended till we went to the dorm. And others could have done the same thing."

"I was on bell duty," said Bainbridge hastily.

"All right," said Trilling from the floor, "you've got an alibi. And so's Watsy. But, hey, I haven't. I left the room and tried to get some of that potash of permanganate mouthwash from Matron to do a scientific experiment with."

"Make a list of those without alibis," Bainbridge directed.

Trilling was about to write when he looked up. "But listen," he said, "I *have* got an alibi. Matron's my alibi."

"All right," Watson said, "leave yourself off then. But I'll tell you two others I saw go out. Hennessy and Forshaw."

"I was with Mr. Prys-Jones," Hennessy said. "I took him my busted plane to mend. Only he never did it. Kept me in his study for half an hour, jawing away about my father conducting. And then in the end, when I asked about my plane for the fiftieth time, he just said he was too busy now."

"Old Prissytoes couldn't mend a flea anyhow," Trilling commented. "He's as clumsy as a herd of elephants. Look at the time Mr. Jespe was ill and he tried to take over Carpentry."

"The point is," said Bainbridge pontifically, "that Hennessy's plane is still out of action. So Prout Major still holds the record."

"Honestly, Bainbridge, you're a nit," Trilling said. "Don't you know that craze has been over for days? It's Treasure Island maps now. Or at least it was. From here on it's Sherlock Holmes Investigates."

"Anyhow, Prout Major's plane shouldn't count," McWilliam put in. "He only got it because his parents buy him anything he asks for. Hennessy made his right from scratch."

"Nobody ever said anything about it having to be a do-it-yourself—" Prout Major began.

Watson cut him short. "We happen to be working out who smashed your robin."

The reminder silenced Prout, and Watson turned to Trilling. "Cross

Hennessy off the list."

Trilling began to scrawl out Hennessy's name. But suddenly he stopped.

"Listen," he said, "alibis like that ought to be checked. Someone should check mine with Matron, and I'll check Hennessy's with Old Prissytoes."

"A fat lot of sense you'll get out of him," Watson said. "But what I want to know is: Where were you, Forshaw?"

Forshaw looked from side to side.

"I went out to the Pavvy," he said. "I left my goalie's gloves there after football."

"Can you prove that?" Trilling asked sharply.

"Of course I can't. But I'm not the only one who went out. McWilliam did for another."

"I just went to the dub," McWilliam said.

Sitting up on his desk, his thin face looking as usual darkly sullen above the frayed collar of his regulation gray shirt, McWilliam glared hard at little Trilling.

"And I can't prove that either," he said. "How could I, up in the dub behind a closed door?"

Trilling wrote down his name.

"Anybody else go out?" Watson asked.

No one admitted it. And no one accused anybody else of lying.

"All right," Watson said, glancing at Trilling's list, "that means it's either Forshaw or McWilliam. We'll just have to try and find out which."

"No, you won't," Prout Major said loudly, as if determined not to be ignored. "It's obvious which of them did it. It was Forshaw."

Forshaw's face, with its large, ill-formed nose and heavy jaw, went suddenly red with rage. He charged toward Prout Major, outstretched fingers reaching for his throat.

Watson jumped between them.

Forshaw stopped. He glared at Watson as if he were ready to fight his way to Prout against any odds. Then he stepped back.

"All right, Prout," Watson said. "Go ahead. Explain."

"Well, look at him," Prout began, a little less sure of himself now. "He's always been as cruel as anything. Think of the way he bullies the juniors whenever he can get his hands on one."

"He bullies you too, Prouty," Trilling said. "Don't pretend it's only juniors."

Prout contrived to ignore this.

247

"And what about last week's Nature Ramble?" he said. "When Forshaw hid from Mr. Prys-Jones behind a bush and pulled the legs off a live frog?"

"Made you look pretty green round the gills," Forshaw said.

"And now you've killed my robin," Prout Major shouted. "You dirty swine!"

Unexpectedly Forshaw did not attempt to punish Prout for the insult. He simply turned away.

"It so happens I didn't kill your stupid bird," he said.

"You did! I know it must have been—"

Prout Major's voice gave out abruptly as the door opened and Mr. Prys-Jones came in with a smiling morning-face.

"Come, boys, to your places, to your places," he said cheerfully. "No time to waste today."

As they all moved slowly to their desks Forshaw murmured one further comment.

"I didn't do it," he said. "But I know who did. And it's someone Watson never thought of."

"Silence," thundered Mr. Prys-Jones.

He turned to the blackboard and vigorously cleaned it with a wooden-backed eraser.

Watson leaned back from his desk toward Forshaw's.

"I bet I'm right and you're wrong," he whispered. "There can't be anybody else without an alibi."

BUT AT BREAK THAT morning young detective Watson was proved wrong. It happened when almost all the top form were crowded into the dub—the school lavatories, tiled and echoing, perpetually smelling of harsh disinfectant. It was Watson's first chance to tackle Forshaw.

"All right," he said, "you think I'm wrong about you and McWilliam being the only ones who could have killed the bird. Prove it."

Forshaw turned to him. Behind them the automatic flush of the urinals squirted loudly.

"Everybody except the top form was in bed at the time the bird was smashed," he said. "And according to you, Bainbridge being on bell duty means no one could have got to the boot-hole unseen. But what you've forgotten is that the beds upstairs aren't the only ones in the school."

After a moment Watson saw it.

"The Sanny," he said. "I forgot the Sanny. And it's only just along the corridor from the boot-hole."

"And who happens to be in the Sanny?" Forshaw asked contemptuously.

"Prout Minor," Watson said.

"If you must play detective," said Forshaw, "you ought to be good at it."

"What do you mean?" Watson said, flushing.

"Just that Prout Minor's in the Sanny because he's got a stinking cold. And he got that because Prout Major held the door to the playing field shut against him when it rained like that on Wednesday. He made him wait outside till he got soaked to the skin for cheeking him. So don't tell me Prout Minor didn't have good reason to smash his brother's stupid bird."

Watson took the setback well.

"All right," he said, "I daresay it was him. But we can't be sure till he's been questioned."

"Then go and question him," Forshaw grinned. "Only don't let Matron catch you in the Sanny. Remember she reported Fitzherbert for being there once, and he got six lashes."

Watson looked at him steadily.

"I'm going there now," he said. "Who's going to come with me to make sure I'm not making it up?"

Bainbridge found it his duty to intervene.

"Listen, Watsy," he said, "this is the worst time of all to go. It's the same time Fitzherbert was caught. They'll be bound to want to know why I didn't stop you."

"Who's coming?" Watson said.

"I will," said Trilling. "But I'll tell you who else ought to come."

"Who?" Forshaw asked. "Not me. I'm not going to get six of the best for nothing."

"No," said Trilling, "it ought to be Prout Major. It's what's called a confrontation."

"Hey, no," Prout Major burst out. "Why should I? It's unfair. I won't go. Why should I risk getting the cane just over a little stinker like Prout Minor?"

"You didn't mind risking being caught out of bed for your robin," Watson said. "Well, your brother probably killed your robin. And if we find out he did, he'll get it all right when he comes out of the Sanny."

Prout Major went.

The Sanatorium, dignified as such in the school prospectus, was simply an isolated room reached by a short corridor running alongside the boot-hole. Since this corridor led nowhere else, there was no excuse for anyone caught there on his way to the forbidden sanatorium.

The setup constituted as nice a trap as the most remorseless hunter could wish.

At the corner near the boot-hole, Watson, Trilling, and Prout Major stood listening. Their rear was guarded by boys stationed at either end of the Long Corridor ready to whistle if anyone came along. But there was no way of telling whether Matron was already in the Sanny.

"I can't hear her talking or anything," Watson said at last. "We'll have to risk it. Come on."

Pushing Prout Major on ahead, he set out on tiptoe. In no time at all, it seemed, they had reached the Sanny door, white and shut. Watson stooped and peered through the keyhole.

"Can't see a thing," he whispered.

They looked at each other.

"Only one thing for it," Watson said.

He took hold of the doorknob and jerked it round.

The Sanny was empty, except for Prout Minor lying in the farthest of the four beds. Watson hauled the others in and quickly closed the door.

"Hey," said Prout Minor loudly, "no one's allowed in here."

Watson crossed over to the bed and thrust his face close to Prout Minor's.

"Keep quiet," he said, "or it'll be the worse for you."

Prout Minor backed away toward the top of the big white-counterpaned bed. He looked not unlike his brother, except that his nose was smaller and sharper and his ears stood out, if possible, even farther. His eyes were wide with fear.

"Now," Watson said, "we've come to find out one thing from you. Did you leave this room yesterday evening? At any time, for any reason at all?"

Prout Minor's face closed up in instant calculation.

"Answer," Watson demanded.

He reached forward and seized Prout Minor's hand as it lay on the top sheet. Holding it hard, he jerked back the middle finger sharply.

"All right, all right," Prout Minor squealed. "I was only thinking."

"Well, did you go out of here? Come on—quickly!"

"No. No, Watson, honest. I never left for a single moment. Cross my heart."

Watson looked at the others.

"That doesn't prove anything either way then," he said. "So we've got three without alibis—Prout Minor here, McWilliam, and Forshaw."

"Except for one thing," Trilling said.

He jumped up on the bed and spoke into Prout Minor's ear.

"How was it I happened to see you out there in the corridor then?" he said.

Prout Minor gave a quick gasp of fright.

"I—I'm sorry. Yes. Yes, I was there. I forgot."

Trilling looked over at Watson with a smile of satisfaction.

"You're a fool, Prout Minor," he said. "I was only bluffing, and now I've caught you. You went out and smashed up your brother's robin, didn't you? Come on, tell us before we really start hurting you."

"No, no. It wasn't that. I went to the dub. That was it. Honest!"

"Don't lie," Watson said. "We've had enough of your lies already. You're meant to use the pot when you're in the Sanny. Everybody knows that."

Prout Minor swallowed and looked from side to side as if some miraculous way of escape must open up.

"Please," he said, "it's really true. I know you have to use the pot here. But I hate doing it. So I just sneaked along to the dub for a moment. I swear that was all—I swear!"

Without another word Watson got to work on Prout's Minor's middle finger. His victim writhed under the bedclothes and tears came into his eyes. But there was too little time.

"It'll be the end of Break in a few seconds," Trilling said urgently. "If we don't get back to the form room, someone will come looking for us."

Watson let Prout Minor's hand go. He went over to the door and listened.

"They're making such a row out in the Long Corridor we'd never hear if Matron was right outside," he said.

Prout Major gave his brother a look of pure malevolence, as if he would like to pay him well for getting him into this jam. Prout Minor glared back spitefully.

"I'm glad someone did smash your bird," he said. "Serves you right for making me catch my cold."

"Shut up," Watson whispered from the door.

"And I think I know who did it," Prout Minor went on.

They wheeled round.

"Who was it?" Watson said. "Quick, or I'll punch you in the face."

He ran back to the bed and held his clenched fist under Prout Minor's pointed little nose.

"I bet it was McWilliam then," Prout Minor shot out. "He's always been jealous of us two, just because our parents are rich and his father's only a village clergyman."

At that moment the bell pealed out.

"Come on!" Watson said.

He darted over and opened the door. The corridor in front of them was clear. They ran.

On the way to the dining room at the end of the morning classes Watson contrived to lag behind. Just ahead of him was McWilliam. For a little while Watson contented himself with walking a yard or two behind. Then just before they got to the dining room he caught hold of his arm.

"Just a sec, McWilliam," he said. "There's something I want to know."

McWilliam turned his dark, narrow face toward him.

"What?"

"Just what were you really doing yesterday evening when you said you were going to the dub?"

For a moment McWilliam stared at him with a look of black fury. Then he answered. "All right, if you must know. I was doing something else. But I'm not going to tell you, or anyone else, what it was. Not so long as I live."

"It's McWilliam," Watson said.

They were changing for football that afternoon. The top formers in their corner of the Changing Room, with its rows of back-to-back lockers, stopped tugging at long colored stockings and turned as one to stare at McWilliam.

He stared back at them, his football clothes much more faded than anyone else's.

"I did not kill Prout's robin," he said.

"All right then," said Watson, "what was it you were doing when you left the form room yesterday?"

"I won't tell you or anyone."

Forshaw went over to him, licking his lips a little, and looking unpleasantly excited.

"How are you going to like getting a top-form beating tonight, McWilliam?" he said.

McWilliam made no reply. It was plain that thoughts were churning in his narrow head behind the two dark brown, fiercely glowing eyes.

Bainbridge, who was ready to go out onto the field, hopped up and down anxiously.

"I say," he called out, "it's time to begin. There'll be an awful row if we don't go now."

"No, just a tick," Trilling said. "Wait everybody."

He looked up from a fantastically tangled knot in the laces of his left boot.

"McWilliam may be in the clear after all. I've just had a theory."

"You'll have more than a theory in a moment, young Trilling."

It was Mr. Jespe, all hearty bounce. In the excitement he had come up completely unnoticed.

"And you, Hennessy," he boomed cheerfully on. "You're independent enough when anybody wants to help with your model airplane. Let's see a bit of independence about getting yourself out of here double quick."

There was a flurry of silent activity as indoor clothes were jammed onto hooks and last knots tied in heavy little boots. Then everyone rushed out.

"Oh, Mr. Jespe, sir," wailed little Trilling, still sitting at his locker. "I can't get this beastly knot undone, sir."

Mr. Jespe, for all his good cheer, did not possess a steady temperament: The standard of football that afternoon disappointed him, and in simple consequence there was no boisterous harrying of his charges back into their indoor clothes afterward. When Mr. Jespe was disappointed in anything, whether it was the standard of play on the football field or young Hennessy's unwillingness to be helped with his model airplane, he plainly sulked.

And so there was plenty of opportunity for Watson to continue his detective investigation.

"All right, Trilling," he said, "what's this theory of yours?"

Trilling heaved off his right boot without undoing the laces.

"It's just a matter of scientific deduction," he said.

"Come on, Trilling," Hennessy said. "Cough up, or I'll give you a hack on the shins you won't forget in a hurry."

"All right, all right. It's just that there's someone we thought had an alibi who hasn't really got one at all."

"You helped to make the list," Watson said.

"Yes, I know. I took his word for it, too."

"Whose word?"

"Bainbridge's. He kept on about his being on bell duty all the time. But there was nothing to stop *him* sneaking down as soon as he'd rung one bell, smashing the robin, then sneaking back again."

"There you are," McWilliam said loudly. "You see, I'm not the only one."

"All right, Trilling," Watson broke in, "I've got to admit it shows there still may be loopholes. So I tell you what: We'll have a proper trial and sort it out that way. We'll have it in the gym, straight after tea. And if we find McWilliam guilty in the end, then he can have the top-form beating there and then on the spot."

There was a stir of excitement. The idea appealed to their savage instincts.

As soon as tea was over, taking advantage of there being no Prep on Saturdays, they all made their way to the gym and set about arranging it to their satisfaction. The dangling ropes were tied together in heavy swaths and fixed to the ribstalls out of the way. The padded-top box was dragged to one corner to make a dock. The long low benches with flapping leather-covered hooks at the ends were ranged neatly opposite as seats for the jury. A thick coconut mat was hauled to the middle of the closely boarded floor as a prosecutor's stand. The beams were lowered to a convenient height and turned on their sides to make an imposing, if precarious, judge's seat. And finally, with a certain air of ceremony, the horse, over which in happier times they vaulted one by one, was placed at the far end of the big room where it could be seen clearly by everybody—the place of execution.

At last they were ready.

"Bainbridge," Watson said, "go and sit in the judge's place."

"Hey," Trilling objected loudly. "He can't be the judge. He's one of the suspects."

"Is he?" said Watson. "Do you really think Bainbridge did it? Can any of you see him smashing up a bird? He's just too soft."

No one attempted to deny it. Bainbridge clambered up to the judge's seat in silence.

Watson went to the prosecutor's mat. McWilliam placed himself sulkily in the dock. The others, even down to Prout Minor who had been allowed up "after tea," went to the benches. There was a sudden silence. They looked at each other uneasily.

"Come on, Bainbridge," Trilling said at last. "At least you ought to start it off."

Bainbridge drew himself up on the high seat and colored a little.

"The court is open," he pronounced. "Watson will begin."

"I accuse McWilliam," Watson said promptly.

Trilling clapped.

"Shut up, Trilling," Bainbridge said. "This is serious."

For once he was listened to.

"It still looks to me," Watson went on, "that McWilliam must be the most likely culprit. There's only three people who haven't got alibis, if you don't count Bainbridge. There's Prout Minor, Forshaw, and McWilliam. Well, McWilliam's the only one who won't say what he was doing at the time the bird was killed. And he's jealous."

He looked steadily at the dark figure of McWilliam behind the padded leather top of the dock. McWilliam did not move a muscle.

"Everyone knows how poor his parents are," Watson resumed. "Look at those awful pajamas he wears with the top and bottom halves different. And then there's his overcoat that comes miles up above the knees. And look at the way he only gives sixpence to the war victims on Poppy Day when everybody else gives at least two shillings. He's just too poor, and Prout's stinking with money. That's why McWilliam tried to get even with him. That's his motive."

He kept his eyes fixed on the target of his accusation. But still McWilliam did not show the least sign of having heard. From the jury benches little Trilling stood up.

"That's all very well," he said, "but McWilliam might just as well smash something belonging to almost anybody. He's jealous of us all. Everyone knows that. It still looks to me as if Prout Minor's just as likely as him."

Prout Minor, crouching inconspicuously at the back of the jury benches and occasionally sniffing loudly, gave a longing glance at the two swing doors of the gym.

"No," said Watson, "you've forgotten McWilliam's birthday cake."

"You mean that rotten old thing made by his mother with only one layer of icing?" Hennessy said.

"Yes, that's exactly it," said Watson. "And only about a fortnight before it was Prout Major's birthday, and he had a specially made cake with a complete rocket-launching base on it."

"And the rocket really fired," said Prout Major.

"Exactly," Watson said. "And everyone knows that the one thing in the world that really meant a lot to you was your robin. Saving it was the only decent thing you've ever done. So naturally that's what McWilliam chose to pay you out with. It's just the mean sort of thing you'd expect from him."

"It isn't! It isn't!"

McWilliam had broken.

He leaned forward and banged the leather top of the box with his clenched fists.

"All right," he shouted, "I was doing something secret when I left the form room. But it *wasn't* killing Prout's robin. I was hiding in the dub for a long time because I was doing something I didn't want anybody else to know about."

"That's not good enough," Watson said. "It doesn't prove a thing. What were you doing?"

"I was sticking a Swiss stamp on a letter I'd got from home," McWilliam said in a voice that could hardly be heard. "It came by the last post yesterday and I hid it and changed the stamp. Then I slipped it into the pile at breakfast today. I wanted it to look as though my parents had gone skiing like everybody else's."

Watson stood considering for a moment.

"All right," he said, "that clears you, McWilliam."

McWilliam did not move from the place of arraignment. For some time no one spoke, though the juniors whispered among themselves. Then McWilliam produced his contribution.

"I suppose I can say it now," he began. "But I've got proof that one of the others without an alibi is a liar. And that's Prout Minor. I was in the dub for hours at that time and no one else came in. You know at once if they do because the door squeaks. So if Prout Minor says he left the Sanny to go to the dub, he's lying!"

"Prout Minor," Bainbridge said from his high seat, "go and take McWilliam's place."

Prout Minor got up and looked round in panic. Slowly, as if he almost lacked the force to walk at all, he began to make his way round the jury benches and toward the dock. Forshaw, sitting in the front row, adroitly kicked him on the ankle.

And he was off. He swung round, put his head down, aimed for the double swing doors, and bolted. He crashed through the doors, leaving them wildly flapping, before anyone could stop him, and darted through the narrow passageway between the ranks of lockers in the Changing Room beyond. But at the far end there were no swing doors. Prout Minor seized the dull brass knob of the single door leading into the Long Corridor, with its half promise of safety, and twisted.

His sweaty little palms revolved on the smooth surface of the knob. Forshaw, first of the hunting pack, pushed a large hand down his collar at the back and twisted.

They lugged him back and shoved him behind the dock.

Bainbridge climbed up to his seat again and heaved himself round to face the body of the court.

"Prout Minor," he said, "have you anything to say before I pass sentence?"

It was at this point that the double swing doors opened again and Mr. Prys-Jones sailed in.

"There's been a terrible amount of noise," he said. "Just what are you boys up to?"

He looked from one to the other, his gaze finally resting on Bainbridge perched on the high beams. Bainbridge looked confused.

Suddenly from the jury benches Trilling bounced up.

"Please, sir, it's a debate, sir," he said. "A sort of debate. You told us about them the other day, sir. And how you used to do so well at the Union of Oxford, sir."

Mr. Prys-Jones laughed tolerantly.

"The Oxford Union, Trilling, the Oxford Union," he corrected him. "Though actually Wadham College Debating Society was more my happy hunting ground up at Oxford."

He looked round with reminiscent pleasure.

"Well, carry on, carry on," he said. "Don't let me interrupt."

And a moment later the double doors swung closed behind him.

"All right, Prout Minor," Bainbridge said. "Now let's hear what you've got to say."

Behind the leather-topped box, quite certainly a dock again, Prout Minor's face went a harsh red from forehead to neck.

"Please, Bainbridge," he said, "it's true what McWilliam told everybody. I never did go to the dub."

"But you did leave the Sanny," Trilling broke in. "I proved that."

"I know," said Prout Minor, beginning to wail. "Matron sent me out. She caught me penciling on the sheets and she made me go up to her room and stand in the corner like a beastly kid."

Even in his present situation the humiliation he had felt the evening before made his voice rise with a sense of intolerable injury. It was totally plain that he was now telling the truth.

"Well," said Trilling, a little uncertainly, "I think Forshaw should go behind the box now."

"No."

It was the unexpected voice of Hennessy, sitting straight and self-contained on the front jury bench.

"No," he repeated, "it's all very well for Trilling and Watson to go putting person after person up like that. But there's someone who ought to be behind the box who's never even been mentioned tonight."

He spoke with quiet confidence. There was a stir among the juniors behind him.

"Well, who is it?" Bainbridge asked. "If you can solve the mystery, Hennessy, you ought to speak up."

"I will," said Hennessy. "It's one of the great detectives themselves. Trilling."

Trilling stiffened.

"Go to the box," Bainbridge said.

Slowly Trilling stood up and walked over.

"It's all very well," he muttered, "But everyone knows I had an alibi. I was with Matron. Watson checked on it."

For a moment it seemed that the quiet Hennessy's hold was loosening. But he stood up without fuss.

"Yes," he said, "Watson checked. And who are just about the best friends in the whole school right now? Watson and Trilling, the pair of detectives."

Watson, still on the prosecutor's mat, was goaded to action.

"You shut up, Hennessy," he said, moving menacingly.

"It's the truth, isn't it?" Hennessy challenged him.

"I may happen to be friends with Trilling," Watson retorted, "but I said I was going to find out who killed Prout's bird, and however much of a friend Trilling is, if he did it I wouldn't do a thing to stop his getting the top-form beating. And you needn't try to make out I would. Whoever did it deserves everything they get."

"All right then," said Hennessy, "let someone else go and check up with Matron."

"That's all very well," Trilling objected, with a show of great reasonableness, "but if people keep going up to Matron and asking her about me, she's going to get ratty and refuse to answer."

"Just what you hope will save your bacon, Trilling," Hennessy said.

"I don't care if—"

But Watson interrupted.

"No, wait a minute, everyone," he said. "I've got it now. And I can prove it completely. It was just this that gave me the solution."

Nobody made the least sound.

"It was what Hennessy said about not being able to get an alibi out of Matron," Watson went on. "I suddenly remembered that someone else had an alibi like that. If it's no use going to Matron to check, it's even less use going to Old Prissytoes. And Old Prissytoes is *your* alibi, Hennessy."

"All right," Hennessy answered.

"And I was with him all the time in his study trying to get my airplane mended."

"Don't give me that," Watson said. "You know quite well, Hennessy, you'd never have gone to Prissytoes for help in a million years. He's as clumsy as a bear. And you wouldn't even let Mr. Jespe help you make your plane in the first place. You're too proud. You're just like your father standing up in front of a whole orchestra making them do what *he* wants."

"And if I say I did go to Mr. Prys-Jones all the same?"

"Then you're a stinking liar," said Watson. "You didn't go near Prissytoes, because Prissytoes wasn't in his study as usual last night. He was in the Television Room watching *World of Ballet*. We've got you, Hennessy."

Hennessy stood his ground, chin jutting forward, eyes blazing.

"All right," he said, "I did smash Prout's robin. I did it because he deserved it. He was the one who smashed my airplane. He wanted to get the record back and he smashed my plane to do it. He deserved to have something of his smashed, and something better than his plane, too."

"Oh, no, he didn't," Watson replied. "Even if he had smashed your plane, all he deserved was to have his own smashed. But he didn't smash your plane."

"Oh, didn't he? Well, who did? If you're so clever."

"Old Prissytoes did in his typical clumsy way," Watson said. "It's obvious. Look at how he suddenly stopped when he was jawing in the dorm last night about owning up. He remembered he'd never owned up to you. Any fool could see that."

They came forward and caught hold of Hennessy. They dragged him up the length of the big gym to the waiting horse. Eagerly they held him down. And then they gave him the top-form beating.

BEYOND THE GREEN BAIZE door in Mr. Prys-Jones's living room the cheerful coal fire hissed and sputtered. From her industrious darning of yet another gray sock, the property of little Trilling, Mrs. Prys-Jones looked up.

"What was that the boys were saying this afternoon about Prout Major's robin being killed or something?" she asked.

Mrs. Prys-Jones took a close interest in all the affairs of the school.

Mr. Prys-Jones held his fine-stemmed sherry glass between himself and the fire and looked at the effect of the warm glow on the delicate color of the wine.

"Oh, the wretched bird just died," he said. "It was bound to, you know. I told the boy so at the time he rescued it. It was simply a matter of natural causes, mere natural causes."

# Medford & Son

DICK LOCHTE

## Dick Lochte's Introduction:

*Ellery Queen's Mystery Magazine likes to keep a running total of the number of "first stories" it has introduced over the years. "Medford & Son," which appeared in the October 1972 issue, was number 373. It was not the first story I'd written. A few years before, while still in college, I'd tried my hand at a couple of hardboiled tales that I submitted to a publication specializing in that type of story, Manhunt. Even though they were returned with a handwritten note from the editor explaining why they'd been rejected and asking to see more, my enthusiasm to become a published writer had given way to the panic accompanying graduation and the looming military draft.*

*It was not until I'd served my Coast Guard tour of duty, kicked around at a few entry-level jobs, and was happily ensconced in the promotion department of Playboy magazine in Chicago that the idea for "Medford" popped into my head. It's the only time, before or since, that a story has arrived unbidden and complete. Those days, I was doing a fair amount of moonlighting at the keys—writing nonfiction for assorted publications including Playboy and pecking away at a semi-autobiographical Great American Novel. But crime fiction wasn't even causing a tiny blip on my to-do radar.*

*Sitting in my apartment that night, watching the news around a plate of pasta (I know what the meal was because it's the only food I ever cooked in what I now refer to as My Bachelor Era), I learned that the yuppie rebels who'd gone on trial for their activities during the Democratic Convention of '68 had been acquitted of conspiracy charges, but some of them were being thrown in the slams for crossing a state line to foment a riot. Having experienced that period of turmoil on a personal level, I was of a mixed mind on the subject. On one hand, I and a friend, the author Robert Coover, while strolling to an Old Town bar, had been treated to tear gas and shoved into an alley by overzealous, baton-wielding cops. On the other, I'd watched a group of Abbie Hoffman wannabes strolling down Elm Street gleefully applying ball peen hammers to automobile windshields, mine included.*

Dick Lochte

*Along with those golden memories, the story suddenly appeared. I didn't put it on paper until a while later. I'm not sure why. Laziness, probably. The typing took less than two hours: spirit-writing, though the identity of the spirit is anybody's guess. I didn't think it was my best work or even that it was all that spectacular a yarn, but it seemed exactly right for the time. I sent it cold to EQMM.*

*I don't remember any more details, such as how many weeks passed before I received notification that they wanted to buy it or if they requested any changes or even how much they wound up paying me. I just remember the thrill of realizing I was suddenly a professional mystery writer, a player in what Ellery Queen liked to call "the grandest game in the world."*

264

# Medford & Son

## DICK LOCHTE

MEDFORD STOOD BEFORE THE desk sergeant, shifting his body nervously, painfully aware of the glances being cast his way by curious cops walking to and from the lockup. It was nearly 7:00 P.M., the end of an imperfect day, appropriately capped off by a report on the TV evening news that his son, Jerry, had been arrested in connection with the bombing of a suburban bank. There had been no phone call from Jerry, just an impersonal broadcaster sharing a news item with two million viewers in the greater metropolitan area.

When the boy appeared, in the company of Steiner, Medford's lawyer, he was barely recognizable. Medford was sure he'd seen his son only a few weeks before. Or had it been a month? In either case, it did not seem possible that Jerry could have let himself go to such a degree in so short a time. His faded and rumpled clothes had been patched by a crude hand. His wiry hair and beard looked like the aftereffects of an electric shock. His eyes, so full of wonder in youth, were now dark and suspicious and sunk deep in a face as gray and immobile as cement. Medford had to look away.

Steiner arranged for bail and, after chastising the boy in a cool and rational manner, left them standing there, father and son, beside Medford's sedan. "If you want to see your mother," Medford said, "I can give you a lift. You'll have to cab it back."

"Why not?" the boy said. "Thanks to your lawyer man's silver tongue, I'm free for the evening."

THE RIDE WAS A particularly difficult one for Medford. He was struggling with a problem that had no solution. The boy mistakenly took his silence as a rebuke. "Well, don't hold back," he said. "I'm a criminal. A disgrace to the family. I heard it all from the lawyer. Might as well hear it from you."

His father had not been expecting a request for conversation. It took a few moments for him to put his mind to it. "I can't even think of you in terms of family anymore," he told the boy. "Everything I've done . . . All I've worked for . . . has been with the hope that one day you'd come into the bond business with me. My God, I used to dream about it. I envisioned a bronze plaque: 'Medford & Son Investments.' Then you dropped out of college and moved in with those long-haired, unwashed drug—"

"Patriots."

"If you say so. Anyway, that's when I gave up my dream."

"Good. You faced up to reality."

"It's time you tried a little of that. You could have killed somebody."

The boy took out a cigarette and lit it with a wooden match that he carelessly dropped to the car's spotless mat. "Since when do people like you care about a little murder or two?"

"What the devil are you talking about, people like me?"

"You know what's going on in the world. The Great God Stock Market rises and falls in direct ratio to the number of deaths in Vietnam. You feed bodies into the war machine, pull the lever, and out pours money."

Medford wearily entered the argument. "That's utter nonsense, Jerry, and you know it."

"I only know what I can see and what I can feel."

"Then you're looking at and feeling the wrong things."

The boy jerked around at him. "Wow, that's smug. You've got yours and the hell with everybody else. Just hang onto that fat bankbook and the sweet, undemanding wife in your vine-covered little mansion in the suburbs."

Medford continued to stare at the road. "It is an idyllic life," he said dryly, "but every now and then something comes along to screw things up."

"Meaning me?"

"Of course, meaning you."

They drove in silence for a while before Medford added, "When you first became involved with those . . . people, burning flags, picketing, was there anything I could have done . . .?"

"To make me see the light? Not likely. But take another shot at it, if you want."

"It's too late. Blowing up a bank. You simplistic young idiot, you've no idea . . ." Medford couldn't finish the thought.

"Forgive me for disturbing your complacent existence, *father*."

"Disturb? Why, boy, you've destroyed it."

"My pleasure," Jerry said nastily.

"Where's all that hostility come from?"

"The condition of life in these United States. Fascist pigs, hypocritical politicians, poisoned air . . . aw, hell, why keep this up?"

"So now, at twenty, you have a police record and the dubious distinction of an impending FBI investigation. But these, in some strange way, will aid man in his quest for a perfect society?"

"Don't try to mess with my head," the boy almost shouted. "Didn't it ever occur to you that things are all screwed up in this country? Haven't you ever wanted to step out of line to make it better?"

"By bombing a bank?"

"By doing *anything*."

"I happen to like the way things are. Correction, make that *were*."

"Didn't you ever believe in something enough to want to defend that belief at any cost?"

When Medford didn't answer the boy slumped back against the leather seat. As the sedan turned onto the blue-gravel drive leading to his home, Medford couldn't help saying, "You've blown it for all of us, Jerry."

"Don't lay that on me. This is my problem, not yours. You and Mom—well, all your cronies at the country club will be properly sympathetic. You'll be like a couple of martyrs—the noble parents whose son went radical freak in spite of all their good efforts."

Jerry's frustration had been building. Suddenly it burst. "This is senseless!" he shouted, jerking open the door of the still-moving car. Medford jammed his foot on the brakes.

"Medford & Son?" Jerry said as he hopped out. "Man, I don't even see how we could have the same blood in our veins."

The boy angrily slammed the car door and ran toward the house. Medford looked after him, trying to remember what it had been like when he was that young.

When Jerry decided not to stay for dinner, Medford felt a sense of relief. He had business to take care of. But first he wanted to spend some time with his wife, to do whatever he could to lift her spirits.

After a slow, almost silent, dinner he sent her to bed with the promise that he would straighten things out. It was a lie, but he felt her owed her at least one more night of hope.

He waited until he heard the bedroom door click shut, then moved to the study. He frowned at the open French doors leading to the patio. Then he saw the plump, balding man at the far end of the room, standing beside his treasured wall of books.

"Some kid you've got," the plump man said in a husky, not unpleasant voice. "A bomber, boy-oh-boy."

"They reach an age when you lose whatever hold you've ever had on them," Medford said.

"I wouldn't know about that," the plump man replied. "I really am sorry."

"So am I," Medford sighed.

His visitor used one gray-gloved finger to brush a speck of dust from a leather-bound volume. "We've worked together for how long? Twenty-five years?"

"Close to twenty-six."

"A long time," the plump man repeated, turning to face his friend. "You got the papers ready?"

"I wasn't expecting you so soon," Medford said. "But they're in order." He crossed the room to a large framed splash of color on the wall and pushed it aside, exposing a small safe. He dialed it open, but before he could reach inside, his visitor pushed him back and removed the pistol that rested just beyond the door.

Medford was amused by the man's caution. "You needn't worry," he said.

"Who's worried?" the plump man said, hefting the weapon.

Medford carefully withdrew a folder containing Photostats and other documents from the safe.

The plump man accepted the folder. "This all?" he asked.

Medford nodded. "Not much for twenty-six years."

"They told me to move quick on this, old friend. A man with too much time to think sometimes does something foolish." Medford wasn't certain which one of them the plump man was talking about.

"Too bad that wild-haired kid of yours had to bring the FBI to your door. The way it works, one thing leads to another. They check him out, they check you out, discover that the real Medford died in the war. Before you know it, all our covers are blown. It has to end with you, friend. They gave me the option of ending it with your kid, but I didn't think you'd go for that."

"You leave him alone."

"That's why I'm here." He flipped through the folder, then gestured with it to an antique desk across the room. "That's where you do your homework, eh? Sit. Take the weight off."

Medford obeyed. The plump man followed. "I'm to make it look like suicide. They'll figure you were despondent over your boy's . . . problems."

"Jerry's got enough hang-ups without having to feel guilty about my death."

"Sorry, but it's how they want it. We follow their decisions. That's the way it works."

"Yes, it is." Medford's neck hurt from twisting it to keep looking up at the man standing at his side. He slumped in the chair and settled for a view of his clean desktop. "They don't seem to matter much any more," he said, "the reasons I volunteered for the mission to come to this country. All so long ago."

"Now we just do as we're told," the plump man said with a wistful sigh. "Personal convictions, who needs 'em? But there was a time, right? We may not have blown up any banks, but all the same we made 'em sit up and take notice."

"That we did."

"It's weird the way life works, isn't it? If your kid hadn't been such a chip off the old block, I wouldn't have to be here tonight."

Medford was amazed. Why hadn't the thought occurred to him before? A chip off the old block. He was immediately lost in a new version of his old fantasy. This time the bronze plaque read "Medford & Son Revolutions."

As he felt the cold barrel of his own gun being pressed against his temple, he was happier than he'd been in years.

# Thieves' Honor

## JOHN LUTZ

## John Lutz's Introduction:

*I was one of those writers who had collected enough rejection slips to stuff a pillow before I finally sold a piece of fiction. So it was with pride, relief, triumph, and amazement when in 1966 I read the contract that arrived in the mail along with a letter informing me that* Alfred Hitchcock's Mystery Magazine *wanted to buy "Thieves' Honor" and was offering a check that could be converted to genuine U.S. currency. Along with the form letter was a brief handwritten note of congratulations from editor Victoria Benham. Victoria had taken a genuine interest in my work and had been writing incisive and encouraging notes on rejection slips for quite a while. For this I am still grateful. Her note said something to the effect that she'd known all along that I could do it.*

*Immediately after this first sale, I doubted for the first time that I'd known it all along. How much had I been psyching myself into thinking I was a good enough writer to be published regularly as a professional? It seemed to me then, as now, that one of the important things to learn in life is how to convince yourself you can't fail at something, then not wear a hair shirt for more than a short while if you fail. I also decided I had a right to feel pride and a sense of accomplishment. It isn't easy breaking into print in a national magazine. I'd thought it was an important thing to do when I set out to do it, and I still thought so. And still think so.*

*After displacing my elbow patting myself on the back, I sat down and tried to figure out what I'd done right. I wanted to do this again. No need to go into the technical stuff here, but I carefully analyzed the story. When I was finished, I'd decided that this was a pretty good short story, but maybe not the best I'd written. "Thieves' Honor" sold, I believe, mainly because I'd taken a contrarian view of a standard piece of writing advice: Carefully study what a magazine publishes before you submit an article or short story to it.*

*But wouldn't this ensure that my story would be too much like everyone else's who'd studied the magazine? Formula is nice in many ways, not the least of which is that it helps to provide a living when you suffer a dearth of ideas. But it* can also be a trap. The thing to do, I'd decided, was to read a publication and try to determine what it didn't publish. What were its taboos?

Every magazine has these forbidden areas that will kill the deal, often reflecting the tastes, fears, and personality of the editor or publisher. Decide what not to write about, then let 'er rip! The important thing is that the editor, if he or she likes the story generally, will then find no reason to reject it. No overt violence or political or religious themes, for instance. Nothing that demeans the aged, the police, or the rich (possibly the publisher is rich—probably not the editor). Nothing to do with fatal diseases or cannibalism. If all this is missing from a story submitted to this particular magazine, even though it might contain elements another magazine would reject, the conclusion will be that this is a good piece of work and "just right for us."

This approach worked for me and might work for any of you who yearn for publication. Don't blithely put your faith in the advice of published writers. Why on earth should you believe anyone whose trade is fiction?

Er, present company excepted.

# Thieves' Honor

## JOHN LUTZ

NED SPANGLER, THAT ANONYMOUS wisp of thievery known to the police only as "the Monkey Burglar," gripped the rope with strong gloved hands as he lowered himself down the brick wall of the apartment building to the Vonderhursts' bedroom window. Eight stories below him the Ninth Avenue traffic continued to stream by, a myriad of moving lights, faint sounds muted by the night air. The office building across the street was dark, no danger of being seen. Cautiously, he moved his head to look into the Vonderhurst apartment.

The light was on in the bedroom, showing it to be unoccupied, but what Spangler was after lay carefully arranged on the oversized bed. He carefully tried the window and it raised with very little noise.

From beyond the closed bedroom door came laughter, a woman's squeal, and the clink of glasses, the sounds of a party. Spangler smiled. The society page was a burglar's best friend. He swung lightly into the room and looked at the guests' expensive furs spread out on the bed. Swiftly he took from inside his shirt a large burlap sack and stepped toward them.

He was hurriedly stuffing the first coat, an expensive sable, into the sack when the door opened. Still bent over the luxurious array of fur, he stared at the girl, then quickly turned to leap for the window. He didn't though, because the girl was now holding a small, deadly looking automatic that she had produced from the evening bag she was carrying.

Keeping beautiful, unblinking gray eyes on him, she closed the half-opened door with her foot. Dressed in a white evening gown that flattered a perfect figure, her blonde hair was pulled back tight from a well-sculpted face that was unmarred by makeup. And now there was a strange gleam in her eyes, a gleam which Spangler didn't understand.

He stood frozen, awaiting the girl's next move. She had him cold. "I believe 'red-handed' is the term," she said coolly. The gun didn't waver.

Spangler relaxed slightly. She wasn't going to shoot or scream, at least not right away. "It's the term," he said, measuring the distance to the window, knowing he couldn't make it even if she were a lousy shot.

"What's your name?" the girl asked, and the question was so unlikely it took Spangler by surprise for a moment.

"The police will fill you in later," he answered after a pause.

"Maybe that doesn't have to happen. Maybe we can make a deal."

Did he see the corners of her mouth lift slightly in a hidden smile? "I'm hardly in a position to make a deal."

"That's exactly why I suggested it," the girl said. There was amusement in her gray eyes. "A man like you, with your novel way of making a living, with that scar on your face, could easily be identified and traced by the police."

Spangler fingered the long scar running down his left cheek, a scar he'd gotten from his partner of ten years ago in a circus brawl. The lady was right. It wouldn't be hard for the police to trace an ex-tumbler who was so marked.

The girl continued, "Even if I were to let you leave this room I'd still have you in an uncompromising position, a position in which you could hardly afford *not* to deal." She leaned back against the closed doors and looked at him appraisingly.

Spangler searched her face, found nothing. "Out with it," he said.

"Yorktown 5-0305, my phone number," the girl said calmly. She repeated it. "You'll call it within three days, or . . ."

"You cry wolf," Spangler interrupted.

She nodded, and he had to admire her poise. Keeping the gleaming automatic aimed at him, she crossed to the bed and picked up a mink stole. "I always leave a party early," she said. Gracefully backing to the door, still watching him, she slipped the gun back into her purse. "I estimate that no other guest will enter this room for at least ten minutes." Again, her lips hinted a smile. "What you do with that time is your business." Then she was gone.

Spangler stood motionless for a moment; still in a kind of relieved shock. Then he went to work. He selected only the finest furs, packing them hastily but expertly into his sack so they'd take up the least possible space. He even checked the closet, where he found the best of the lot, Mrs. Vonderhurst's long, dark mink with her monogram in the lining.

Tying the drawstrings of the now-bulging sack, Spangler stepped to the window and took a last look around. Then he tied the sack to his belt, reached for the waiting rope, and climbed out of the window. Despite his encounter with the girl, he felt the familiar thrill and satisfaction. He had only to climb two stories to the roof, then use the rope to lower himself down the back of the building to the fire escape that led into the alley where his car was parked. In forty-five minutes he'd be home sipping his customary after-the-job drink, a good five thousand dollars richer.

ON THE THIRD DAY he called her. He had to tell her his name and, surprisingly, she told him hers—Veronica Ackling. When Spangler heard the name he realized why she would be at a cocktail party given by a wealthy art patron like Mrs. Vonderhurst. Veronica's husband, Herbert Ackling, was a well-known collector of rare books, and the Ackling name appeared quite often on the society page.

Veronica wasn't coy. She told Spangler what his part of the deal would be. She simply wanted him to rob her of her jewelry, without her husband's knowledge, and Spangler would get 10 percent of the insurance money plus 10 percent of the price he could get for the jewels. Her husband, she said, was a miser who clung selfishly to every dollar, and she was on an allowance that was hardly suitable to her tastes. The robbery and insurance settlement, she assured Spangler, could be handled without her husband's knowledge, since he would be in Europe for the next month tracking down a rare first edition.

There was something about the deal that didn't smell right. Spangler, by nature a methodical and solitary operator, would rather have skipped it. A partner was something he didn't need or want, least of all an imponderable woman like Veronica Ackling. But, damnit, she had him trapped.

He felt much better about the deal when Veronica told him the jewelry was insured for ninety thousand dollars. That meant nine thousand guaranteed, and his other 10 percent would add up to a worthwhile sum, even after the cut he'd have to take on the value of the jewels when he sold them. Spangler had stolen jewelry before, while traveling with the circus, so he knew ninety thousand dollars' worth of jewelry sometimes amounted to less than thirty thousand when it reached the greedy but hesitant hands of a wary fence. Veronica told him the incredibly simple plan for the robbery, and he left the phone booth from which he was calling and walked preoccupied out the door, already turning over the details of the theft in his mind.

At 2:00 A.M. Spangler climbed noiselessly on rubber-soled shoes up the five flights of stairs to the top floor of the Freemont Apartment Building. The Freemont was not quite so exclusive as the Barton Arms next door, where the Acklings lived, so there was no doorman. He walked quickly down the long corridor and found the service passage to the roof, just where Veronica said it would be. He picked the crude mechanism of the cheap padlock that barred his way and in a few seconds opened the rooftop door to the sudden, cold blast of winter.

The gangway between the Barton Arms and the Freemont Apartments was ten feet wide, but Spangler leaped easily onto the roof of the Barton Arms. Wasting no time, he paced off the proper distance along the edge of the roof to be sure he was over the window of the Acklings' third-floor apartment, then moved about four feet to the side to be certain the rope wouldn't be visible from the windows on the upper floors. He tied one end of his rope to the sturdy base of a lightning rod, then let the other end, weighted so it would not be affected by the wind, down the side of the building.

The window to Herbert Ackling's den was locked, as Spangler and Veronica had agreed it would be, and Spangler quickly solved that with the aid of an efficient glass cutter. Wearing gloves, he turned the lock, slowly raised the window, and entered Herbert Ackling's den.

THERE WAS NO ONE home, of course. Ackling was in Europe, and Veronica was out establishing a firm alibi for herself to dispel any suspicions the insurance company might have. By the thin yellow beam of his flashlight, Spangler rummaged through the den to make the robbery look genuine, even pocketing an expensive lighter from the desktop for effect. Then he made his way into the bedroom and pulled open all the dresser drawers. In the top drawer, behind an unruly tangle of scarves and nylon hose, he found the jewelry box.

Spangler set the box on the floor and easily sprung the flimsy lock. In the beam of the flashlight the jewelry sparkled dazzlingly. He could well believe there was ninety thousand dollars' worth here. Admiring each sparkling piece, he hurriedly filled the special pocket he had sewn into the lining of his jacket.

As he stood by the den window, feeling the comfortable weight of the jewelry against his side, Spangler flashed the beam of his light around with satisfaction. As far as the police and the insurance company were concerned, this would be just one more bit of work by "the Monkey Burglar." Then, silently, he left.

"Do turn out the light, darling." Veronica lay on Spangler's bed with the covers pulled up around her chin. Her eyes were closed to the light and, though there was a delicate frown line between her eyebrows, she was smiling faintly.

It was early morning, and Spangler sat on the edge of the bed contemplating his good fortune. He loved Veronica, he knew. When she had delivered the money, they'd had a few drinks, talked, and discovered they were very attracted to each other. Veronica's social position in no way awed Spangler. Though Spangler loved with a certain reserve, he was completely fascinated by this woman whose aristocratic coolness could turn like the flip of a card to deep passion.

Spangler, already dressed, turned off the bedside lamp and the half-light of dawn filtered through the slanted blinds. He propped a pillow behind his head and smiled at the fragrance of her expensive perfume.

"I have an idea," Veronica said, and rested her head against his shoulder. "I want you to rob me again."

"Did I hear you right?"

"It's not really a bad idea, darling." Her eyes caught the sunlight in the room. "You've robbed the same place twice on occasion. It's part of your 'modus operandi.'"

"I'm not worried about getting away with it," Spangler said, "and I suppose the insurance company would come through again; there'd be no doubt it was the work of the same man. But why be greedy?"

Veronica said calmly, "Herbert's going to France again next week, and if there's one more robbery, if I can have just that much more money, I'll leave him. They're my jewels. Let him just try to get the insurance money back—if he can find me."

"And you'll be?"

"With you."

Spangler was silent for a few minutes. That part of him that looked at things objectively knew he didn't really have any more choice this time than he'd had before. There was no way he could involve Veronica if she chose to turn him in, no way he could prove their alliance. He wondered if there were some detached and aloof part of Veronica's mind that thought the same thing.

"How much are your new jewels insured for?" Spangler asked.

"Eighty thousand. I used my share of the insurance money to replace the stolen ones. Herbert's unaware of the whole thing, of course. He never noticed what kind of jewelry I wore, or if I wore any, for that matter."

Spangler reached over to the nightstand and rooted through Veronica's purse for a pack of cigarettes. "I don't know," he said.

"This time you can have half of whatever you get for the jewels."

Another payday like the last appealed to Spangler. He wouldn't have to take a risk for a long time with that kind of money, and the thought of going away with Veronica appealed to him almost as much.

"Agreed," he said, and gently pulled her to him.

Veronica smiled. "We'll spend it together," she said before she kissed him.

A week later Spangler was at work again. He'd climbed the stairway of the Freemont and onto the roof. He'd leaped the gangway again and repeated his pacing off of distance and securing and lowering of the rope. Now he hung against the cold, unyielding wall, buffeted by a brisk winter wind that made his ears ache. He'd be glad to get inside.

He inched his way toward the window with his free hand and foot, surprised to see that this time a light burned in Herbert Ackling's den. Had Veronica forgotten to turn it off? Spangler cautiously looked into the room.

There was Herbert Ackling, his head resting on his desktop like that of a schoolboy taking an afternoon nap—only a brilliant scarlet pool of blood covered the top of the desk and the open book he'd been reading. On the thick carpet, just inside the window that Spangler now saw was flung wide open, lay the glinting automatic that Veronica always carried in her purse, the gun that Spangler had handled a dozen times. Then he knew.

Suddenly Veronica stood in the doorway, screaming loud and long. There was no expression of shock on her face as she looked at Spangler and the body; she would save that for an appreciative audience. She turned and ran.

With lightning speed Spangler pulled himself hand-over-hand up the rope. *Why hadn't he thought of it?* Now Veronica, the Veronica he loved, would have Ackling's insurance money. She also had something more important: a made-to-order murderer for the police.

Spangler reached the roof and ran over the tar and gravel surface toward the opposite edge. As he leaped the gangway with a yard to spare, he heard the wavering wail of a siren. Then he was in the Freemont building, descending the stairs in long, desperate leaps. The wail of sirens grew steadily louder. It would be close, close. He didn't care if he made noise now.

As his feet hit the bottom floor, Spangler raced down the long corridor toward the rear door. There was a sudden whooshing of air and a burst of sound as the front door opened. Spangler faintly heard a voice call "Halt!" He didn't hear a shot, but something ricocheted off the tile wall next to him, sending ceramic chips flying. He didn't hesitate, but hit the back door hard. It opened, and he was in the gangway that he'd just leaped, five stories above, a few seconds ago.

He stood still for a split second, gasping, then ran again. From a window high in one of the buildings a woman's voice screamed, "Murderer!" and a flashing red light suddenly appeared at the end of the gangway toward which Spangler was running. He spun on his heel, but this time as he heard the shots he experienced a searing pain.

Still conscious, Spangler lay on his back looking up at the narrow band of bright winter stars between the two buildings. The cement was hard and cold against his back, but his hands rested in something warm and sticky. He knew he was losing blood fast.

He heard a deep, authoritative voice say, "Out, out. Keep everyone out of the gangway until the ambulance arrives."

Spangler didn't care about the ambulance. He was thinking of Veronica, and strangely he felt no anger toward her. It was the game. She'd outwitted him, and for that he could only admire her. Damned if he didn't hope she'd enjoy the insurance money.

# Not All Brides Are Beautiful

## SHARYN MCCRUMB

## Sharyn McCrumb's Introduction:

*Short stories come in flashes of lightning.*

*They are very different from novels, not just in length and complexity but also in the germination of the idea itself. For me a novel is an organic creation which may grow slowly out of the illumination of a character (Malcolm MacCourry in* The Songcatcher) *or from the examination of a theme (the motif of journeys in* She Walks These Hills). *I follow a thread of thoughts to see how a novel will unfold, and often I have only a vague idea of what the ending will be.*

*A short story comes all at once, like the glimpse of a dark landscape suddenly lit by lightning, and for me the lightning that provides the inspiration is a strong emotion. Anger works well.*

*Although I had published and won awards for my more literary works, "Not All Brides Are Beautiful" was the first short story I published in crime fiction. It appeared in Ellery Queen's Mystery Magazine, and I wrote it at the request of EQMM's editor, Eleanor Sullivan, whom I met when she lectured at a writers convention in West Virginia.*

*"Why don't you send me a story?" she said.*

*I was such a novice in those days that I would have written anything for anybody, and I promptly agreed to send her a story without having the least idea what I would write about. I can never force short story ideas to materialize. I can only put myself in the way of inspiration and hope something turns up. In trolling for stories I read nonfiction, newspapers, technical journals, magazines like Smithsonian and Discover, because I agree with Louis Pasteur that "Chance favors the prepared mind."*

*The idea for "Not All Brides Are Beautiful" turned up in my local newspaper in the form of a very odd wedding announcement. A prisoner on death row was getting married to a woman activist from a neighboring state. The groom's name was chillingly familiar. A few months earlier, banner headlines on page one of the local newspaper had announced a prison escape from the death row of Virginia's maximum security prison, and this prisoner had been one of the escapees. After a*

**Sharyn McCrumb**

weeks-long manhunt, all the escapees had been apprehended and returned to the prison, but apparently this fellow—weeks away from his scheduled execution—had arranged to marry a woman he'd never met, so he was back in the headlines.

The paper carefully explained that the ceremony was just a formality. The newlyweds weren't going to be let out for a honeymoon at Myrtle Beach, or even a make-out session in the visitors lounge. The prison chaplain would be performing the ceremony while the bride and groom gazed at each other through the bars.

I thought the whole stunt deserved an award for bad taste. He was a dangerous killer who had slaughtered half a dozen women and young children, and she was a publicity hound who planned to parlay her brief marriage into a book deal and a round of talk shows. The wedding wouldn't inconvenience her too much, I thought. After all, he's going to die in six weeks.

And then it hit me: the flash of inspirational lightning. Wouldn't it be great if he didn't die? Or better yet, if they let him out? Then, instead of a having media-eventful widowhood, the new bride would have a murdering psychopath on her hands until death did them part. . . . (Which would be at his discretion, I thought.)

I wrote the story my way, and sent it to Eleanor Sullivan, who published it in the December 1986 issue of Ellery Queen's Mystery Magazine. In real life, of course, the killer was executed on schedule, and his bride made the rounds of talk shows, just as I had predicted, but I like my version better. Poetic justice is rare, but satisfying, even if you have to invent it.

# Not All Brides Are Beautiful

## SHARYN MCCRUMB

THEY SAY THAT ALL brides are beautiful, but I didn't like the look of this one. She came into the prison reception area wearing a lavender suit and a little black hat with a veil. Her figure was okay, but when she went up to Tracer and that other photographer from the wire service, there was a hard look about her, despite that spun-sugar smile. I knew it would be easy to get an interview—she'd *insist* on it—but that didn't mean I was going to enjoy talking to her.

"Is it true you're going to marry Kenny Budrell?" I called out.

She redirected her smile at me, and her dark eyes lit up like miners' lamps.

"You're here for the wedding, honey?" she purred. "Have you got something I could borrow? I already have something old, and new, and blue."

Just a regular old folksy wedding. I was about to tell her what I'd like to lend her when I felt a nudge in my side. Tracer—reminding me that good reporters get stories any way they can. I managed a faint smile. "Sure, I'll see what I can find. Why don't we go into the ladies' room and get acquainted?"

She smiled back. "This is my day to get acquainted."

"That's right," said Tracer. "You've never met the groom, have you?"

Kenny Budrell had been a newsroom byword since before I joined the paper. By the time he was eighteen, his clip-file in the newspaper morgue was an inch thick: car theft, assault and battery, attempted murder. He did some time in the state penitentiary about the same time I was at the university, and it seems we both graduated with honors. The next news of Kenny was that he'd robbed a local convenience store and taken the female clerk hostage. Tracer was the photographer on assignment when they found her body; he says it's one of the few times he's been sick on duty. It took three more robberies, each followed by the brutal murder of a hostage, before the police finally caught up with Kenny. He didn't make it through the roadblock and

287

took a bullet in the shoulder trying to shoot his way past.

The trial took a couple of weeks. The paper sent Rudy Carr, a much more seasoned reporter than I, to cover it, but I followed the coverage and listened to the office gossip. The defense had rounded up a psychologist who said Kenny must have been temporarily insane, and he never did confess to the killings, but the jury had been looking at that cold, dead face of Kenny's for two weeks and they didn't buy it. They found him guilty in record time, and the judge obliged with a death sentence.

After that, the only clippings added to Kenny's file were routine one-column stories about his appeal to the State Supreme Court, and then to Washington. That route having failed, it was official: In six weeks Kenny Budrell would go to the electric chair.

That's when *she* turned up.

Varnee Sumner—sometime journalist and activist, full-time opportunist. In between her ecological-feminist poetry readings and her grant proposals, Varnee had found time to strike up a correspondence with Kenny. The first we heard of it was when the warden sent out a press release saying that Kenny Budrell had been granted permission to get married two weeks before his execution.

It shouldn't have come as a surprise to me that Varnee Sumner wanted to be pals—that's probably what my city editor was counting on when he assigned me to cover the story.

"What's your name?" she asked me as she applied fuchsia lipstick to her small, tight mouth.

"Lillian Robillard. Tell me—are you nervous?" I decided against taking notes. That might make her more careful about what she said.

She smoothed her hair. "Nervous? Why should I be nervous? It's true I've never met Kenny, but we've become real close through our letters—I've come to know his soul."

I winced. Kenny Budrell's soul should come with a Surgeon General's warning. Maybe *she* wasn't nervous about marrying a mass murderer, but I would have been.

My thoughts must have been obvious, because she said, "Besides, they're not going to let him come near me, you know. Even during the wedding ceremony he'll be on one side of a wire screen and we'll be on the other."

"Will they let you spend time alone with him?"

That question did faze her. "Lord, I hope—" I'd swear she was going to say *not*, but she caught herself and said, "Perhaps we'll have a quiet talk through the screen—Honey, would you like to be my maid of honor?"

"I'd love to," I said. "And would you like to give me an exclusive pre-wedding interview?"

"I wish I could," she said, "but I've promised the story to *Personal World* for ten thousand dollars." She straightened her skirt and edged past me and out the door.

I didn't think it was possible, but I was beginning to feel sorry for Kenny Budrell.

"YOU LOOKED REAL GOOD out there as maid of honor," Tracer told me as we left the prison. "I got a good shot of you and the warden congratulating the bride."

"Well, if I looked happy for them, pictures *do* lie." The television crews had arrived just as we were leaving and Varnee was granting interviews right and left, talking about Kenny's beautiful soul and how she was going to write to the president about his case. "You know why she's doing this, don't you?"

Tracer gave me a sad smile. "Well, I ruled out love early on."

"It's a con game. She stays married to him for two weeks, after which the state conveniently executes him, and she's a widow who stands to make a fortune on movie rights and book contracts. *I Was a Killer's Bride!*"

"Maybe they deserve each other," said Tracer mildly. "Kenny Budrell is no choirboy."

I pulled open the outside door fiercely. "He grew up poor and tough, and for all I know he *may* not be in his right mind. But there's nothing circumstantial about what she's doing!"

Tracer grinned at me. "I can see you're going to have a tough time trying to write up this wedding announcement."

He was right. It took the two hours to get the acid out of my copy. But I managed. I wanted to stay assigned to the story.

I DIDN'T SEE THE new Mrs. Budrell for the next two weeks, but I kept track of her. She went to Washington and gave a couple of speeches about the injustices of the American penal system. She tried to get in to see the vice president and a couple of Supreme Court justices, but that didn't pan out. She managed to get plenty of newspaper space, though, and even made the cover of a supermarket newspaper. They ran a picture of her with the caption COURAGEOUS BRIDE FIGHTS FOR HUSBAND'S LIFE.

Because of the tearjerker angle, her efforts on Kenny's behalf received far more publicity than those of the court-appointed attorney assigned to his case. Allen Linden, a quiet, plodding type just out of law school, had been filing stacks of appeals and doing everything he could do, but nobody paid any attention. He wasn't newsworthy, and he shied away from the media blitz. He hadn't attended Budrell's wedding, and he declined all interviews to discuss the newlyweds. I know because I tried to talk with him three times. The last time he'd brushed past me in the hall outside his office, murmuring, "I'm doing the best I can for him, which is more than I can say for—"

He swallowed the rest but I knew what he had been about to say. Varnee wasn't doing a thing to really help her husband's case, although she'd been on two national talk shows and a campus lecture tour, and there was talk of a major book contract. Varnee was doing just fine—for herself.

THE WHOLE SIDESHOW WAS due to end on April third, the date of Kenny's execution. The editor was sending Rudy Carr to cover that and I was going along to do a sidebar on the widow-to-be. I wondered how she was going to play her part: grieving bride or impassioned activist?

"I'm glad to see it's raining," said Tracer, hunched down in the backseat with his camera equipment. "That ought to keep the demonstrators away."

Rudy, at the wheel, glanced at him in the rearview mirror and scowled. He had hardly spoken since we started.

I watched the windshield wipers slapping the rain. "It won't keep *her* away," I said, feeling the chill, glad I'd worn my sheepskin coat.

"You've got to give the woman credit, though," Tracer said. "She's been using this case to say a lot of things that need saying about capital punishment."

I sighed. If you gave Tracer a sack of manure, he'd spend two hours looking for the pony.

"She's getting rich off this," I pointed out. "Did you know that Kenny Budrell has a mother and sisters?"

"And so did two of the victims," added Rudy with such quiet intensity that it shut both Tracer and me up for the rest of the trip.

THE PRISON RECEPTION ROOM was far more crowded for the execution than it had been for the wedding. By now Varnee had received so much publicity she was a national news item, and when we arrived she was three-deep in reporters. She was wearing a black designer suit and the same hat she'd worn for the wedding. I knew she wouldn't give me the time of day with all the bigger fish waving microphones and cameras in her face, but I did get a photocopy of her speech on capital punishment from a stack of copies she'd brought with her.

"You'd better talk to her now," Tracer said. "In a few minutes they're taking the witnesses in to view the execution and you're not cleared for that."

I stared at him. "You mean she's going to watch?"

"Oh, yeah. They agreed on that from the start."

I might have gone over and talked with her then, but I noticed Allen Linden, Kenny's attorney, sitting on a bench by himself, sipping coffee. He looked tired, and his gray suit might have been slept in for all its wrinkles.

He looked up warily as I approached.

"You don't have to talk to me if you don't want," I said.

He managed a wan smile. "Have I seen you somewhere before?"

I introduced myself. "You've dodged me in the hall outside your office a few times," I admitted. "But I didn't come over here to give you a hard time. Honest."

He let out a long sigh. "This is my first capital murder case," he said in a weary voice. "It's hard to know what to do."

"I'm sure you did your best." He was very young and I wasn't sure how good his best was, but he seemed badly in need of solace.

"Kenny Budrell isn't a very nice person," he mused.

I was puzzled. I thought lawyers always spoke up for their clients. "You don't think he's innocent?"

"He never claimed to be," said Linden. "At one point he expressed

291

surprise at all the fuss being made over a couple of broads, as he put it. No, he's not a very nice person. But he was entitled to the best defense he could get. To every effort I could make."

I guess it's inevitable for a lawyer to feel guilty if his client is about to die. He must wonder if there is something else he could have done. "I'm sure you did everything you could," I said. "And if Varnee couldn't get him a stay of execution, it must have been hopeless."

He grimaced at the sound of her name. "She's not a very nice person, either, is she?"

I hesitated. "How does Kenny Budrell feel about her?"

"Very flattered." Linden smiled. "Here is a minor celebrity making his case a prime-time issue. He has a huge scrapbook of her—he keeps her letters under his pillow. He said to me once, 'She loves me, so I must be a hero. I've worried a lot about that.'"

There was a stir in the crowd and the warden, flanked by two guards, came into the room. I stiffened, dreading the next deliberate hour.

"It will be over soon," I whispered.

"I know. I hope I've done the right thing."

"Are you going to watch the execution?"

Linden shut his eyes. "There isn't going to be one. I found an irregularity in the police procedure and got the case overturned. I've just made Kenny Budrell a free man."

"But he's guilty!" I protested.

"But he's still entitled to due process, same as anyone else, and it's my job to take advantage of anything that will benefit my client." He shook his head. "I can't even take credit for it. It just fell into my lap."

"What happened?"

"Remember when they captured Kenny at the roadblock?"

"Yes. He was wounded in the shoot-out."

"Right. Well, in all the excitement nobody remembered to read him his rights. Later, in the hospital, when he was questioned, the police assumed it had already been done. One of the state troopers got to thinking about the case and came forward to tell me he thought there had been a slipup. I checked, and he was right: Kenny wasn't Mirandized, so the law says there's no case. The trooper told me he came forward because of all this business with Varnee. He said maybe the guy deserved a break, after all."

Tracer got a first-class series of pictures of the warden telling Varnee that her new husband was now a free man until death do them part, and of Varnee eventually starting to scream right there in front of the TV cameras. As far as I'm concerned, they deserve a Pulitzer.

# Manslaughter

JOYCE CAROL OATES

## Joyce Carol Oates's Introduction:

"Manslaughter" is set in a fictionalized Lockport, New York, the city of my birth. As a young girl I'd attended a trial in the Niagara County Courthouse and was fascinated by the proceedings, but also by the people involved, and by the setting. A young man of about twenty-one was being tried for murder; he was by no means an isolated individual, but surrounded by family and friends. I was struck by the way in which the young murderer was regarded by these people, who must have compartmentalized his actions, incapable or unwilling to judge him. It seemed to me, at about the age of thirteen, that no code of morality or ethics really prevailed beyond the personal.

I imagine the events of "Manslaughter" evolving out of a mysterious conjunction of time, place, and character. The time is decades ago, the place is upstate New York, and the characters are composites of people I've known and imagined. The story had a fluid, cinematic quality in my imagination, and was fairly quickly written in dramatic scenes.

In my family history, long before I was born, there had been a never-explained act of violence, the murder of my mother's father. Though the murder was never spoken of, nor even alluded to, in my presence, it seemed to permeate the atmosphere of our household. I grew up with a sense that sudden, inexplicable, and irrevocable acts could devastate ordinary life. I accepted without question the possibility that acts of violence, even murder, have occurred in most families, if one traces history back far enough. A benign amnesia allows us to imagine ourselves fully civilized.

We are fascinated and repelled by "mystery." Something in us yearns to solve the inexplicable, even as we realize that motives can probably never be comprehended. As in "Manslaughter," like the hapless Beatrice, we find ourselves unable to resist the very evil that had repelled us. In the end, it isn't even evil, but something like ordinary life, seen from a different perspective.

Beatrice of "Manslaughter" becomes, like the murdered Rose Ann, a victim of what might be called an eroticized violence. She, too, will be "man-slaughtered."

# Manslaughter

## JOYCE CAROL OATES

EDDIE FARRELL, TWENTY-SIX, temporarily laid off from Lackawanna Steel, had been separated from his wife, Rose Ann, for several months, off and on, when the fatal stabbing occurred. This was on a January afternoon near dusk. Most of the day snow had been falling lightly, and the sun appeared at the horizon for only a few minutes, the usual dull red sulfurous glow beyond the steel mills.

According to Eddie's sworn testimony, Rose Ann had telephoned him at his mother's house and demanded he come over, she had something to tell him. So he went over and picked her up—while he was driving his brother's 1977 Falcon—they went to the County Line Tavern for a drink—then drove around, talking, or maybe quarreling. Suddenly, Rose Ann took out a knife and went for him—no warning—but he fought her off—he tried to take the knife away—*she* was stabbed by accident—he panicked and drove like crazy for twenty, twenty-five minutes—until he was finally flagged down by a state trooper out on the highway, doing eighty-eight miles an hour in a fifty-five-mile zone. By then Rose Ann had bled to death in the passenger's seat—she'd been stabbed in the throat, chest, belly, thighs, thirty or more times.

"I guess I lost control," Eddie said repeatedly, referring to the drive in the "death car" (as the newspapers called it), not to stabbing his wife: He didn't remember stabbing his wife. It seemed to him he had only defended himself against her attack, somehow she had managed to stab herself. Maybe to punish him. She was always criticizing him, always finding fault. She called up his mother, too, and bitched over the telephone—*that* really got to him.

When asked by police officers how his wife had come into possession of a hunting knife belonging to his brother, Eddie replied at first that he didn't have any idea, then he said she must have stolen it and hidden it away in the apartment. He really didn't know. She did crazy things. She threatened all kinds of crazy things. The knife was German-made, with an eight-inch stainless steel blade and a black sealed wood handle, a beautiful thing, expensive. Lying on a little table at the front of the courtroom, beneath the judge's high bench, it looked like it might be for sale—the last of its kind, after everything else had been bought.

At first Eddie Farrell was booked for second-degree murder, with $45,000 bail (which meant 10 percent bond); then the charges were lowered to third, with $15,000 bail. Midway in the trial the charges would be lowered further to manslaughter, voluntary.

IT WAS BEATRICE GRAZIA'S bad luck to happen to see the death car as it sped along Second Avenue in her direction. She was on her way home from work, crossing the street, when the car approached. She jumped back onto the curb, she said. The driver was a goddamned maniac, and she didn't want to get killed.

Sure, she told police, she recognized Eddie Farrell driving—she got a clear view of his face as he drove past. But it all happened so quickly, she just stood on the curb staring after the car. Her coat was splashed with slush and dirt; he'd come that close to running her down.

At the trial five months later Beatrice swore to tell the truth, the whole truth, and nothing but the truth, but it all seemed remote now—insignificant. Her voice was so breathless it could barely be heard by the spectators in the first row. She was the tenth witness for the prosecution, out of twenty-seven, and her testimony seemed to add little to what had already been said. She hadn't wanted to appear—the district attorney's office had issued her a subpoena. Yes, she'd seen Eddie Farrell that day. Yes, he was driving east along Second. Yes, he was speeding. Yes, she had recognized him. Yes, he was in the courtroom today. Yes, she could point him out. Yes, she had seen someone in the passenger's seat beside him. No, she hadn't recognized the person. She believed it was a woman—she was fairly certain it was a woman—but the car passed by so quickly, she couldn't see.

Her voice was low, rapid, sullen, as if she were testifying against her will. Both the district attorney's assistant and the defense lawyer repeatedly asked her to speak up. The defense lawyer grew visibly irritated, his questions were edged with malice: How could she be certain she recognized the driver of the car?—wasn't it almost dark?—did she have *perfect* vision?

Blood rushed into her cheeks; she stammered a few words and went silent.

Eddie Farrell was sitting only a few yards away, staring dully into a corner of the courtroom—he didn't appear to be listening. His hair was slickly combed and parted on the side. He wore a pinstriped suit that fitted his skinny body loosely, as if he had put it on by mistake. His eyes were deep-set, shadowed; there was a queer oily sheen to his skin. Beatrice wasn't sure she would have recognized him, now.

THOUGH EVERYONE WAITED FOR Eddie to take the stand, to testify for himself, it wasn't his lawyer's strategy to allow him to speak: This disappointed many of the spectators. In all, the defense called only six people, four of them character witnesses. They spoke of Eddie Farrell as if they didn't realize he was in the courtroom with them; they didn't seem to have a great deal to say.

The most articulate witness was a young man named Ron Boci who had known Eddie, he said, for ten, twelve years, since grade school. He spoke rapidly and fluently, with a faint jeering edge to his voice; his swarthy skin had flushed darker. Yeah, he was a friend of Eddie's, they went places together—yeah, Eddie'd told him there was trouble with his wife—but it wasn't ever serious trouble, not from Eddie's side. He loved his wife, Ron Boci said, looking out over the courtroom, he wouldn't ever hurt her. He put up with a lot from her. Rose Ann was the one, he said. Rose Ann was always going on how she'd maybe kill herself, cut her throat, take an overdose or something, just to get back at Eddie, but Eddie never thought she meant it, nobody did—that was just Rose Ann shooting off her mouth. Yeah, Ron Boci said, moving his narrow shoulders, he knew her, kind of. But not like he knew Eddie.

Ron warmed as he spoke; he crossed his legs, resting one high-polished black boot lightly on his knee. He had a handsome beakish face, quick-darting eyes, hair parted in the center of his head so that it could flow thick and wavy to the sides, where it brushed against his collar. His hair was so black it looked polished. He too was wearing a suit—a beige checked suit with brass buttons—but it fitted his slender body snugly. His necktie was a queer part-luminous silver that might have been metallic.

DURING ONE OF THE recesses, when Beatrice went to the drinking fountain, Ron Boci appeared beside her and offered to turn on the water for her. It was a joke, but Beatrice didn't think it was funny. "No thank you," she said, her eyes sliding away from his, struck by how white the whites were, how heavy the eyebrows. "No thank you, I can turn it on myself," Beatrice said, but he didn't seem to hear. She saw, stooping, lowering her pursed lips to the tepid stream of water, that there was a sprinkling of small warts on the back of Ron Boci's big-knuckled hand.

IT WAS SHORTLY AFTER the New Year that Beatrice's husband, Tony, drove down to Port Arthur, Texas, on the Gulf, to work for an offshore oil drilling company. He'd be calling her, he said. He'd write, he'd send back money as soon as he could.

A postcard came in mid-February, another at the end of March. Each showed the same Kodacolor photograph of a brilliant orange-red sunset on the Gulf of Mexico, with palm trees in languid silhouette. Not much news, Tony wrote, things weren't working out quite right, he'd be telephoning soon. No snow down here, he said, all winter. If it snows it melts right away.

Where is Tony? people asked, neighbors in the building, Beatrice's parents, her girlfriends, and she said with a childlike lifting of her chin, "Down in Texas where there's work." Then she tried to change the subject. Sometimes they persisted, asking if she was going to join him, if he had an apartment or anything, what their plans were. "He's supposed to call this weekend," Beatrice said. Her narrow face seemed to thicken in obstinacy; the muscles of her jaws went hard.

He did call, one Sunday night. She had to turn the television volume down but, at the other end of the line, there was a great deal of noise—as if a television were turned up high. A voice that resembled Tony's lifted incoherently. Beatrice said, "Yes? Tony? Is that you? What?" but the line crackled and went dead. She hung up. She waited awhile, then turned the television back up and sat staring at the screen until the phone rang again. This time, she thought, I know better than to answer.

"WHAT ARE YOU DOING about the rent for July?—and you still owe for June, don't you?" Beatrice's father asked.

Beatrice was filing her long angular nails briskly with an emery board. Her face went hot with blood but she didn't look up.

"*I* better pay it," Beatrice's father said. "And you and the baby better move back with us."

"Who told you what we owe?" Beatrice asked.

She spoke in a flat neutral voice though her blood pulsed with anger. People were talking about them—her and Tony—it was an open secret now that Tony seemed to have moved out.

"Tony won't like it if I give this place up," Beatrice said, easing the emery board carefully around her thumbnail, which had grown to an unusual length. To provoke her father a little she said, "He'll maybe be mad if he comes back and somebody else is living here, and he's got to go over to our house to find me and Danny. You know how his temper is."

Beatrice's father surprised her by laughing. Or maybe it was a kind of grunt—he rose from his chair, a big fleshy man, hands pushing on his thighs as if he needed extra leverage. "I can take care of your wop husband," he said.

It was a joke—it really *was* a joke because Beatrice's mother was Italian—but Beatrice hunched over the emery board and refused even to smile. "You wouldn't talk like that if Tony was here," she said.

"I wouldn't need to talk like this if Tony was here," her father said. "But the point is, he isn't here. That's what we're talking about."

"That's what *you're* talking about," Beatrice said.

When her father was leaving, Beatrice followed after him on the stairs, pulling at his arm, saying, "Momma wants Danny with her and that's okay, Momma is wonderful with him, but, you know, this was supposed to be . . ." She made a clumsy pleading gesture indicating the stairs, the apartment on the landing, the building itself. She swallowed hard so that she wouldn't start to cry. "This was supposed to be a new place, a different place," she said. "That's why we came here. That's why we got married."

"I already talked to the guy downstairs," her father said, rattling his car keys. "He said you can move any time up to the fifteenth. I'll rent one of them U-Hauls and we'll do it in the morning."

"I don't think I can," Beatrice said, wiping angrily at her eyes. "I'm not going to do that."

"Next time he calls," Beatrice's father said, "tell him the news. Tell him your old man paid the rent for him. Tell him to look me up, he wants to cause trouble."

"I'm not going to do any of that," Beatrice said, starting to cry.

"It's already halfway done," her father said.

ONE NIGHT AROUND TEN o'clock Beatrice was leaving the 7-Eleven store up the street when she heard someone approach her. As she glanced back an arm circled her shoulders, which were almost bare—she was wearing a red halter top—and a guy played at hugging her as if they were old pals. She screamed and pushed him away—jabbed at him with her elbow.

It was Ron Boci, Eddie Farrell's friend. He was wearing a T-shirt and jeans, no shoes. No belt, the waist of the jeans was loose and frayed, you could see how lean he was—not skinny exactly but lean, small-hipped. His hair was a little longer than it had been in the courtroom but it was still parted carefully in the center of his head; he had a habit of shaking it back, loosening it, when he knew people were watching.

"Hey, you knew who it was," he said. "Come on."

"You scared the hell out of me," Beatrice said. Her heart was knocking so hard she could feel her entire body rock. But she stooped and picked up the quart of milk she'd dropped, and the carton of cigarettes, and Ron Boci stood there with his knuckles on his hips, watching. He meant to keep the same kidding tone, but she heard an edge of apology in his voice, or maybe it was something else.

"You knew who it was," he said, smiling, lifting one corner of his mouth. "You saw me in there but you wouldn't say hello."

"Saw you in where?" Beatrice asked. "There wasn't anybody in there but the salesclerk."

"I was in there; I stood right in the center of the aisle, where the soda pop and stuff is, but you pretended not to see me, you looked right through me," Ron Boci said. "But I bet you remember my name."

"I don't remember any name," Beatrice said. Her voice sounded so harsh and frightened, she added quickly, "It's just a good thing I wasn't carrying any bottles or anything, it'd all be broke now." She said, "Well, I know the name Boci. Your sister Marian."

"Yeah. Marian," Ron Boci said.

Beatrice started to walk away and Ron Boci followed close beside her. He was perhaps six inches taller than Beatrice and walked with his thumbs hooked into the waist of his jeans, an easy sidling walk, self-conscious, springy. His smell was tart and dry like tobacco mixed with something moist: hair oil, shaving lotion. Beatrice knew he was watching her but she pretended not to notice.

He was a little high, elated. He laughed softly to himself.

"Your telephone got disconnected or something," Ron Boci said after a pause. He spoke with an air of slight reproach.

"I don't live there anymore," Beatrice said quickly.

She saw a sprinkling of glass on the sidewalk ahead but she didn't intend to warn him: Let him walk through it and slice up his filthy feet.

"Where do you live, then, Beatrice?" he asked casually. "I know Tony is in Texas."

"He's coming back in a few weeks," Beatrice said. "Or I might fly down."

"I used to know Tony," Ron Boci said. "The Grazias over on Market Street—? Mrs. Grazia and my mother used to be good friends."

Beatrice said nothing. Ron Boci's elbow brushed against her bare arm and all the fine brown hairs lifted in goose bumps.

"Where are you living now, if you moved?" Ron Boci asked.

"It doesn't matter where I live," Beatrice said.

"I mean, what's their name? You with somebody, or alone?"

"Why do you want to know?"

"I'm just asking. Where are you headed now?"

"My parents' place, I'm staying overnight. My mother helps out sometimes with the baby," Beatrice said. She heard her voice becoming quick, light, detached, as if it were a stranger's voice, overheard by accident. She was watching as Ron Boci walked through the broken glass—saw his left foot come down hard on a sliver at least four inches long—but he seemed not to notice, didn't even flinch. His elbow brushed against her again.

He was watching her, smiling. He said, in a slow, easy voice. "I didn't know Tony Grazia had a kid, how long ago was that? *You* don't look like you ever had any baby."

Beatrice said stiffly, "There's lots of things you don't know."

303

"I SAW YOU LAST night at the Hi-Lo but you sure as hell didn't see me," Beatrice's father told her across the supper table. His face was beefy and damp with perspiration. "Ten, ten-thirty. You sure as hell didn't notice *me*."

It was late July and very hot. They'd had a heat spell for almost a week. Beatrice and her mother had set up a table in the living room, where it was cooler, but the effort hadn't made much difference. Beatrice's arms stuck unpleasantly to the surface of the table and her thighs stuck against her chair. She could see that her father was angry—his face was red and mottled with anger—but he didn't intend to say much in front of Beatrice's mother.

"I wasn't at the Hi-Lo very long," Beatrice said. "I don't even remember."

"Wearing sunglasses in the dark, *dark* glasses," Beatrice's father said with a snort of laughter, "like a movie star or something."

"That was just a joke," Beatrice said. "For five minutes. I had them on for five minutes and then I took them off."

"Okay," her father said, chewing his food. "Just wanted you to know."

"I just went out with some friends," she said.

"Okay," her father said.

After a while Beatrice said, "I don't need anybody spying on me, I'm not a kid. I'm twenty years old."

"You're a married woman," Beatrice's father said.

Beatrice's mother tried to interrupt, but neither of them paid her any attention.

"If I want to go out with some friends," Beatrice said, her voice rising, "that's my business."

"I didn't see any *friends*, I saw only that one guy," Beatrice's father said. "As long as you know what you're doing."

Beatrice had stopped eating. She said nothing. She sat with her elbows on the table, staring and staring until her vision slipped out of focus. She could look at something—a glass saltshaker, a jar of mustard—until finally she wasn't seeing it and she wasn't thinking of anything and she wasn't aware of her surroundings either. In the past, when she lived at home, lapsing into one of these spells at the supper table could be dangerous—her father had slapped her awake more than once. But now he wouldn't. Now he probably wouldn't even touch her.

304

"Do you like this?" Ron Boci was saying.

Beatrice woke slowly. "No," she said. "Wait."

"Do you like *this*?" Ron said, laughing.

"No. Please. Wait." Her voice was muffled, groggy, she had dreamed she was suffocating and now she couldn't breathe. "Wait," she said.

After a while he said, "Christ, are you crying?" and she said no. She was sobbing a little, or maybe laughing. Her head spun, Jesus she was hung over. At first she almost didn't know where she was, only that she didn't ever want to leave.

At work in the post office those long hours—waiting for the Clinton Street bus—changing the baby's diaper, her fingers so swift and practiced my God you'd think she had been doing this all her life—she found herself thinking of him. Of him and of it, what he did to her. That was it. That was the only thing. Sometimes the thought of him hit her so hard she felt a stabbing sensation in the pit of the belly, between her legs. She never thought of her husband, sometimes she went for hours without thinking of her baby. Once, changing his diaper, she pricked him and he began to cry angrily, red-faced, astonished, furious; she picked him up she held him in her arms she buried her face against him begging to be forgiven but the baby just kept crying: hot and wriggling and kicking and crying. *Like he doesn't know who I am*, Beatrice thought. *Like he doesn't trust me.*

Ron Boci's driver's license had been suspended for a year but in his line of work, as he explained, he had to use a car fairly often, especially for short distances in the city. He needed to make deliveries and he couldn't always trust his buddies.

He made his deliveries at night, he told Beatrice.

During the day there was too much risk, his face was too well known in certain neighborhoods.

He usually borrowed his brother's '84 Dodge. Not in the best condition, it'd been around, Ron said, had taken some hard use. His own car, a new Century, white, red leather inside, wire wheels, vinyl roof, stereo— he'd totaled it last January out on the highway. Hit some ice, went into a skid, it all happened pretty fast. Totaled, Ron said with a soft whistle, smiling at Beatrice. He'd walked away from the crash, though, just a few scratches, bloody nose—"Not like the poor fuckers in the other car."

Beatrice stared. "So you were almost killed," she said.

"Hell no," Ron said, "didn't I just tell you? I walked away on my own two feet."

*(Once Beatrice had happened to remark to Tony that he was lucky, real lucky about something. The precise reason for the remark she no longer remembered, but she remembered Tony's quick reply: "Shit," he said, "you make your own luck.")*

MANSLAUGHTER SHOULD HAVE MEANT—how many years in prison? Not very many compared to a sentence for first-degree murder, or even second-degree murder, but, still, people in the neighborhood were astonished to hear that a governing board called the state appeals court had overturned Eddie Farrell's conviction. Like that!—"overturned" his conviction on a technicality that had to do with the judge's remarks while the jury was in the courtroom!

"Christ, I can't believe it," Beatrice's father said, tapping the newspaper with a forefinger. "I mean—*Jesus.* How do those asshole lawyers do it?"

So Eddie Farrell was free, suddenly. Released from the county house of detention and back home.

It was no secret that Eddie had killed his wife, but people had been saying all along she'd asked for it, she'd asked for it for years, knowing Eddie had a nasty temper (like all the Farrells). Beatrice was stunned, didn't know what to think. And didn't want to talk about it. Her father said, laughing angrily, "It says here that Eddie Farrell told a reporter 'I was innocent before, and I'm innocent now.'"

Word got around the neighborhood: Eddie hadn't any hard feelings toward people who'd testified against him at the trial. He guessed they had to tell the truth as they saw it, they'd been subpoenaed and all. He guessed they didn't mean him any personal injury.

Now, he said, he hoped everybody would forget. *He* wasn't the kind of guy to nurse a grudge.

BEATRICE'S MOTHER HEARD FROM a woman friend that Tony was back in town—someone had seen him with one of his brothers over on Holland Avenue. One day, pushing Danny in the stroller, Beatrice thought she heard someone come up behind her, she had a feeling it was Tony, but she didn't look around: just kept pushing the stroller.

In Woolworth's window she saw the reflection of a young kid in a T-shirt striding past her. It wasn't Tony, and she was happy with herself for not being frightened. *You don't have any claim on me*, she would tell him. *I'm twenty years old. I have my own life.*

The rumor that Tony Grazia was back in town must have been a lie, because Beatrice received another postcard from him at the beginning of August. He'd written only hello, asked how she and Danny were, how the weather was up north—it was hot as hell, he said, down there. *Hot as hell* was underscored. Since there was no return address, Beatrice couldn't reply to the card. *I have my own life*, she was going to tell him, all her anger gone quiet and smooth.

It was meant to be a joke in the household, Tony's three postcards Scotch-taped on the back of the bathroom door, each the same photo of a Gulf of Mexico sunset.

"You're getting a strange sense of humor," Beatrice's father told her.

"Maybe I always had one," Beatrice said.

LATER THAT WEEK BEATRICE was in the shower at Ron Boci's, lathering herself vigorously under her arms, between her legs, between her toes, when she felt a draft of cooler air—she heard the bathroom door open and close.

"Hey," she called out, "don't come in here. I don't want you in here."

He'd said he was going out for a pack of cigarettes, but now he yanked open the scummy glass door to the stall and stepped inside, naked, grinning. He clapped his hands over his eyes and said, "Don't you look at me, honey, and I won't look at you." Beatrice laughed wildly. They were so close she couldn't see him anyway—the skinny length of him, the hard fleshy rod erect between his legs, the way coarse black hairs grew on his thighs and legs, even on the backs of his pale toes.

They struggled together, they nipped and bit at each other's lips, still a little high from the joint they'd shared, and the bottle of dago wine. Beatrice wanted to work up a soapy lather on Ron Boci's chest, but he knocked the bar of soap out of her hands. He gripped her hard by the buttocks, lifted her toward him, pushed and poked against her until he entered her, already thrusting, pumping, hard. Beatrice clutched at him, her arms around his neck, around his shoulders, her eyes shut tight in pain. It was the posture, the angle, that hurt. The rough tile wall of the shower stall against her back. "Hold still," he said, and she did. She locked herself against him in terror of falling. "Hold still," he said, grunting, his voice edged with impatience.

Later they shared another joint, and Beatrice cut slices of a melon, a rich seedy overripe cantaloupe she'd brought him from the open-air market. Though it was on the edge of being rotten it still tasted delicious; juice ran down their chins. Beatrice stared at herself in Ron Boci's bread knife, which must have been newly purchased, it was so sharp, the blade so shiny.

"I can see myself in it," Beatrice said softly, staring. "Like a mirror."

ONE SATURDAY NIGHT IN the fall Ron Boci played a sly little trick on Beatrice.

They were going out, they were going on a double date with another couple, and who should come by to Ron's apartment to pick them up but Eddie Farrell? He was driving a new green Chevy Camaro; his girlfriend was a slight acquaintance of Beatrice's from high school, named Iris O'Mara.

Beatrice's expression must have been comical because both Eddie and Ron burst out laughing at her. Eddie stuck out his hand, grinning, and said, "Hey Beatrice, no hard feelings, okay? Not on *my* side." Ron nudged her forward, whispered something in her ear she didn't catch. She saw her hand go out and she saw Eddie Farrell take it, as if they were characters in a movie. *Was this happening? Was she doing this?* She didn't even know if, beneath her shock, she was surprised.

"No hard feelings, honey: not on *my* side," Eddie repeated.

He was cheery, expansive, his old self. Grateful to be out, he said, and to be *alive*.

The focus of attention, however, was Eddie's new Camaro. He demonstrated, along lower Tice, how powerfully it accelerated—from zero to forty miles an hour *in under twenty seconds*. Hell, these were only city streets, traffic lights, and all that shit; he'd really cut loose when they got out on the highway.

Ron and Beatrice were sitting in the backseat of the speeding car but Ron and Eddie carried on a conversation in quick staccato exchanges. Iris shifted around to smile back at Beatrice. She was a redhead, petite, startlingly pretty, Beatrice's age though she looked younger. Her eyelids were dusted with something silvery and glittering and her long, beautifully shaped fingernails were painted frosty pink. To be friendly she asked Beatrice a few questions—about Beatrice's baby, about her parents—*not* about Tony—but with all the windows down and the wind rushing in it was impossible to talk.

Eddie drove out of town by the quickest route, using his brakes at the intersections, careful about running red lights: He wasn't going to take any chances ever again, he said. It was a warm muggy autumn night, but Beatrice had begun to shiver and couldn't seem to stop. She wore stylish white nylon trousers that flared at the ankle, a light-textured maroon top, open-toed sandals with a two-inch heel; she looked good but the goddamned wind was whipping her hair like crazy and it seemed to be getting colder every minute. Ron Boci noticed her shivering finally and laid his arm warm and heavy and hard around her shoulders, pulling her against him in a gesture that was playful, but loving: "Hey honey," he said, "is this a little better?"

# You Don't Know What It's Like

## BILL PRONZINI

# Bill Pronzini's Introduction:

*I was twenty-two and working as a warehouseman for a San Francisco plumbing supply company when I wrote "You Don't Know What It's Like." It was the second story I attempted as therapy after the breakup of a brief, grim first marriage. (In my teens I perpetrated half a dozen stories, all slanted for hardboiled mystery magazines such as* Manhunt; *they came bouncing back with printed rejection slips, speedily and deservedly.) The first of the therapeutic tales, the title of which I no longer remember, was pretty terrible; on the advice of the literary agency to which I paid a reading fee for analysis, it was never submitted to any magazine. The fee-desk reader was more enthusiastic about my second submission, pronouncing it salable and agreeing to market it.*

*(The fee man was Barry Malzberg, with whom I would later collaborate on four novels and more than forty shorter works. But that's another story.)*

*"You Don't Know What It's Like" was bought on its first submission by Cylvia Kleinman and Leo Margulies, editor and publisher respectively of several digest-size mystery and western periodicals. They paid me sixty dollars and published the story in the November 1966 issue of* Shell Scott Mystery Magazine—*the last issue of SSMM and the first of a dozen magazines I have inadvertently helped to kill off. Leo and Cylvia, good and nurturing friends to many young writers, asked to see more of my stories and eventually commissioned lead novellas for* Mike Shayne Mystery Magazine, The Man From U.N.C.L.E., *and* Zane Grey Western Magazine. *More than anyone else, they were responsible for my becoming, in the phrase of irreverent literary sage Jack Woodford, a "professional fiction racketeer."*

*In those early days, my ability was both raw and limited. I was at that highly impressionable age when novice writers imitate what they read and admire. One of my passions was Hemingway; another, my having eclectic tastes then and now, was paperback original mystery and adventure novels published under the Fawcett Gold Medal imprint—in particular those by Gil Brewer, who owned a spare, clipped, Hemingwayesque style of his own. The noir plot and style of "You Don't*

Know What It's Like," therefore, is a shameless melding of bad Hemingway, passable Brewer, and pubescent Pronzini.

Still, for a maiden effort, the story seems to hold up reasonably well. At least, I didn't cringe more than half a dozen times when I reread it recently. I was tempted to rewrite it, but opted instead for a few minor editorial changes to remove the worst of my youthful offenses. It is what it is, and ought to more or less remain that way. A caring parent should not be ashamed of his firstborn, after all, no matter what it may look like to him thirty-five years later.

# You Don't Know What It's Like

## BILL PRONZINI

THE SKY WAS THE color of a steel bar when I got down to Bay Fisheries that morning. The air smelled wet and damp. A sharp wind kicked down from the north, and the bay was all spread with white froth. We were in for some blow.

I came up onto the pier and Alf, this half-wit I use for a mate, was already there. He spotted me.

"Jack," he said. "Hey, Jack."

"Listen," I said. "Did you get the bait?"

"It's trouble," Alf said. "Big trouble."

I looked at him.

"No bait, Jack. Old Charley, he said no more bait. The Greek told him."

Well, now, wasn't this the topper? I said to Alf, "What about the fuel?"

Alf shook his head. "No diesel either," he said. "It's big trouble, Jack." He put his hand on my arm.

I shook it off. He was pretty rumdum, Alf, but as fine a mate as you could ever want. I was giving him five bucks a day.

"All right," I said to him. "I'm going to see the Greek. You wait here."

"Okay, Jack."

I went across the pier. They had big iron crab pots stacked to one side of the main building. Beyond them was a door set into the side of the corrugated iron. It was the Greek's office.

I stood there. This Greek had taken over Bay Fisheries six months ago, and he'd put on the screws. He'd cut the rate on salmon to low base, and jacked up the prices on bait and diesel.

It was slack season, too. The worst in eight years.

And now he'd cut me off.

315

I shoved open the door and went in there.

The Greek was behind his wide gun-metal gray desk opposite the door, bent over some kind of ledger. A fat blowfish in shirt sleeves, with a blob of colorless putty for a nose, tongue held between stained teeth and glistening wet like a pink eel. Black ringlets lay on his skull like oiled springs.

He looked up.

"Jack," he said. "Hello, boy."

I slammed the door.

"All right," I said. "Let's hear about it."

"Take it easy," the Greek said. "Sit down."

"The hell with that."

He licked his lips. They were the color of spoiled liver sausage. He said, "I'm sorry about the credit, Jack. It was all I could do."

"Sure."

"You're a month behind. You're into me for four hundred."

"McGivern carried me for three months. And for twice that."

"That was McGivern."

"Listen," I said, "I can't operate without bait and fuel. And I can't pay you. What the hell do you want?"

"You got to look at it my way, Jack," he said. "I can't make any money with you owing me and going in deeper every day. These are hard times, boy. First thing you know, I'm carrying the whole fleet. It's just bad business."

"Look," I said. "There's rumors of a big salmon run. Down from Alaska. Give me another couple of weeks."

"I can't do it."

"So that's the way you want it," I said. "All right." There was no use in pushing it. He was a hard one, this Greek. I turned for the door.

"Wait a minute," he said. "Maybe we can work something out."

I came around.

"Sit down, Jack."

I just stood there. He got out a cigar and bit off the end. He lit it with some kind of gold thing on his desk.

He said, "I need somebody to do a job for me. A good man with a boat."

I stared at him. "What kind of job?"

"Nothing much. Just pick up some goods. That's all."

"What goods?"

"That's not important."

I could smell dead fish. "What's the pitch?"

"You meet a boat," he said. "This boat will have a crate. You deliver the crate here to Bay Fisheries. That's it. Nothing at all."

I didn't like the sound of it. Not a bit. You could figure what it was. Contraband. Whiskey, maybe. They smuggle it out of Canada and bring it in on the coast. There's nice money in a deal like that.

It didn't surprise me much to see the Greek in on it.

I said, "You picked the wrong guy."

He blew out green smoke.

"Look," he said, "this thing's worth five hundred to me. Five hundred big ones, Jack."

I chewed that around.

"That squares you on the books," the Greek said. "And you got another hundred besides. All for a couple hours' work."

I said, "I don't like it."

"You don't have to like it. Just do the job and take the five hundred."

I shook my head.

"No," I said. "Count me out."

"You better think about it, boy. You better think hard."

"Meaning what?"

"Just that," the Greek said. "You're cut off now, Jack. You don't play right with me, I can see you don't get a job cutting bait."

He was some boy all right. He'd set me up for this. He'd pulled my credit, shoved me over the barrel. I didn't have a pot the way it was. It was either go along with him, or I was through. Some choice.

I clamped my teeth down tight together and took a breath. I said, "All right."

The Greek gave me a wide, yellow smile. He said, "Good boy, Jack."

I just looked at him. Then I said, "What about the credit?"

"I'll take care of that with Charley," he said.

I went to the door and opened it. Behind me the Greek said, "You stick with me, Jack. You'll do okay."

"Sure," I said.

I went back to the pier. Alf was still there. "What happened, Jack?"

"Go see Charley," I said to him. "Pick up the bait. I'm going to have her gassed."

"We got credit again, Jack?" Alf said. "We all right?"

"We're all right," I said. "We're fine now."

THE THING CAME OFF with no trouble.

I put out from Bay Fisheries with the *Marietta II* at a little past ten that Friday. It was a nice night, the stars laid out like bits of silver on black crepe. The storm had blown through now.

Up on the bridge I lit a cigarette. In the flare of the match I could see the brown envelope the Greek had given me, up there on the wheel housing. I knew what was inside, all right.

I took the *Marietta II* across the harbor and out past the breakwater. It was calm, and the bow, cutting through, spun just a few drops of spray against the open windshield.

They had it rigged up about five miles out, west by southwest. The Greek had given me the compass reading.

I cut the throttle down when I neared the place, like the Greek had said. They had this signal to identify us, two short flicks with the spot. I couldn't see much in the black, but then the light came on about five hundred yards to my right and falling southward. They blinked it on and off and I gave it back to them.

They held on the spot for a second to let me see where they were. I took the *Marietta II* up alongside. It was this big cruiser, about thirty-six foot, sitting low in the water. I could make out two of them in the stern, standing at the rail.

I cut the engines and came down off the bridge. One of them tossed me a line and I made it fast.

This one jumped over onto the *Marietta II*. He stood there, looking at me.

"Jack," he said. "That right?" The Greek had given them the word.

"That's right," I said.

"Okay, Jack," this guy said. "Let's see what you've got."

I went up on the bridge and got the envelope and gave it over. He tore off the top and looked inside.

"Okay," he said. "Let's get at it."

I followed him over onto the cruiser. The other one was standing there, near the cabin. He had a big Thompson gun slung over one arm.

I stopped, looking at him. I felt cold.

This guy moved the Thompson gun just a little.

"Well?" he said. "Do you think this is a picnic?"

We went down the companionway and aft to the main quarters. It was dark. The guy turned on a pencil flash. I could see a big wooden crate against one of the bulkheads, strapped in heavy band iron. Stenciled across the face in black letters was: *Martins and Kelleher, Vancouver, British Columbia*, and below that, in smaller print, *Quality Fishing Line*.

The crate was pretty heavy. We got it over onto the *Marietta II* and into the wheelhouse, just the two of us. The other one stood out of the way with the Thompson gun, watching.

When it was done, the guy climbed back aboard the cruiser. He untied the line.

"Shove off, Jack," he said.

I fired up and turned her around and headed back. A sharp north wind had come up. It was pretty cold now.

My stomach felt a little queasy, the way it had there on the cruiser. Those two had been a real pair of red-hots, for a fact. I got the bottle I kept inside and had a long one to ease me down.

I wasn't cut out for this kind of thing at all.

HAVE YOU EVER SEEN the way it can get?

The salmon run down from Alaska petered out. It was as if they had all died there in spawn. I was into the Greek again before two weeks were out.

I didn't have a place to turn. The Greek had me six ways from Sunday on this smuggling thing. I couldn't get back out.

I didn't like to think much about it. But there was plenty of risk. It scared me, all right.

But what could I do?

There was the money, too. It was five hundred for every run I made. Two a month, was the way the Greek put it to me. A thousand bucks.

I didn't like it. It was black money, sure enough. But you can see that I just didn't have any choice. I was caught up in it, and I didn't have any choice at all.

The Greek sent down word for me one morning after I'd brought in the second crate. He was stewing on something. He wanted to know, was anything said to me when I was out there on the cruiser? I said no. But that was all. You could see this thing eating him.

He sat there behind his desk. He said, "There's another meet a week from Monday night."

"All right."

"I'm coming along."

I looked at him. I wondered what it was about. But I didn't say anything. It was the best for me if I didn't know any more about it.

THE FOG HAD COME in early, and by ten-thirty it was a gray blanket over the harbor. The Greek was there. He had a dead green cigar shredded between his teeth, a blue mackinaw buttoned up to his throat.

We boarded the *Marietta II*. I got her warmed up, then backed her and got her turned around. The Greek came up on the bridge and stood with me at the wheel. He just stared straight ahead, out over the black water. It was eating him bad.

We got past the breakwater. The wind was pretty strong. I put her wide open and lashed down the wheel. I got out a smoke.

The Greek said, "Listen, have you got anything to drink? I could use one, boy."

"Some whiskey," I said. I turned, and my arm brushed against the pocket of his mackinaw.

I backed off. "Hey," I said. "What have you got?"

He stared at me.

"It's a gun," I said. "What the hell?"

"Forget it, Jack."

"Listen, what's it for?"

"It's nothing for you."

"Is it trouble? Is that it?"

"Let it alone," the Greek said.

I didn't like this. I hadn't figured for it. The Greek looked at me. "Get me that drink, will you?"

I went into the wheelhouse and got the jug and brought it to him. He took a slug and handed me the bottle.

I had a long one. It trailed fire. I didn't like this at all.

I stood at the wheel. I tried to figure it. Something had gone wrong. It looked bad.

After awhile, we came near the spot. I cut the throttle, and the *Marietta II*'s bow sloughed down and she settled in her wake. The Greek was peering into the darkness. "See anything?"

"No."

"Are we on course?"

"We're out about five and right on. This is it."

I shut her off. It was quiet. All you could hear was the wind.

We waited. I lit another smoke and pulled one out of the bottle. I was pretty nervous, waiting.

And then this light came on, dead ahead of us, blinking the signal. I kicked my spot on and off, and I could hear the whine of their engines as they came toward us. After a minute I could see them, black against the lighter gray of the sky, and they came alongside. The two of them were at the rail. One tossed the line over and the Greek took it.

The first guy jumped over the rail, onto the *Marietta II*. He stared at the Greek.

"What the hell?" he said.

"Stow it," the Greek said. "Where's the shipment?"

"Did you bring the money?"

"Let's see the stuff first."

"All right," the guy said. "Come aboard."

We did that. The other guy stood a little way off, and he still had that Thompson gun. We went below decks and into the main quarters.

"Turn on some lights," the Greek said. "You can't see a damn thing."

"You're nuts," the guy said. "What if somebody should see?"

"The hell with it. Turn on some lights, I say."

The guy went over and switched on a lamp on the port bulkhead. The crate was there, like always. The Greek went to it.

"Get me a crowbar," he said to the guy.

"Are you nuts?" the guy said.

"Just get it."

"Listen—"

"Goddamn it!" the Greek said.

The other guy had come inside, and the first one looked at him.

"Get him the bar," the other guy said.

The first one went outside, and I could hear him on the bridge. He came back with a crowbar. The Greek took it. He pried up a couple of boards across the top of the crate, and then used the bar to twist the band iron until it snapped.

There were spools of fishing line inside, what looked like number nine linen. I watched him. I had a crawly feeling on the back of my neck.

The Greek emptied about half the crate, then he came up with this little metal box. It was taped shut.

He took the box and set it on the table aft. He looked pretty grim. He cut the tape and got the box open. The two guys just watched, not saying anything.

The Greek wet his finger and stuck it inside the box. He brought it out and licked it again. He looked at the two guys, and his eyes were black coal chips.

"It's been cut," he said.

Nobody said anything.

"Milk sugar," the Greek said.

"Well?" the guy with the Thompson gun said.

"Forty percent milk sugar," the Greek said. "The last two shipments the same way. You've been cutting it."

"What's with him?" the other guy said.

"Nuts," the guy with the Thompson gun said.

"Listen, you bastards," the Greek said. He was getting pretty worked up. A tic jumped along his jaw. "I've got contacts on my neck over this cut stuff. I'm in hot water. I won't stand for it, you hear?"

"That's your troubles," the guy with the Thompson gun said.

"It's damn well your troubles, too," the Greek said. His voice was like a knife. "I want the pure, see? From now on, nothing but the pure. You got that?"

"You just got nothing to say about it," the guy with the Thompson gun said.

"I got plenty to say about it!" the Greek snapped. You could see it in his face. He'd gone over, all right. "I got this to say about it!"

It happened so fast then you didn't have time to think.

The Greek's hand jumped to the pocket of his mackinaw and he got the gun out and came up with it. The guy jumped on one side, his face a mask, and let go with a burst from the Thompson gun. There was an awful roar, and the cabin lit up in orange flame.

I pitched sideways against the bulkhead, went down with something stinging my shoulder, and covered up my head with my hands.

But I could still see the Greek, on his knees now, next to the table, with the gun still up and he fired twice. The guy came up on his toes, like you see dancers do, and then spun in a half-circle, and then he dropped and the Thompson gun clattered on the deck. The other one went after it, got his hands on the muzzle. The Greek cut loose with two more and blew away the side of the guy's head.

It was very quiet. All you could hear was the slap of water against the hull as the cruiser rocked in the swells.

I lay there against the bulkhead. I couldn't move. The air was seared with burnt gunpowder.

The Greek got to his feet. He stood looking down at the two of them. His face was paste-white. He turned to me.

"We've got to get out of here," he said.

I got to my feet and leaned there. I was shaking like the palsy. I couldn't stop shaking.

The Greek grabbed the metal box off the table. He pushed me ahead of him down the companionway and up on deck. We climbed over onto the *Marietta II* and the Greek got the bottle and drank deep and then gave it to me. I got some down. My hand kept shaking and spilling it over my chest.

There was blood on my windbreaker. I opened it up. It was just a narrow groove in the skin. I rubbed my face. "God," I said.

"Come on," the Greek said. "Let's get out of here."

I went on the bridge and started her. The Greek cast off the line. I opened her full bore.

The Greek came up beside me. I had another one out of the bottle. I wished I could stop shaking.

We'd gone a way. There was nothing in sight. The wind was chill. I could feel the sweat drying on my body. I looked at the Greek.

"You killed them," I said. "You killed them both."

"Take it easy," the Greek said.

"What did you want to go and bring that damn gun for?"

"I wasn't going to use it," the Greek said. He looked scared some, too. "I lost my head."

"What are we going to do?"

"Nothing. It's done now."

"What happens when they're found?"

"They can't tie them to us," the Greek said.

"But what if somebody saw us go out tonight?"

"None of that, now."

It was silent for a minute. I looked over at that metal box the Greek had.

"What have you got in there?" I said. "It's drugs, isn't it? Heroin, or something."

"What did you think?"

Oh, Lord. I took a pull on the bottle.

"Listen," I said. "I want out of this. I don't want any part of it."

"You don't have a choice, Jack."

"I can't take this kind of thing," I said. "I figured it for booze-running. But drugs. And now murder, and almost dying out there. It's too much. I can't take it, I tell you."

The Greek's eyes glared black. "Now, listen, boy. If you know what's good for you, you'll do what I tell you. You just keep your mouth shut. That's all you have to do."

I was shaking so bad now I couldn't keep my hands on the wheel. *What happens now?* I thought. *Where does it go from here?*

YOU DON'T REALLY FEEL it all at once.

It takes some time. There is the shock at first. You put it out of your mind. You don't think about it.

I was sitting at the table in the kitchen after we'd come in, with a bottle of whiskey, when it came on me. I got to shaking so bad I had no control over my body. I was cold. It was like I was done up in a block of ice.

After awhile it went away. But I couldn't stop thinking. I began to drink the whiskey. I drank it straight and very fast. The bottle was empty. I got up to get another one from the cupboard. That's all I remember.

I came awake on the kitchen floor. Hot white light from the sun filtered in through the window. I felt very bad with it. I found the other bottle and took a drink.

I had to get out of there. It was like the walls were closing in on me. I drove down to Bay Fisheries. It was only seven-thirty.

Alf was already there, washing down the *Marietta II* with a hose. I came down off the pier and onto the board float leading to my slip. Alf waved. "Hey, Jack."

I climbed aboard. Alf shut off the hose. He looked at me with his head kind of hanging loose to one side in that way he had.

"Jack," he said. "You don't look so good. You sick, Jack? You all right, boy?"

"Yeah," I said. "I'm okay."

He came up close to me. His eyes were bright. He kind of gave you the willies, being this half-wit and all.

"Did you hear about what happened, Jack?" he said. "Did you hear the news?"

"No," I said.

"There was a shooting last night. The Coast Guard found this boat. There was two men dead on her. All shot up. Murdered."

I could feel sweat in my armpits.

"One of the commercials come in with the news," Alf said. "Saw 'em towing her into the Coast Guard station at Bodega Bay."

My head pounded.

"It's a real mystery, Jack," Alf said. "Ain't it something? Ain't it really something?"

"Sure," I said. "It's something, all right."

I got away from there and went to the Greek's office. He looked like he hadn't slept at all. I said, "You know they found the cruiser?"

"I know," he said. "What did you expect?"

"I don't know."

"The Coast Guard will be along pretty soon," he said. "They'll ask questions."

"I can't take that," I said. "I can't talk to them."

The Greek said, "Now you take it easy."

"I can't talk to them."

"Look," the Greek said. "I don't like this any more than you do. But that's the way it is. I'll handle things."

"How?"

"Take the *Marietta II* out. Stay out all day. When the Coast Guard comes I'll fix up a story. You were with me last night. Playing poker. You stick to that."

"All right."

He looked at me. "You been on the booze?"

"Some."

"Well, you lay off. Hear that? You get on that stuff and go popping off to somebody, the both of us are stuck."

"All right," I said.

We took the *Marietta II* out, north toward Jenner. It was a bad morning. Alf had the lines out, chattering away. It felt like the top of my head would come off.

After a time I told him to lock up the outriggers. He wanted to know why, and if I was all right, and did I want to go in to see the doc. I yelled at him to shut it. He got all pouty like a little kid, and went into the stern and sat there and didn't say anything.

I stuck it out until three. I killed what was left in the bottle there in the wheelhouse. I got a little edge on. I felt a little better.

We came in across the harbor. I figured sure to see the big gray Coast Guard cutter docked at the pier there. But there was no sign.

I found the Greek in the warehouse.

"What happened?" I said.

"They were here," he said. "It's all right. They hit a blank. Nobody saw or heard anything."

"What do they know?"

"They hit on the smuggling angle. But they won't find much."

"What's going to happen?"

"Nothing. We just have to play it tight for awhile."

"Sure."

He looked at me.

"Listen," he said. "I thought I told you to lay off the booze. What's the matter with you?"

"I'm scared," I said. "It's got me down."

"Just take it slow," the Greek said. "Everything's all right."

I nodded. But I knew everything wasn't all right. I knew it wasn't all right at all.

I SAT IN A rear booth in a little roadhouse a mile or two up the highway from Bay Fisheries. It's this place where the commercial crews hang out. But it was only just after six, and too early for the crowd.

I had a bottle there in the booth with me. I'd been there four hours. I hadn't taken the *Marietta II* out in two days, since that afternoon.

Mostly I'd been on the bottle. The Greek was plenty sore at me for it. But I couldn't help it with the thing on me the way it was. It was the only way.

I sloshed whiskey into the glass and had it off. Up at the bar a hooker who worked the fleet spots along the coast was sitting sideways on her stool, smiling, giving me the eye.

I lit a cigarette. The smoke was bitter. This girl got up from her stool and went over and put a quarter in the juke. She stood there for a time, listening. Then she came over to where I was and sat down across from me.

"Hello, Jack," she said. "Buy me a drink?"

"Sure," I said.

"Thanks." She poured one and hit it, and brushed this black hair away from her face. She looked at me over the glass. She wasn't a bad kid. I knew she liked me.

I could feel her leg against mine under the table. "You look sick, Jack," she said. "Troubles?"

I laughed. "No," I said. "Nothing like that."

She lifted her glass again.

"Well," she said. "Cheers."

I poured another drink and lifted it. I saw her smiling at me. I put the drink down. The girl's face began to dissolve in this white fog. There was sudden pain in back of my eyes. Gulls screamed in my ears.

"Jack," I heard her say. "Are you all right?"

I covered my face with my hands and pressed a finger hard over each eye. The pain dimmed. I took my hands away. The white fog was gone.

The hooker's eyes were wide.

"I'm okay," I said to her. "I just need some air."

I stood up. My right leg felt numb. I took a step on it, caught onto the back of the booth. I took another step, and I had some balance. I went across to the door and outside.

It was very hot. The air was still and choked with heat; you could see this kind of dark haze, like gossamer, over the sky.

I took deep breaths. The air smelled of salt and kelp and dark rain. It bit into the back of my nose. I could hear my heart thumping like a jackpump.

I went to my car and stood with my hands on the cold metal of the hood. I felt very strange. I wondered if it could be that I were losing my mind.

I started the car and swung up on to the highway. I had to see the Greek. There had to be a way for me to get away from here. I couldn't take much more of this.

I drove out past the cottage the Greek had. It was dark. His car was gone. Maybe he was late at Bay Fisheries on something.

There was sweat in my eyes, down my back. I stared at the white line. After a time I could see the lot in front of Bay Fisheries. There was the Greek's car, and this other one. I had never seen it before. It was pulled in close to the building.

I could feel dark things on my skin. I slowed the car and pulled off the side of the road. I had a feeling there was something wrong; you could smell it on the heavy air.

I went across the lot and up on to the pier. The Greek's office was up ahead. The door stood open a bit, and there was a light on inside. I swung the door. It was empty.

I wiped sweat off my face. The gulls were back at my ears. I went along the pier, and around to the rear of the main building. The corrugated-iron doors into the warehouse were unlocked and open about a foot. I went up to them and looked inside. A night light on a post burned up near the front.

I stepped inside. The single light cast quivering black shadows. The silence was the crash of angry surf.

And then gray shadows detached from the black, looming shapes angling across the concrete floor. Another light came on, this from a big flash, and I saw the Greek.

He stood with his back to a long conveyor belt that stretched the width of the warehouse. His face was fishbelly white in the light.

I crouched down behind a forklift standing silent near another of the posts. The shapes, still moving, came into the circle of light from the night lamp.

There were two of them, in dark suits and wide snap brims. One of them held the flash, the other this tan leather suitcase.

The Greek's eyes had hidden in the fat of his face. His lips worked. His voice carried across to me, echoing.

"All right. You've got the stuff. You've got what you came for. What happens now?"

"What do you think?" one of them said.

"Listen," the Greek said. He was sweating like somebody had poured water over him. "What happened there on the boat, it was an accident. You got to believe that."

"Doesn't make any difference," this one said. "Either way."

"Don't you see?" the Greek said. "It was cut stuff. They were cutting it."

"We know all about it."

"You know?"

"What did you think?" the guy said. "This is no two-bit deal."

"But I was paying for the pure."

"Oh, hell," the one who did the talking said. "You were paying our price for the cut. Just like the rest."

The Greek shook his head.

"Who did you think you were dealing with?" the guy said.

The Greek looked sick.

"No," he said. "Oh, God, I didn't know."

The other guy, the one who hadn't said anything before, turned to the first one.

"He's dumb," he said. "He's about the dumbest boy I ever saw."

"But nothing was said. Nothing!"

"That's too bad for you," the first one said. "You should have stayed out of it."

"Please," the Greek said.

"Come on," the second one said to the first. "Let's get it done."

"All right," the first one said.

"Please," the Greek said again.

I saw the two of them back off a step, and then I could see the guns. The barrels looked a foot long. The one said, "This is it."

They planted their feet, with their arms straight out, stiff, and the Greek made a sound like an animal in the night, and they opened up with the guns.

They made little popping sounds, not like a gun should sound at all, and the Greek slipped down to one knee, his hands coming up in front of him, and then one took him in the chest and another in the face, and he pitched forward and rolled on his back and lay still. But they kept pouring it into him until both guns were empty.

Then the two of them put the guns inside their coats. One went over and knelt down by the Greek and the other snapped the flash on him. He didn't have a face anymore.

I lurched to my feet and stumbled over to the door and got outside. I went around the building and down off the pier. A gale wind had come up. It whipped my face.

I made it to my car and fell down by the rear tire. I pressed my face on the cold ground and lay there like that for a time.

Then I got to my knees and pulled the door open and sprawled inside. I started the car and let out the clutch. The tires screamed.

I saw the darkened windows of my cabin. I couldn't remember driving there. The lower part of my face had begun to tremble. I parked and got out and went inside.

The bottle was on the table where I had left it. I tilted it up. My stomach recoiled. I held onto the edge of the table. The smell was raw. I got more of the whiskey down and squeezed my eyes shut and it stayed there.

I took the bottle and went over and sat by the window. My head ached with pain I had never known before. I couldn't think. I drank more of the whiskey.

I knew they had killed the Greek because of the two men on the cruiser. But there was more to it than that. I didn't understand what it was. But it didn't matter now.

I knew they would be coming for me soon. It was the way they did things. I had been scared watching them do it to the Greek, but I wasn't scared now. It was too late for that.

*If I'm going to get away it has to be now.*

*But how far can you run?*

*Not that far. Not ever that far.*

I couldn't do it. I'd seen too much of it.

You don't know what it's like.

I sat there by the window and drank. Out on the street, at the far end, I could see headlights.

It had begun to rain.

# The Disappearance of Penny

## ROBERT J. RANDISI

The Intemperance
of Penny

ROBERT A. RANDISI

## Robert J. Randisi's Introduction:

*"The Disappearance of Penny" was my second story sale. The first was a story called "Murder Among Witches" which was, indeed, about just that. So I consider "Penny" to actually be my first straight mystery story.*

*"Penny" appeared in Alfred Hitchcock's Mystery Magazine. At the time that I sold it I was sitting on the MWA Edgar committee for Best Mystery TV Show with, among others, Eleanor Sullivan, who at that time was editing both Hitchcock and EQMM. So the sale falls under two categories: the "Right Place at the Right Time" category, and the "It's Not What You Know, But Who" category. Of course, I had to have written a good story in order to take advantage of my situation, i.e., serving on a committee with possibly the most powerful and influential short story editor of that time.*

*In all I sold three stories to Eleanor and they appeared in three consecutive issues of AHMM, beginning with this story, which was in the December 1976 issue—also, the Twentieth Anniversary issue of the magazine. To this day I have never sold them another story, whether the editor was Eleanor or the current editor, Cathleen Jordan. No complaint, mind you, just a "by the way."*

*In addition to being my first straight mystery sale, "Penny" was also my very first private-eye story. The P.I. in the story is named "Frank Tucker," but later, when I sold the idea as a novel and it actually became my first novel sale, I changed his name to "Henry Po." Four Po books were planned, but alas, The Disappearance of Penny—published in 1980—was the only one to see the light of day. You see, those were the days of Fluctuating Editorial Policies, and the series of Po books fell victim. I did go on to write five Po stories, two of which have been published just over the past five years. As a matter of fact, "The Girl Who Talked To Horses," which appeared in 1996, went on to be nominated for a Shamus Award, and appeared in one Best of . . . collection for that year.*

*However, "The Disappearance of Penny" short story made its appearance without a ripple in a sea of mystery short stories published that year, so here it is, twenty-five years later, for your enjoyment.*

# The Disappearance of Penny

## ROBERT J. RANDISI

PENNY'S PENNY WAS HOPKINS Stable's Triple Crown hopeful for 1976. The colt had been named after Benjamin Hopkins's daughter, Penny Hopkins.

"Penny won nine out of ten races as a two-year-old, Mr. Tucker," Benjamin Hopkins bragged to me. "Her only loss was to Paul Lassiter's Bold Randy—"

"Whose only loss as a two-year-old was to Penny's Penny," I finished for him. "I follow the horses, Mr. Hopkins." Hopkins and Lassiter were chief rivals in the world of thoroughbred racing. "Could we get down to why you asked me to come here?"

"As I told you on the phone, Mr. Tucker, she left the house yesterday morning and has not returned. She's never done that before. I tried to report her missing to the police, but they inform me that she's overage."

"What they mean is that she is between eighteen and sixty-five and therefore they cannot accept a missing-persons report on her unless there is some physical evidence of foul play," I explained, "or a history of mental illness."

He waved his hand impatiently. "Yes, yes, they explained that to me. They also suggested I hire a private investigator."

He had called me that morning at my office and asked me if I would come to his office at the track. He promised me a two-hundred-dollar consultation fee even if I turned down his case.

"They told me you are a specialist in missing persons."

I nodded. "I worked with the Missing Persons Unit as a detective for six years until they changed their policy to this eighteen-to-sixty-five age limit. I disagree with the new policy, which claims it is against the constitutional rights of the missing person for us to look for him if he doesn't want to be found. How are we supposed to determine whether a person wants to be found or not?" I shrugged. "I decided to go out on my own."

He tapped the desktop with a pencil.

"I will pay you one thousand dollars to find her for me," he told me.

I didn't hesitate. "You've got yourself a detective, Mr. Hopkins."

"Fine. First I'd like you to—"

"We'd better get something straight right from the beginning," I interrupted, holding up my hand. "You've hired yourself a detective, not a leg man. You'll have to let me run the investigation my own way."

He digested that a moment, then nodded curtly. "Agreed."

I took some preliminary information from him, about his daughter's favorite places and people. He paid me the promised fee, plus a retainer, and walked me to the door. He was tall and stately looking, with plentiful snow-white hair, big shoulders, and a barrel chest. He must have been a hell of a figure twenty years before, but now he was sixty-five and showed every year of it.

"Please, Mr. Tucker," he said before I left, "find my daughter."

I had a feeling his concern was artificial, but I told him I'd try.

HOPKINS HAD SAID THAT Penny was a regular at almost every stable on the track, so that's where I began asking questions about who'd seen her and when.

I saved Paul Lassiter's stable until last.

As I approached, I saw a man come out of one of the stalls. He was tall, at least six foot one, and he was remarkably handsome. Paul Newman eyes. In his early forties.

"Paul Lassiter?" I asked on a hunch.

He turned and gave me an easy kind of grin.

"That's me. What can I do for you?"

"My name is Frank Tucker. I'm working for Benjamin Hopkins."

"In what capacity?" he asked.

I took out one of my cards and handed it to him.

"What would Benny need with a private eye?" he asked, pocketing the card.

"He's looking for his daughter. She's disappeared."

"Penny?" He seemed surprised.

"How many daughters does he have?"

"Just Penny that I know of."

"Have you seen her in the last few days?" I asked him.

"Come over to my office, Mr. Tucker. Maybe we can rustle up a drink." I followed him to the far end of the grounds where we stepped into an office very much like the one where I'd spoken to Hopkins. I turned down his offer of a drink and settled into a seat while he made one for himself. I had the feeling he was stalling for time.

He turned around, a drink in his hand, a smile on his face, and said, "I think I saw her, let me see, the day before yesterday. That would be Thursday, wouldn't it?"

"How friendly were you?"

"An old man like me?" he said. If he was acting he was doing it very well. "I'm her father's mortal—well, professional rival."

"What were you going to say?" I prodded.

He shrugged, sipped his drink. "Mortal enemy. But that's a little strong. That may be the way Benny thinks of me, but it's not the way I think of him."

"You call him Benny."

He sipped his drink again before answering. "I used to work for him. Then I branched out for myself, took some people with me. He never forgave me for that. I think he wanted me to be his protégé forever. That wasn't for me. I learned everything he could teach me, then went out on my own. I guess he considered me a traitor, probably still does."

"What was Penny doing when you saw her Thursday?"

"It was at the track lounge. She was having a drink with one of her friends, Louis Melendez."

"The jockey?"

He laughed. "Some people think of him that way."

Which didn't say much for Lassiter's opinion of Melendez's riding ability.

I thanked him for his time and left, promising myself I'd be getting back to him soon.

I couldn't locate Louis Melendez anywhere on the track grounds. He seemed to have vanished right along with Penny Hopkins. Before checking out his apartment, I decided to try the lounge where Lassiter had said he'd seen them together.

"What'll it be?" the bartender asked. He might have been an ex-jockey, judging from his size.

"A ginger ale and some information," I told him, sliding a ten across the bar. "Louis Melendez. Have you seen him?"

"Little Louie? Let me think—Thursday," he answered finally.

"Was he with anyone?" I asked.

"Sure was. That little fox, Penny Hopkins."

"Benjamin Hopkins's daughter?"

"The same. Hey, if there were two of her, wouldn't that be something?" .

"Why so?"

His eyebrows went up and almost touched his hairline.

"Haven't you ever seen her?" he asked. I shook my head. Old man Hopkins hadn't had a picture of his daughter in his office.

"Come with me," the little barkeep beckoned, coming around the bar. I followed him to a wall covered with framed photographs.

He pointed to one and I zeroed in on it. It was a shot of a curvaceous young girl surrounded by a group of jockeys. She was taller than all of them and her red hair was tied with a green ribbon. Her grin was wide, her nose slightly snubbed. Her face was that of a young girl, but the body was definitely a woman's.

"If that don't make your blood boil, you're made of stone," the bartender said.

"Is Melendez in that picture?" I asked.

"He sure is—he's the guy practically drooling into her lap." He pointed to a little guy whose hang-dog look bespoke a man hopelessly in love with someone he couldn't possibly have.

"Was he in love with her?"

"Hey, you're pretty good. Just from the picture you can tell, huh?" I stared at him until *he* got the picture. "Okay, sure he was crazy for her. I mean, everybody was a little in love with her, but he was sick."

"How'd she treat him?" I asked.

"Like a trained puppy. He was her gopher, but that was his choice, you know?" He shook his head and a faraway look came into his eyes. "I'd've been her gopher, she give me half a chance."

I turned around and went back to the bar to finish my ginger ale. It was still early and the place was empty, so he came back with me and leaned on the bar while I drained my glass.

"Thanks for the information," I told him.

"Of course, I never would have had a chance with her, same as everybody else," he said and droned on. I shut him off and was about to leave when he said something that made me stop and back up.

337

"What?" I said.

He had good instincts, that boy. As soon as he saw my interest he clammed up, waiting for the green. I reached across the bar and grabbed his tie with the horse's face on it and twisted it just a trifle.

"Repeat, please."

"Hey, okay, okay. All I said was nobody had a chance because everybody knew she was tied to Paul Lassiter."

"Yeah," I half whispered, letting loose of his tie.

I laid a five down on the bar and left.

"IT WAS A STUPID lie, Lassiter," I snapped. "If it was all over the track, you had to know I'd come back with it sooner or later. Why make it later?"

He shrugged his shoulders and reached for the drink he'd been drinking when I burst into his office. "I saw no reason to volunteer any information—besides, isn't that an occupational hazard with you? Being lied to?"

"Only by people who have something to hide," I told him.

"I have nothing to hide, Tucker." He shook his head. "I didn't think Benny would mention it to you because he was furious at the idea. He wouldn't admit to anyone that his daughter loved me. I saw no reason to admit it either."

"You've made me think you have something to hide, Lassiter. If you do, I'll find out what, I promise."

I left him and went looking for Benjamin Hopkins. He had lied to me also, even if it was a lie of omission.

He wasn't in his office and I didn't see him on the grounds.

"Where's Hopkins?" I asked his trainer, Mickey Rivers.

Rivers glared at me. He was a man of about thirty-five, retired from the races because of a bad fall some years before. Hopkins took him on as trainer because of his love for horses and it had worked out to their mutual advantage. "*Mr.* Hopkins," he began, "went home earlier. I imagine he's still there . . ."

Hopkins greeted me, asking, "Have you found out something already?"

"Yes, I have. I found out about Penny and Paul Lassiter. That was something you should have told me, Mr. Hopkins."

"I don't see why that—" he began imperiously.

"I can see why you might not want to admit that Lassiter was taking something from you, especially your daughter, but if you are really concerned about finding her, your pride shouldn't interfere. That is, if your real interest is in finding her."

"What do you mean by that?" he demanded.

"Just that your main interest may not be in *where* she is, but in whether or not she's with Lassiter."

The look on his face told me I had him pegged right. He wasn't concerned about his daughter's welfare; his real concern was in finding out if Lassiter had taken a "property" away from him.

"I'd like to see her room," I told him, before he could gather his thoughts and decide he wanted to fire me.

"Come this way," he muttered. I followed him up a long winding flight of stairs and into a room larger than my entire apartment. The walls were covered with framed photographs of Penny with horses, Penny with jockeys, and Penny in the Winners Circle with her father.

"I have some paperwork to attend to downstairs," Hopkins told me. "If you need anything, call me."

When he left I began to prowl about the room, attempting to get a bead on how the girl's mind worked.

On her dressing table was a hardcover novel called *Price, Pride, and Passion* by someone I'd never heard of. The bookmark was between the last page and the back cover. I leafed through the book and decided to take it home with me. I continued to prowl and came up with a locked diary—under the mattress. I put it in my jacket pocket.

Nothing else in the room interested me except a framed picture of Paul Lassiter, at his very probable handsomest. He was smiling and it was signed, *Love, Paul.*

He was a phony, just like her old man. He didn't love her, or he wouldn't have attempted to hide the fact that they were a "thing." Neither of them loved her. They both considered her a prize to be won from one another. I took a close-up of Penny from the wall, removed it from its frame, and slid it into the book to take with me, and found myself wondering if Penny Hopkins's disappearance had been her own idea.

WHEN I CALLED MY service, there was a message from "Ray the bartender." He said he had some information for me. I didn't know a bartender named "Ray," so it had to be the one at the track lounge.

When I walked in, his face lit up in a smile. Considering the way I'd left him, it was a bit of a surprise, but it also meant he had something to sell and he thought he could sell it big.

"Hey," he said, "I been trying to find you. I got your number out of the book."

"Pour me the same as before," I told him. "Why did you want to see me?"

"I remembered something after you left this morning." He stopped and backed away so that his horseface tie was not within easy reach. I took out a five and slid it across the bar.

"To start," I told him. He nodded and gobbled it up.

"I saw Melendez after Thursday."

"When?"

"Yesterday. He came in here for a drink and he was filthy."

"What do you mean by filthy?"

"He looked as if he'd just ridden the feature in the mud and got thrown, you know? Only it ain't rained in weeks."

I digested that and swallowed some ginger ale. "He had a drink?"

"Yep. He came running in, all upsetlike. He even ordered in Spanish. I hadda ask him to repeat it in English. After he drank it, he looked around, scaredlike, you know? Then he ran out like somebody was chasing him."

"Why didn't you remember that this morning?" I asked.

"Hell, it happened so fast. He was in and gone in a couple of minutes." He shrugged. "Slipped my mind."

I thought about it. If what Ray had just told me was true and Melendez was that scared, chances are he wouldn't be at his place. He'd probably be hiding out somewhere.

"Who's he hang out with the most?" I asked. Another jock named Ramirez, Ray said. I asked him to get a message to Ramirez, telling him I had to talk to Melendez. I slid him one of my cards wrapped in a ten-dollar bill.

"He's to call me anytime, got it?"

He snatched up the ten. "I got it. What's it all about anyway?"

"The way I figure it, that's about thirty bucks you've made already. If I hear from Melendez, it could go up to fifty. Got it?"

He widened his eyes. "You got it!"

I went home and fixed myself a steak with onions, a baked potato, and a salad. Then I settled down with my night's reading.

I got a little deeper into the book and caught the drift of it. It was about a girl with a dominant father who didn't like her choice of a fiancé. The two, father and fiancé, hated each other. One night the girl was raped and murdered. The book ends with the two men crying on each other's shoulder.

The diary was next. I used a steak knife on the flimsy lock, got it open, and started reading. It was written in a little-girl scrawl that made the reading a task. It started when she was about seventeen, about two years before. Most of it was about her love of the racetrack, the horses, and the jockeys. There was a segment that said, "Little Louie brought me flowers again today. I know he loves me, and he is sweet, but Paul would never understand."

Another part lamented: "If only Paul and Daddy could become friends again, like they used to be." These, or words to the same effect, were repeated again and again.

Later on, dated just a few weeks before:

"I can't take it much longer. I feel as if I'm being torn apart, I love them both so much."

The last pages grew even more anguished, until the last page: "I finished the book this afternoon, and I think I finally have the solution. I must go see Little Louie and ask him for his help."

That was dated Thursday. On Friday Penny had disappeared. She had been seen in the track lounge with Little Louie Melendez on Thursday. On Friday Louie was seen again in the lounge, this time dirty and agitated.

I closed the diary and set it aside.

"ARE YOU THE GUY that called?" he asked. His nameplate identified him as Officer Doyle.

"That's right, officer." I took out my photostat and showed it to him. His partner, Parker, came along and took a look for himself. They'd pulled their radio car right into the meadow behind the track.

"What's this about a homicide?" Parker asked.

I shook my head. "I didn't say homicide. I said I'd found a body. It's over here."

They followed me into the brush where I had found Penny Hopkins's final resting place. I'd driven there early and had started my search of the meadow about eight-thirty. I found her at ten. I dug just deep enough to free her arm, then stopped and went back to the track to call the police. They'd sent a patrol car first, to decide whether or not the call was a crank, but as soon as Doyle saw her arm he had called to his partner to get Homicide and the lab people.

I asked him if we could wait for Homicide before I told my story so that I'd only have to tell it once. He was agreeable and we spent the time between talking horses. Neither of us looked at the grave while we spoke.

When Homicide arrived I told my story to two detectives I didn't know, Homes and Williams. I told them why I was hired, who I'd spoken to, and what led me to believe the girl was buried where she was.

"You say Melendez showed up in the bar covered with dirt?" Homes remarked. "I'll put out a wanted on him, but meanwhile if you hear anything from him, let us know."

"Would *you* let *me* know what the lab comes up with on her?" I asked him. He agreed to keep me informed.

"You got any ideas?" he asked, as we walked from the meadow.

I nodded. "Some. But I need a little more time. Ask Lieutenant Joe Garvey about me. He'll tell you it will be worth your while to give me a little rope." Garvey was my old boss at Missing Persons.

He poked a cigar into his mouth and said, "That's a pretty good recommendation. Were you on the force?"

I nodded. "Ten years."

When we reached his car he told me, "I'll talk to Garvey. If you don't hear from me, be in my office tonight." He pointed his cigar at me and added, "Ready to spill."

I GOT TO A phone and called my service. It was a little like calling OTB to see if your horse has come in—and mine had. Melendez had called and left a message for me to meet him at the opposite end of the track, beneath the grandstand. The time he wanted was twelve-thirty, and it was a quarter-past now.

The grandstand was, as I've said, at the other end of the track so that you couldn't see the meadow from there. I hoped Melendez hadn't seen the police from somewhere else and been scared off.

But when I got there he was waiting. He was like a scared deer, ready to run at any moment.

"Meester Tucker?" he asked, primed to run if I said no.

"That's right," I told him. I let him see my ID and he relaxed.

"I got message saying you want to help me." He was almost five feet tall and must have weighed all of ninety pounds.

"That's right, Louis, I do."

He nodded. "That is good. I can use help."

Just then he spotted something behind me and he froze. I turned. It was Homes with his partner and two uniformed cops.

"Damn it!" I yelled. They had tailed me.

"Don't move, Melendez!" Homes shouted. "We're the police!"

Louis glared at me and yelled, "You trick me!"

"No, Louis, I didn't!" He started to run and I hollered, "Don't run, they can't hurt you!"

"You've got nowhere to go, Melendez!" Homes shouted, coming up beside me. He had his gun out and was pointing it at the fleeing jockey. "Halt!"

"Don't shoot, damn it!" I yelled, knocking his arm up. His shot went wild and I started after Louis. I had to get to him before Homes or anyone else killed him.

I knew he hadn't killed Penny Hopkins.

He had only buried her.

"DETECTIVE HOMES AND DETECTIVE Williams, Mr. Hopkins. They're from Homicide."

Hopkins backed away from the door into his stable office and said, "Homicide! You mean he killed her?"

"Who killed her, Mr. Hopkins?" Homes asked. Williams stepped inside after us but kept the door open.

"Why, Lassiter, of course. She probably came to her senses about marrying him and he killed her!" He sat. "She is dead, isn't she?"

"Yes, Mr. Hopkins, she's dead," Homes answered. "Mr. Tucker found her buried in the meadow behind the track."

Hopkins nodded. "So he did kill her."

"You're ridiculous," came a voice from outside. Lassiter stepped into the room and faced Hopkins, a younger version of his former mentor. "You know I didn't love her, Benny. Why would I kill her?"

"Because you couldn't take her from me," Hopkins snapped.

"That's all she was to both of you, something to take from each other," I told them.

Hopkins took no offense. "I don't have to justify myself to you, Tucker. I didn't ask for a daughter, I wanted a son. And on top of that, my wife died in childbirth. How could anyone expect me to love her?" It made so much sense to him that I pitied him.

"What about you?" I asked Lassiter. "What did she mean to you?"

Lassiter shrugged. "I liked her, but I didn't love her. She knew that—"

I shook my head. "No, she didn't know that. It says in here that she loved you both." I tossed the diary at Hopkins.

"What's this?" he asked.

"It's the diary of a young girl who was being pulled apart by the only two men in the world she really cared about."

"All right, Tucker," Homes snapped, "you brought us here to convince us Melendez didn't kill the girl—so do it." Melendez was in custody, but he hadn't been charged yet.

"Melendez only buried her," I said, suddenly bone-tired. I indicated Hopkins and Lassiter and added, "They killed her."

"What?" Hopkins barked.

"You fool," Lassiter said.

"Tucker—" Homes began, but I interrupted.

"I'm sorry. I should have said they caused her death. They didn't actually murder her, but they *were* the cause."

I picked up the diary and began to explain. "Penny Hopkins was a very emotional, impressionable, unstable young girl. She loved her father and she loved Lassiter, but to them she was just something to fight over, like a beautiful colt. That confused her. She wanted them to love her and she wanted them to be friends.

"I don't know exactly how long their battle for Penny went on, but this diary goes back two years and it was happening then. That's two years she was pushed and pulled between the two people she cared most about, not knowing which way to go, which one to be loyal to . . .

"Then she read a book about a girl with very much the same problem as hers. The girl in the book had her problem solved for her. She was raped and murdered and this brought her father and boyfriend closer together. It was a terrible, romantic solution, but Penny was very much alone and very

344

much in need of a solution."

"You mean she went out and got herself raped and murdered?" Williams asked.

"I mean she shot herself."

"What?" It was a collective statement.

I turned to the last page of her diary. "The last page in her diary says she finished the book and had found her solution, but she needed Melendez's help. Melendez was in love with her, he'd do anything for her. He got her the gun she asked for and afterward he buried her."

I shut the diary and concluded.

Penny, Louis had told me, had chosen the meadow for her suicide because it was behind the track and out of sight and chances were good the shot would not be heard. After it was over, after he had watched her put the gun to her head, and pull the trigger, and he had buried her, he began to realize what he'd done. Penny had not wanted to be buried—she had wanted to be found. It was part of the plan to make her father and Lassiter think she'd been murdered, which, to her disturbed way of thinking, would bring them closer together. Instead, he, Melendez, had panicked and buried her in the meadow, along with the gun—as a result of which, he was as guilty in the eyes of the law as if he had pulled the trigger.

And so the man who had really loved Penny Hopkins would pay for Hopkins's and Lassiter's lack of love for her, and they would go scot-free. I took the photograph of the girl from my pocket and looked at it.

The two men she had adored were playing a perpetual game of chess.

She had thought she was their queen.

I'm glad she never discovered she was just another pawn.

# A Victim Must Be Found

## HENRY SLESAR

## Henry Slesar's Introduction:

*I was a victim myself back in 1955, recuperating from an illness and reading everything in sight, including my own teenage attempt at science fiction called "The Brat." I had once presumptuously mailed it to* The Magazine of Fantasy and Science Fiction, *received a cordial rejection, and immediately given up the idea of a writing career.*

*Now, with time on my hands, I aimed lower and sent it to a new publication called* Imaginative Tales. *I was so exhilarated by the fifty-dollar check that arrived a month later that I ran into the bathroom where my wife was showering, stuck the check through the curtain, and almost obliterated the signature.*

*Inspired, I dug out all my early fiction and began composing new stories at the rate of one every two weeks. Fortunately, I didn't give up my day job as creative director of a middle-sized ad agency. It was more than a year before I sold my next offering, this one written even earlier than "The Brat." I called it "The List."*

*One afternoon my secretary walked in with a befuddled expression and said that "Ellery Queen" was on the phone. It was Fred Dannay, of course, who thought his pseudonym was the easiest way to get my attention. He asked about "The List," hoping it was suitable for his cherished Department of First Stories. I could only tell him the truth, that my "first" story was published almost a year ago. He was disappointed, and so was I.*

*Dannay was a persistent man, however. He extracted the information that "The List" was actually written prior to "The Brat." The technicality was meticulously explained in his lengthy introduction to the story, which was (and is) quite short. It also appeared under a new and better title, "A Victim Must Be Found." Evidently, Fred Dannay was a Gilbert and Sullivan fan.*

*I'll always regret that I never got to meet Fred Dannay in person. (I did get to meet another great-hearted editor of the genre, Leo Margulies.) But I'm happy with my long-term relationship to Ellery Queen's fine magazine, which has now published more than fifty of my stories since "A Victim Must Be Found."*

# A Victim Must Be Found

## HENRY SLESAR

THE LOOKS HURT MOST. The quizzical one from Dennis, the Account Supervisor. The knowing, falsely sympathetic one from Hargrove, the head Art Director. The amused, poor henpecked-slob look from Mead, research man of the advertising agency.

Bill Hendricks looked disapprovingly at his secretary. "I told you not to interrupt me," he said. "Tell Mrs. Hendricks I'll call her back."

"She said it was very important, Mr. Hendricks." Her own face registered neither approval nor disapproval.

Hendricks scraped back his chair. Dennis waved permission to leave. "It's all right, Bill," he said emotionlessly. "We're almost through here, anyway."

"I'll be right back," Hendricks promised.

He went to his office. The receiver was lying on the blotter, and when he picked it up he could almost feel the presence of his wife quivering inside the instrument.

"Karen? For God's sake!" he snapped. "I was in a meeting. I've told you a thousand times—"

"Don't shout at me." The metallic reply was automatic. "It's almost four o'clock and I've just *got* to know . . ."

"Know what?"

"About dinner—what do you suppose? You said you'd call me at three. What do you think I am, a mind reader?"

Hendricks squeezed the telephone receiver. He pulled out the tangled wire and inched his way around the desk and into his swivel chair. With his free hand he reached absently for a pencil and stabbed at a memo pad, the point breaking and rolling off the desk.

"Now listen to me, Karen," he said in controlled tones, looking at the open doorway. "You've just got to stop yanking me out of meetings this way. A million dinners aren't worth it, do you understand?"

"I'm not going to argue with you over the phone." Karen spaced the words carefully, in that annoying way she had. Hendricks gritted his teeth.

"I'm not arguing," he said. "I'm telling you. You're making me look like a complete fool—"

"Darling, you give me too much credit."

Hendricks started to hang up. But he jerked the telephone back from its cradle just in time.

"I'm not coming home tonight," he said.

"Goodbye," said Karen.

"Goodbye!"

He slammed the receiver down too loudly, and looked up guiltily at the doorway. His hands were shaking, so he shoved them into the pockets of his jacket and leaned back in the chair. There were low muttered sounds in the hallway outside, and he realized that the meeting had broken up. He was glad of it.

Mead popped his head into the office.

"Get your call okay?" he smiled.

"Yeah," said Hendricks.

"Nothing much happened after you left. The old man read over the decisions of the plans board—that's about all. You took notes, I expect."

"I made a list," said Hendricks. "Must have left it in the conference room—"

Mead held up a yellow pad with ruled blue lines. "This it?" he grinned.

"Yes, that's it," said Hendricks. He caught the pad from Mead's easy toss. "Thanks a lot, Ralph."

"Nice-looking notes," said Mead, hanging around. Hendricks pretended that he was immersed in the long lines of script on the pad. "Nice and neat," said Mead. "You ought to be in Research, Bill."

"I have to take notes. Got a lousy memory."

"Yeah," Mead said. There was a vacant sort of satisfaction in his round face, and he stood in the doorway, rolling back and forth on the balls of his feet. *What was he waiting for?* Hendricks thought angrily.

"Drink tonight, Bill?" Mead said finally. "Harry, Lew, and I are going downstairs. Join us?"

Hendricks shook his head. "No, thanks. Got some things to clear up before I go home. This bakery account of mine is in one hell of a mess."

"Sure," said Mead. "Okay, Bill. See you Monday, right?"

"Right," said Hendricks.

He sighed when the research man was out of sight, and then, as if to justify the refusal he had given him, buried himself in his notes.

The minutes ticked past five, and the office sounds slowly diminished. The secretaries bustled into their going-home costumes, their laughter shriller and gayer than usual, for this was Friday afternoon. There was the inevitable jocularity at the elevators, and the isolated laughter of a small after-hours group in some cubicle on the floor. Then they, too, went their way, and the cushioned silence so peculiar to a deserted skyscraper office surrounded Bill Hendricks as he sat in his chair, staring blankly at his own tight scrawls on the yellow pad.

He mused that way for some ten minutes, then snapped out of it with a start. He looked at the pad again, and the detailed instructions he had noted during the conference now seemed strangely meaningless and unimportant. He dropped the pad, and pushed it away from him loathingly. Then he took a key from the top drawer and unlocked the deep file drawer to the bottom left of his desk.

A thin manila folder was all that was in the drawer, and its contents were still another kind of notes.

Bill Hendricks read them over with grim pleasure.

1. Nagging at me every damn night.
2. Spending $500 on a coat she didn't need.
3. Calling me a liar in front of my friends.
4. Throwing out a good set of golf clubs.
5. Ripping my best sports shirt, deliberately.
6. Keeping the car home so that I have to walk or take a taxi from the station.
7. Refusing to go wherever I want to go every damn vacation.
8. Making me sleep in the living room whenever she gets mad.
9. Insulting my secretary.
10. Calling Joe Dennis a windbag loud enough for him to hear.
11. Never making my breakfast in the morning.
12. Always hiding the damn ashtrays.
13. Calling my family a bunch of leeches.

14.   Slapping me in the face when I told her the truth about herself.

15.   Using my toilet things without permission.

16.   Never giving a damn about my clothes—too much starch in the shirts, holes in the socks and underwear.

17.   Acting like a damn fool at important business parties.

He came to the last notation and his nostrils flared. Then he picked up his ball-point pen and made an addition to the list.

18.   Always calling me up at the worst possible times with phony urgent messages.

He read the list through once more, satisfied at its increasing length. Then he carefully replaced the sheet in the manila folder, returned both to the file drawer, locked it, and put the key back where it belonged.

Then he went home.

"BILL?"

"LATER," HE SAID. He went past the living room and up the stairway to the bedroom. There had been a glass in his wife's hand—he had not missed that. Drinking, of course. That was something else. She could really pour that stuff down, all right. Wouldn't be surprised if she lowered the bourbon a good three inches every day he was away at work.

*That's Number 19*, he told himself with sardonic smugness.

He went into the bedroom.

"Twenty," he said aloud, looking around the untidy room. *Her* clothes, mostly; some of his, of course, but whose job was that? It was the least she could do. What else did she have to do all day?

He picked up some kind of lacy underthing from the floor and slammed it onto a chair. He picked up a crumpled covey of facial tissues and threw them into the narrow wastebasket. He lifted up a pair of his trousers, whipped the belt out from the loops, and hung them up in the closet. Then he took off his shirt, rolled it into a ball, and flung it onto the chair that held her lingerie.

He took a heavyweight wool shirt from his drawer and slowly put it on. Then he remembered the gun, and dug through the pile of clothing to see if the box was still there. It was there, of course, tightly sealed with strips of Scotch tape.

"I thought you said you weren't coming home," Karen accused, as he came down the stairs.

"I changed my mind," he said.

"Don't expect any dinner—I took you at your word, you know."

He dropped heavily into an armchair and picked up the evening paper from the table alongside. "I had a bite at the Shack," he said.

"Fried food?" She put down her glass and it rang on the marble top of the coffee table. "Fried potatoes and gravy and things?"

"Yes, fried potatoes and things!" He rattled the paper in annoyance.

"Well, it's your stomach," she said with a shrug. "I'd offer you a drink, but I suppose that would be more than that colon of yours could stand right now."

"Worry about your own colon," he said savagely, over the top of the paper. "I notice you don't spare it any alcohol!"

"Well, well! *Now* what are we getting at?"

"You know damn well what," he said, the words boiling slowly out his mouth. "You can really knock hell out of a bottle of bourbon these days, can't you? It's the big suburban hobby now, isn't it? A bunch of the girls getting nice and tight while hubby's at work—"

"Bill!"

He dropped the paper to the floor. "Don't give me that outraged innocence routine," he fumed. "Do you think I'm blind? You can tip a jug with the best of 'em, kid, and I know it!"

"Now we're *really* feeling guilty, aren't we?" Karen said. "What's the matter, dear? Had a tough day? Or did you have a fight with that honey-dripping secretary of yours?"

"Damn it to—"

"Oh, don't explode for my benefit!" she said. "Keep it under control, sweetie. If I had only one eye and three pints of bourbon in the bargain I could see what's going on between you and that mealymouthed—"

"That's enough!"

"Sure, it's enough!" she shouted. "I think it's enough and plenty! Now you come home and want Faithful Annie to trot out the pipe and slippers and drink her Ovaltine like a good little girl. Well, Faithful Annie's good and sick of it, let me tell you!" She picked up her glass and swallowed the remains of her drink.

Hendricks stood up.

"Where are you going?"

"Upstairs," he said quietly. "I'll be right back."

He went up the stairs deliberately. In the bedroom, he went straight to his shirt drawer and opened it. He lifted out the folded shirts carefully and put them on the bed. Then he took out the tightly wrapped package in the rear of the drawer and brought it with him to Karen's dressing table.

He fumbled with the Scotch tape until he snapped one of his finger-nails on the rim of the box. He swore softly, and then put the box on the table and went looking for a pair of scissors.

He couldn't locate them, nor anything else with a sharp enough edge. He tried one of his wife's nail files on the box, but it didn't do the trick.

"Damn!" he said to himself.

He went through all the drawers now, looking for some sort of tool to get to the weapon cozily nestling in its container. He was careless about the search, strewing the jumbled contents of his wife's bureau and vanity table all around the bedroom. *It didn't matter now*, he told himself. In fact, it would be helpful when he told the police about the sudden entrance of the burglar, the hoodlum who had held him at bay and killed his poor Karen . . .

He cursed so loudly at his fruitless hunt that he was afraid his wife would hear him.

Then he spotted Karen's sewing basket, a floral-decorated straw bag he had given her on some long forgotten occasion. He went to it quickly, and turned it upside down, spilling the contents on the rug.

A spool of thread, a thimble, a tape measure, a small revolver, and a piece of folded paper had dropped out and fallen to the floor.

He picked up the paper first, unfolded it, and read:

1.  Never talking to me when he gets home at night.
2.  Carrying on with his secretary.
3.  Never paying any attention to me at parties.
4.  Never letting me. . .

# Blue Rose

## PETER STRAUB

## Peter Straub's Introduction:

*In the fall of 1984, I stopped writing for a year to blow off some steam and, almost as an afterthought, do some research about Vietnam and combat veterans for a novel to be called Koko, which, as I saw it then, would deal with a number of former soldiers wandering around the Far East. By the summer of 1985, I had filled several notebooks with details about the characters and the general shape of the story, but the notebooks failed to address a crucial issue, that of how to resume writing prose fiction after so long a break from it. I answered my growing anxiety in a fashion typical of the mid-eighties me, i.e. by ignoring it while spending hour after hour drinking Saint Pauli Girl beer, devouring stacks of books, and deepening my suntan in a lounger on the front lawn of the house I then inhabited, located in Westport, Connecticut, a village I had gleefully demolished in my previous solo flight,* Floating Dragon. *I needed a push, badly, and one of those books, E. M. Thornton's* The Freudian Fallacy, *provided it.*

*A grumpy neuroscientist fed up with what he saw as the grandiose claims made by Sigmund Freud and his followers, Thornton had elected to squander several years of his life disproving psychoanalytic theory on scientific grounds. That this effort missed the point entirely missed Thornton entirely. I read his bad-tempered, furiously impacted sentences with increasing wonderment, right up to the moment when two or three of those sentences pushed an internal button that caused me to roll off the lounger, march into the house, and trot upstairs to my office, there to write down the idea that occurred to me when the author of* The Freudian Fallacy *had mentioned the similarity in brain patterns between hypnotic subjects and victims of asphyxiation.*

*During his childhood, former Lieutenant Harry Beevers, by far the least sympathetic member of* Koko's *cast, had murdered his younger brother after placing him in a hypnotic trance. This idea suggested an indirect way into the maze: by writing a story about Harry's terrible boyhood, I could at least warm up my writing muscles, knock the rust off the internal machinery.*

359

*Once begun, the story quickly took me over. Because the very act of writing had become difficult after a year off, I was forced to pay great attention to every phrase; this intensity of concentration almost instantly demanded a kind of transparency of style that felt to me like a form of narrative responsibility. I wanted no mediation, no stylistic filter between the reader and the events depicted on the page. The reader was supposed, simply, to see.*

*The story took four months to write. Not long after it was completed, Dennis Etchison asked if I had anything to contribute to* Prime Evil, *an anthology he was editing, and I gave him "Blue Rose." The anthology—containing my first published short story—came out in 1986, when I was forty-three.* Koko, *the novel to which the story had given me access, appeared two years later.*

# Blue Rose

## PETER STRAUB

### 1

ON A STIFLING SUMMER day the two youngest of the five Beevers children, Harry and Little Eddie, were sitting on cane-backed chairs in the attic of their house on South Sixth Street in Palmyra, New York. Their father called it "the upstairs junk room," as this large irregular space was reserved for the boxes of tablecloths, stacks of diminishingly sized girls' winter coats, and musty old dresses Maryrose Beevers had mummified as testimony to the superiority of her past to her present.

A tall mirror that could be tilted in its frame, an artifact of their mother's onetime glory, now revealed to Harry the rear of Little Eddie's head. This object, looking more malleable than a head should be, was just peeking above the back of the chair. Even the back of Little Eddie's head looked tense to Harry.

"Listen to me," Harry said. Little Eddie squirmed in his chair, and the wobbly chair squirmed with him. "You think I'm kidding you? I had her last year."

"Well, she didn't kill *you*," Little Eddie said.

"Course not, she liked me, you little dummy. She only hit me a couple of times. She hit some of those kids every single day."

"But teachers can't *kill* people," Little Eddie said.

At nine, Little Eddie was only a year younger than he, but Harry knew that his undersized fretful brother saw him as much a part of the world of big people as their older brothers.

"Most teachers can't," Harry said. "But what if they live right in the same building as the principal? What if they won *teaching awards*, hey, and what if every other teacher in the place is scared stiff of them? Don't you think they

**361**

can get away with murder? Do you think anybody really misses a snot-faced little brat—a little brat like you? Mrs. Franken took this kid, this runty little Tommy Golz, into the cloakroom, and she killed him right there. I heard him scream. At the end, it sounded just like bubbles. He was trying to yell, but there was too much blood in his throat. He never came back, and nobody ever said boo about it. She killed him, and next year she's going to be your teacher. I hope you're afraid, Little Eddie, because you ought to be." Harry leaned forward. "Tommy Golz even looked sort of like you, Little Eddie."

Little Eddie's entire face twitched as if a lightning bolt had crossed it.

In fact, the young Golz boy had suffered an epileptic fit and been removed from school, as Harry knew.

"Mrs. Franken especially hates selfish little brats that don't share their toys."

"I do share my toys," Little Eddie wailed, tears beginning to run down through the delicate smears of dust on his cheeks. "Everybody *takes* my toys, that's why."

"So give me your Ultraglide Roadster," Harry said. This had been Little Eddie's birthday present, given three days previous by a beaming father and a scowling mother. "Or I'll tell Mrs. Franken as soon as I get inside that school, this fall."

Under its layer of grime, Little Eddie's face went nearly the same white-gray shade as his hair.

An ominous slamming sound came up the stairs.

"Children? Are you messing around up there in the attic? Get down here!"

"We're just sitting in the chairs, Mom," Harry called out.

"Don't you bust those chairs! Get down here this minute!"

Little Eddie slid out of his chair and prepared to bolt.

"I want that car," Harry whispered. "And if you don't give it to me, I'll tell Mom you were foolin' around with her old clothes."

"I didn't do nothin'!" Little Eddie wailed, and broke for the stairs.

"Hey, Mom, we didn't break any stuff, honest!" Harry yelled. He bought a few minutes more by adding, "I'm coming right now," and stood up and went toward a cardboard box filled with interesting books he had noticed the day before his brother's birthday, and which had been his goal before he had remembered the Roadster and coaxed Little Eddie upstairs.

When, a short time later, Harry came through the door to the attic steps, he was carrying a tattered paperback book. Little Eddie stood quivering with misery and rage just outside the bedroom the two boys shared with their older brother Albert. He held out a small blue metal car, which Harry instantly took and eased into a front pocket of his jeans.

"When do I get it back?" Little Eddie asked.

"Never," Harry said. "Only selfish people want to get presents back. Don't you know anything at all?" When Eddie pursed his face up to wail, Harry tapped the book in his hands and said, "I got something here that's going to help you with Mrs. Franken, so don't complain."

HIS MOTHER INTERCEPTED HIM as he came down the stairs to the main floor of the little house—here were the kitchen and living room, both floored with faded linoleum, the actual "junk room" separated by a stiff brown woolen curtain from the little makeshift room where Edgar Beevers slept, and the larger bedroom reserved for Maryrose. Children were never permitted more than a few steps within this awful chamber, for they might disarrange Maryrose's mysterious "papers" or interfere with the rows of antique dolls on the window seat which was the sole, much-revered architectural distinction of the Beevers house.

Maryrose Beevers stood at the bottom of the stairs, glaring suspiciously up at her fourth son. She did not ever look like a woman who played with dolls, and she did not look that way now. Her hair was twisted into a knot at the back of her head. Smoke from her cigarette curled up past the big glasses like bird's wings, which magnified her eyes.

Harry thrust his hand into his pocket and curled his fingers protectively around the Ultraglide Roadster.

"Those things up there are the possessions of my family," she said. "Show me what you took."

Harry shrugged and held out the paperback as he came down within striking range.

His mother snatched it from him and tilted her head to see its cover through the cigarette smoke. "Oh. This is from that little box of books up there? Your father used to pretend to read books." She squinted at the print on the cover. "*Hypnosis Made Easy*. Some drugstore trash. You want to read this?"

Harry nodded.

"I don't suppose it can hurt you much." She negligently passed the book back to him. "People in society read books, you know—I used to read a lot, back before I got stuck here with a bunch of dummies. My father had a lot of books."

Maryrose nearly touched the top of Harry's head, then snatched back her hand. "You're my scholar, Harry. You're the one who's going places."

"I'm gonna do good in school next year," he said.

"*Well.* You're going to do well. As long as you don't ruin every chance you have by speaking like your father."

Harry felt that particular pain composed of scorn, shame, and terror that filled him when Maryrose spoke of his father in this way. He mumbled something that sounded like acquiescence, and moved a few steps sideways and around her.

## 2

THE PORCH OF THE Beevers house extended six feet on either side of the front door, and was the repository for furniture either too large to be crammed into the junk room or too humble to be enshrined in the attic. A sagging porch swing sat beneath the living room window, to the left of an ancient couch whose imitation green leather had been repaired with black duct tape; on the other side of the front door through which Harry Beevers now emerged stood a useless icebox dating from the earliest days of the Beeverses' marriage and two unsteady camp chairs Edgar Beevers had won in a card game. These had never been allowed into the house. Unofficially, this side of the porch was Harry's father's, and thereby had an entirely different atmosphere—defeated, lawless, and shameful—from the side with the swing and couch.

Harry knelt down in neutral territory directly before the front door and fished the Ultraglide Roadster from his pocket. He placed the hypnotism book on the porch and rolled the little metal car across its top. Then he gave the car a hard shove and watched it clunk nose-down onto the wood. He repeated this several times before moving the book aside, flattening himself out on his stomach, and giving the little car a decisive push toward the swing and the couch.

The Roadster rolled a few feet before an irregular board tilted it over on its side and stopped it.

"You dumb car," Harry said, and retrieved it. He gave it another push deeper into his mother's realm. A stiff, brittle section of paint that had separated from its board cracked in half and rested atop the stalled Roadster like a miniature mattress.

Harry knocked off the chip of paint and sent the car backward down the porch, where it flipped over again and skidded into the side of the icebox. The boy ran down the porch and this time simply hurled the little car back in the direction of the swing. It bounced off the swing's padding and fell heavily to the wood. Harry knelt before the icebox, panting.

His whole head felt funny, as if wet hot towels had been stuffed inside it. Harry picked himself up and walked across to where the car lay before the swing. He hated the way it looked, small and helpless. He experimentally stepped on the car and felt it pressing into the undersole of his moccasin. Harry raised his other foot and stood on the car, but nothing happened. He jumped on the car, but the moccasin was no better than his bare foot. Harry bent down to pick up the Roadster.

"You dumb little car," he said. "You're no good anyhow, you low-class little jerky thing." He turned it over in his hands. Then he inserted his thumbs between the frame and one of the little tires. When he pushed, the tire moved. His face heated. He mashed his thumbs against the tire, and the little black doughnut popped into the tall thick weeds in front of the porch. Breathing hard more from emotion than exertion, Harry popped the other front tire into the weeds. Harry whirled around and ground the car into the wall beside his father's bedroom window. Long deep scratches appeared in the paint. When Harry peered at the top of the car, it too was scratched. He found a nail head that protruded a quarter of an inch out from the front of the house, and scraped a long paring of blue paint off the driver's side of the Roadster. Gray metal shone through. Harry slammed the car several times against the edge of the nail head, chipping off small quantities of paint. Panting, he popped off the two small rear tires and put them in his pocket because he liked the way they looked.

Without tires, well-scratched and dented, the Ultraglide Roadster had lost most of its power. Harry looked it over with a bitter, deep satisfaction and walked across the porch and shoved it far into the nest of weeds. Gray metal and blue paint shone at him from within the stalks and leaves. Harry thrust his hands into their midst and swept his arms back and forth. The car tumbled away and fell into invisibility.

When Maryrose appeared scowling on the porch, Harry was seated serenely on the squeaking swing, looking at the first few pages of the paper-back book.

"What are you doing? What was all that banging?"

"I'm just reading, I didn't hear anything," Harry said.

## 3

"WELL, IF IT ISN'T the shitbird," Albert said, jumping up the porch steps thirty minutes later. His face and T-shirt bore broad black stripes of grease. A short, muscular thirteen-year-old, Albert spent every possible minute hanging around the gas station two blocks from their house. Harry knew that Albert despised him. Albert raised a fist and made a jerky, threatening motion toward Harry, who flinched. Albert had often beaten him bloody, as had their two older brothers, Sonny and George, now at army bases in Oklahoma and Germany. Like Albert, his two oldest brothers had seriously disappointed their mother.

Albert laughed, and this time swung his fist within a couple of inches of Harry's face. On the backswing he knocked the book from Harry's hands.

"Thanks," Harry said.

Albert smirked and disappeared around the front door. Almost immediately Harry could hear his mother beginning to shout about the grease on Albert's face and clothes. Albert thumped up the stairs.

Harry opened his clenched fingers and spread them wide, closed his hands into fists, then spread them wide again. When he heard the bedroom door slam shut upstairs, he was able to get off the swing and pick up the book. Being around Albert made him feel like a spring coiled up in a box. From the upper rear of the house, Little Eddie emitted a ghostly wail. Mary-rose screamed that she was going to start smacking him if he didn't shut up, and that was that. The three unhappy lives within the house fell back into silence. Harry sat down, found his page, and began reading again.

A man named Dr. Roland Mentaine had written *Hypnosis Made Easy*, and his vocabulary was much larger than Harry's. Dr. Mentaine used words like "orchestrate" and "ineffable" and "enhance," and some of his sentences wound their way through so many subordinate clauses that Harry lost his way. Yet Harry, who had begun the book only half-expecting that he would comprehend anything in it at all, found it a wonderful book. He had made it most of the way through the chapter called "Mind Power."

Harry thought it was neat that hypnosis could cure smoking, stuttering, and bed-wetting. (He himself had wet the bed almost nightly until months after his ninth birthday. The bed-wetting stopped the night a certain lovely dream came to Harry. In the dream he had to urinate terribly, and was hurrying down a stony castle corridor past suits of armor and torches guttering on the walls. At last Harry reached an open door, through which he saw the most splendid bathroom of his life. The floors were of polished marble, the walls white-tiled. As soon as he entered the gleaming bathroom, a uniformed butler waved him toward the rank of urinals. Harry began pulling down his zipper, fumbled with himself, and got his penis out of his underpants just in time. As the dream-urine gushed out of him, Harry had blessedly awakened.) Hypnotism could get you right inside someone's mind and let you do things there. You could make a person speak in any foreign language they'd ever heard, even if they'd only heard it once, and you could make them act like a baby. Harry considered how pleasurable it would be to make his brother Albert lie squalling and red-faced on the floor, unable to walk or speak as he pissed all over himself.

Also, and this was a new thought to Harry, you could take a person back to a whole row of lives they had led before they were born as the person they were now. This process of rebirth was called reincarnation. Some of Dr. Mentaine's patients had been kings in Egypt and pirates in the Caribbean, some had been murderers, novelists, and artists. They remembered the houses they'd lived in, the names of their mothers and servants and children, the locations of shops where they'd bought cake and wine. Neat stuff, Harry thought. He wondered if someone who had been a famous murderer a long time ago could remember pushing in the knife or bringing down the hammer. A lot of the books remaining in the little cardboard box upstairs, Harry had noticed, seemed to be about murderers. It would not be any use to take Albert back to a previous life, however. If Albert had any previous lives, he had spent them as inanimate objects on the order of boulders and anvils.

*Maybe in another life Albert was a murder weapon*, Harry thought.

"Hey, college boy! Joe College!"

Harry looked toward the sidewalk and saw the baseball cap and T-shirted gut of Mr. Petrosian, who lived in a tiny house next to the tavern on the corner of South Sixth and Livermore Street. Mr. Petrosian was always shouting genial things at kids, but Maryrose wouldn't let Harry or Little Eddie talk to him. She said Mr. Petrosian was common as dirt. He worked as a janitor in the telephone building and drank a case of beer every night while he sat on his porch.

"Me?" Harry said.

"Yeah! Keep reading books and you could go to college, right?"

Harry smiled noncommittally. Mr. Petrosian lifted a wide arm and continued to toil down the street toward his house next to the Idle Hour.

In seconds Maryrose burst through the door, folding an old white dish towel in her hands. "Who was that? I heard a man's voice."

"Him," Harry said, pointing at the substantial back of Mr. Petrosian, now half of the way home.

"What did he say? As if it could possibly be interesting, coming from an Armenian janitor."

"He called me Joe College."

Maryrose startled him by smiling.

"Albert says he wants to go back to the station tonight, and I have to go to work soon." Maryrose worked the night shift as a secretary at Saint Joseph's Hospital. "God knows when your father'll show up. Get something to eat for Little Eddie and yourself, will you, Harry? I've just got too many things to take care of, as usual."

"I'll get something at Big John's." This was a hamburger stand, a magical place to Harry, erected the summer before in a vacant lot on Livermore Street two blocks down from the Idle Hour.

His mother handed him two carefully folded dollar bills, and he pushed them into his pocket. "Don't let Little Eddie stay in the house alone," his mother said before going back inside. "Take him with you. You know how scared he gets."

"Sure," Harry said, and went back to his book. He finished the chapter on "Mind Power" while first Maryrose left to stand up at the bus stop on the corner, and then while Albert noisily departed. Little Eddie sat frozen before his soap operas in the living room. Harry turned a page and started reading "Techniques of Hypnosis."

4

AT EIGHT-THIRTY THAT night the two boys sat alone in the kitchen, on opposite sides of the table covered in yellow bamboo Formica. From the living room came the sound of Sid Caesar babbling in fake German to Imogene Coca on *Your Show of Shows*. Little Eddie claimed to be scared of Sid Caesar, but when Harry had returned from the hamburger stand with a Big Johnburger (with "the works") for himself and a Mama Marydog for Eddie, double fries, and two chocolate shakes, he had been sitting in front of the television, his face moist with tears of moral outrage. Eddie usually liked Mama Marydogs, but he had taken only a couple of meager bites from the one before him now, and was disconsolately pushing a french fry through a blob of ketchup. Every now and then he wiped at his eyes, leaving nearly symmetrical smears of ketchup to dry on his cheeks.

"Mom *said* not to leave me alone in the house," said Little Eddie. "I heard. It was during *The Edge of Night* and you were on the porch. I think I'm gonna tell on you." He peeped across at Harry, then quickly looked back at the french fry and drew it out of the puddle of ketchup. "I'm ascared to be alone in the house." Sometimes Eddie's voice was like a queer speeded-up mechanical version of Maryrose's.

"Don't be so dumb," Harry said, almost kindly. "How can you be scared in your own house? You live here, don't you?"

"I'm ascared of the attic," Eddie said. He held the dripping french fry before his mouth and pushed it in. "The attic makes noise." A little squirm of red appeared at the corner of his mouth. "You were supposed to take me with you."

"Oh, jeez, Eddie, you slow everything down. I wanted to just get the food and come back. I got you your dinner, didn't I? Didn't I get you what you like?"

In truth, Harry liked hanging around Big John's by himself because then he could talk to Big John and listen to his theories. Big John called himself a "renegade Papist" and considered Hitler the greatest man of the twentieth century, followed closely by Paul XI, Padre Pio who bled from the palms of his hands, and Elvis Presley.

All these events occurred in what is usually but wrongly called a simpler time, before Kennedy and feminism and ecology, before the Nixon presidency and Watergate, and before American soldiers, among them a twenty-one-year-old Harry Beevers, journeyed to Vietnam.

"I'm still going to tell," said Little Eddie. He pushed another french fry into the puddle of ketchup. "And that car was my birthday present." He began to snuffle. "Albert hit me, and you stole my car, and you left me alone, and I was scared. And I don't wanna have Mrs. Franken next year, cuz I think she's gonna hurt me."

Harry had nearly forgotten telling his brother about Mrs. Franken and Tommy Golz, and this reminder brought back very sharply the memory of destroying Eddie's birthday present.

Eddie twisted his head sideways and dared another quick look at his brother. "Can I have my Ultraglide Roadster back, Harry? You're going to give it back to me, aren'cha? I won't tell Mom you left me alone if you give it back."

"Your car is okay," Harry said. "It's in a sort of a secret place I know."

"You hurt my car!" Eddie squalled. "You did!"

"Shut up!" Harry shouted, and Little Eddie flinched. "You're driving me crazy!" Harry yelled. He realized that he was leaning over the table, and that Little Eddie was getting ready to cry again. He sat down. "Just don't scream at me like that, Eddie."

"You did something to my car," Eddie said with a stunned certainty. "I knew it."

"Look, I'll prove your car is okay," Harry said, and took the two rear tires from his pocket and displayed them on his palm.

Little Eddie stared. He blinked, then reached out tentatively for the tires.

Harry closed his fist around them. "Do they look like I did anything to them?"

"You took them *off*!"

"But don't they look okay, don't they look fine?" Harry opened his fist, closed it again, and returned the tires to his pocket. "I didn't want to show you the whole car, Eddie, because you'd get all worked up, and you gave it to me. Remember? I wanted to show you the tires so you'd see everything was all right. Okay? Got it?"

Eddie miserably shook his head.

"Anyway, I'm going to help you, just like I said."

"With Mrs. Franken?" A fraction of his misery left Little Eddie's smeary face.

"Sure. You ever hear of something called hypnotism?"

"I heard a hypmotism." Little Eddie was sulking. "Everybody in the whole world heard a that."

"Hypnotism, stupid, not hypmotism."

"Sure, hypmotism. I saw it on the TV. They did it on *As the World Turns*. A man made a lady go to sleep and think she was going to have a baby."

Harry smiled. "That's just TV, Little Eddie. Real hypnotism is a lot better than that. I read all about it in one of the books from the attic."

Little Eddie was still sulky because of the car. "So what makes it better?"

"Because it lets you do amazing things," Harry said. He called on Dr. Mentaine. "Hypnosis unlocks your mind and lets you use all the power you really have. If you start now, you'll really knock those books when school starts up again. You'll pass every test Mrs. Franken gives you, just like the way I did." He reached across the table and grasped Little Eddie's wrist, stalling a fat brown french fry on its way to the puddle. "But it won't just make you good in school. If you let me try it on you, I'm pretty sure I can show you that you're a lot stronger than you think you are."

Eddie blinked.

"And I bet I can make you so you're not scared of anything anymore. Hypnotism is real good for that. I read in this book, there was this guy who was afraid of bridges. Whenever he even *thought* about crossing a bridge he got all dizzy and sweaty. Terrible stuff happened to him, like he lost his job and once he just had to ride in a car across a bridge and he dumped a load in his pants. He went to see Dr. Mentaine, and Dr. Mentaine hypnotized him and said he would never be afraid of bridges again, and he wasn't."

Harry pulled the paperback from his hip pocket. He opened it flat on the table and bent over the pages. "Here. Listen to this. 'Benefits of the course of treatment were found in all areas of the patient's life, and results were obtained for which he would have paid any price.'" Harry read these words haltingly, but with complete understanding.

"Hypmotism can make me strong?" Little Eddie asked, evidently having saved this point in his head.

"Strong as a bull."

"Strong as Albert?"

"A lot stronger than Albert. A lot stronger than me, too."

"And I can beat up on big guys that hurt me?"

"You just have to learn how."

Eddie sprang up from the chair, yelling nonsense. He flexed his string-like biceps and for some time twisted his body into a series of muscleman poses.

"You want to do it?" Harry finally asked.

Little Eddie popped into his chair and stared at Harry. His T-shirt's neck band sagged all the way to his breastbone without ever actually touching his chest. "I wanna start."

"Okay, Eddie, good man." Harry stood up and put his hand on the book. "Up to the attic."

"Only, I don't wanna go in the attic," Eddie said. He was still staring at

Harry, but his head was tilted over like a weird little echo of Maryrose, and his eyes had filled with suspicion.

"I'm not gonna *take* anything from you, Little Eddie," Harry said. "It's just, we should be out of everybody's way. The attic's real quiet."

Little Eddie stuck his hand inside his T-shirt and let his arm dangle from the wrist.

"You turned your shirt into an armrest," Harry said.

Eddie jerked his hand out of its sling.

"Albert might come waltzing in and wreck everything if we do it in the bedroom."

"If you go up first and turn on the lights," Eddie said.

5

HARRY HELD THE BOOK open on his lap, and glanced from it to Little Eddie's tense smeary face. He had read these pages over many times while he sat on the porch. Hypnotism boiled down to a few simple steps, each of which led to the next. The first thing he had to do was to get his brother started right, "relaxed and receptive," according to Dr. Mentaine.

Little Eddie stirred in his cane-backed chair and kneaded his hands together. His shadow, cast by the bulb dangling overhead, imitated him like a black little chair-bound monkey. "I wanna get started, I wanna get to be strong," he said.

"Right here in this book it says you have to be relaxed," Harry said. "Just put your hands on top of your legs, nice and easy, with your fingers pointing forward. Then close your eyes and breathe in and out a couple of times. Think about being nice and tired and ready to go to sleep."

"I don't wanna go to sleep!"

"It's not really sleep, Little Eddie, it's just sort of like it. You'll still really be awake, but nice and relaxed. Or else it won't work. You have to do everything I tell you. Otherwise everybody'll still be able to beat up on you, like they do now. I want you to pay attention to everything I say."

"Okay." Little Eddie made a visible effort to relax. He placed his hands on his thighs and twice inhaled and exhaled.

"Now close your eyes."

Eddie closed his eyes.

Harry suddenly knew that it was going to work—if he did everything the book said, he would really be able to hypnotize his brother.

"Little Eddie, I want you just to listen to the sound of my voice," he said, forcing himself to be calm. "You are already getting nice and relaxed, as easy and peaceful as if you were lying in bed, and the more you listen to my voice the more relaxed and tired you are going to get. Nothing can bother you. Everything bad is far away, and you're just sitting here, breathing in and out, getting nice and sleepy."

He checked his page to make sure he was doing it right, and then went on.

"It's like lying in bed, Eddie, and the more you hear my voice the more tired and sleepy you're getting, a little more sleepy the more you hear me. Everything else is sort of fading away, and all you can hear is my voice. You feel tired but good, just like the way you do right before you fall asleep. Everything is fine, and you're drifting a little bit, drifting and drifting, and you're getting ready to raise your right hand."

He leaned over and very lightly stroked the back of Little Eddie's grimy right hand. Eddie sat slumped in the chair with his eyes closed, breathing shallowly. Harry spoke very slowly.

"I'm going to count backward from ten, and every time I get to another number, your hand is going to get lighter and lighter. When I count, your right hand is going to get so light it floats up and finally touches your nose when you hear me say 'One.' And then you'll be in a deep sleep. Now I'm starting. Ten. Your hand is already feeling light. Nine. It wants to float up. Eight. Your hand really feels light now. It's going to start to go up now. Seven."

Little Eddie's hand obediently floated an inch up from his thigh.

"Six." The grimy little hand rose another few inches. "It's getting lighter and lighter now, and every time I say another number it gets closer and closer to your nose, and you get sleepier and sleepier. Five."

The hand ascended several inches nearer Eddie's face.

"Four."

The hand now dangled like a sleeping bird half of the way between Eddie's knee and his nose.

"Three."

It rose nearly to Eddie's chin.

"Two."

Eddie's hand hung a few inches from his mouth.

"One. You are going to fall asleep now."

The gently curved, ketchup-streaked forefinger delicately brushed the tip of Little Eddie's nose, and stayed there while Eddie sagged against the back of the chair.

Harry's heart beat so loudly that he feared the sound would bring Eddie out of his trance. Eddie remained motionless. Harry breathed quietly by himself for a moment. "Now you can lower your hand to your lap, Eddie. You are going deeper and deeper into sleep. Deeper and deeper and deeper."

Eddie's hand sank gracefully downward.

The attic seemed hot as the inside of a furnace to Harry. His fingers left blotches on the open pages of the book. He wiped his face on his sleeve and looked at his little brother. Little Eddie had slumped so far down in the chair that his head was no longer visible in the tilting mirror. Perfectly still and quiet, the attic stretched out on all sides of them, waiting (or so it seemed to Harry) for what would happen next. Maryrose's trunks sat in rows under the eaves far behind the mirror, her old dresses hung silently within the dusty wardrobe. Harry rubbed his hands on his jeans to dry them, and flicked a page over with the neatness of an old scholar who had spent half his life in libraries.

"You're going to sit up straight in your chair," he said.

Eddie pulled himself upright.

"Now I want to show you that you're really hypnotized, Little Eddie. It's like a test. I want you to hold your right arm straight out before you. Make it as rigid as you can. This is going to show you how strong you can be."

Eddie's pale arm rose and straightened to the wrist, leaving his fingers dangling.

Harry stood up and said, "That's pretty good." He walked the two steps to Eddie's side and grasped his brother's arm and ran his fingers down the length of it, gently straightening Eddie's hand. "Now I want you to imagine that your arm is getting harder and harder. It's getting as hard and rigid as an iron bar. Your whole arm is an iron bar, and nobody on earth could bend it. Eddie, it's stronger than Superman's arm." He removed his hands and stepped back.

"Now. This arm is so strong and rigid that you can't bend it no matter how hard you try. It's an iron bar, and nobody on earth could bend it. Try. Try to bend it."

Eddie's face tightened up, and his arm rose perhaps two degrees. Eddie grunted with invisible effort, unable to bend his arm.

"Okay, Eddie, you did real good. Now your arm is loosening up, and when I count backward from ten, it's going to get looser and looser. When I get to "one," your arm'll be normal again." He began counting, and Eddie's fingers loosened and drooped, and finally the arm came to rest again on his leg.

Harry went back to his chair, sat down, and looked at Eddie with great satisfaction. Now he was certain that he would be able to do the next demonstration, which Dr. Mentaine called "The Chair Exercise."

"Now you know that this stuff really works, Eddie, so we're going to do something a little harder. I want you to stand up in front of your chair."

Eddie obeyed. Harry stood up too, and moved his chair forward and to the side so that its cane seat faced Eddie, about four feet away.

"I want you to stretch out between these chairs, with your head on your chair and your feet on mine. And I want you to keep your hands at your sides."

Eddie hunkered down uncomplainingly and settled his head back on the seat of his chair. Supporting himself with his arms, he raised one leg and placed his foot on Harry's chair. Then he lifted the other foot. Difficulty immediately appeared in his face. He raised his arms and clamped them in so that he looked trussed.

"Now your whole body is slowly becoming as hard as iron, Eddie. Your entire body is one of the strongest things on earth. Nothing can make it bend. You could hold yourself there forever and never feel the slightest pain or discomfort. It's like you're lying on a mattress, you're so strong."

The expression of strain left Eddie's face. Slowly his arms extended and relaxed. He lay propped string-straight between the two chairs, so at ease that he did not even appear to be breathing.

"While I talk to you, you're getting stronger and stronger. You could hold up anything. You could hold up an elephant. I'm going to sit down on your stomach to prove it."

Cautiously, Harry seated himself down on his brother's midriff. He raised his legs. Nothing happened. After he had counted slowly to fifteen, Harry lowered his legs and stood. "I'm going to take my shoes off now, Eddie, and stand on you."

He hurried over to a piano stool embroidered with fulsome roses and carried it back; then he slipped off his moccasins and stepped on top of the stool. As Harry stepped on Eddie's exposed thin belly, the chair supporting his brother's head wobbled. Harry stood stock-still for a moment, but the chair held. He lifted the other foot from the stool. No movement came from the chair. He set the other foot on his brother. Little Eddie effortlessly held him up.

Harry lifted himself experimentally up on his toes and came back down on his heels. Eddie seemed entirely unaffected. Then Harry jumped perhaps half an inch into the air, and since Eddie did not even grunt when he landed, he kept jumping, five, six, seven, eight times, until he was breathing hard. "You're amazing, Little Eddie," he said, and stepped off onto the stool. "Now you can begin to relax. You can put your feet on the floor. Then I want you to sit back up in your chair. Your body doesn't feel stiff anymore."

Little Eddie had been rather tentatively lowering one foot, but as soon as Harry finished speaking he buckled in the middle and thumped his bottom on the floor. Harry's chair (Maryrose's chair) sickeningly tipped over, but landed soundlessly on a neat woolen stack of layered winter coats.

Moving like a robot, Little Eddie slowly sat upright on the floor. His eyes were open but unfocused.

"You can stand up now and get back in your chair," Harry said. He did not remember leaving the stool, but he had left it. Sweat ran into his eyes. He pressed his face into his shirtsleeve. For a second, panic had brightly beckoned. Little Eddie was sleepwalking back to his chair. When he sat down, Harry said, "Close your eyes. You're going deeper and deeper into sleep. Deeper and deeper, Little Eddie."

Eddie settled into the chair as if nothing had happened, and Harry reverently set his own chair upright again. Then he picked up the book and opened it. The print swam before his eyes. Harry shook his head and looked again, but still the lines of print snaked across the page. He pressed the palms of his hands against his eyes, and red patterns exploded across his vision.

He removed his hands from his eyes, blinked, and found that although the lines of print were now behaving themselves, he no longer wanted to go on. The attic was too hot, he was too tired, and the toppling of the chair had been too close a brush with actual disaster. But for a time he leafed purposefully through the book while Eddie tranced on, and then found the subheading "Posthypnotic Suggestion."

"Little Eddie, we're just going to do one more thing. If we ever do this again, it'll help us go faster." Harry shut the book. He knew exactly how this went; he would even use the same phrase Dr. Mentaine used with his patients. *Blue rose*—Harry did not quite know why, but he liked the sound of that.

"I'm going to tell you a phrase, Eddie, and from now on whenever you hear me say this phrase, you will instantly go back to sleep and be hypnotized again. The phrase is 'Blue rose.' Blue rose. When you hear me say 'Blue rose,' you will go right to sleep, just the way you are now, and we can make you stronger again. 'Blue rose' is our secret, Eddie, because nobody else knows it. What is it?"

"Blue rose," Eddie said in a muffled voice.

"Okay. I'm going to count backward from ten, and when I get to 'one' you will be wide awake again. You will not remember anything we did, but you will feel happy and strong. Ten."

As Harry counted backward, Little Eddie twitched and stirred, let his arms fall to his sides, thumped one foot carelessly on the floor, and at "one" opened his eyes.

"Did it work? What'd I do? Am I strong?"

"You're a bull," Harry said. "It's getting late, Eddie—time to go downstairs."

Harry's timing was accurate enough to be uncomfortable. As soon as the two boys closed the attic door behind them they heard the front door slide open in a cacophony of harsh coughs and subdued mutterings followed by the sound of unsteady footsteps proceeding to the bathroom. Edgar Beevers was home.

6

LATE THAT NIGHT THE three homebound Beevers sons lay in their separate beds in the good-sized second-floor room next to the attic stairs. Directly above Maryrose's bedroom, its dimensions were nearly identical to it except that the boys' room, the "dorm," had no window seat and the attic stairs shaved a couple of feet from Harry's end. When the other two boys had lived at home, Harry and Little Eddie had slept together, Albert had slept in a bed with Sonny, and only George, who at the time of his induction into the Army had been six feet tall and weighed two hundred and one pounds, had slept alone. In those days, Sonny had often managed to make Albert cry out in the middle of the night. The very idea of George could still make Harry's stomach freeze.

Though it was now very late, enough light from the street came in through the thin white net curtains to give complex shadows to the bunched muscles of Albert's upper arms as he lay stretched out atop his sheets. The voices of Maryrose and Edgar Beevers, one approximately sober and the other unmistakably drunk, came clearly up the stairs and through the open door.

"*Who* says I waste my time? I don't say that. I don't waste my time."

"I suppose you think you've done a good day's work when you spell a bartender for a couple of hours—and then drink up your wages! That's the story of your life, Edgar Beevers, and it's a sad sad story of W-A-S-T-E. If my father could have seen what would become of you . . ."

"I ain't so damn bad."

"You ain't so damn good, either."

"Albert," Eddie said softly from his bed between his two brothers.

As if galvanized by Little Eddie's voice, Albert suddenly sat up in bed, leaned forward, and reached out to try to smack Eddie with his fist.

"I didn't do nothin'!" Harry said, and moved to the edge of his mattress. The blow had been for him, he knew, not Eddie, except that Albert was too lazy to get up.

"I hate your lousy guts," Albert said. "If I wasn't too tired to get out of this here bed, I'd pound your face in."

"Harry stole my birthday car, Albert," Eddie said. "Makum gimme it back."

"One day," Maryrose said from downstairs, "at the end of the summer when I was seventeen, late in the afternoon, my father said to my mother, 'Honey, I believe I'm going to take out our pretty little Maryrose and get her something special,' and he called up to me from the drawing room to make myself pretty and get set to go, and because my father was a gentleman, and a Man of His Word, I got ready in two shakes. My father was wearing a very handsome brown suit and a red bow tie and his boater. I remember just like I can see it now. He stood at the bottom of the staircase, waiting for me, and when I came down he took my arm and we just went out that front door like a courting couple. Down the stone walk, which my father put in all by himself even though he was a white-collar worker, down Majeski Street, arm in arm down to South Palmyra Avenue. In those days all the best people, all the people who counted, did their shopping on South Palmyra Avenue."

"I'd like to knock your teeth down your throat," Albert said to Harry.

"Albert, he took my birthday car, he really did, and I want it back. I'm ascared he busted it. I want it back so much I'm gonna die."

Albert propped himself up on an elbow and for the first time really looked at Little Eddie. Eddie whimpered. "You're such a twerp," Albert said. "I wish you *would* die, Eddie, I wish you'd just drop dead so we could stick you in the ground and forget about you. I wouldn't even cry at your funeral. Prob'ly I wouldn't even be able to remember your name. I'd just say, 'Oh, yeah, he was that little creepy kid used to hang around cryin' all the time, glad he's dead, whatever his name was.'"

Eddie had turned his back on Albert and was weeping softly, his unwashed face distorted by the shadows into an uncanny image of the mask of tragedy.

"You know, I really wouldn't mind if you dropped dead," Albert mused. "You neither, shitbird."

". . . realized he was taking me to Allouette's. I'm sure you used to look in their windows when you were a little boy. You remember Allouette's, don't you? There's never been anything so beautiful as that store. When I was a little girl and lived in the big house, all the best people used to go there. My father marched me right inside, with his arm around me, and took me up in the elevator and we went straight to the lady who managed the dress department. 'Give my little girl the best,' he said. Price was no object. Quality was all he cared about. 'Give my little girl the best.' *Are you listening to me, Edgar?*"

ALBERT SNORED FACEDOWN into his pillow; Little Eddie twitched and snuffled. Harry lay awake for so long he thought he would never get to sleep. Before him he kept seeing Little Eddie's face all slack and dopey under hypnosis—Little Eddie's face made him feel hot and uncomfortable. Now that Harry was lying down in bed, it seemed to him that everything he had done since returning from Big John's seemed really to have been done by someone else, or to have been done in a dream. Then he realized that he had to use the bathroom.

Harry slid out of bed, quietly crossed the room, went out onto the dark landing, and felt his way downstairs to the bathroom.

When he emerged, the bathroom light showed him the squat black shape of the telephone atop the Palmyra directory. Harry moved to the low telephone table beside the stairs. He lifted the phone from the directory and opened the book, the width of a Big 5 tablet, with his other hand. As he had done on many other nights when his bladder forced him downstairs, Harry leaned over the page and selected a number. He kept the number in his head as he closed the directory, and replaced the telephone. He dialed. The number rang so often Harry lost count. At last a hoarse voice answered. Harry said, "I'm watching you, and you're a dead man." He softly replaced the receiver in the cradle.

7

HARRY CAUGHT UP WITH his father the next afternoon just as Edgar Beevers had begun to move up South Sixth Street toward the corner of Livermore. His father wore his usual costume of baggy gray trousers cinched far above his waist by a belt with a double buckle, a red-and-white plaid shirt, and a brown felt hat stationed low over his eyes. His long fleshy nose swam before him, cut in half by the shadow of the hat brim.

"Dad!"

His father glanced incuriously at him, then put his hands back in his pockets. He turned sideways and kept walking down the street, though perhaps a shade more slowly. "What's up, kid? No school?"

"It's summer, there isn't any school. I just thought I'd come with you for a little."

"Well, I ain't doing much. Your ma asked me to pick up some hamburg on Livermore, and I thought I'd slip into the Idle Hour for a quick belt. You won't turn me in, will you?"

"No."

"You ain't a bad kid, Harry. Your ma's just got a lot of worries. I worry about Little Eddie too, sometimes."

"Sure."

"What's with the books? You read when you walk?"

"I was just sort of looking at them," Harry said.

His father insinuated his hand beneath Harry's left elbow and extracted two luridly jacketed paperback books. They were titled *Murder, Incorporated* and *Hitler's Death Camps*. Harry already loved both of these books. His father grunted and handed *Murder, Incorporated* back to him. He raised the other book nearly to the top of his nose and peered at the cover, which depicted a naked woman pressing herself against a wall of barbed wire while a uniformed Nazi aimed a rifle at her back.

Looking up at his father, Harry saw that beneath the harsh line of shadow cast by the hat brim, his father's whiskers grew in different colors and patterns. Black and brown, red and orange, the glistening spikes swirled across his father's cheek.

"I bought this book, but it didn't look nothing like that," his father said, and returned the book.

"What didn't?"

"That place. Dachau. That death camp."

"How do you know?"

"I was there, wasn't I? You wasn't even born then. It didn't look anything like that picture on that book. It just looked like a piece a shit to me, like most of the places I saw when I was in the army."

This was the first time Harry had heard that his father had been in the service.

"You mean, you were in World War II?"

"Yeah, I was in the Big One. They made me corporal over there. Had me a nickname, too. 'Beans.' 'Beans' Beevers. And I got a Purple Heart from the time I got a infection."

"You saw Dachau with your own eyes?"

"Damn straight I did." He bent down suddenly. "Hey—don't let your ma catch you readin' that book."

Secretly pleased, Harry shook his head. Now the book and the death camp were a bond between himself and his father.

"Did you ever kill anybody?"

His father wiped his mouth and both cheeks with one long hand. Harry saw a considering eye far back in the shadow of the brim.

"I killed a guy once."

A long pause.

"I shot him in the back."

His father wiped his mouth again, and then motioned forward with his head. He had to get to the bar, the butcher, and back again in a very carefully defined period of time. "You really want to hear this?"

Harry nodded. He swallowed.

"I guess you do, at that. Okay—we was sent into this camp, Dachau, at the end of the war to process the prisoners and arrest the guards and the commandant. Everything was all arranged. A bunch of brass hats from division were going to come on an inspection, so we had to wait there a couple days. We had these guards lined up, see, and these skinny old wrecks would come up and give 'em hell. We wasn't supposed to let 'em get too near."

They were passing Mr. Petrosian's little tar-paper house, and Harry felt a spasm of relief that Mr. Petrosian was not out on his tiny porch, working on his case of beer. The Idle Hour was only a few paces ahead.

"Anyhow, one of these guards, one of the worst ones, suddenly decided he's going to run for it. He takes off, runnin' like crazy toward the woods. What do I do? I ask. Nobody knows what the hell to do. Shoot him, somebody says. So I shot him in the back. That was all she wrote."

Now they had reached the screen door that led into the Idle Hour, and the smells of malt and hops filled the air. "See you back at the house," his father said, and disappeared through the screen door like a magician.

## 8

AFTER HARRY HAD READ a hundred pages of *Murder, Incorporated*, his favorite murderers were Louis "Lepke" Buchalter and Abe "Kid Twist" Reles. They were dependable professionals. A kind of black light surrounded them and made them glitter. Lepke Buchalter and Abe Reles looked out at the world from the shadows of their hat brims. They lived in shadowy rooms and peered out through the curtains. They appeared on a dark corner before their terrified victim, did their work, and walked away, turning up their coat collars.

*Suppose you had some kind of job that took you around the country, like a salesman's job,* Harry thought as he read away the afternoon in the porch swing; *suppose you had a job that took you from one town to another. Suppose you killed someone in each one of those towns, carefully and quietly, and hid the bodies so it would take people a long time to find them. Your work would never be done.*

## 9

"BLUE ROSE," HARRY SAID.

Little Eddie sagged openmouthed against the cane of his chair, his hands loose in his lap.

It had worked. Harry looked around as if he expected applause, and did feel that all the things in the attic looked back at him with warm approval. It was nine-thirty at night; he and Eddie, alone in the house, occupied the attic in perfect safety. Harry wanted to see if he could put other people under and make them do things, but for now, for tonight, he was content to experiment with Eddie.

"You're going deeper and deeper asleep, Eddie, deeper and deeper, and you're listening to every word I say. You're just sinking down and down, hearing my voice come to you, going deeper and deeper with every word, and now you are real deep asleep and ready to begin."

Little Eddie sat sprawled over Maryrose's cane-backed chair, his chin touching his chest and his little pink mouth drooping open. He looked like a slightly undersized seven-year-old, like a second-grader instead of the fourth-grader he would be when he joined Mrs. Franken's class in the fall. Suddenly he reminded Harry of the Ultraglide Roadster, scratched and dented and stripped of its tires.

"Tonight you're going to see how strong you really are. Sit up, Eddie."

Eddie pulled himself upright and closed his mouth, almost comically obedient.

Harry thought it would be fun to make Little Eddie believe he was a dog and trot around the attic on all fours, barking and lifting his leg. Then he saw Little Eddie staggering across the attic, his tongue bulging out of his mouth, his own hands squeezing and squeezing his throat. Maybe he would try that too, after he had done several other exercises he had discovered in Dr. Mentaine's book. He checked the underside of his collar for maybe the fifth time that evening, and felt the long thin shaft of the pearl-headed hat pin he had stopped reading *Murder, Incorporated* long enough to smuggle out of Maryrose's bedroom after she had left for work.

"Eddie," he said, "now you are very deeply asleep, and you will be able to do everything I say. I want you to hold your right arm straight out in front of you."

Eddie stuck his arm out like a poker.

"That's good, Eddie. Now I want you to notice that all the feeling is leaving that arm. It's getting number and number. It doesn't even feel like flesh and blood anymore. It feels like it's made out of steel or something. It's so numb that you can't feel anything there anymore. You can't even feel pain in it."

Harry stood up, went toward Eddie, and brushed his fingers along his arm. "You didn't feel anything, did you?"

"No," Eddie said in a slow gravel-filled voice.

"Do you feel anything now?" Harry pinched the underside of Eddie's forearm.

"No."

"Now?" Harry used his nails to pinch the side of Eddie's bicep, hard, and left purple dents in the skin.

"No," Eddie repeated.

"How about this?" He slapped his hand against Eddie's forearm as hard as he could. There was a sharp loud smacking sound, and his fingers tingled. If Little Eddie had not been hypnotized, he would have tried to screech down the walls.

"No," Eddie said.

Harry pulled the hat pin out of his collar and inspected his brother's arm. "You're doing great, Little Eddie. You're stronger than anybody in your whole class—you're probably stronger than the whole rest of the school." He turned Eddie's arm so that the palm was up and the white forearm, lightly traced by small blue veins, faced him.

Harry delicately ran the point of the hat pin down Eddie's pale, veined forearm. The pinpoint left a narrow chalk-white scratch in its wake. For a moment Harry felt the floor of the attic sway beneath his feet; then he closed his eyes and jabbed the hat pin into Little Eddie's skin as hard as he could.

He opened his eyes. The floor was still swaying beneath him. From Little Eddie's lower arm protruded six inches of the eight-inch hat pin, the mother-of-pearl head glistening softly in the light from the overhead bulb. A drop of blood the size of a watermelon seed stood on Eddie's skin. Harry moved back to his chair and sat down heavily. "Do you feel anything?"

"No," Eddie said again in that surprisingly deep voice.

Harry stared at the hat pin embedded in Eddie's arm. The oval drop of blood lengthened itself out against the white skin and began slowly to ooze toward Eddie's wrist. Harry watched it advance across the pale underside of Eddie's forearm. Finally he stood up and returned to Eddie's side. The elongated drop of blood had ceased moving. Harry bent over and twanged the hat pin. Eddie could feel nothing. Harry put his thumb and forefinger on the glistening head of the pin. His face was so hot he might have been standing before an open fire. He pushed the pin a further half-inch into Eddie's arm, and another small quantity of blood welled up from the base. The pin seemed to be moving in Harry's grasp, pulsing back and forth as if it were breathing.

"Okay," Harry said. "Okay."

He tightened his hold on the pin and pulled. It slipped easily from the wound. Harry held the hat pin before his face just as a doctor holds up a thermometer to read a temperature. He had imagined that the entire bottom section of the shaft would be painted with red, but saw that only a single winding glutinous streak of blood adhered to the pin. For a dizzy second he thought of slipping the end of the pin in his mouth and sucking it clean.

He thought: *Maybe in another life I was Lepke Buchalter.*

He pulled his handkerchief, a filthy square of red paisley, from his front pocket and wiped the streak of blood from the shaft of the pin. Then

he leaned over and gently wiped the red smear from Little Eddie's under-
arm. Harry refolded the handkerchief so the blood would not show, wiped
sweat from his face, and shoved the grubby cloth back into his pocket.

"That was good, Eddie. Now we're going to do something a little bit
different."

He knelt down beside his brother and lifted Eddie's nearly weightless,
delicately veined arm. "You still can't feel a thing in this arm, Eddie, it's
completely numb. It's sound asleep and it won't wake up until I tell it to."
Harry repositioned himself in order to hold himself steady while he knelt,
and put the point of the hat pin nearly flat against Eddie's arm. He pushed
it forward far enough to raise a wrinkle of flesh. The point of the hat pin
dug into Eddie's skin but did not break it. Harry pushed harder, and the
hat pin raised the little bulge of skin by a small but appreciable amount.

Skin was a lot tougher to break through than anyone imagined.

The pin was beginning to hurt his fingers, so Harry opened his hand
and positioned the head against the base of his middle finger. Grimacing,
he pushed his hand against the pin. The point of the pin popped through
the raised wrinkle.

"Eddie, you're made out of beer cans," Harry said, and tugged the head
of the pin backward. The wrinkle flattened out. Now Harry could shove the
pin forward again, sliding the shaft deeper and deeper under the surface
of Little Eddie's skin. He could see the raised line of the hat pin marching
down his brother's arm, looking as prominent as the damage done to a cartoon lawn by a cartoon rabbit. When the mother-of-pearl head was perhaps
three inches from the entry hole, Harry pushed it down into Little Eddie's
flesh, thus raising the point of the pin. He gave the head a sharp jab, and
the point appeared at the end of the ridge in Eddie's skin, poking through a
tiny smear of blood. Harry shoved the pin in further. Now it showed about
an inch and a half of gray metal at either end.

"Feel anything?"

"Nothing."

Harry jiggled the head of the pin, and a bubble of blood walked out
of the entry wound and began to slide down Eddie's arm. Harry sat down
on the attic floor beside Eddie and regarded his work. His mind seemed
pleasantly empty of thought, filled only with a variety of sensations. He *felt*
but could not hear a buzzing in his head, and a blurry film seemed to cover
his eyes. He breathed through his mouth. The long pin stuck through Little
Eddie's arm looked monstrous seen one way; seen another, it was sheerly
beautiful. Skin, blood, and metal. Harry had never seen anything like it

before. He reached out and twisted the pin, causing another little blood-snail to crawl from the exit wound. Harry saw all this as if through smudgy glasses, but he did not mind. He knew the blurriness was only mental. He touched the head of the pin again and moved it from side to side. A little more blood leaked from both punctures. Then Harry shoved the pin in, partially withdrew it so that the point nearly disappeared back into Eddie's arm, moved it forward again; and went on like this, back and forth, back and forth as if he were sewing his brother up, for some time.

Finally he withdrew the pin from Eddie's arm. Two long streaks of blood had nearly reached his brother's wrist. Harry ground the heels of his hands into his eyes, blinked, and discovered that his vision had cleared.

He wondered how long he and Eddie had been in the attic. It could have been hours. He could not quite remember what had happened before he had slid the hat pin into Eddie's skin. Now his blurriness really was mental, not visual. A loud uncomfortable pulse beat in his temples. Again he wiped the blood from Eddie's arm. Then he stood on wobbling knees and returned to his chair.

"How's your arm feel, Eddie?"

"Numb," Eddie said in his gravelly sleepy voice.

"The numbness is going away now. Very very slowly. You are beginning to feel your arm again, and it feels very good. There is no pain. It feels like the sun was shining on it all afternoon. It's strong and healthy. Feeling is coming back into your arm, and you can move your fingers and everything."

When he had finished speaking Harry leaned back against the chair and closed his eyes. He rubbed his forehead with his hand and wiped the moisture off on his shirt.

"How does your arm feel?" he said without opening his eyes.

"Good."

"That's great, Little Eddie." Harry flattened his palms against his flushed face, wiped his cheeks, and opened his eyes.

*I can do this every night,* he thought. *I can bring Little Eddie up here every single night, at least until school starts.*

"Eddie, you're getting stronger and stronger every day. This is really helping you. And the more we do it the stronger you'll get. Do you understand me?"

"I understand you," Eddie said.

"We're almost done for tonight. There's just one more thing I want to try. But you have to be really deep asleep for this to work. So I want you to go deeper and deeper, as deep as you can go. Relax, and now you are really deep asleep, deep deep, and relaxed and ready and feeling good."

Little Eddie sat sprawled in his chair with his head tilted back and his eyes closed. Two tiny dark spots of blood stood out like mosquito bites on his lower right forearm.

"When I talk to you, Eddie, you're slowly getting younger and younger, you're going backward in time, so now you're not nine years old anymore, you're eight, it's last year and you're in the third grade, and now you're seven, and now you're six years old . . . and now you're five, Eddie, and it's the day of your fifth birthday. You're five years old today, Little Eddie. How old are you?"

"I'm five." To Harry's surprised pleasure, Little Eddie's voice actually seemed younger, as did his hunched posture in the chair.

"How do you feel?"

"Not good. I hate my present. It's terrible. Dad got it, and Mom says it should never be allowed in the house because it's just junk. I wish I wouldn't ever have to have birthdays, they're so terrible. I'm gonna cry."

His face contracted. Harry tried to remember what Eddie had gotten for his fifth birthday, but could not—he caught only a dim memory of shame and disappointment. "What's your present, Eddie?"

In a teary voice, Eddie said, "A radio. But it's busted and Mom says it looks like it came from the junkyard. I don't want it anymore. I don't even wanna *see* it."

*Yes,* Harry thought, *yes, yes, yes.* He could remember. On Little Eddie's fifth birthday, Edgar Beevers had produced a yellow plastic radio which even Harry had seen was astoundingly ugly. The dial was cracked, and it was marked here and there with brown circular scablike marks where someone had mashed out cigarettes on it.

The radio had long since been buried in the junk room, where it now lay beneath several geological layers of trash.

"Okay, Eddie, you can forget the radio now, because you're going backward again, you're getting younger, you're going backward through being four years old, and now you're three."

He looked with interest at Little Eddie, whose entire demeanor had changed. From being tearfully unhappy, Eddie now demonstrated a self-sufficient good cheer Harry could not ever remember seeing in him. His arms were folded over his chest. He was smiling, and his eyes were bright and clear and childish.

"What do you see?" Harry asked.

"Mommy-ommy-om."

"What's she doing?"

"Mommy's at her desk. She's smoking and looking through her

papers." Eddie giggled. "Mommy looks funny. It looks like smoke is coming out of the top of her head." Eddie ducked his chin and hid his smile behind a hand. "Mommy doesn't see me. I can see her, but she doesn't see me. Oh! Mommy works hard! She works hard at her desk!"

Eddie's smile abruptly left his face. His face froze for a second in a comic rubbery absence of expression; then his eyes widened in terror and his mouth went loose and wobbly.

"What happened?" Harry's mouth had gone dry.

"No, Mommy!" Eddie wailed. "Don't, Mommy! I wasn't spying, I wasn't, I promise—" His words broke off into a screech. *"No, Mommy! Don't! Don't, Mommy!"* Eddie jumped upward, sending his chair flying back, and ran blindly toward the rear of the attic. Harry's head rang with Eddie's screeches. He heard a sharp *crack!* of wood breaking, but only as a small part of all the noise Eddie was making as he charged around the attic. Eddie had run into a tangle of hanging dresses, spun around, enmeshing himself deeper in the dresses, and was now tearing himself away from the web of dresses, pulling some of them off the rack. A long-sleeved purple dress with an enormous lace collar had draped itself around Eddie like a ghostly dance partner, and another dress, of dull red velvet, snaked around his right leg. Eddie screamed again and yanked himself away from the tangle. The entire rack of clothes wobbled and then went over in a mad jangle of sound.

*"No!"* he screeched. *"Help!"* Eddie ran straight into a big wooden beam marking off one of the eaves, bounced off, and came windmilling toward Harry. Harry knew his brother could not see him.

"Eddie, stop," he said, but Eddie was past hearing him. Harry tried to make Eddie stop by wrapping his arms around him, but Eddie slammed right into him, hitting Harry's chest with a shoulder and knocking his head painfully against Harry's chin; Harry's arms closed on nothing and his eyes lost focus, and Eddie went crashing into the tilting mirror. The mirror yawned over sideways. Harry saw it tilt with dreamlike slowness toward the floor, then in an eyeblink drop and crash. Broken glass sprayed across the attic floor.

*"Stop!"* Harry yelled. *"Stand still, Eddie!"*

Eddie came to rest. A ripped and dirty dress of dull red velvet still clung to his right leg. Blood oozed down his temple from an ugly cut above his eye. He was breathing hard, releasing air in little whimpering exhalations.

"Holy shit," Harry said, looking around at the attic. In only a few seconds Eddie had managed to create what looked at first like absolute devastation. Maryrose's ancient dresses lay tangled in a heap of dusty fabrics from which wire hangers skeletally protruded; gray Eddie-sized footprints lay like a pattern over the muted explosion of colors the dresses now created. When the rack had gone over, it had knocked a section the size of a dinner plate out of a round wooden coffee table Maryrose had particularly prized for its being made from a single section of teak—"a single piece of *teak*, the rarest wood in all the world, all the way from Ceylon!" The much-prized mirror lay in hundreds of glittering pieces across the attic floor. With growing horror, Harry saw that the wooden frame had cracked like a bone, showing a bone-pale, shockingly white fracture in the expanse of dark stain.

Harry's blood tipped within his body, nearly tipping him with it, like the mirror. "Oh God, oh God, oh God."

He turned slowly around. Eddie stood blinking two feet to his side, wiping ineffectually at the blood running from his forehead and now covering most of his left cheek. He looked like an Indian in war paint—a defeated, lost Indian, for his eyes were dim and his head turned aimlessly from side to side.

A few feet from Eddie lay the chair in which he had been sitting. One of its thin curved wooden arms lay beside it, crudely severed. It looked like an insect's leg, Harry thought, like a toy gun.

For a moment Harry thought that his face too was red with blood. He wiped his hand over his forehead and looked at his glistening palm. It was only sweat. His heart beat like a bell. Beside him Eddie said, "Aaah . . . what . . . ?" The injury to his head had brought him out of the trance.

The dresses were ruined, stepped on, tangled, torn. The mirror was broken. The table had been mutilated. Maryrose's chair lay on its side like a murder victim, its severed arm ending in a bristle of snapped ligaments.

"My head *hurts*," Eddie said in a weak, trembling voice. "What happened? Aaah! I'm all blood! I'm all blood, Harry!"

"You're all blood, you're all blood?" Harry shouted at him. "Everything's *all blood*, you dummy! Look around!" He did not recognize his own voice, which sounded high and tinny and seemed to be coming from somewhere else. Little Eddie took an aimless step away from him, and Harry wanted to fly at him, to pound his bloody head into a pancake, to destroy him, smash him. . . .

Eddie held up his bloodstained palm and stared at it. He wiped it vaguely across the front of his T-shirt and took another wandering step. "I'm ascared, Harry," his tiny voice uttered.

"Look what you did!" Harry screamed. "You wrecked everything! Damn it! What do you think is going to happen to us?"

"What's Mom going to do?" Eddie asked in a voice only slightly above a whisper.

"You don't know?" Harry yelled. "You're dead!"

Eddie started to weep.

Harry bunched his hands into fists and clamped his eyes shut. They were both dead, that was the real truth. Harry opened his eyes, which felt hot and oddly heavy, and stared at his sobbing, red-smeared, useless little brother. "Blue rose," he said.

10

LITTLE EDDIE'S HANDS FELL to his sides. His chin dropped, and his mouth fell open. Blood ran in a smooth wide band down the left side of his face, dipped under the line of his jaw, and continued on down his neck and into his T-shirt. Pooled blood in his left eyebrow dripped steadily onto the floor, as if from a faucet.

"You are going deep *asleep*," Harry said. Where was the hat pin? He looked back to the single standing chair and saw the mother-of-pearl head glistening on the floor near it. "Your whole body is *numb*." He moved over to the pin, bent down, and picked it up. The metal shaft felt warm in his fingers. "You can feel no *pain*." He went back to Little Eddie. "Nothing can *hurt* you." Harry's breath seemed to be breathing itself, forcing itself into his throat in hot, harsh, shallow pants, then expelling itself out.

"Did you *hear* me, Little Eddie?"

In his gravelly, slow-moving, hypnotized voice, Little Eddie said, "I heard you."

"And you can feel no *pain*?"

"I can feel no pain."

Harry drew his arm back, the point of the hat pin extending forward from his fist, and then jerked his hand forward as hard as he could and stuck the pin into Eddie's abdomen right through the blood-soaked T-shirt. He exhaled sharply, and tasted a sour misery on his breath.

"You don't feel a thing."

"I don't feel a thing."

Harry opened his right hand and drove his palm against the head of the pin, hammering it in another few inches. Little Eddie looked like a voodoo doll. A kind of sparkling light surrounded him. Harry gripped the head of the pin with his thumb and forefinger and yanked it out. He held it up and inspected it. Glittering light surrounded the pin, too. The long shaft was painted with blood. Harry slipped the point into his mouth and closed his lips around the warm metal.

He saw himself, a man in another life, standing in a row with men like himself in a bleak gray landscape defined by barbed wire. Emaciated people in rags shuffled up toward them and spat on their clothes. The smells of dead flesh and of burning flesh hung in the air. Then the vision was gone, and Little Eddie stood before him again, surrounded by layers of glittering light.

Harry grimaced or grinned, he could not have told the difference, and drove his long spike deep into Eddie's stomach.

Eddie uttered a small *oof*.

"You don't feel anything, Eddie," Harry whispered. "You feel good all over. You never felt better in your life."

"Never felt better in my life."

Harry slowly pulled out the pin and cleaned it with his fingers.

He was able to remember every single thing anyone had ever told him about Tommy Golz.

"Now you're going to play a funny, funny game," he said. "This is called the Tommy Golz game because it's going to keep you safe from Mrs. Franken. Are you ready?" Harry carefully slid the pin into the fabric of his shirt collar, all the while watching Eddie's slack, blood-streaked person. Vibrating bands of light beat rhythmically and steadily about Eddie's face.

"Ready," Eddie said.

"I'm going to give you your instructions now, Little Eddie. Pay attention to everything I say and it's all going to be okay. Everything's going to be okay—as long as you play the game exactly the way I tell you. You understand, don't you?"

"I understand."

"Tell me what I just said."

"Everything's gonna be okay as long as I play the game exactly the way you tell me." A dollop of blood slid off Eddie's eyebrow and splashed onto his already soaked T-shirt.

"Good, Eddie. Now the first thing you do is fall down—not now, when I tell you. I'm going to give you all the instructions, and then I'm going to count backward from ten, and when I get to "one," you'll start playing the game. Okay?"

"Okay."

"So first you fall down, Little Eddie. You fall down real hard. Then comes the fun part of the game. You bang your head on the floor. You start to go crazy. You twitch, and you bang your hands and feet on the floor. You do that for a long time. I guess you do that until you count to about a hundred. You foam at the mouth, you twist all over the place. You get real stiff, and then you get real loose, and then you get real stiff, and then real loose again, and all this time you're banging your head and your hands and feet on the floor, and you're twisting all over the place. Then when you finish counting to a hundred in your head, you do the last thing. You swallow your tongue. And that's the game. When you swallow your tongue you're the winner. And then nothing bad can happen to you, and Mrs. Franken won't be able to hurt you ever ever ever."

Harry stopped talking. His hands were shaking. After a second he realized that his insides were shaking, too. He raised his trembling fingers to his shirt collar and felt the hat pin.

"Tell me how you win the game, Little Eddie. What's the last thing you do?"

"I swallow my tongue."

"Right. And then Mrs. Franken and Mom will never be able to hurt you, because you won the game."

"Good," said Little Eddie. The glittering light shimmered about him.

"Okay, we'll start playing right now," Harry said. "Ten." He went toward the attic steps. "Nine." He reached the steps. "Eight."

He went down one step. "Seven." Harry descended another two steps. "Six." When he went down another two steps, he called up in a slightly louder voice, "Five."

Now his head was beneath the level of the attic floor, and he could not see Little Eddie anymore. All he could hear was the soft, occasional plop of liquid hitting the floor.

"Four."

"Three."

"Two." He was now at the door to the attic steps. Harry opened the door, stepped through it, breathed hard, and shouted "One!" up the stairs.

He heard a thud, and then quickly closed the door behind him.

Harry went across the hall and into the "dormitory" bedroom. There seemed to be a strange absence of light in the hallway. For a second he saw—was sure he saw—a line of dark trees across a wall of barbed wire. Harry closed this door behind him, too, and went to his narrow bed and sat down. He could feel blood beating in his face; his eyes seemed oddly warm, as if they were heated by filaments. Harry slowly, almost reverently, extracted the hat pin from his collar and set it on his pillow. "A hundred," he said. "Ninety-nine, ninety-eight, ninety-seven, ninety-six, ninety-five, ninety-four . . ."

When he had counted down to "*one*," he stood up and left the bedroom. He went quickly downstairs without looking at the door behind which lay the attic steps. On the ground floor he slipped into Maryrose's bedroom, crossed over to her desk, and slid open the bottom right-hand drawer. From the drawer he took a velvet-covered box. This he opened, and jabbed the hat pin in the ball of material, studded with pins of all sizes and descriptions, from which he had taken it. He replaced the box in the drawer, pushed the drawer into the desk, and quickly left the room and went upstairs.

Back in his own bedroom, Harry took off his clothes and climbed into his bed. His face still burned.

HE MUST HAVE FALLEN asleep very quickly, because the next thing he knew Albert was slamming his way into the bedroom and tossing his clothes and boots all over the place. "You asleep?" Albert asked. "You left the attic light on, you fuckin' dummies, but if you think I'm gonna save your fuckin' asses and go up and turn it off, you're even stupider than you look."

Harry was careful not to move a finger, not to move even a hair.

He held his breath while Albert threw himself onto his bed, and when Albert's breathing relaxed and slowed, Harry followed his big brother into sleep. He did not awaken again until he heard his father half-screeching, half-sobbing up in the attic, and that was very late at night.

### 11

SONNY CAME FROM FORT SILL, George all the way from Germany. Between them, they held up a sodden Edgar Beevers at the grave site while a minister Harry had never seen before read from a Bible as cracked and rubbed as an old brown shoe. Between his two older sons, Harry's father looked bent and ancient, a skinny old man only steps from the grave himself. Sonny and George despised their father, Harry saw—they held him up on sufferance, in part because they had chipped in thirty dollars apiece to buy him a suit and did not want to see it collapse with its owner inside onto the lumpy clay of the graveyard. His whiskers glistened in the sun, and moisture shone beneath his eyes and at the corners of his mouth. He had been shaking too severely for either Sonny or George to shave him, and had been capable of moving in a straight line only after George let him take a couple of long swallows from a leather-covered flask he took out of his duffel bag.

The minister uttered a few sage words on the subject of epilepsy.

Sonny and George looked as solid as brick walls in their uniforms, like prison guards or actual prisons themselves. Next to them, Albert looked shrunken and unfinished. Albert wore the green plaid sport jacket in which he had graduated from the eighth grade, and his wrists hung prominent and red four inches below the bottoms of the sleeves. His motorcycle boots were visible beneath his light gray trousers, but they, like the green jacket, had lost their flash. Like Albert, too: ever since the discovery of Eddie's body, Albert had gone around the house looking as if he'd just bitten off the end of his tongue and was trying to decide whether or not to spit it out. He never looked anybody in the eye, and he rarely spoke. Albert acted as though a gigantic padlock had been fixed to the middle of his chest and *he* was damned if he'd ever take if off. He had not asked Sonny or George a single question about the army. Every now and then he would utter a remark about the gas station so toneless that it suffocated any reply.

Harry looked at Albert standing beside their mother, kneading his hands together and keeping his eyes fixed as if by decree on the square foot of ground before him. Albert glanced over at Harry, knew he was being looked at, and did what to Harry was an extraordinary thing. Albert *froze*. All expression drained out of his face, and his hands locked immovably together. He looked as little able to see or hear as a statue. *He's that way because he told Little Eddie that he wished he would die*, Harry thought for the tenth or eleventh time since he had realized this, and with undiminished awe. Then was he lying? Harry wondered. And if he really did wish that Little Eddie would drop dead, why isn't he happy now? Didn't he get what he wanted? Albert would never spit out that piece of his tongue, Harry thought, watching his brother blink slowly and sightlessly toward the ground.

Harry shifted his gaze uneasily to his father, still propped up between George and Sonny, heard that the minister was finally reaching the end of his speech, and took a fast look at his mother. Maryrose was standing very straight in a black dress and black sunglasses, holding the straps of her bag in front of her with both hands. Except for the color of her clothes, she could have been a spectator at a tennis match. Harry knew by the way she was holding her face that she was wishing she could smoke. *Dying for a cigarette*, he thought, *ha ha, the Monster Mash, it's a graveyard smash.*

The minister finished speaking and made a rhetorical gesture with his hands. The coffin sank on ropes into the rough earth. Harry's father began to weep loudly. First George, then Sonny, picked up large damp shovel-marked pieces of the clay and dropped them on the coffin. Edgar Beevers nearly fell in after his own tiny clod, but George contemptuously swung him back. Maryrose marched forward, bent and picked up a random piece of clay with thumb and forefinger as if using tweezers, dropped it, and turned away before it struck. Albert fixed his eyes on Harry—his own clod had split apart in his hand and crumbled away between his fingers. Harry shook his head *no*. He did not want to drop dirt on Eddie's coffin and make that noise. He did not want to look at Eddie's coffin again. There was enough dirt around to do the job without him hitting that metal box like he was trying to ring Eddie's doorbell. He stepped back.

"Mom says we have to get back to the house," Albert said.

Maryrose lit up as soon as they got into the single black car they had rented through the funeral parlor, and breathed out acrid smoke over everybody crowded into the backseat. The car backed into a narrow graveyard lane and turned down the main road toward the front gates.

In the front seat, Edgar Beevers drooped sideways next to the driver and leaned his head against the window, leaving a blurred streak on the glass.

"How in the name of hell could Little Eddie have epilepsy without anybody knowing about it?" George asked.

Albert stiffened and stared out the window.

"Well, that's epilepsy," Maryrose said. "Eddie could have gone on for years without having an attack." That she worked in a hospital always gave her remarks of this sort a unique gravity, almost as if she were a doctor.

"Must have been some fit," Sonny said, squeezed into place between Harry and Albert.

"*Grand mal*," Maryrose said, and took another hungry drag on her cigarette.

"Poor little bastard," George said. "Sorry, Mom."

"I know you're in the Armed Forces, and Armed Forces people speak very freely, but I wish you would not use that kind of language."

Harry, jammed into Sonny's rock-hard side, felt his brother's body twitch with a hidden laugh, though Sonny's face did not alter.

"I said I was sorry, Mom," George said.

"Yes. Driver! Driver!" Maryrose was leaning forward, reaching out one claw to tap the chauffeur's shoulder. "Livermore is the next right. Do you know South Sixth Street?"

"I'll get you there," the driver said.

*This is not my family*, Harry thought. *I came from somewhere else and my rules are different from theirs.*

HIS FATHER MUMBLED SOMETHING inaudible as soon as they got in the door and disappeared into his curtained-off cubicle. Maryrose put her sunglasses in her purse and marched into the kitchen to warm the coffee cake and the macaroni casserole, both made that morning, in the oven. Sonny and George wandered into the living room and sat down on opposite ends of the couch. They did not look at each other—George picked up a *Reader's Digest* from the table and began leafing through it backward, and Sonny folded his hands in his lap and stared at his thumbs. Albert's footsteps plodded up the stairs, crossed the landing, and went into the dormitory bedroom.

"What's she in the kitchen for?" Sonny asked, speaking to his hands. "Nobody's going to come. Nobody ever comes here, because she never wanted them to."

"Albert's taking this kind of hard, Harry," George said. He propped the magazine against the stiff folds of his uniform and looked across the room at his little brother. Harry had seated himself beside the door, as out of the way as possible. George's attentions rather frightened him, though George had behaved with consistent kindness ever since his arrival two days after Eddie's death. His crew cut still bristled and he could still break rocks with his chin, but some violent demon seemed to have left him. "You think he'll be okay?"

"Him? Sure." Harry tilted his head, grimaced.

"He didn't see Little Eddie first, did he?"

"No, Dad did," Harry said. "He saw the light on in the attic when he came home, I guess. Albert went up there, though. I guess there was so much blood Dad thought somebody broke in and killed Eddie. But he just bumped his head, and that's where the blood came from."

"Head wounds bleed like bastards," Sonny said. "A guy hit me with a bottle once in Tokyo, I thought I was gonna bleed to death right there."

"And Mom's stuff got all messed up?" George asked quietly.

This time Sonny looked up.

"Pretty much, I guess. The dress rack got knocked down. Dad cleaned up what he could the next day. One of the cane-back chairs got broke, and a hunk got knocked out of the teak table. And the mirror got broken into a million pieces."

Sonny shook his head, and made a soft whistling sound through his pursed lips.

"She's a tough old gal," George said. "I hear her coming, though, so we have to stop, Harry. But we can talk tonight."

Harry nodded.

## 12

AFTER DINNER THAT NIGHT, when Maryrose had gone to bed—the hospital had given her two nights off—Harry sat across the kitchen table from a George who clearly had something to say. Sonny had polished off a six-pack by himself in front of the television and gone up to the dormitory bedroom by himself. Albert had disappeared shortly after dinner, and their father had never emerged from his cubicle beside the junk room.

"I'm glad Pete Petrosian came over," George said. "He's a good old boy. Ate two helpings, too."

Harry was startled by George's use of their neighbor's first name—he was not even sure that he had ever heard it before.

Mr. Petrosian had been their only caller that afternoon. Harry had seen that his mother was grateful that someone had come, and despite her preparations wanted no more company after Mr. Petrosian had left.

"Think I'll get a beer, that is if Sonny didn't drink it all," George said, and stood up and opened the fridge. His uniform looked as if it had been painted on his body, and his muscles bulged and moved like a horse's. "Two left," he said. "Good thing you're underage." George popped the caps off both bottles and came back to the table. He winked at Harry, then tilted the first bottle to his lips and took a good swallow. "So what the devil was Little Eddie doing up there, anyhow? Trying on dresses?"

"I don't know," Harry said. "I was asleep."

"Hell, I know I kind of lost touch with Little Eddie, but I got the impression he was scared of his own shadow. I'm surprised he had the nerve to go up there and mess around with Mom's precious stuff."

"Yeah," Harry said. "Me, too."

"You didn't happen to go with him, did you?" George tilted the bottle to his mouth and winked at Harry again.

Harry just looked back. He could feel his face getting hot.

"I was thinking maybe you saw it happen to Little Eddie, and got too scared to tell anybody. Nobody would be mad at you, Harry. Nobody would blame you for anything. You couldn't know how to help someone who's having an epileptic fit. Little Eddie swallowed his tongue. Even if you'd been standing next to him when he did it and had the presence of mind to call an ambulance, he would have died before it got there. Unless you knew what was wrong and how to correct it. Which nobody would expect you to know, not in a million years. Nobody'd blame you for anything, Harry, not even Mom."

"I was asleep," Harry said.

"Okay, okay. I just wanted you to know."

They sat in silence for a time, then both spoke at once.

"Did you know—"

"We had this—"

"Sorry," George said. "Go on."

"Did you know that Dad used to be in the army? In World War II?"

"Yeah, I knew that. Of course I knew that."

"Did you know that he committed the perfect murder once?"

"*What?*"

"Dad committed the perfect murder. When he was at Dachau, that death camp."

"Oh, Christ, is that what you're talking about? You got a funny way of seeing things, Harry. He shot an enemy who was trying to escape. That's not murder, it's war. There's one hell of a big difference."

"I'd like to see war someday," Harry said. "I'd like to be in the army, like you and Dad."

"Hold your horses, hold your horses," George said, smiling now. "That's sort of one of the things I wanted to talk to you about." He set down his beer bottle, cradled his hands around it, and tilted his head to look at Harry. This was obviously going to be serious. "You know, I used to be crazy and stupid, that's the only way to put it. I used to look for fights. I had a chip on my shoulder the size of a house, and pounding some dipshit into a coma was my idea of a great time. The army did me a lot of good. It made me grow up. But I don't think you need that, Harry. You're too smart for that—if you have to go, you go, but out of all of us, you're the one who could really amount to something in this world. You could be a doctor. Or a lawyer. You ought to get the best education you can, Harry. What you have to do is stay out of trouble and get to college."

"Oh, college," Harry said.

"Listen to me, Harry. I make pretty good money, and I got nothing to spend it on. I'm not going to get married and have kids, that's for sure. So I want to make you a proposition. If you keep your nose clean and make it through high school, I'll help you out with college. Maybe you can get a scholarship—I think you're smart enough, Harry, and a scholarship would be great. But either way, I'll see you make it through." George emptied the first bottle, set it down, and gave Harry a quizzical look. "Let's get one person in this family off on the right track. What do you say?"

"I guess I better keep reading," Harry said.

"I hope you'll read your ass off, little buddy," George said, and picked up the second bottle of beer.

### 13

THE DAY AFTER SONNY left, George put all of Eddie's toys and clothes into a box and squeezed the box into the junk room; two days later, George took a bus to New York so he could get his flight to Munich from Idlewild. An hour before he caught his bus, George walked Harry up to Big John's and stuffed him full of hamburgers and french fries and said, "You'll probably miss Eddie a lot, won't you?" "I guess," Harry said, but the truth was that Eddie was now only a vacancy, a blank space. Sometimes a door would close and Harry would know that Little Eddie had just come in; but when he turned to look, he saw only emptiness. George's question, asked a week ago, was the last time Harry had heard anyone pronounce his brother's name.

In the seven days since the charmed afternoon at Big John's and the departure on a southbound bus of George Beevers, everything seemed to have gone back to the way it was before, but Harry knew that really everything had changed. They had been a loose, divided family of five, two parents and three sons. Now they seemed to be a family of three, and Harry thought that the actual truth was that the family had shrunk down to two, himself and his mother.

Edgar Beevers had left home—he too was an absence. After two visits from policemen who parked their cars right outside the house, after listening to his mother's muttered expressions of disgust, after the spectacle of his pale, bleary, but sober and clean-shaven father trying over and over to knot a necktie in front of the bathroom mirror, Harry finally accepted that his father had been caught shoplifting. His father had to go to court, and he was scared. His hands shook so uncontrollably that he could not shave himself, and in the end Maryrose had to knot his tie—doing it in one, two, three quick movements as brutal as the descent of a knife, never removing the cigarette from her mouth.

GRIEF-STRICKEN AREA MAN FORGIVEN OF SHOPLIFTING CHARGE read the headline over the little story in the evening newspaper that at last explained his father's crime. Edgar Beevers had been stopped on the sidewalk outside the Livermore Avenue National Tea, T-bone steaks hidden inside his shirt and a bottle of Rhinegold beer in each of his front pockets. He had stolen two steaks! He had put beer bottles in his pockets! This made Harry feel like he was sweating inside. The judge had sent him home, but home was not where he went. For a short time, Harry thought, his father had hung out on Oldtown Road, Palmyra's skid row, and slept in vacant lots with winos and bums. (Then a woman was supposed to have taken him in.)

Albert was another mystery. It was as though a creature from outer space had taken him over and was using his body, like *Invasion of the Body Snatchers*. Albert looked like he thought somebody was always standing behind him, watching every move he made. He was still carrying around that piece of his tongue, and pretty soon, Harry thought, he'd get so used to it that he would forget he had it.

Three days after George left Palmyra, Albert actually tagged along after Harry on the way to Big John's. Harry turned around on the sidewalk and saw Albert in his black jeans and grease-blackened T-shirt halfway down the block, shoving his hands in his pockets and looking hard at the ground. That was Albert's way of pretending to be invisible. The next time he turned around, Albert growled, "Keep walking."

Harry went to work on the pinball machine as soon as he got inside Big John's. Albert slunk in a few minutes later and went straight to the counter. He took one of the stained paper menus from a stack squeezed in beside a napkin dispenser and inspected it as if he had never seen it before.

"Hey, let me introduce you guys," said Big John, leaning against the far side of the counter. Like Albert, he wore black jeans and motorcycle boots, but his dark hair, daringly for the 1950s, fell over his ears. Beneath his stained white apron he wore a long-sleeved black shirt with a pattern of tiny azure palm trees. "You two are the Beevers boys, Harry and Bucky. Say hello to each other, fellows."

Bucky Beaver was a toothy rodent in an Ipana television commercial. Albert blushed, still grimly staring at his menu sheet.

"Call me 'Beans,'" Harry said, and felt Albert's gaze shift wonderingly to him.

"Beans and Bucky, the Beevers boys," Big John said. "Well, Buck, what'll you have?"

"Hamburger, fries, shake," Albert said.

Big John half-turned and yelled the order through the hatch to Mama Mary's kitchen. For a time the three of them stood in uneasy silence. Then Big John said, "Heard your old man found a new place to hang his hat. His new girlfriend is a real pistol, I heard. Spent some time in County Hospital. On account of she picked up little messages from outer space on the good old Philco. You hear that?"

"He's gonna come home real soon," Harry said. "He doesn't have any new girlfriend. He's staying with an old friend. She's a rich lady and she wants to help him out because she knows he had a lot of trouble and she's going to get him a real good job, and then he'll come home, and we'll be able to move to a better house and everything."

He never even saw Albert move, but Albert had materialized beside him. Fury, rage, and misery distorted his face. Harry had time to cry out only once, and then Albert slammed a fist into his chest and knocked him backward into the pinball machine.

"I bet that felt real good," Harry said, unable to keep down his own rage. "I bet you'd like to kill me, huh? Huh, Albert? How about that?"

Albert moved backward two paces and lowered his hands, already looking impassive, locked into himself.

For a second in which his breath failed and dazzling light filled his eyes, Harry saw Little Eddie's slack, trusting face before him. Then Big John came up from nowhere with a big hamburger and a mound of french fries on a plate and said, "Down, boys. Time for Rocky here to tackle his dinner."

That night Albert said nothing at all to Harry as they lay in their beds. Neither did he fall asleep. Harry knew that for most of the night Albert just closed his eyes and faked it, like a possum in trouble. Harry tried to stay awake long enough to see when Albert's fake sleep melted into the real thing, but he sank into dreams long before that.

He was rushing down the stony corridor of a castle past suits of armor and torches guttering in sconces. His bladder was bursting, he had to let go, he could not hold it more than another few seconds. . . . At last he came to the open bathroom door and ran into that splendid gleaming place. He began to tug at his zipper, and looked around for the butler and the row of marble urinals. Then he froze. Little Eddie was standing before him, not the uniformed butler. Blood ran in a gaudy streak from a gash high on his forehead over his cheek and right down his neck, neat as paint. Little Eddie was waving frantically at Harry, his eyes bright and hysterical, his mouth working soundlessly because he had swallowed his tongue.

Harry sat up straight in bed, about to scream, then realized that the bedroom was all around him and Little Eddie was gone. He hurried downstairs to the bathroom.

14

AT TWO O'CLOCK THE next afternoon Harry Beevers had to pee again, and just as badly, but this time he was a long way from the bathroom across from the junk room and his father's old cubicle. Harry was standing in the humid sunlight across the street from 45 Oldtown Way. This short street connected the bums, transient hotels, bars, and seedy movie theaters of Oldtown Road with the more respectable hotels, department stores, and restaurants of Palmyra Avenue—the real downtown. Forty-five Oldtown Way was a four-story brick tenement with an exoskeleton of fire escapes. Black iron bars covered the ground-floor windows. On one side of 45 Oldtown Way were the large soap-smeared windows of a bankrupt shoe store, on the other a vacant lot where loose bricks and broken bottles nestled amongst dandelions and tall Queen Anne's Lace. Harry's father lived in that building now. Everybody else knew it, and since Big John had told him, now Harry knew it, too.

He jigged from leg to leg, waiting for a woman to come out through the front door. It was as chipped and peeling as his own, and a broken fanlight sat drunkenly atop it. Harry had checked the row of dented mailboxes on the brick wall just outside the door for his father's name, but none bore any names at all. Big John hadn't known the name of the woman who had taken Harry's father in, but he said that she was large, black-haired, and crazy, and that she had two children in foster care. About half an hour ago a dark-haired woman had come through the door, but Harry had not followed her because she had not looked especially large to him. Now he was beginning to have doubts. What did Big John mean by "large," anyhow? As big as he was? And how could you tell if someone was crazy? Did it show? Maybe he should have followed that woman. This thought made him even more anxious, and he squeezed his legs together.

His father was in that building now, he thought. Harry thought of his father lying on an unmade bed, his brown winter coat around him, his hat pulled low on his forehead like Lepke Buchalter's, drawing on a cigarette, looking moodily out the window.

Then he had to pee so urgently that he could not have held it in for more than a few seconds, and trotted across the street and into the vacant lot. Near the back fence the tall weeds gave him some shelter from the street. He frantically unzipped and let the braided yellow stream splash into a nest of broken bricks. Harry looked up at the side of the building beside him. It looked very tall, and seemed to be tilting slightly toward him. The four blank windows on each floor looked back down at him. Just as he was tugging at his zipper, he heard the front door of the building slam shut.

His heart slammed, too. Harry hunkered down behind the tall white weeds. Anxiety that she might walk the other way, toward downtown, made him twine his fingers together and bend his fingers back. If he waited about five seconds, he figured, he'd know she was going toward Palmyra Avenue and would be able to get across the lot in time to see which way she turned. His knuckles cracked. He felt like a soldier hiding in a forest, like a murder weapon.

He raised up on his toes and got ready to dash back across the street, because an empty grocery cart closely followed by a moving belly with a tiny head and basketball shoes, a cigar tilted in its mouth like a flag, appeared past the front of the building. He could go back and wait across the street. Harry settled down and watched the stomach go down the sidewalk past him. Then a shadow separated itself from the street side of the fat man, and the shadow became a black-haired woman in a long loose dress now striding past the grocery cart. She shook back her head, and Harry saw that she was tall as a queen and that her skin was darker than olive. Deep lines cut through her cheeks. It had to be the woman who had taken his father in. Her long rapid strides had taken her well past the fat man's grocery cart. Harry ran across the rubble of the lot and began to follow her up the sidewalk.

His father's woman walked in a hard, determined way. She stepped down into the street to get around groups too slow for her. At the Oldtown Road corner she wove her way through a group of saggy-bottomed men passing around a bottle in a paper bag and cut in front of two black children dribbling a basketball up the street. She was on the move, and Harry had to hurry along to keep her in sight.

"I bet you don't believe me," he said to himself, practicing, and skirted the group of winos on the corner. He picked up his speed until he was nearly trotting. The two black kids with the basketball ignored him as he kept pace with them, then went on ahead. Far up the block, the tall woman with bouncing black hair marched right past a flashing neon sign in a bar window. Her bottom moved back and forth in the loose dress, surprisingly big whenever it bulged out the fabric of the dress; her back seemed as long as a lion's. "What would you say if I told you," Harry said to himself.

A block and a half ahead, the woman turned on her heel and went through the door of the A & P store. Harry sprinted the rest of the way, pushed the yellow wooden door marked "Enter," and walked into the dense, humid air of the grocery store. Other A & P stores may have been air-conditioned, but not the little shop on Oldtown Road.

What was foster care, anyway? Did you get money if you gave away your children?

*A good person's children would never be in foster care,* Harry thought. He saw the woman turning into the third aisle past the cash register. He took in with a small shock that she was taller than his father. If I told you, you might not believe me. He went slowly around the corner of the aisle. She was standing on the pale wooden floor about fifteen feet in front of him, carrying a wire basket in one hand. He stepped forward. What I have to say might seem. For good luck, he touched the hat pin inserted into the bottom of his collar. She was staring at a row of brightly colored bags of potato chips. Harry cleared his throat. The woman reached down and picked up a big bag and put it in the basket.

"Excuse me," Harry said.

She turned her head to look at him. Her face was as wide as it was long, and in the mellow light from the store's low-wattage bulbs her skin seemed a very light shade of brown. Harry knew he was meeting an equal. She looked like she could do magic, as if she could shoot fire and sparks out of her fierce black eyes.

"I bet you don't believe me," he said, "but a kid can hypnotize people just as good as an adult."

"What's that?"

His rehearsed words now sounded crazy to him, but he stuck to his script.

"A kid can hypnotize people. I can hypnotize people. Do you believe that?"

"I don't think I even care," she said, and wheeled away toward the rear of the aisle.

"I bet you don't think I could hypnotize you," Harry said.

"Kid, get lost."

Harry suddenly knew that if he kept talking about hypnotism the woman would turn down the next aisle and ignore him no matter what he said, or else begin to speak in a very loud voice about seeing the manager. "My name is Harry Beevers," he said to her back. "Edgar Beevers is my dad."

She stopped and turned around and looked expressionlessly into his face.

"I wonder if maybe you call him Beans," Harry said.

"Oh, great," she said. "That's just great. So you're one of his boys. Terrific. *Beans* wants potato chips, what do you want?"

"I want you to fall down and bang your head and swallow your tongue and *die* and get buried and have people drop dirt on you," Harry said. The woman's mouth fell open. "Then I want you to puff up with *gas*. I want you to *rot*. I want you to turn green and *black*. I want your *skin* to slide off your bones."

"You're crazy!" the woman shouted at him. "Your whole family's crazy! Do you think your mother wants him anymore?"

"My father shot us in the back," Harry said, and turned and bolted down the aisle for the door.

Outside, he began to trot down seedy Oldtown Road. At Oldtown Way he turned left. When he ran past number 45, he looked at every blank window. His face, his hands, his whole body felt hot and wet. Soon he had a stitch in his side. Harry blinked, and saw a dark line of trees, a wall of barbed wire before him. At the top of Oldtown Way he turned into Palmyra Avenue. From there he could continue running past Allouette's boarded-up windows, past all the stores old and new, to the corner of Livermore, and from there, he only now realized, to the little house that belonged to Mr. Petrosian.

## 15

ON A SWELTERING MID-AFTERNOON eleven years later at a camp in the central highlands of Vietnam, Lieutenant Harry Beevers closed the flap of his tent against the mosquitoes and sat on the edge of his temporary bunk to write a long-delayed letter back to Pat Caldwell, the young woman he wanted to marry—and to whom he would be married for a time, after his return from the war to New York State.

This is what he wrote, after frequent crossings-out and hesitations. Harry later destroyed this letter.

Dear Pat:

First of all I want you to know how much I miss you, my darling, and that if I ever get out of this beautiful and terrible country, which I am going to do, that I am going to chase you mercilessly and unrelentingly until you say that you'll marry me. Maybe in the euphoria of relief (YES!!!), I have the future all worked out, Pat, and you're a big part of it. I have eighty-six days until DEROS, when they pat me on the head and put me on that big bird out of here. Now that my record is clear again, I have no doubts that Columbia Law School will take me in. As you know, my law board scores were pretty respectable (modest me!) when I took them at Adelphi. I'm pretty sure I could even get into Harvard Law, but I settled on Columbia because then we could both be in New York.

My brother George has already told me that he will help out with whatever money I—you and I—will need. George put me through Adelphi. I don't think you knew this. In fact, nobody knew this. When I look back, in college I was such a jerk. I wanted everybody to think my family was well-to-do, or at least middle class. The truth is, we were damn poor, which I think makes my accomplishments all the more noteworthy, all the more loveworthy!

You see, this experience, even with all the ugly and self-doubting and humiliating moments, has done me a lot of good. I was right to come here, even though I had no idea what it was really like. I think I needed the experience of war to complete me, and I tell you this even though I know that you will detest any such idea. In fact, I have to tell you that a big part of me loves being here, and that in some way, even with all this trouble, this year will always be one of the high points of my life. Pat, as you see, I'm determined to be honest—to be an honest man. If I'm going to be a lawyer, I ought to be honest, don't you think? (Or maybe the reverse is the reality!) One thing that has meant a lot to me here has been what I can only call the close comradeship of my friends and my men—I actually like the grunts more than the usual officer types, which of course means that I get more loyalty and better performance from my men than the usual lieutenant. Someday I'd like you to meet Mike Poole and Tim Underhill and Pumo the Puma and the most amazing of all, M. O. Dengler, who of course was involved with me in the Ia Thuc cave incident. These guys stuck by me. I even have a nickname, "Beans." They call me "Beans" Beevers, and I like it.

There was no way my court-martial could have really put me in any trouble, because all the facts, and my own men, were on my side. Besides, could you see me actually killing children? This is Vietnam and you kill people, that's what we're doing here—we kill Charlies. But we don't kill babies and children. Not even in the heat of wartime—and Ia Thuc was pretty hot!

Well, this is my way of letting you know that at the court-martial, of course I received a complete and utter vindication. Dengler did, too. There were even unofficial mutterings about giving us medals for all the BS we put up with for the past six weeks—including that amazing story in *Time* magazine. Before people start yelling about atrocities, they ought to have all the facts straight. Fortunately, last week's magazines go out with the rest of the trash.

Besides, I already knew too much about what death does to people.

I never told you that I once had a little brother named Edward. When I was ten, my little brother wandered up into the top floor of our house one night and suffered a fatal epileptic fit. This event virtually destroyed my family. It led directly to my father's leaving home. (He had been a hero in WWII, something else I never told you.) It deeply changed, I would say even damaged, my older brother Albert. Albert tried to enlist in 1964, but they wouldn't take him because they said he was psychologically unfit. My mom, too, almost came apart for a while. She used to go up in the attic and cry and wouldn't come down. So you could say that my family was pretty well destroyed, or ruined, or whatever you want to call it, by a sudden death. I took it, and my dad's desertion, pretty hard myself. You don't get over these things easily.

The court-martial lasted exactly four hours. Big deal, hey?, as we used to say back in Palmyra. We used to have a neighbor named Pete Petrosian who said things like that, and against what must have been million-to-one odds, died exactly the same way my brother did, about two weeks after—lightning really did strike twice. I guess it's dumb to think about him now, but maybe one thing war does is to make you conversant with death. How it happens, what it does to people, what it means, how all the dead in your life are somehow united, joined, part of your eternal family. This is a profound feeling, Pat, and no damn whipped-up, failed court-martial can touch it. If there were any innocent children in that cave, then they are in my family forever, like little Edward and Pete Petrosian, and the rest of my life is a poem to them. But the Army says there weren't, and so do I.

I love you and love you and love you. You can stop worrying now and start thinking about being married to a Columbia Law student with one hell of a good future. I won't tell you any more war stories than you want to hear. And that's a promise, whether the stories are about Nam or Palmyra.

Always yours,
Harry
(aka "Beans!")

# A Bad Night
# for Burglars

## LAWRENCE BLOCK

Lawrence Block's Introduction:

*Quandary time . . .*

*A couple of years ago, when I edited* Death Cruise, *my first anthology, several readers expressed disappointment that I hadn't included a story of my own. I decided they were right, and since then I've managed to shoehorn something of mine into each anthology I've put together.*

*Until now, this hasn't been terribly difficult. For the Seven Deadly Sins series, I've written original novellas for each volume. For* Master's Choice, *volumes One and Two, I've followed the formula and picked a favorite story by another writer and a favorite of my own. One can, after all, have more than one favorite, and I intend to have as many as there are volumes of* Master's Choice.

*With* Opening Shots, *however, there would appear to be a problem. How many first stories can one person have? Only one, it would seem. Oh, there's some leeway here; one's first written story need not be the first one sold, which in turn need not be the first one published. But in my own case one story, "You Can't Lose," was first across the wire in all three categories—first written, first sold, and first published. And so I tucked it into the first volume of* Opening Shots, *spent the money for it, and was altogether quite happy about the whole thing.*

*But how can I get a story of mine into* Opening Shots 2?

*As my contributors sent in their own first efforts, along with their excellent introductions, inspiration struck. I could not help noticing how many of the writers sold their first stories to* Ellery Queen's Mystery Magazine, *and included fascinating reminiscences of the late Fred Dannay, who with his cousin Manfred Lee was Ellery Queen, and who all by himself created and edited EQMM.*

*My own first story sold to* Manhunt, *back in 1957, and it wasn't until 1976 that I finally placed a story in EQMM. By then I'd sold a few dozen stories—to* Manhunt, *to its imitators, to Alfred Hitchcock, to various men's magazines, but never to Ellery Queen. I don't know that I particularly aimed stories there, and I don't recall eating my heart out because I hadn't cracked that market, but I don't know that I was entirely sanguine about it, either.*

*Sometime in 1975 I started thinking about burglary.*

*I've said this before. I'd reached a low point in my career, and was ready to try something else, and couldn't avoid the realization that there was nothing else I was suited for. I had no training, no experience. All I'd ever done was write.*

*Well, suppose I tried crime? Burglary, specifically, as I had no appetite for violence, and preferred the idea of working alone and avoiding human contact, both good ideas when you're breaking into other people's houses.*

*I was in Rodanthe, a fishing village on the North Carolina Outer Banks, when I wrote "A Bad Night for Burglars." I wrote several short stories during the month I spent there, and sent all of them off to my then-agent, Henry Morrison.*

*And I continued thinking about burglary. In an attempt at a Matthew Scudder novel, stillborn after twenty or thirty pages, a loser of a burglar surrenders to the cops when they catch him in mid-job, then bolts when they find a corpse on the premises. He seeks out Scudder, who arrested him years ago and is now working private, and engages him to help him beat the murder charge.*

*Sound familiar? The plot, without Scudder and with a much hipper and sassier burglar, wound up driving my first Bernie Rhodenbarr novel, Burglars Can't Be Choosers. By the time I started writing that book, in the early months of 1976, I was living in Los Angeles and even more inclined toward burglary as a career. I taught myself to open the locked door of my hotel room with a credit card that no longer had any other practical use, and eventually did in fact finish BCBC, just in time for Bernie to save me from a life of crime.*

*Meanwhile, though, Fred Dannay had bought "A Bad Night for Burglars" for EQMM. I got the news, and the check, while I was at that hotel in LA, and it may well have spurred me to recycle my aborted Scudder effort into Burglars Can't Be Choosers. I can't swear it played a role, but I rather think it did.*

*Fred, who never met a title he didn't want to change, published the story as "Gentlemen's Agreement." Never mind the fact that Laura Z. Hobson had already made excellent use of that title. It's not that great a title for the story to begin with. I restored my original title when I collected the story in Sometimes They Bite, and that's how it appears here.*

*In the years that followed, until his death in 1982, Fred Dannay published quite a few more stories of mine, many of them about Martin Ehrengraf. Eleanor Sullivan was editing the magazine and doing the heavy lifting, but Fred always oversaw the entire operation, saying the final yea or nay on the stories she presented to him—and, as often as not, changing the titles.*

*My first story? Well, no, obviously not. First appearance of Bernie Rhoden-barr? Obviously not, as you'll see when you read the story; it is quite clearly this burglar's last appearance. But I daresay we might call him a Bernie Rhodenbarr prototype or forerunner, and the story was indeed my first in Ellery Queen, and I think that's enough to earn it a place here.*

*And, after all, who's editing this book?*

# A Bad Night for Burglars

## LAWRENCE BLOCK

THE BURGLAR, A SLENDER and clean-cut chap just past thirty, was rifling a drawer in the bedside table when Archer Trebizond slipped into the bedroom. Trebizond's approach was as catfooted as if he himself were the burglar, a situation which was manifestly not the case. The burglar never did hear Trebizond, absorbed as he was in his perusal of the drawer's contents, and at length he sensed the other man's presence as a jungle beast senses the presence of a predator.

The analogy, let it be said, is scarcely accidental.

When the burglar turned his eyes on Archer Trebizond, his heart fluttered and fluttered again, first at the mere fact of discovery, then at his own discovery of the gleaming revolver in Trebizond's hand. The revolver was pointed in his direction, and this the burglar found upsetting.

"Damn it all," said the burglar, approximately. "I could have sworn there was nobody home. I phoned, I rang the bell—"

"I just got here," Trebizond said.

"Just my luck. The whole week's been like that. I dented a fender on Tuesday afternoon, overturned my fish tank the night before last. An unbelievable mess all over the carpet, and I lost a mated pair of African mouthbreeders so rare they don't have a Latin name yet. I'd hate to tell you what I paid for them."

"Hard luck," Trebizond said.

"And just yesterday I was putting away a plate of fettuccine and I bit the inside of my mouth. You ever done that? It's murder, and the worst part is you feel so stupid about it. And then you keep biting it over and

414

over again because it sticks out while it's healing. At least I do." The burglar gulped a breath and ran a moist hand over a moister forehead. "And now this," he said.

"This could turn out to be worse than fenders and fish tanks," Trebizond said.

"Don't I know it. You know what I should have done? I should have spent the entire week in bed. I happen to know a safecracker who consults an astrologer before each and every job he pulls. If Jupiter's in the wrong place or Mars is squared with Uranus or something he won't go in. It sounds ridiculous, doesn't it? And yet it's eight years now since anybody put a handcuff on that man. Now who do you know who's gone eight years without getting arrested?"

"I've never been arrested," Trebizond said.

"Well, you're not a crook."

"I'm a businessman."

The burglar thought of something but let it pass. "I'm going to get the name of his astrologer," he said. "That's just what I'm going to do. Just as soon as I get out of here."

"If you get out of here," Trebizond said. "Alive," Trebizond said.

The burglar's jaw trembled just the slightest bit. Trebizond smiled, and from the burglar's point of view Trebizond's smile seemed to enlarge the black hole in the muzzle of the revolver.

"I wish you'd point that thing somewhere else," he said nervously.

"There's nothing else I want to shoot."

"You don't want to shoot me."

"Oh?"

"You don't even want to call the cops," the burglar went on. "It's really not necessary. I'm sure we can work things out between us, two civilized men coming to a civilized agreement. I've some money on me. I'm an open-handed sort and would be pleased to make a small contribution to your favorite charity, whatever it might be. We don't need policemen to intrude into the private affairs of gentlemen."

The burglar studied Trebizond carefully. This little speech had always gone over rather well in the past, especially with men of substance. It was hard to tell how it was going over now, or if it was going over at all. "In any event," he ended somewhat lamely, "you certainly don't want to shoot me."

"Why not?"

"Oh, blood on the carpet, for a starter. Messy, wouldn't you say? Your wife would be upset. Just ask her and she'll tell you shooting me would be a ghastly idea."

"She's not at home. She'll be out for the next hour or so."

"All the same, you might consider her point of view. And shooting me would be illegal, you know. Not to mention immoral."

"Not illegal," Trebizond remarked.

"I beg your pardon?"

"You're a burglar," Trebizond reminded him. "An unlawful intruder on my property. You have broken and entered. You have invaded the sanctity of my home. I can shoot you where you stand and not get so much as a parking ticket for my trouble."

"Of course you can shoot me in self-defense—"

"Are we on *Candid Camera*?"

"No, but—"

"Is Allen Funt lurking in the shadows?"

"No, but I—"

"In your back pocket. That metal thing. What is it?"

"Just a pry bar."

"Take it out," Trebizond said. "Hand it over. Indeed. A weapon if I ever saw one. I'd state that you attacked me with it and I fired in self-defense. It would be my word against yours, and yours would remain unvoiced since you would be dead. Whom do you suppose the police would believe?"

The burglar said nothing. Trebizond smiled a satisfied smile and put the pry bar in his own pocket. It was a piece of nicely shaped steel and it had a nice heft to it. Trebizond rather liked it.

"Why would you want to kill me?"

"Perhaps I've never killed anyone. Perhaps I'd like to satisfy my curiosity. Or perhaps I got to enjoy killing in the war and have been yearning for another crack at it. There are endless possibilities."

"But—"

"The point is," said Trebizond, "you might be useful to me in that manner. As it is, you're not useful to me at all. And stop hinting about my favorite charity or other euphemisms. I don't want your money. Look about you. I've ample money of my own—that should be obvious. If I were a poor man you wouldn't have breached my threshold. How much money are you talking about, anyway? A couple of hundred dollars?"

"Five hundred," the burglar said.

"A pittance."

"I suppose. There's more at home but you'd just call that a pittance too, wouldn't you?"

"Undoubtedly." Trebizond shifted the gun to his other hand. "I told you I was a businessman," he said. "Now if there were any way in which you could be more useful to me alive than dead—"

"You're a businessman and I'm a burglar," the burglar said, brightening.

"Indeed."

"So I could steal something for you. A painting? A competitor's trade secrets? I'm really very good at what I do, as a matter of fact, although you wouldn't guess it by my performance tonight. I'm not saying I could whisk the Mona Lisa out of the Louvre, but I'm pretty good at your basic hole-and-corner job of everyday burglary. Just give me an assignment and let me show my stuff."

"Hmmmm," said Archer Trebizond.

"Name it and I'll swipe it."

"Hmmmm."

"A car, a mink coat, a diamond bracelet, a Persian carpet, a first edition, bearer bonds, incriminating evidence, eighteen-and-a-half minutes of tape—"

"What was that last?"

"Just my little joke," said the burglar. "A coin collection, a stamp collection, psychiatric records, phonograph records, police records—"

"I get the point."

"I tend to prattle when I'm nervous."

"I've noticed."

"If you could point that thing elsewhere—"

Trebizond looked down at the gun in his hand. The gun continued to point at the burglar.

"No," Trebizond said, with evident sadness. "No, I'm afraid it won't work."

"Why not?"

"In the first place, there's nothing I really need or want. Could you steal me a woman's heart? Hardly. And more to the point, how could I trust you?"

"You could trust me," the burglar said. "You have my word on that."

"My point exactly. I'd have to take your word that your word is good, and where does that lead us? Down the proverbial garden path, I'm afraid. No, once I let you out from under my roof I've lost my advantage. Even if I have a gun trained on you, once you're in the open I can't shoot you with impunity. So I'm afraid—"

"No!"

Trebizond shrugged. "Well, really," he said. "What use are you? What are you good for besides being killed? Can you do anything besides steal, sir?"

"I can make license plates."

"Hardly a valuable talent."

"I know," said the burglar sadly. "I've often wondered why the state bothered to teach me such a pointless trade. There's not even much call for counterfeit license plates, and they've got a monopoly on making the legitimate ones. What else can I do? I must be able to do something. I could shine your shoes, I could polish your car—"

"What do you do when you're not stealing?"

"Hang around," said the burglar. "Go out with ladies. Feed my fish, when they're not all over my rug. Drive my car when I'm not mangling its fenders. Play a few games of chess, drink a can or two of beer, make myself a sandwich—"

"Are you any good?"

"At making sandwiches?"

"At chess."

"I'm not bad."

"I'm serious about this."

"I believe you are," the burglar said. "I'm not your average wood-pusher, if that's what you want to know. I know the openings and I have a good sense of space. I don't have the patience for tournament play, but at the chess club downtown I win more games than I lose."

"You play at the club downtown?"

"Of course. I can't burgle seven nights a week, you know. Who could stand the pressure?"

"Then you *can* be of use to me," Trebizond said.

"You want to learn the game?"

"I know the game. I want you to play chess with me for an hour until my wife gets home. I'm bored, there's nothing in the house to read, I've never cared much for television, and it's hard for me to find an interesting opponent at the chess table."

"So you'll spare my life in order to play chess with me."

"That's right."

"Let me get this straight," the burglar said. "There's no catch to this, is there? I don't get shot if I lose the game or anything tricky like that, I hope."

"Certainly not. Chess is a game that ought to be above gimmickry."

"I couldn't agree more," said the burglar. He sighed a long sigh. "If I didn't play chess," he said, "you wouldn't have shot me, would you?"

"It's a question that occupies the mind, isn't it?"

"It is," said the burglar.

THEY PLAYED IN THE front room. The burglar drew the white pieces in the first game, opened King's Pawn, and played what turned out to be a reasonably imaginative version of the Ruy Lopez. At the sixteenth move Trebizond forced the exchange of knight for rook, and not too long afterward the burglar resigned.

In the second game the burglar played the black pieces and offered the Sicilian Defense. He played a variation that Trebizond wasn't familiar with. The game stayed remarkably even until in the end game the burglar succeeded in developing a passed pawn. When it was clear that he would be able to queen it, Trebizond tipped over his king, resigning.

"Nice game," the burglar offered.

"You play well."

"Thank you."

"Seems a pity that—"

His voice trailed off. The burglar shot him an inquiring look. "That I'm wasting myself as a common criminal? Is that what you were going to say?"

"Let it go," Trebizond said. "It doesn't matter."

They began setting up the pieces for the third game when a key slipped into a lock. The lock turned, the door opened, and Melissa Trebizond stepped into the foyer and through it to the living room.

Both men got to their feet. Mrs. Trebizond advanced, a vacant smile on her pretty face. "You found a new friend to play chess with. I'm happy for you."

Trebizond set his jaw. From his back pocket he drew the burglar's pry bar. It had an even nicer heft than he had thought. "Melissa," he said, "I've no need to waste time with a recital of your sins. No doubt you know precisely why you deserve this."

She stared at him, obviously not having understood a word he had said to her, whereupon Archer Trebizond brought the pry bar down on the top of her skull. The first blow sent her to her knees. Quickly he struck her three more times, wielding the metal bar with all his strength, then turned to look into the wide eyes of the burglar.

"You've killed her," the burglar said.

"Nonsense," said Trebizond, taking the bright revolver from his pocket once again.

"Isn't she dead?"

"I hope and pray she is," Trebizond said, "but I haven't killed her. You've killed her."

"I don't understand."

"The police will understand," Trebizond said, and shot the burglar in the shoulder. Then he fired again, more satisfactorily this time, and the burglar sank to the floor with a hole in his heart.

Trebizond scooped the chess pieces into their box, swept up the board and set about the business of arranging things. He suppressed an urge to whistle. He was, he decided, quite pleased with himself. Nothing was ever entirely useless, not to a man of resources. If fate sent you a lemon, you made lemonade.

# Authors' Biographies

Doug Allyn is an accomplished author whose short fiction regularly graces years' best collections. His work has appeared in *Once Upon a Crime*, *Cat Crimes Through Time*, and *The Year's 25 Finest Criman and Mystery Stories*, volumes 3 and 4. His stories of Tallifer, the wandering minstrel, have appeared in *Ellery Queen's Mystery Magazine* and *Murder Most Scottish*. His story "The Dancing Bear," a Tallifer tale, won the Edgar award for short fiction for 1994. His other series character is veterinarian Dr. David Westbrook, whose exploits have been collected in the anthology *All Creatures Dark and Dangerous*. Allyn lives with his wife in Montrose, Michigan.

William E. Chambers is the executive vice president of the Mystery Writers of America. He has had two novels published, and his short fiction has appeared in such venues as *Ellery Queen's Mystery Magazine*, *Alfred Hitchcock's Mystery Magazine*, and several mystery and suspense anthologies published in the United States and the United Kingdom. He writes and edits "Vital Signs" for MWA's monthly newsletter, "The 3rd Degree," and "Bloodlines" for the New York Chapter newsletter. He has served as a labor organizer for the Communications Workers of America while employed by New York's Bell System. He and his wife Marie also owned and operated Chambers Pub, a bar-restaurant in Greenpoint, Brooklyn, where he is a community activist and lifelong resident.

Winner of the Edgar Award, Shamus Award, and Anthony, Harlan Coben has authored critically acclaimed Myron Bolitar novels that have been called "poignant and insightful" (*Los Angeles Times*), "consistently entertaining" (*Houston Chronicle*), "superb" (*Chicago Tribune*), and "must reading" (*Philadelphia Inquirer*). Coben's *Tell No One*, a *New York Times* bestseller that made the front pages of the Hollywood trade when it created a four-studio bidding war, was released nationally in June 2001. Harlan's books are published in well over a dozen countries. He lives in New Jersey with his pediatrician wife Anne and their young children.

Michael Collins is the most famous pseudonym of author Dennis Lynds, the creator of Dan Fortune, the one-armed private investigator who has sleuthed his way through more than fifteen novels, including *Cassandra in Red*, which was nominated for the Shamus Award. His creator served in World War II, earning the Bronze Star, Purple Heart, Combat Infantry Badge, and three battle stars. After the war he used his bachelor's degree in chemistry to forge various careers including editing several chemistry magazines. In the 1960s he turned to mystery writing and has been at it ever since. A former president of the Private Eye Writers of America, he received the MWA's Edgar Award in 1967 for his novel *Act of Fear*.

Jeffery Deaver's novels have appeared on a number of best-seller lists around the world, including the *New York Times*, the *London Times*, and the *Los Angeles Times*. The author of sixteen novels, he's been nominated for four Edgar Awards from the Mystery Writers of America (two of them for short stories) and an Anthony Award (also for a short story) and is the two-time recipient of the Ellery Queen Reader's Award for Best Short Story of the Year. His novel *The Bone Collector* was a feature release from Universal Pictures starring Denzel Washington and Angelina Jolie. And his latest novel, *The Blue Nowhere*, is soon to be a feature film from Warner Brothers. He is now at work on his latest Lincoln Rhyme novel.

There is little Harlan Ellison has not done in the field of writing. He has authored more than seventeen hundred short stories, four novels, essays, criticisms, movies, and teleplays, and been a constant force for excellence and experimentation in science fiction and fantasy. His works have pushed and often broken through the borders of what would be considered safe fiction by today's society. Having won just about every award in the fiction field, including multiple Nebulas, Hugos, Edgars, and Writers Guild of America awards, he shows no sign of slowing down. He has also made his mark in the editing field, having put together the groundbreaking collection *Dangerous Visions* and following that up with *Again, Dangerous Visions*, both books containing stories that at the time were deemed too controversial to publish elsewhere. Currently, an enormous fifty-year retrospective,

*The Essential Ellison*, is garnering rave reviews.

Joe Gores is the only writer to have won the Mystery Writers of America's Edgar Award in three categories: short story, for "Goodbye, Pops"; television drama, for an episode of the *Kojak* television series; and novel, for his first book, *A Time of Predators*. Along the way he has also written episodes for many 1980s television mystery shows, including *Magnum, P.I.*, *Remington Steele*, and *Columbo*. His DKA series of novels are classic procedural novels of the men working at an auto repossession company and the crimes they get involved in as a result. He has also written a tour-de-force historical mystery entitled *Hammett*, which tours the seedy side of San Francisco during the 1920s, with a lifelong resident's passion and eye for detail. He lives in Fairfax, California, with his family.

If versatility is a virtue, then Ed Gorman is virtuous indeed. He has written steadily in three different genres—mystery, horror, and westerns—for almost twenty years. He has also written a large number of short stories, with six of his collections of wry, poignant, unsettling fiction in print in the USA and UK. Kirkus said "Gorman is one of the most original crime writers around," taking particular note of his Sam McCain-Judge Whitney series, which is set in small-town Iowa in the 1950s, and winning rave reviews from coast to coast. It is no surprise that he captures the essence of life in the Midwest, since he lives in Cedar Rapids, Iowa. As for the wealth of detail he brings to every novel and story he writes, well, he's been there and back again, and the observations he shares about life, love, and loss make his books all the richer. His most recent novel is *Will You Still Love Me Tomorrow?*, the third Sam McCain book.

Double award winner Jan Grape has five mystery award nominations: in 1998, her Anthony winner for Best Short Story, "A Front Row Seat," from *Vengeance Is Hers*, was also nominated for a Shamus. *Deadly Women*, a nonfiction book coedited with Dean James, won the McCavity and was nominated for both an Edgar and an Agatha. After numerous short stories and articles, Jan's first full-length novel, *Austin City Blue*, is an October 2001 release from Five Star Mysteries. A regular columnist for *Mystery Scene*, Jan has held offices in Mystery Writers and Private-Eye Writers, and she is a cofounder/life member of Heart of Texas Chapter, Sisters-in-Crime. Other memberships include American and International Crime Writers and the Independent Mystery Booksellers. In 1999 Jan and her husband sold Mysteries & More bookstore in Austin, Texas, to spend more time with their five grandchildren and to travel in an RB with their black cats, Nick and Nora.

David Handler was born and raised in Los Angeles and began his career in New York as a journalist and critic. He published two highly acclaimed novels about growing up, *Kiddo* and *Boss*, before resorting to a life of crime fiction. He has written eight novels featuring the witty and dapper celebrity ghostwriter Stewart Hoag, including the Edgar and American Mystery Award-winning "The Man Who Would Be F. Scott Fitzgerald." He has also written extensively for television and films and coauthored the international best-selling thriller *Gideon* under the pseudonym Russell Andrews. With the publication of *The Cold Blue Blood* in the fall of 2001, he launched a new mystery series featuring the mismatched crime-fighting duo of Mitch Berger and Desiree Mitry. Mr. Handler presently lives in a two-hundred-year-old carriage house in Old Lyme, Connecticut.

Jeremiah Healy is one of the private-eye writers who helped change a moribund mystery field in the eighties. A former professor at the New England School of Law, his debut novel about private detective John Francis Cuddy, *Blunt Darts*, announced that here was a wise new kid on the block. Since then he has written more than a dozen novels featuring his melancholy P.I. His books and stories have done nothing but enhance his reputation as an important and sage writer whose work has taken the private-eye form to an exciting new level. Winner of the Shamus Award in 1986 for *The Staked Goat*, he is one of those writers who packs the poise and depth of a good mainstream novel into an even better genre novel. Recent books include *The Stalking of Sheilah Quinn* and the latest Cuddy mysteries, *The Only Good Lawyer* and *Spiral*.

Edward D. Hoch is probably the only man in the world who supports himself exclusively by writing short stories. He has appeared in every issue of *Ellery Queen's Mystery Magazine* since the late 1970s, and manages to write for several other markets as well. He has probably created more short-story series characters than anybody who ever worked in the crime fiction field. And what great characters, too—Nichael Vlado, a Gypsy detective; Dr. Sam Hawthorne, a small-town GP of the 1920s who solves impossible crimes while dispensing good health; and, among many others, his outré and bedazzling Simon Ark, who claims, in the proper mood, to be two thousand years old. Locked room, espionage, cozy, hard-boiled, suspense, Ed Hoch has done it all and done it well.

The word *prolific* has been used to describe Evan Hunter so many times you might think it was part of his name. Mr. Evan "Prolific" Hunter. But there's no denying that Hunter—aka Ed McBain—has amassed a body of work that stuns the senses when one sits down to reckon with it. That so much of it is excellent, and that some of it is possessed of true genius, and that every single piece of it makes for enjoyable reading, is a testament to the man's prowess as an author. He is like watching a world-class boxer at his peak; he knows all the moves. Because of such bestsellers as *The Blackboard Jungle* and *A Matter of Conviction*, Hunter's early fame was for his mainstream novels. But over the years he became better known for the 87th Precinct series. It's impossible to choose the "best" of the 87th books—there are just too many good ones—but one might suggest a peek at *He Who Hesitates* (1965), *Blood Relatives* (1975), *Long Time No See* (1977), and *The Big Bad City* (1999). He wrote the screenplay of *The Birds* for Alfred Hitchcock and his powerful novel *Last Summer* became one of the seminal films of the seventies. His recent novels include another 87th Precinct book, *The Last Dance*.

Stuart Kaminsky's four mystery series characters include Inspector Por-firy Rostnikov, an intelligent Moscow policeman always being assigned "impossible" cases, which he solves with aplomb; private detective Toby Peters, who takes on cases for stars like Judy Garland and the Marx Brothers in 1940s' Hollywood; Florida P.I. Lou Fonesca; and philosophical police detective Abe Lieberman. A former president of Mystery Writers of America, he has also written plays, screenplays, and biographies on noted celebrities such as Clint Eastwood and director John Huston. His short fiction has appeared in anthologies such as *Guilty as Charged*, *The Mysterious West*, and *Death by Espionage*.

Henry Reymond Fitzwalter, or H. R. F. Keating, has been writing the Inspector Ganesh Ghote series for more than thirty years, chronicling a world that would seem foreign to many mystery readers, that of India through the past three decades, but which he makes vibrant and just as dangerous as any other metropolitan area. His Inspector Ghote is not cast in the mold of the usual brilliant police sleuths; he is fallible, emotional, and all-too-human, which has endeared him to readers through more than twenty novels, including one where Ghote travels to America. Keating is also a splendid writer of short fiction,with another series character, Mrs. Cragg, whose exploits are collected in the collection *Mrs. Craggs: Crime Cleaned Up*. He is also a reviewer and editor of repute, having assembled several volumes on mystery writing and writers, including *Agatha Christie: First Lady of Crime* and *Crime and Mystery: The 100 Best Books*.

Dick Lochte is the creator of world-weary private eye Leo Bloodworth and his precocious teen assistant Serendipity Dalhquist, who have appeared in two novels, *Sleeping Dog* and *Laughing Dog*, and New Orleans detective Terry Manion, whose adventures are chronicled in *Blue Bayou* and *The Neon Smile*. He has also been a promotional copywriter for *Playboy* magazine, a theater critic for *Los Angeles* magazine, and a book columnist for the *Los Angeles Times*. Recently, he has teamed up with former L.A. prosecutor Christopher Darden on a series of crime novels, the first of which, *The Trials of Nikki Hill*, won rave reviews.

When John Lutz won the Edgar for his short story "Ride the Lightning," a number of critics pointed out that such recognition was long overdue. Whether writing his Fred Carver or Alo Nudger books—or his suspense novels, one of which, *SWF Seeks Same*, was the basis for the hit movie "Single White Female"—Lutz brings to the noir school of writing a sympathy for the average man rarely seen in contemporary fiction of any kind. Lutz knows how most of us live and manages to give engaging (and sometimes sad, sometimes violent) portraits of life lived here in the cities and suburbs of the United States at the start of the new Millennium. Novels such as *The Ex*, recently produced as a made-for-cable movie, illustrate how the characters and situations, in his skillful hands, can come back to haunt you.

Sharyn McCrumb is a *New York Times* best-selling author whose critically acclaimed success in southern fiction has been both scholarly as well as popular. Her novels are studied in universities throughout the world, translated into German, Dutch, Japanese, French, Greek, Czech, Russian, Danish, Spanish, and Italian, in addition to being national best-sellers in the United States. She has won more awards in crime fiction than any other author, including all of the major U.S. awards in the field, although critics and scholars are also now recognizing her as an author of serious, nonmystery fiction. She has been awarded the Edgar, two Anthony Awards, two Macavity Awards, three Agatha Awards, and the Nero. She is the author of sixteen novels, including the "Ballad Books," consisting of *If I Ever Return*

*Pretty Peggy O* and *The Hangman's Beautiful Daughter*, and the *New York Times* best-sellers *She Walks These Hills* and *The Rosewood Casket*, all of which were named *New York Times* or *Los Angeles Times* Notable Books. Recent books include *The Ballad of Frankie Silver* and *The Songcatcher*.

Joyce Carol Oates is widely regarded as one of America's premier authors and leading literary critics. Her articles have appeared in The *New York Review of Books* and other prestigious literary forums. Her novels and short stories deconstruct modern life as we know it, magnifying seemingly inconsequential events and showing the motives and rationalizations behind it all. She can make everyday life seem horrifying, and when she decides to actually write suspenseful fiction, there are few who are her equal. Recent books include *We Were the Mulvaneys*, recently chosen by the Oprah Winfrey Book Club, and *The Barrens*.

While the Nameless Detective series is very well written, cleverly plotted, and steeped with fascinating characters, it is also, one senses, a kind of diary for its author. Stretching over several decades now, the series spotlights both San Francisco and an unnamed detective, and charts how both have changed over this period of time. *Shackles* and *Sentinels* are two of the series highlights. And author Bill Pronzini has proved he can write nonseries novels, too: *Blue Lonesome* and *A Wasteland of Strangers* being among the most creative and moving novels of the 1990s—in or out of crime fiction. Nameless makes his most recent appearances in *Illusions* and *Crazybone*. Also, as you are about to discover, from his very first published fiction, Pronzini is a master of the short story.

Robert J. Randisi cofounded *Mystery Scene* magazine, single-handedly created the Private Eye Writers of America, and has created a number of cutting-edge anthologies showcasing contemporary hardboiled fiction at its best. While Randisi's early crime novels were swift, sure, singular looks at working-class Brooklyn (two of which were deservedly nominated for Shamus Awards), his more recent books demonstrate the true width and depth of his skills, in particular his novels about detective Joe Keough, which include *In the Shadow of the Arch*. The Keough books work both as excellent thrillers and serious novels. He is also an excellent western writer, with a number of novels to his credit in that genre, most notably perhaps *The Ham Reporter*, about Bat Masterton's days in New York City as a sports reporter.

## Authors' Biographies

Henry Slesar was a mainstay of the fiction magazines of the late 1950s and early 1960s, the last big boom of the digests, which were just the pulps in more convenient size. He did it all and he did it well. A collection of his crime work is long overdue. In the course of his career he has won the Mystery Writers of America Edgar Allan Poe Award for novel (1960), for a TV serial (1977), and an Emmy Award for a continuing daytime series (1974). He has written for many TV series such as *Alfred Hitchcock Presents* and *Twilight Zone*. And he survived many years as the head writer of a long-running soap opera, *The Edge of Night*.

Peter Straub is the best-selling author of more than a dozen novels, including *The Hellfire Club* and *Mr. X*. Combining the best elements of mainstream fiction with tropes of horror, suspense, or both, he has attained both critical and popular success with novels such as *Ghost Story*, *The Throat*, and *Koko*. Born in Milwaukee, Wisconsin, he attended the University of Wisconsin, Columbia University, and University College, Dublin. He was an English teacher for three years before turning to writing full time in 1972. His short fiction has been collected in *Houses Without Doors*, and *Magic Terror: Seven Tales*. He lives with his family in New York City.

Lawrence Block's novels range from the urban noir of Matthew Scudder (*Hope to Die*) to the urbane effervescence of Bernie Rhodenbarr (*The Burglar in the Rye*), while other characters include the globe-trotting insomniac Evan Tanner (*Tanner on Ice*) and the introspective assassin Keller (*Hit List*). A Grand Master of Mystery Writers of America, he has won the Edgar and Shamus Awards four times each and the Japanese Maltese Falcon Award twice, as well as the Nero Wolfe and German Philip Marlowe Awards. In France, he has been proclaimed a *Grand Maitre du Roman Noir* and has twice been awarded the Societe 813 trophy. He has been a guest of honor at Bouchercon and at book fairs and mystery festivals in France, Germany, Australia, Italy, New Zealand, and Spain, and, as if that were not enough, he was publicly presented with the key to the city of Muncie, Indiana.

# Copyrights and Permissions

Printed in the USA
CPSIA information can be obtained
at www.ICGtesting.com
JSHW052014140824
68134JS00027B/2473